Not Only
Good Boys

Also by Jo Eames

The Faithless Wife

Not Only the Good Boys

Jo Eames

 NotOnlyTheGoodBoys

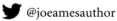 @joeamesauthor

*For all those who served under
Major-General Sir Percy Cleghorn Stanley Hobart
in the 79th Armoured Division, 1942–45
'Hobo's Funnies'*

1

AUGUST 1942, DIEPPE

The last thing he expected was that they would come on bicycles. Crouching in the ripe wheat, its dust raised and made to dance by the big gun, he had been straining for nearly an hour to hear the clank and rumble that would mean tanks or half-tracks coming down the road from Dieppe. But his ears were stunned, his other senses too, every time the corn rippled before a great wave of blast and the head-splitting roar of the gun. Hot wind blasted an entire summer's accumulation of dust into his eyes, nose and mouth and each time he caught himself scrabbling at the baked earth, driven by instinct to burrow away from danger.

In a brief interval of silence – while the German gunners were easing another freight-wagon-sized shell into the breach of the great gun – he heard it. A faint jingling, bumping sound. Maybe it was because he was lying in a cornfield that he knew immediately what it was: Pat Jacques riding her mother's sturdy nurse's bicycle down through the stubble to where he and the others leaned on their rakes and watched her, parched for the flasks of tea clinking together in the big basket over her front wheel. Except when he knelt up and peered through the trembling ears of wheat in the direction of the sound, it wasn't Pat he saw but the coal-scuttle helmets of the enemy. Thirty or more of them, shoulders hunched as they pedalled hard along the grass headland at the edge of the field, rifles slung over their backs.

He dropped back to the ground and swam awkwardly through the wheat till he came up to the soles of handmade boots. 'Sir?'

The CO twisted round. His face was covered in pale dust. 'What is it, Mike?'

'They're coming up, sir. Reinforcements.'

'Tanks?'

'No, push-bikes, sir.'

The major frowned. 'Pulling my leg, Dixon?'

'No, sir. I swear. About thirty of 'em. Maybe more behind. The ones I could see were pedalling like billy-o.'

The CO pushed himself on to his knees and raised his head to look. Then the corn thrashed them in a sudden frenzy and the sky split in two with a crash that should have ended the world. The blast threw him face down beside Mike and they lay there, hands squeezed hard against their ears, as the roar enveloped them. When it finally faded and they could speak again, Major Young nodded.

'Trying to out-flank us. Time to get back to the beach. Hope some more of our chaps have turned up by now.'

The CO wriggled forward, calling to the rest of the men as he went. Mike peered out through the still-shivering corn again. The enemy was continuing to advance along the field edge, toiling away at their pedals. It was a strange sight, the first he'd had of real Germans. In the newsreels, they were never on push-bikes.

Somebody knocked him on the shoulder. It was Sergeant Peat, who said: 'Come on lad, let's get out of it before they rumble us. No more good we can do here.'

Mike got on to his feet and they went on side by side in a crouching run. The camouflage paint had mingled with sweat and dust and run into the grooves on the older man's face. Mike grinned at him. 'He who fights and runs away, eh?'

Peat grunted. 'Nowt wrong with living to fight another day. There'll be plenty more before this lot's over.'

'Let's hope so,' muttered Mike. He'd waited a long time for his first day in action, and it hadn't gone at all the way he'd expected.

When they made it back to the cliff edge, Mike glanced at his watch and saw it was exactly three hours since he'd first set foot in France. Next second he was running hell for leather down a gulley towards the beach, shoulders hunched, head low, chalk scree crunching under his boots. Hollings was in front and Sergeant Peat's heavy breathing close behind. The cyclists had never got off a shot at them, but now they were in clear view of the cliff batteries. Bullets zipped over their heads, whistling and whining off the rocks. Then there was a thud-thud and something crashed into his heel. He sprawled his length, slamming the knuckles of his right hand into the sharp stones, almost dropping his weapon. He lay a moment, panting, waiting for the pain. Someone had told him you didn't feel it when you were hit. Not at first. He rolled over and stared down at his feet, fearful at what he'd see. But there was no blood or exposed white bone. And still no pain. Then he saw Henry Peat lying right behind him. Holes ripped in the back of his battledress. One over his shoulder and another round his ribs. Blood soaking the battledress all down his right side.

'Henry?'

The sergeant moaned. Mike dropped his rifle and scrambled to his knees. He crawled back and pulled at the sergeant's collar: 'Henry, come on!' Peat moaned again. Tried to push himself up using his left arm. He got his elbow straight, then collapsed. Another volley of bullets hammered down around them, throwing up sandy soil and whining chips of chalk. Mike let go of Peat's collar and threw himself flat, hands protecting his head. When the firing stopped, he tried to move but his fingers seemed stuck to his head. He couldn't remember how to call on the muscles to move. Even his eyes refused to open.

'Mike?'

Someone was saying his name, a long way off, beyond the bass-drum racket of his heart thundering in his ears.

3

'Lieutenant Dixon. Sir!'

Something thudded into his shoulder. With a massive effort, he slowly moved one hand, putting his fingers out to feel where he'd been hit.

'Lieutenant Dixon, come on. Move, sir! It's time to go.'

Peat punched him in the arm again, using his good hand. Mike winced and opened his eyes. The sergeant's face, glassy with sweat, was a foot away. His voice was low but urgent. 'You have to get to the boats, sir. Quick as you can. I'll be all right.' The concern on the wounded man's face made it seem as if it was Mike who had been hit and not him. It occurred to Mike, vaguely, that that was the wrong way round. He blinked a few times and tried to think what to do. No thoughts came. Peat thumped him again. 'Go on now. Get out of it.'

Mike wanted to tell Henry something, but found he'd forgotten how to talk. He had two arms and two legs and he wasn't sure how to make them move. Slowly, shifting one limb at a time, he crawled forward to his rifle and closed his hand around it. The familiar weight and feel of it against his palm restored him to himself a little. Without looking back, he launched himself from all fours and started to run. The beach was still twenty yards ahead. Six feet from the end of the gulley a line of bullets came dancing across in front of him. He pulled up, skidding, eyes stinging from the flying stone dust. When he'd blinked away a mixture of dust and tears, he saw there were boats beached on the shore and men running through the surf in both directions. A few of his lot had taken cover behind a rock and were firing up at the cliff.

The stretch of sand between him and the others heaved and puffed like boiling porridge as bullets struck it. He stood still for a minute, looking at it. Then, hardly knowing how or why, he turned and scrambled back up the gulley. Peat was lying where he'd fallen,

4

clutching his steel helmet to his head with one hand, the other arm lying useless at his side. Mike grabbed the good arm and pulled it round his shoulders. The sergeant groaned once and went heavy and inert as a sack of King Edwards. The steel helmet rolled away.

He set off for the beach again, bent nearly double under the bigger man's weight. Spandau fire kept on hammering away and his legs felt they might give any minute, but he clenched his teeth and staggered forward. Where the gulley dropped away, scree turned to shingle. He stumbled at the change in the going and almost fell. Hauled Peat higher so that he could run without the man's legs dragging. Had taken no more than five paces across the shifting stones when he was punched in the back and his cheek smashed against the cold pebbles. Wetness and warmth spilled over him in a wave. Liquid ran into his eyes and he tasted salt and iron on his lips. He tried to get up. The weight on top of him was too heavy to shift. 'Henry!' he yelled. 'Henry, get off me, would you?' And Henry did. Miraculously, the weight lifted. He tried again to get up, but still couldn't do it.

'We've got you, sir' said a voice, and he looked up to find not Henry but Hollings and one of the other sergeants, Ogden-Smith, grabbing his arms. Pulling his stupidly unresponsive legs over the shingle.

'What about Henry?'

'Henry's had it,' said Hollings, panting.

He tried to look back. A shocking bolt of pain ran up his back as he twisted his neck. He shut his eyes and didn't open them for a long time.

MARCH 1943, YORKSHIRE

'Stop at the station on your way back, would you?'

Lt-Colonel Burton spoke quietly in Charlie's ear as he poked one long leg into the back of the staff car and prepared to fold himself in after it. 'New chap's due this afternoon. Be good if we could save him waiting for the bus. He's likely to be on it again soon enough.'

The driver looked up from pulling on her gloves. 'Surely one of them has to hang about some time, sir.'

Burton tapped the roof. Droplets of rain that had settled there shivered and ran together under his fingers. He stirred the little pool distractedly: 'If only one would. War Office is getting downright shirty about finding endless replacements. Trouble is, this chap's straight out of a convalescent ward.'

Frowning, the girl adjusted the peak of her cap a fraction of an inch, though it was already irreproachably straight. 'I'm not sure that's the best run-up for this job, sir. Is it?'

Burton shook his head. 'No, and if they've decided to send us crocks from now on, I don't see how we're ever going to find one the Old Man thinks is up to snuff.'

'What in blazes are you two gassing about?'

A face that was all black spectacles, heavy eyebrows and ill-temper loomed out of the dark interior and Charlie was reminded, not for the first time, of the troll in The Three Billy Goats Gruff. Burton flicked the wet from his fingers and telescoped himself into the car.

'Sorry, sir.' He turned to meet his commanding officer's petrifying glare as if it was the mildest manner in the world: 'I was just tasking Charlie with tracking down your new aide-de-camp once she's dropped us at the airfield.'

This idea was greeted by something between a snort and a grunt. Something bullish, thought Burton, or possibly wild-boarish.

'Let's hope he's more use than the last one. I suppose there's no chance he's regular army. Another bloody civilian, I expect.'

Burton's shoulders twitched, but he stilled them before the movement amounted to a shrug, a gesture the CO detested. 'Can't say, sir. He's been in action. I do know that.' He judged it best not to mention the convalescent hospital.

'That's something, I suppose.' The General switched his attention to the girl, who had started the engine but not yet moved off. 'Why are we still hanging about? Charlie, for heaven's sake, we haven't got all day.'

'Course not, sir. Sorry.'

As the car started to roll, Howard Burton crossed his legs awkwardly and sent up a prayer that the new man would last the month.

'Next station's Rawdon.' The conductor came swaying down the corridor, his shoulder rattling the glass in the window to Mike's compartment as the locomotive's heavy braking threw him off his stride. 'Next station's Rawdon. Rawdon, next stop.'

Mike shoved a dog-eared copy of *David Copperfield* into the pocket of his greatcoat and stared out through the dirty glass. It was only just after four but the light had already drained away down the plughole of a late winter's day. All he could make out was a long blackened wall and the usual rubbish of weeds and old sleepers by the trackside.

He lowered the window as the train coasted in. Leaned out to turn the handle. Waited a moment in the open doorway to gauge how fast the platform was moving. Twenty feet per second. Ten feet per second. Then he jumped. The onward pull of the train made the ground lurch under his feet and sent pain jarring up his bad leg. He swayed, steadied and hefted his kit-bag higher on to his shoulder. At the entrance to the waiting room the turnstile gave reluctantly, click by click, with just enough resistance at each turn for him to stagger slightly as it finally let him through. Nobody was waiting. The black-out was already in place and the blinds were down over the ticket windows. Even the narrow coal grate at the end was bare black bars. As he opened the door to go outside, Rawdon's only greeting was a bitter gust of wind.

He glanced round the empty station yard and wondered if anyone was expecting him. He couldn't imagine why they would be. He had been left by the wayside of the war, the world, life even, for so long that the arrival of a new posting, finally, had taken him by surprise. Who could want him now? What was he good for? Not a hell of a lot, by his own estimate. What was the phrase the moving finger wrote in the Bible? 'Thou art weighed in the balance and found wanting.' That was about the size of it. After the raid, there had been days of nothingness, weeks of lying around in feebleness and pain, months of being coaxed and bullied by nurses and therapists. Through it all he had felt less like a man than a machine, a motorcar that had been in a smash-up and was being worked on to get it fit for the road again. For his own part, he wouldn't have protested if they'd declared him a total write-off. But the mechanics had seemed determined to get him going again. What's more, they must have boasted of their progress to someone outside the closed world of the hospital for that someone to have posted him here.

He'd never heard of Rawdon. The movement order placed it somewhere in the West Riding. That was all he knew. He'd changed at Leeds, out of a train full of grumbling servicemen on their way to Scotland, and waited an hour for the stopping train to Harrogate. He had been to Harrogate once before, when he was fifteen, cadging a lift with a mate of his dad who was making a run up from Loughborough with machine parts from the Brough. Then, he remembered pulling into a handsome town in open country, but coming from Leeds the view was all squat suburbs and factory chimneys that only began to be punctuated by fields and hills in the last couple of miles before the conductor named Rawdon and he pulled his bag off the luggage rack.

He'd never heard of the 79th Armoured Division either. Nor had anyone at the hospital. New outfit. Must be. It was bloody cold in Rawdon. He knew that by now. Dark and deserted. There was a bus-stop, but no sign of a bus. No signs at all, as per. He hadn't a clue how far it was to Rawdon Hall, or if there was a bus that went near. With no one around to ask, he stamped his feet and delved in his pockets for cigarettes and matches. Slid the match box open. Four left. He stood still for a moment, assessing the wind before turning his back on it. The match flared at the third attempt but the thin blue flame danced and died in a wisp of smoke that the wind snatched away. He fumbled for another and went to strike it. It jolted against the scratch-board and missed. He took a deep breath and tried to line it up again. The job was more difficult than it had any right to be. He wanted to blame the blasted wind, but he couldn't conceal from himself that his hands were trembling. Willing them to give over, he jammed match and box hard together, and snapped the match in two. He swore. Pushed open the box for the last-but-one match, which skated away from him.

Just out of his field of concentration he was vaguely aware of engine noise, coming closer. He didn't turn to look. It had become the most important thing in the world to light this bloody fag. He steadied the hand that had finally got a grip on the match, cupped it hard against the one holding the box. He took a deep breath, dropped his shoulders, stroked match against emery board. It caught with a fizz. Flickered for a moment in the wind. Then he had it, steady, against the cigarette and saw the tip start to glow orange and sparks fly off into the dark.

He shoved his hands deep in his pockets, raised his chin, took a long drag, and noticed the car. Though it was no more than a bulk of shadow behind blinkered headlamps, he thought it was one of the big Humbers. Stationary, engine running, a straight six by the sound, the pale face of the driver peering out at him. He heard the window rattle down.

'Lieutenant Dixon?' said a female voice he instantly placed as home counties genteel. His hackles stirred. He dragged his bag on to his shoulder and sloped towards the car.

'You're lucky, sir. I've just dropped the GOC off at the airfield. Thought I'd run past the station and see if there was any sign of the Leeds train. They said you should be here this afternoon but the trains are such a mess you can never tell. Jump in, sir. But not with that ciggie, I'm afraid. The Old Man goes ape at the smell of tobacco in the car. Finish it first. I can wait. You look like you needed it. And at least the rain's stopped for once.'

Mike leaned down to the window, but the driver had already turned away to deal with something on the dashboard. All he could see in the gloom was an ATS cap, and a pale neck with a twist of fair hair disappearing up under the cap's brim. That and a waft of unmistakably expensive French scent, a perfume that hung rare and tremulous in the cold Yorkshire air, like a bar of Schubert heard in the most unexpected place. He felt a fool, ashamed that she had watched him struggle to light a damn cigarette.

'Doesn't matter,' he said, throwing the stupid thing into the gutter, where it fizzed in a grey puddle. 'Is it far? To the camp?'

She laughed: 'Not far, sir. Not the way I drive. Hop in.'

As she waited to turn out of the station yard, Charlie stole a look through the rear-view mirror at the new arrival. He wasn't a bad looker, sturdy, well-balanced features in a squarish face, yet there was something of 'what the cat dragged in' about him. He was maybe five feet ten, and either he'd been issued the wrong size greatcoat or he'd lost a lot of weight since he got it. There was definitely the shadow of a limp as he'd carried his bag over to the car. Not the dot-and-carry limp that betrayed an artificial leg, like her father's, but an unmistakable gingerness about one side. To put the tin lid on it, she could have sworn his hands were shaking as he tried to light his cigarette. 'Poor devil,' she thought, 'Hobo'll snap you up for breakfast.' He was staring out of the window now, though it was too dark to see much. Charlie thought she might as well try and break the ice. 'Ever been here before, sir? Yorkshire, I mean?'

'Once,' he said. Then hesitated. 'Before the war. Harrogate.'

'Oh, Harrogate's quite smart. Compared to Rawdon. It's all mills and factories round here. Ugly as sin. I never knew grim places like this existed till I came here.'

'I bet you didn't,' thought Mike, glaring at the darkness. 'Your sort'd have no idea where the steel comes from, the textiles, the coal, all the things that have kept us in the war, just about.' There had been nothing smart about his bit of Harrogate. His cousin Fred had a tiny, filthy mechanic's workshop under the railway arches near the station. Shut up for the duration, probably, with Fred called up. He remembered the oily taste of sandwiches eaten with hands wiped on an ancient bit of rag. His first real chance to work on engines, take things apart and put them back together again. Excited to find he had a natural bent for it that had made the older man shake his head and smile. Learning to ride Fred's Velocette up and down the cobbled approach. He could still feel the rattle in his jaw.

'He doesn't say much,' thought Charlie. 'But I think he almost smiled then. He doesn't look so bad when he stops scowling.' 'Where are you from, sir? Where's home, I mean?'

Mike sighed without realising it. Ever since he walked through the door at his Officer Cadet Training Unit he'd been learning that there was never a right answer to this question. Not with a girl like this one. People who asked this question were always trying to make a connection. Trying to lead up to the shout of recognition and the eager: 'Oh, but you must know so-and-so.' He never did know so-and-so. Never did know anyone that anyone else knew. 'Leicestershire.'

'Leicestershire? Gosh, I'm terrible at geography. Leicestershire's one of those places I wouldn't have a clue where to stick on the map. Sort of northern, but not as far north as here. Is that right?'

'It's generally thought to be in the Midlands.'

If she heard sarcasm she gave no sign. 'Yes, well, there you are. I have a sort of mental blank about the Midlands. Never been entirely sure where they are.'

Mike leaned his head against the seat and wondered if it was very far to Rawdon Hall. But the weight of the silence embarrassed him into an answer at last. 'Clue's in the name. The Midlands are in the middle of the country. If you cut out a map of Britain and tried to balance it on your fingertip, you'd find Leicestershire just about over the point of balance.'

'Oh, that's rather clever,' said the girl. She took one hand off the wheel and held it out, palm up, gloved forefinger outstretched, as she tried to imagine Britain balancing on the tip. 'That's the sort of thing I'd never think of in a million years. There must be something I know about Leicestershire though. Surely. Even I can't be that dim.' They drove on a little way, testing the point, before she hopped in her seat. 'I've got it. The Quorn. And The Belvoir. They hunt in Leicestershire, don't they?'

'That's right,' he said. How could he not, when he'd grown up right in the middle of Quorn country. Times, when he and his brother Frank were out picking cabbage plants in Fred Mee's fields, they'd stopped to watch the hunt work the cover at the bottom of Flight Hill. He could feel it now, the agonising stiffness in his lower back as he straightened up, legs wide, one foot either side of the row of wet muddy leaves. Frozen fingers that would throb and burn later with chilblains and the bitter cold in his toes, his left foot always worse because of the hole in his father's old pit-boot his mother had stuffed with a wad of newspaper that had turned cold and soggy hours ago. The weird monotony of counting, twenty-five plants to a bunch, bunches stacked with a ninety-degree turn each time, till they formed piles of ten bunches, two hundred and fifty plants, a monotony that took up all your attention to start with but then, becoming automatic, freed your thoughts to roam to all sorts of strange places. When his mind was ever so far away, there they'd be at the bottom of the hill, the hounds first, a brown and white river of dogs, followed by the sound of the horn and the first riders, taking the gate or the hedge from the long pasture with a drumbeat of hooves that carried up the hill to where they were working. Little Frank always used to run down the hill to get a better look, wheeling his arms as he went. Michael would just stand there and watch the procession of red and green coats, the sweating horses, plumes of steam puffing from their nostrils, still half away with the fairies, numbers spinning in his head.

'So do you hunt, sir?'

'What?'

As soon as she said it, as soon as she saw through her mirror the way his face stiffened to a cold slab, she realised it was a stupid question but, once asked, she couldn't un-ask it. 'Before the war, I mean. Did you hunt?'

'No,' he said. 'I didn't hunt.' And they both heard the almost dropped 'h' and the shaded northern 'u', his accent stronger than it had been in years.

They drove on in silence, Charlie putting her foot down as hard as she dared in the dark, anxious to get the new officer delivered before she made another balls-up. She dropped him at the front of the Hall, reversing a little to throw a weak path of light towards the door. He limped up the steps as she swung around and headed down the hill to the motor pool.

'Well,' she thought, as bare tree trunks loomed out of the dark on either side of the drive, 'I don't give much for that one's chances. Even if he does stay, I don't think we're going to be great pals. "Do you hunt," indeed? Charlotte Carrington, you are a Class One Idiot.'

4

Daylight gave Mike only a slightly better idea of where he had landed. He slept badly, tormented by the usual dream, and rose at seven out of hospital habit. Pulling aside the black-out curtains revealed a dirty sort of morning. The sky was a featureless grey and the dormer window of his attic room looked out over the hips and gullies of an undulating roof of old stone slates that had seen far, far better days. Deep green moss hugged the leaded valleys and a mat of sodden leaves blocked the drain hopper directly beneath the window.

He dressed, found a bathroom at the end of the corridor and shaved in water so cold it made his face smart. As he scraped away, he could hear the slamming of doors, footsteps on lino and the general hubbub of a begrudged awakening – the morning noises of any boarding school, any army billet, any hospital. He had no experience of the first, a fair amount of the second and far too much, recently, of the third. To that extent, and to that extent only, Rawdon Hall already felt familiar.

Downstairs there was no one about, so he crossed the hall, boots ringing on the flagstones, and hauled open the battered front door. At the bottom of raddled steps ran a drive that was crying out for a ton or twelve of gravel. The recent passage of heavy tracked vehicles hadn't helped its condition. Stepping over deep corrugated ruts filled with muddy water, he turned to look up at the house. It was an ancient place built of Yorkshire sandstone, long dirtied by smoke from the local mill chimneys and colonised by mouldy greenish lichen. The date-stone over the door claimed '1654'. He had no grounds to disagree.

'Filthy old hovel, ain't it?'

He turned to see a round-faced schoolboy, dressed as a second lieutenant in the 22nd Dragoons, wheeling a bicycle up the drive. 'Owners haven't lived here for two hundred years at least and some of the tenants have been ghastly, by all accounts. Still, probably none as ghastly as the Seventy Ninth Armoured Division. You new?'

Mike nodded.

'Well, you're more than welcome to the place. My advice? Find yourself a billet in the village. Food's better for a start, especially if you can land on a farmer's wife. God, they know how to feed a chap. Rationing or no. Plus there's less risk of getting button-holed by the Old Man, which is a definite bonus.'

'The Old Man?'

The schoolboy stopped abruptly, as if the new man had displayed some startling piece of ignorance, like not knowing the earth was round. 'The General Officer Commanding,' he said slowly, as if to a dim child. 'Hobo. Major-General Percy Hobart. Everybody calls him Hobo – not within his hearing, of course. I'm Babington-Browne, by the way.'

'Dixon. What's he like, the Old Man? I'm supposed to be his new aide.'

The subaltern snorted with laughter: 'Good Lord. Whatever have you done to deserve that? Forget what I said about a nice billet. I wouldn't even bother unpacking. Hobo goes through staff officers like billy-o. You may have noticed – there's not a spot of rust on that station turnstile. It hardly ever stops turning. He's sacked more chaps in the last five months than I've had hot dinners. Hundreds. Literally. You must have heard of old Hobo. He's legendary in the world of tanks.'

Mike shook his head. 'Sorry, I'm not a tank man.'

'What are you doing here then? It's nobbut tanks round here.' He flourished his Yorkshire 'nobbut' the way a traveller to exotic lands shows off a gimcrack souvenir: 'Hobo can't talk about anything else, and no one else is allowed to either. What outfit were you with before?'

'Three Commando. I was wounded. RTU'd. No idea why I was posted here.'

The schoolboy giggled. 'At least it shows the Gabardine Swine have a sense of humour. Sending Hobo a commando as his ADC. That's a beauty. They've tried everyone else – must have finally worked out it's a job for the silent killing brigade.'

'Glad you find it entertaining.'

Babington-Browne, who was busy shoving the front wheel of his bicycle between two ancient stones beside the doorway, heard Mike's tone and turned back hastily: 'Sorry, old man. No need to take umbrage. Come and have breakfast and I'll fill you in on the Seventy Ninth. Not that any of us really knows what it's all about, but still. In the kingdom of the blind and all that … '

So saying, the one-eyed man hopped up the steps and led the way down a dingy corridor in the direction of the unmistakable smell of army cooking. The officers' mess occupied a draughty room with tall, many-paned windows that overlooked a wreck of a garden. Breakfast sat congealing in dented silver chafing dishes on a massive mahogany buffet of ornate ugliness, presumably a relic of one of the Victorian tenants who had lacked the fortitude to drag it any further. A scrubbed oak refectory table in the centre of the room was host to a handful of morose-looking officers, forking in a mixture of greyish scrambled egg and toast between gulps from large mugs of tea. Babington-Browne made the introductions and the men nodded at Mike with little effort at interest.

'Sorry,' muttered Babington-Browne as they foraged at the buffet. 'Hearts are a tad in boots. It's a bit of a rag-bag. Division was only formed in October and no one's sure if it's going to last. We've hardly any equipment, and what we do have is pretty useless. There are two rumours going around. Smart money's on the one that says we'll be broken up shortly and used as replacements in the Desert Rats or the Black Bulls. They both used to be Hobo's outfits, you know. For some reason the top brass never let him take a division into action. Too kind to Jerry by half, I say. If he was as vile to the enemy as he is to his own chaps they'd run a mile.'

'Bit of a martinet is he?'

Babington-Browne laughed bleakly. 'Let's just say Hobo makes Captain Bligh look like a famous philanthropist. Frankly, the man's obsessed. The equipment's a load of useless old scrap and yet he expects us to pull off the most incredible coups. Insists every officer should be able to strip down his tank and fix it, so we spend half our time in overalls covered in engine oil like common grease monkeys. And if you do the slightest thing to incur his displeasure he sets you a course across the foulest terrain to make sure your tank throws a track and it takes you hours to get home. I tell you, the fellow's a titanic pain in the arse.'

He pulled out a chair and threw himself at it, clattering his plate on to the table in front of him: 'Funny thing, though … '

'What's that?'

Babington-Browne's chubby choirboy features rumpled in puzzlement. Mike wondered how old he was. Nineteen, he guessed. Twenty at the outside.

'The other ranks seem to quite like him. I mean, fear of God and all that, but they do seem oddly inclined to be fond of the old horror. Beats me. They get stuck out on Ilkley Moor baht 'at in all weathers just as much as we do. Don't seem to take it to heart.'

Mike found himself smiling down at his appalling breakfast.

'Something funny, old man?' Babington-Browne sounded slightly hurt.

Mike shook his head and attacked his powdered egg. He doubted anything old Hobo could come up with on the Yorkshire Moors would compete with commando training in the Scottish Highlands in winter. He'd moaned with the rest about the sheer bloody-mindedness of it, until the results began to show and he'd realised he was getting fit enough for anything. Strong enough, maybe, to beat his father, with his coal-miner's iron forearms, in an arm-wrestle. If he'd ever gone home on leave. He felt a pang of homesickness suddenly, not for home, but for 3 Commando – the only place in the British Army where it was how good you were at the job that mattered, not where you came from or what your name was. And now he was out of it. Because of Dieppe. Because of his stupid leg. Unfit to be a commando any more. Unfit for anything useful. Posted to the very last job on earth he'd have chosen – a glorified secretary to exactly the kind of fossilised brass hat responsible for Dieppe, Calais and every other disaster of the last four years. He dropped his fork on to the plate and looked up. 'Any idea when he'll be back?'

'Oh, he comes and goes all the time. His other HQ's down in Suffolk. Division's littered around the country so he's always on the bloody move. Seems to have the energy of a kid, even though he's nearly sixty. Sixty. Just think of it … ' He paused, fork halfway to his fleshy lips, to ponder the nonsensicality of a sixty-year-old believing he had a part to play in a young man's war. He blinked twice, slowly, gave it up as a bad job and put the fork-load down to add more pepper: 'I heard they tried to retire him once, until Churchill himself insisted they bring him back. I mean, I'm as big an admirer of Winston as anyone, but I'm not sure that doesn't rank as one of his more crackpot ideas.'

'So you don't know when he's due back here?'

'Not an earthly. Sorry. Tell you who might. There's a corker of a girl who drives him around. ATS. She seems to keep tabs on him better than most. Motor pool's down the hill, big old stable-block in the farmyard. Should be there if she's on duty.'

'Is she a blonde?'

'I'll say. Though I can't tell you for sure whether it comes out of a bottle. There's a few chaps who've tried to find out, but she's engaged to a fly boy. Actually … ' His face rumpled again. 'Now I come to think of it, someone told me the chap'd been posted missing. A few weeks ago. Might be worth having a crack now. I say, does that sound awful?'

Mike shrugged. He had the feeling Babington-Browne's crack at a self-possessed blonde would be a long time progressing from the planning stage to an actual assault on the ground. He chewed and swallowed without the slightest pleasure. 'I met her, I think, last night. She brought me here from the station. Drove like a maniac.'

'That's Charlie. Hobo eggs her on. Kicks up a stink if she isn't doing at least twice the speed limit at all times. Seems to think sane driving is the hallmark of a fifth columnist. It's no good though, Dixon. She is promised to another. And even if that's off, be a good chap and remember there's a queue.'

After breakfast Mike poked about looking for someone to tell him what to do, but the General had taken his GSO1, Burton, with him to Suffolk and everybody else was out. It struck him as gloomily amusing that the unit he'd washed up in was disorganised, disillusioned and unfit for purpose, whatever that purpose might turn out to be. It seemed the War Office had sent him to the right place after all.

Since he had no idea yet where to find the servant who would put up his badges, he dumped his kit on his bunk and wandered back downstairs to read the paper in the empty mess. He was halfway through the death notices in *The Times* when Babington-Browne's head appeared round the door: 'Ah, Dixon, look lively. Old Man's back. I thought we were safely shot of him for a few days. No such luck. I wouldn't let him catch you loafing around with the paper if I were you.'

Mike shoved *The Times* down the side of the armchair and scrambled to his feet. Footsteps were approaching rapidly down the corridor accompanied by a loud, impatient voice. The voice was saying, 'Why the blazes isn't it ready for me to look at? Horley told me they were building it nearly two days ago. I've flown back from Suffolk specifically to inspect it.' It didn't seem to wait for any kind of answer before it went on: 'Get on to Horley immediately. And my new ADC was supposed to arrive last night. Anybody set eyes on the fellow?'

Babington-Browne had hidden himself behind the door and was using it as a shield against the approaching threat. Mike saw that the young lieutenant was genuinely nervous. He glanced down at his own hands. They were steady. Odd, the things that brought on the shakes. Apparently, the sound of a Major-General on the warpath wasn't one of them. He walked to the doorway without a glance at the subaltern and stepped out. 'Lieutenant Dixon, sir. I think it's me you're looking for.' He saluted smartly, for the first time in a long time, and immediately felt annoyed with himself.

When he relaxed from the salute and looked at his new boss, the General both was and wasn't what Mike had expected. A lean man of just over the middle height, his weathered face fitted the career soldier. Strong prominent nose. Large fleshy ears. Eyebrows that no barber had recently had chance (or possibly the courage) to tame. A neat but by no means fastidious moustache sat between deepish grooves running from nose to mouth. So far, so conventional, but it was the eyes that were striking. Even behind heavy-rimmed spectacles the eyes showed a fierce curiosity that seemed to be coupled with a readiness to find whatever they rested on wanting. At that moment they rested on Lt Michael Dixon.

'Is it true you've seen action, Dixon? Or are you fresh from Civvy Street?'

Mike stared for a second or two more than was polite before answering. 'Not fresh, sir. Joined up after Dunkirk. Last in action six months ago. Been recovering from wounds pretty much full time since then.'

'North Africa?'

'No, sir. Operation Jubilee.'

'Dieppe?' The expressive eyebrows rose above the spectacles and waggled for a moment.

'Sir.'

'But all the armour at Dieppe was Canadian. You were seconded?'

'No, sir. I was with a commando unit.'

'Commando? You transferred from a tank unit to the commando? For God's sake, why?'

Mike almost fell back a pace under this barrage: 'Sir, I think there's some misunderstanding. I've never been in tanks before now.'

'Never been in tanks? Then what in God's name are you doing here? I've no use for a commando.'

He did take a step back now, checked himself and glared back. 'I was proud to be in Three Commando, sir.'

Hobo stared at him for a long minute and seemed to reach a decision: 'So you were at Dieppe. Well, that's some use, I suppose.

You can fill me in later. Damn fool nonsense. I don't approve of sideshows, Dixon. Let me tell you that for nothing. We don't have the men and equipment to spare on sideshows. Do you know how many tanks we lost at Dieppe?'

The glare he gave his new aide suggested he thought Operation Jubilee had been all Dixon's idea.

'No, sir.'

'All of them. Every single bloody one! And for what?' He snorted, the lenses of his spectacles magnifying the intensity of his glare. Mike felt his face burn. It wasn't embarrassment or fear that pulsed through him. It was anger. Rage, even. Baby Babington-Browne was right. The man cared for nobbut tanks – but it wasn't only tanks they'd left destroyed or abandoned on the beaches at Dieppe.

'We lost a lot of good men that morning too, sir.'

A tall officer standing behind Hobart gave a warning shake of the head. 'Hardly surprising,' snapped the General. 'When the thing had no sensible objectives, no proper bombardment and no air support. Damn waste, when we couldn't afford it. Still, you got out – wounded, you say?'

'Yes, sir. I was Returned To Unit. Then they sent me here.'

'And before the Commando?'

'Royal Engineers is where I started, sir.'

Something eased in Hobo's expression. 'Well, that's not too bad I suppose. I was in the Royal Engineers myself till twenty-three. Then I saw that the armoured idea was the future. Been in tanks ever since. Now,' he pointed at Dixon's battledress, 'Get yourself properly dressed and report to my office in an hour. Last chap left in a hurry. You'll need to get stuck in.'

'Sir.' Mike saluted again and watched as the General and his silent entourage set off again down the corridor at a smart lick. When they were a safe distance away Babington-Browne appeared in the doorway to the mess. 'You like to live dangerously, I must say. Giving the Old Man back-word on your first day. This is going to be interesting. Short and sweet, probably, but definitely interesting.'

'Glad you're amused. Now,' and he felt a surge of satisfaction in pulling rank on the subaltern, 'be a good chap and find a servant to fix my kit, would you?'

5

One thing was clear. Hobo's arrival had a galvanic effect on the unseen inhabitants of Rawdon Hall. The place echoed with the sound of hurrying feet and urgent conversations. It seemed nobody relished examination by that belligerent stare. Even if they didn't know what they ought to be doing, each man understood he'd better look as if he was doing something.

Up in the cold, cheerless bunk-room where he'd dumped his kit, Mike found himself re-tying his tie a third time. His reflection in the fragment of mirror hung up on an old nail took him by surprise, as it sometimes did these days, because the face that looked back at him displayed little mark of war. The weariness, the dismay, the sense of having failed, so strong within him, must, he felt, be obvious to all. But on this evidence he doubted even those who knew him best would be able to tell all the ways in which he had changed. Frank would soon spot them, he thought. Except it was three years since he'd seen Frank and who knew how much he must have changed too. He turned away before he started to brood any more on that.

As he clattered down the stairs, favouring his good leg, he wondered if old Hobo was one of those officers for whom ceaseless motion masked a chronic lack of ideas. All heat and no light. He couldn't be much good if he was still a Major-General at sixty and never trusted to lead a unit in action. As he was thinking this, he arrived outside the library. A little clerk sat by the door at a deal desk, dwarfed by a huge typewriter. The corridor was freezing. He looked perished.

'Lieutenant Dixon to see General Hobart. I'm his new ADC. Can you let him know I'm here, er … ?'

'Piddington, sir. Go straight in. Knock and enter is how he likes it. Unless he tells you otherwise.'

Mike knocked and pushed the door open, reckoning that too much hesitation would probably be worse than too little. General Hobart was sitting behind a desk placed opposite the door. There were no chairs on the visitor's side. Mike approached the desk and saluted, a little more sloppily than before.

The CO looked up from a letter he was writing: 'Ah, Dixon, is it? About time. We can talk in the car.'

He scribbled his name and stood up, screwing the top back on to his fountain pen. 'Piddington!' The clerk's head appeared round the door faster than Mike would have thought possible. 'Letters. And have that report typed up for when I get back. We'll be three or four hours. I'm expecting something from the CIGS, so keep your eyes peeled.'

They were out of the library and halfway down the corridor before this instruction was complete. In the same time, Hobart had put on a beret and was climbing into his greatcoat. 'I told Horley to be ready for us at fifteen hundred. We'll have two hours before the light goes. There's never enough time, damn it. I may have to shoot down to Whitehall at any minute and there's another day wasted at least. Nobody seems to see how imperative it is that we use every hour of every day. You can be damn sure the Germans aren't sitting around drinking tea and complaining about the difficulties of tank procurement. We need men. We need new equipment and the trouble is everything's in the shop window and none to spare.'

They arrived at the front door. It had come on to rain now, an opaque moorland rain falling without sound from a sky that looked as if it was perfectly capable of raining forever. Hobo gave no sign of noticing and plunged down the steps to the car. The driver opened her door but he waved her to stay where she was before she could do more than put one foot to the ground. She pulled it back in and shut the door, not before Mike had noticed that the foot came with a shapely ankle attached, only partly camouflaged by a heavy brown lace-up shoe and thick beige stocking. It was the girl who had picked him up from the station. He felt he was piecing her together like a jigsaw – cut-glass accent, fair hair on the nape of her neck, eyes in the rear-view mirror, now a foot.

Hobo motioned Mike in impatiently. 'Let's not keep Major Horley waiting any longer than we have to, shall we?'

The big car moved smoothly off. Leafless trees lined the narrow drive, less an avenue than a motley gang of grey trunks bullying in at either side. As they gathered speed, Mike glimpsed moss-covered rocks and a few clumps of sooty, wind-battered snowdrops cowering between the tree roots. The girl swept the Humber round the tight turn at the end of the drive between two tumbled stone pillars on to a narrow lane that headed steeply uphill as if she had yards, not inches, to spare.

'So, Dixon. What have you heard about us so far?'

Mike almost spluttered. If he told the commanding officer that his men believed they were in a rag, tag and bobtail outfit with not much chance of ever fighting together he could see the car making a rapid diversion via Rawdon station. 'Truth is, sir, I've hardly had a chance to speak to anyone yet.'

'Nonsense,' said Hobart. 'The truth is they've told you that no one has a clue what's going on, that our equipment is thin on the ground and mostly obsolete, that the commanding officer is an awkward old bugger whom the Army Council would love to push into retirement once and for all, and that hardly anyone expects the Seventy Ninth to last till summer.'

Mike felt himself between the devil and a patch of very deep blue sea. He looked around for inspiration and found it in an unexpected place. Blue eyes were staring at him in the rear-view mirror and the driver's head nodded imperceptibly. Was she trying to tell him that honesty was the best policy? He hoped he was reading her right. It hardly seemed likely that she'd go out of her way to help him after last night, but he had no other leads, so he gulped air and said: 'Something along those lines, sir.'

Hobart nodded sharply, once, and turned away to look out of the window. A row of soot-blackened labourers' cottages climbed the hillside in saw-tooth steps. In the uncomfortable silence Mike wondered if self-pity was one of the Old Man's fatal flaws. But when Hobo turned back to face him his eyes were alight. 'Fact is the rumour mill's not far wrong. There aren't enough resources to equip an extra front-line division at the moment. General Brooke insists there is a job for us to do though. Something new. That's why it's interesting to have you here. I'm sure it's a complete bloody coincidence. Nobody in Whitehall would ever send me a useful officer on purpose. Still, we must take our lucky chances where we may. There's damned few of them.'

Mike didn't have an earthly what he was talking about and his cluelessness must have shown in his expression.

'Dieppe, man. You said you were on the Dieppe raid.'

'I was, sir. But I don't see how that helps.'

The General bounced in his seat. 'For a start, you're one of the few who came back, which makes you one of the few with experience of assaulting a heavily-defended French beach. What happened to our tanks? Did they get ashore safely or were they swamped? Were they able to start firing straightaway? What were the minefields like? There's been so much arse-covering, it's almost impossible to identify what mistakes were made and, consequently, no hope of learning from them.'

Mike frowned. It was the first time since he was dragged aboard a wallowing landing craft in a slick of blood that anyone had asked him what had happened that August morning. He had tried to push it away, as far as he could, until all that obtruded into his daily life was a sharp corner of inarticulate anger at the disaster that had unfolded so terribly fast.

'Well, man? Speak up. You don't have to worry about offending anyone. It's just the two of us. Unless you count my driver and I doubt she's a spy for Dickie Mountbatten. Are you, Charlie? Spying for the Head of Combined Ops?'

'He is rather handsome, sir. In the newsreels.'

'Handsome be damned. Handsome is as handsome does. Ignore her, Dixon. Speak as you find. I always have. Not that I recommend it if you crave a glittering career in the army.'

Mike felt the prick of anger again. 'I don't care about my career, sir.'

'Well, care about it enough to give me some answers.'

'It's difficult, sir. I … '

'Rubbish. Just tell me what you observed. Raw intelligence is the best, before the statisticians and the regimental historians get their hands on it.'

Mike straightened his bad leg and felt the re-connected ligaments pull taut. Raw intelligence? He supposed you could call it that. He eased his foot down on to the floor of the car and tried to remember what he'd spent the last seven months trying to forget. 'Well, we went in earlier than the main force. Before first light, so I didn't see the main assault. The nearest Canadian beach to us was Blue Beach, I think. They were supposed to be the flanking attack – most of them were dead or had given up by the time we came off.'

'But did you see anything of what happened?'

Mike tried to think. How could he explain what he'd never understood? It had all been such a mess. 'The main thing was the confusion going in, I suppose. One minute it was pitch black then a star-shell went up. We'd run into a Jerry convoy coming down the coast. Their escort put the gun-boat leading us pretty much out of action, shot away its radio and steering. When it quietened down a bit we'd lost touch with the rest of our flotilla. Didn't know if they'd kept going or turned back, or been sunk. The CO and naval commander in our boat decided we should stick to the plan and head into shore anyway.'

'How many men were you?'

'Twenty-five. Including the boat's crew. Eighteen commando.'

'And how many should you have been?'

'The plan was for two hundred and fifty commando to assault the gun at Berneval.'

The eyebrows rose and waggled again: 'Go on.'

'We beached just after first light. Jerry didn't seem to have taken much notice of the commotion – I suppose they're used to ships tangling in the Channel. We cut the wire and worked our way round behind the battery. The CO decided to harass them from the cornfields beyond. Said a few yards of standing corn could stop a bullet. We knew we probably couldn't take the gun, but if we could keep it off the main assault force for a while, that'd be worth something. We kept them amused for a while. They even got brassed off enough to haul the gun around and start firing into the cornfield. A few yards of corn wouldn't have stopped one of those big shells. Luckily they couldn't depress the gun enough to be in danger of hitting us. That wasted a good bit of time. We hung about until they brought up reinforcements to out-flank us. That's when Major Young decided it was time to go.'

He stopped, his throat suddenly dry. He stared out of the window and tried to swallow. His heart was pounding and he felt heat rising into his face.

'Dixon? You've ground to a halt, man. What happened then?'

Rain streaked the car window. 'Sorry, sir. I was ... sorry.' He shook his head and slowly came back to Yorkshire. 'I was hit as we reached the beach. Spandau fire. Lucky it was then, or I suppose I'd be in a POW camp now. Chaps in those other boats weren't so lucky – they landed as we were coming off and were pretty much all killed or captured, so I heard.'

Hobo grunted: 'Stupidity. How did you run into a German convoy without any warning? Why didn't the landing craft have radio contact with their HQ?'

'Don't know, sir.' Mike's voice was low and numb.

'Of course *you* don't know, man. Wasn't your job to know. It was the planners' job. Fact is, Mountbatten couldn't persuade the Air Force to back his operation – so he went ahead without them. Idiotic. What possible qualification has a naval captain for planning an amphibious assault of all arms? Sometimes I wonder why we demand such sacrifices from our merchant marine, our coal-miners, our steel-workers, agriculture – only for the British officer class to throw all their work away on grandstanding. This war's not won, Dixon. Not by a long chalk. I believe there are some who would sooner see us lose it than put the running of it in the right hands. I mean, what was the point of trying to storm Dieppe? Tell me that. We never expected to be able to hold the port for long, so why go? To knock out a few guns? To give the Canadians a run out, because they'd been kicking their heels in England for too long?'

'Don't know, sir.'

It was like being back at school, being quizzed about the causes of the Great War. He'd never had a clue about that sort of thing and it struck him that he still didn't, even when he had been on the spot as the history was being made.

'Nor do I, Dixon. What I do know is: if we're to beat Hitler, we will have to go back to France one day soon. We'll have to move men and armour across beaches no less difficult than the ones at Dieppe. We'll have to do it on a huge scale – and if we fail we may never muster the strength for another try. The PM has promised the Americans an invasion next year. That means spring or summer, so we don't have much more than a year to get ready. In the next twelve months we have to build the biggest invasion force ever seen and work out a way for it not to end in carnage like Dieppe. Whereas all Hitler and his cronies have to do is wait for us to show our hand.'

Mike went to ask a question. Then he hesitated. Dixon the commando would never have thought to ask it. Dixon the Dieppe veteran couldn't help it: 'Do you think we're up to it?'

Hobo glared at him for a long time. Mike had the feeling he was about to get the sack before he'd even started. Wondered what would happen to him then. He wondered, but he couldn't find it in himself to care much.

'We have to be, Dixon. Every single one of us has to work for it with every ounce of our strength. I hope to God the Seventy Ninth gets a chance to play its part. Brooke's ideas for this Division aren't bad. We have to wait and see whether he can square it with the Army Council. If he pulls that off maybe we can start to get things moving in the right direction.'

The car came sharply to a halt. The driver turned and gave Mike his first good look at her face. As jigsaw pieces go, it was better than a bit of sky. It was like finding all four corners at once. What had Babington-Browne called her? A corker? He hadn't exaggerated.

'Here we are, sir,' she said. 'Major Horley.'

Mike looked out of the window to see an officer standing in a field gateway. Major Horley wasn't the copybook image of a happy man. The leather belt fastened round the middle of his greatcoat appeared to be holding his contents together like the strap on an over-stuffed travelling trunk. Rainwater ran towards a slight dent on the peak of his cap and dripped off at a steady rate. The General flung open the door. 'Everything ready, Horley?'

'Sir,' said Horley, voice muffled by his sodden British Warm riding up under his chin as he stuffed himself into the seat facing Hobo, his back to the driver. The car filled with the powerful stink of wet wool, as if a sheep had just climbed in. 'Of course, we weren't expecting to do the first test so soon. I only told you my idea of the thing yesterday morning, sir.'

'Well, what have you been doing since then, man? You've got an engineering shop, local blacksmiths and metal bashers. Initiative is what we need here. If we're ever to get these things into production we can't wait for the official machinery to grind its way to perdition. We need to tell the War Office exactly what we want, or we'll only get what they think will do for us. And do for us they probably will. Now where the devil is it? Miss Carrington has a pretty decent sense of direction, for a woman, but she's not a mind-reader.'

Horley sighed, then swallowed it in a rapid gulp as the GOC's head snapped up. 'Through the gateway to the right and about three fields over. We found some soft ground down in a hollow that seemed about right. It's not sand, of course, but it isn't too claggy either.'

'What are we waiting for?'

The car took off with a leap that threw the unhappy Major towards his CO. He yelped and grabbed the door handle. Hobo gave him a withering look and turned back to Mike. 'The only way we're going to win this war is by using our brains. Very underrated military equipment, brain-power. Especially, I'm afraid, in the British army. It's fair to say that the kind of vision and elasticity of thinking that would be most useful right now is generally viewed by the Army Council with the utmost suspicion, which is why we shall be best telling them as little as possible about what we're doing until we know exactly what we need.

'Horley here is working on the mine-sweeping side of the job. It's already been tried in North Africa, using a tank to clear mines out of sand, but it's hellish slow and does away with the main gun. I want to get it rolling along at a better lick and without losing the right to return fire. I'm not in favour of sending men into the vanguard of an attack as sitting ducks.'

A copse of trees was approaching fast. It had had a large hole torn in it, with trees uprooted and cast aside. Mike had never seen the damage a herd of elephants could do, but he thought it might look similar. The spoor of at least one large tracked vehicle headed into the mangled woodland.

'We've laid mines,' shouted Horley, over the engine and the protests of the Humber's suspension, 'and we've managed to mount the pipes on the tank. Now we need to see if we can propel them with enough force to detonate the mines. I was hoping to have a couple of goes before … '

Wasted breath. The door was open before the car had come to a standstill and Hobo was in amongst the men, peppering them with a heavy fire of questions, while Major Horley was still getting down. As Mike climbed out last, the ATS girl turned her head and said lightly, 'I hear they're calling it The Mighty Wurlitzer.'

'What?'

'Major Horley's contraption. On account of the organ pipes. I should stand well clear when they're testing it, if I were you, sir. The GOC likes to get really close but some of these things are a bit experimental. Stand back, or be ready to get clear sharpish.' She smiled. 'Welcome to the Seventy Ninth, Lieutenant. Never a dull moment.'

Glad somebody seems to be enjoying this war, he thought. Then he remembered the gossip about her fiancé being posted missing and wondered if it was true.

The debate as to who should play The Mighty Wurlitzer on its debut was quickly settled by a captain deferring to a sergeant. The NCO climbed up on to the little tank, an old Matilda, with an expression that suggested this was exactly the sort of good turn he had come to expect from life. The tank lurched into motion and the clanking of the tracks sent a flock of rooks protesting noisily off their roost on a big elm. Mike watched them go, a black squadron cawing resentment into the wet sky, as General Hobart gripped Major Horley by the elbow and hurried him into a clear position to observe. Mike glanced back at the girl driver, who was standing on the door sill of the car, resting her arms on the top of the window frame. She lifted her chin and shook her head. He shrugged and went after the CO. It wasn't much of a job, but it was his for now.

The sergeant stood on the control step behind the driver holding two triggers, each one leading to a bank of metal pipes mounted either side of the turret. The Matilda trundled towards a line marked with two red flags. As it reached the line there was an almighty bang, a series of whooshes and the tank disappeared in a dense grey fog. The first big explosion was followed by four or five lesser ones as explosive tubes scorched along the ground detonating mines as they went.

'I say,' shouted Hobo, over the reverberations. 'Good show. Was that just one side?'

'Think so, sir,' said Horley. 'Other side should follow now.'

They were standing level with the Matilda's right forequarter, about a dozen yards away. As the smoke began to drift up into the trees, the same thing dawned on each of them at the same moment. Firing the first salvo had slewed the tank round so that it was now facing away from the minefield and pointing directly at its lords and masters. Horley was the first to move, scrambling down the side of the bank. Mike pressed himself deep into the turf, but shutting his eyes was a mistake. Every hair on his body bristled, the blood thundered in his ears and he forgot how to move. Above it all, he heard a stentorian voice bellowing, 'Cease fire! Cease fire!' but it seemed a long way off and hardly to do with him. How could it be? He was in Dieppe with Henry Peat lying next to him.

'What the devil are you doing down there?' A hand was shaking his arm. He thought hard about it and managed to force his eyes open. The Major-General was standing over him, pulling on his arm, trying to get him to his feet. He realised he had curled up almost into a ball and quickly pushed himself up off the bank, trying to steady the beating of his heart, clenching his fists to hide the tremor in his hands.

'You're white as a sheet, man. I think Sergeant Hall knows better than to fire on his commanding officer. Come on.'

As he followed the General over to the tank, he saw Horley labouring up from the rear. While they waited for him to arrive back, Mike turned his face up to the sky for the rain to rinse away the cold sweat on his face. His hands he jammed in his greatcoat pockets until his heart stopped pounding and he could be sure they wouldn't betray him.

'What happened, Hall?'

'First side was fine, sir. No go with the right-hand side, though. Must be a loose connection. Good job too, seeing as I was banging away at the trigger well before the smoke cleared. Didn't realise the old girl had swung round so much. Reckon I'd have potted the lot of you if the thing had gone off.'

'Better luck next time. Where the devil's Horley?'

'Here, sir.' The Major was still out of breath from his sprint away from danger and his almost-as-athletic return. Hobo was standing at the edge of the minefield. Ahead of him were several furrows ploughed in the soft earth and five smallish craters. He addressed Horley over his shoulder. 'Did you mark the mines?'

'I told the sappers to mark the positions on a plan as they laid them, sir.'

'Well, let's have a look. This system's only going to work if it detonates all the mines in a lane. Otherwise we shall have to go back to the idea of a rotor drum with flails. Looks like they've only gone thirty feet or so. Would it be better if we could get them rocket-powered?'

'We don't have any rockets, sir.' Horley's voice was high with surprise. 'It's hard enough getting hold of High Explosive.'

Hobo snorted. 'Of course it's hard to get these things. There's a legion of people in Whitehall who think it's their job to make it hard. Whereas it's our job to get the things we need to beat the Germans and train men to use them. If that's rockets, I'll find rockets. If you need more HE, I'll get hold of it. Christ, man, if it's cuckoo clocks you need, I'll find cuckoo clocks – and bugger Swiss neutrality. Now, can we pack more punch into that second set of tubes and see if that helps?'

'We'll need to take them back to the shop to re-load them.'

Hobo kicked the ground in frustration and peered at his watch: 'For God's sake, Horley. Must everything go at a snail's pace? I want the whole set-up back here at 0600 tomorrow. Assess the results of this afternoon, re-lay the minefield, boost the explosives and do something about that side-thrust. Could be nasty if you have tanks advancing in line.'

'Yes, sir. 0600,' said Horley, as the General turned and headed back towards his car.

'Could have been pretty nasty this afternoon,' said Mike, half to himself, as he prepared to follow.

'Bloody lunatic'll get us all killed one of these days,' hissed Horley, his eyes on the CO's retreating back. 'You'd think the Second Front was due next week. If I had enough time to get things ready I'd be able to put on a decent show, but the old fool always wants it yesterday. Shame Hall didn't blow his damned head off!'

With a resentful glare, Horley turned back to his minefield, leaving Mike to follow the General's rapidly departing back.

6

Back at Rawdon Hall, Piddington was keeping a gloomy vigil in the corridor. 'It's come, sir. General Brooke's despatch rider got here about an hour ago. I've put it on your desk. He's waiting in case there's a reply.'

'Right, might as well see what Brooke has managed to do for us.'

The General threw off his greatcoat and gloves and snatched up the buff envelope that lay on his blotter. He tore it open and drew out a folder Mike saw was stamped 'Top Secret'. Holding it down into the pool of light cast by the desk light, he began to read where he stood. When he reached the end he flicked straight back to the beginning, frowning. Now he sat, reached for his pen and started annotating the pages in a surprisingly small, civilised hand. At one point he scored heavily through two lines with a grunt. Mike, in the relative safety of deep shadow on the other side of the desk, raised his eyebrows. If these were orders from the highest ranking officer in the British army, it took some nerve for a mere major-general to take an editor's blue pencil to them. Perhaps Hobo's lack of advancement had as much to do with lack of tact as his temper and lack of care for his men's safety.

In under five minutes the amendments were done and Hobart looked up. 'Well,' he said. 'It's not bad. Not bad at all. We're lucky to have Brooke, I suppose. If Dill was still Chief of the Imperial General Staff we'd be hopelessly dished. But I think Brooke will do his best for us.

'Of course, as a mandate, it doesn't go far enough. They don't see how vital it is for us to run our own show. And they haven't thought of flame-throwers. Plus, of course, there's nothing about the divisional HQ being capable of close support in the field. Nobody else has trained three armoured divisions from scratch. I'm damned well going into action with this one.'

'You've added that, have you?' asked Mike.

'Not in words of one syllable, Dixon. I'm not a complete ass. I added something fairly anodyne about Divisional HQ being capable of functioning operationally. No need to make a song and dance of it at this stage. Piddington!'

'Sir?' said the orderly, his head appearing round the door like a rabbit out of a conjuror's hat.

'Give this back to the despatch rider and get him on his way.'

'Right you are, sir. Poor beggar should have about thawed out by now. I sent him round to the kitchen to scrounge some food and a hot drink.'

'Good,' said Hobo, but Mike could see that his mind was already elsewhere. Piddington saw it too and withdrew, taking the Division's new charter away with him. Hobo stood up and began to pace, turning irritably on his heel as though the room was too small to contain his urge for action. 'Time to get started, Dixon. It will take a great effort to get things on the move, especially as the Division's not known what it was for all these months. Inertia is the thing we have to get over. I suppose you could say inertia is the greatest force in the universe. Some would argue for entropy – and that might be the thing in Whitehall – but I think, in general, inertia has the edge.'

'Inertia, sir?'

'Yes. And we don't have any damn time for it. So let's shake them up a bit.'

His eyes flashed behind thick lenses. 'I want to talk to every man in the Division within the next week. We've units here in Yorkshire, Cumberland, Suffolk, Wales – don't forget Scotland. Commandeer the largest venue close to each of our bases – cinemas, town halls, anywhere with a decent auditorium. Not just officers, the men too. If we're to stand a chance of pulling this thing off we're going to need ideas from all ranks. I want every man to have a direct line of communication to me if he has a theory that can help us get across those beaches. I'll speak to the first lot tomorrow – straight after Horley's next trial.'

Mike glanced at his watch. It was 6.45pm. He had no idea where the nearest town was, let alone the nearest decent auditorium. And still no real idea of what the Division was about, beyond the semi-suicidal display of home-made weaponry earlier. He felt a pang of fellow-feeling with Major Horley.

'What the hell are you waiting for, man? Jump to it.'

Mike looked up and down the corridor. There was no sign of Piddington. He'd probably found something to detain him in the kitchen. Something warming. He didn't feel like seeking out Babington-Browne, who would be all too pleased to demonstrate his superior local knowledge. And he didn't know anyone else. Except for the ATS girl. Charlie. She'd tried to help him twice today already, which was more than he deserved after last night. He wondered if it was too late to make a better impression. He wasn't sure if he'd be able to find the motor-pool in the dark, or if she'd still be there – but it was worth a try. As the front door of the Hall swung to behind him he saw he was in luck. There was a good slice of moon to help him find his way. He tripped down the hill on a cobbled track until he came to a metal gate that led into a farmyard. By the moonlight he could just make out a double-height stable block to the rear of a lower, rambling farmhouse. Everything was shut up tight, except for a fine line of yellowish light under the doors of the cart shed where the cobbles dipped with wear. He slipped and squelched across the yard, the smell of it even more pungent in the dark. For the second time in as many days he thought of Fred Mee's farm – and his brother's sweetheart, Beattie, the dairymaid who always had a little whiff of farmyard about her. He used to tease Frank that she put a little dab of it behind her ears, but he always swore he liked it. 'Nowt wrong wi' a gel that smells a bit. She's a real gel, any road, wi' a real smell. Not like the gels in your 'ead. They may smell of fancy scent, but you can't gie 'em a squeeze like I can Beattie.' Frank had been right, as usual. Back then, Mike's girls were all theoretical – High School girls who wouldn't give him the time of day in his too-short, too-obviously second-hand blazer. Frank had had real girlfriends since he was twelve. It had always been the same with them, long before Mike won his scholarship to the Junior College and their paths split: Mike the looker and Frank the leaper. He wished his brother was here. He'd wished it every day for three years and he knew he'd be wishing it longer yet.

When he reached the stable block, he ran his hand over the rough wood of the door, feeling for the latch. Finding it, he pulled the door open and stepped smartly inside, jamming it shut again before anyone could yell at him for showing a light.

Four cars were parked in a line. He was in luck. Someone was working on the big Humber. One side of the bonnet was folded back. A figure in overalls bent low over the cylinder block and by the light of the wire-shaded work-lamp that hung over the car a rolled sleeve and a pale elbow was working furiously with a box spanner. He coughed and the mechanic jumped, dropping the spanner into the engine with a clang.

'Bugger!' said a cut-glass voice. The girl peered into the engine for a moment, crouched down and fished under the car, coming up with the spanner. Only then did she turn to see who was there. At the sight of Mike she said, 'Sorry, sir. For the language.'

He decided to take the high ground – he didn't expect to hold it long – and said, 'It's not quite what we expect from the ladies, I must say.'

'Sorry, sir. It won't happen again.' Then she seemed to reach the limits of contrition. 'Though if you will go creeping up on people in the dark and making them jump I don't know quite what you do expect.'

He laughed. It felt good. Seemed to open a space in his chest that had been closed up for too long. 'Something wrong with the car?'

She opened her hand and showed him a spark-plug. The hand was small and neat and etched with oil. 'Just cleaning the plugs and draining the rad for the night. Have to keep the old Killing Bottle in fighting fettle. The GOC can't abide being stuck on the side of the road. Gets in an awful bait. Really, if you think my language is bad, you should hear his when he gets held up. So I try to make sure his car's always ready to go.'

'Why's it called the Killing Bottle?'

'Oh, that's Lieutenant-Colonel Burton's name for it. He's spent so much time cooped up in it with nothing to eat or drink, he says he feels like an insect in a botanist's killing bottle. I try and make sure there are sandwiches if I know it's going to be a long trip, but poor Colonel Burton hates sandwiches and the GOC will never stop for something proper to eat.'

'It must be hard on you too, having to drive non-stop like that.'

She smiled and tucked a stray piece of hair behind her ear, leaving a glistening smear of oil on her cheekbone. Mike found himself wanting to step forward and smooth the oil away with his thumb. He realised she was watching him look at her, but all she said was, 'I don't mind. Sometimes I take him down to Suffolk or up to Scotland. It's better than being stuck up here all the time. He flies a lot too. There's a Polish pilot he likes. You're sure to meet him. Jakub.

He's a bit of a barn-stormer.'

He opened his eyes wide in mock disbelief. 'I don't suppose his flying can be much more terrifying than your driving.'

She pointed her spanner at him indignantly. 'I'll have you know I scored top marks on the advanced driving course at Camberley.'

'I've no doubt it's advanced. It advances a damn sight too fast for me. But I dare say I'll get used to it. If I've learnt one thing in the army, it's that you can get used to anything, given time.'

'They say you were in the Commando. That you were seriously wounded. Is that right?'

'They're saying that, are they?' he thought. 'I'm a topic of conversation. Saying I'm crocked, I suppose. I wonder what else they're saying.' He shrugged. 'I don't know about "seriously". Leg's a bit stiff, that's all. I hope I'll be passed fit enough for something besides a desk job soon. Then I can get a transfer out of here.'

She giggled. 'You'll probably find working for the CO's a bit more than a desk job. And I'd think twice before putting in for a transfer if I were you. Last but one chap did that, decided he wasn't up to the job. Hobo tore a strip off him for having the nerve to second-guess him. He did it in the car, said,' – and here she scowled and put on a mock-gruff voice – '"If I'd thought you were no bloody good, I'd have sacked you myself. I'll tell you soon enough if you're not up to it." Ripped up the transfer request right in front of his nose.'

'We'll soon see if he thinks I'm up to it. He's just given me my first job and I don't have a clue where to start. I was hoping you might help me.'

'I'll try, sir. If I can. So long as it's not about the inner workings of tanks. Keeping the Killing Bottle running's about my limit.'

'No, the tanks I could probably work out on my own. This is about local knowledge. He wants to talk to all the men in the Division and he's told me to book halls or cinemas where he can lecture at them. Only I don't even know where we are, exactly, let alone where the nearest big hall is – and he wants to start tomorrow morning.'

She grinned. 'Of course. I'm surprised he didn't want to start tonight. Let's think.'

She tapped her front teeth with the spark plug, and stuck out her tongue at the taste: 'I should say, for the units based round Rawdon, the Ritz at Keighley would be your best bet. It's the biggest cinema round here, and it's easy to get to – you don't want everybody traipsing into Leeds, you'd lose half on the way back.'

'How many's it seat, do you reckon?'

'Oh Lord, now you're asking. I haven't a clue. I don't go to count the seats. I go for the romance, the glamour. Squint hard enough and you could almost be in Piccadilly.'

'Could you?' Mike had never been in Piccadilly. The girl laughed at him. 'No, of course not. It's a Yorkshire flea pit. But it's better than spending every night in a cold billet.'

'Would you, er … ' his throat dried and he coughed, 'Would you consider going with me one night?'

Her smile faltered. She looked down sharply at the spanner in her right hand and turned away to hang it up on a peg-board fixed to the wall.

'I mean to say, we could go in a gang. You and the other ATS girls, some of the chaps here. That's all I … ' He tailed off as she turned back to look at him. It was clear that he'd overstepped the mark by more than a yard. Idiot. Of course, she wouldn't want to go to the pictures with the likes of him.

'I'm sorry, sir,' she said. 'You weren't to know. I'm engaged, you see. At least I was, before my chap went and got himself posted missing. Don't know what I am now, officially. In limbo, I'd say if I was Roman Catholic. God, that sounds dreadfully melodramatic. It's just … difficult, I suppose. There don't seem to be any rules for this situation. Or, if there are, no one's explained them to me.'

'I'm sorry.' He felt a full two inches tall. 'Can we forget I said anything?'

She nodded, and the smile flickered faintly back to life. 'Keighley,' she said. 'There must be somewhere decent in Beverley for the East Riding Yeomanry. You'll have to ring round. Get Piddington to help. He's a brick.'

'Looked more like an ice cube when I saw him. Freezing his backside off in that corridor.'

'Poor Piddington. He's a martyr to chilblains. Wears little mittens when the GOC's out of the way but hides them as soon as he hears him coming. Hobo's a stickler for uniform. He's your man, though. He's a great fixer-upper. If you can't find him, he'll be in the Duke of Westmorland later. Always is.'

Mike wondered if she went there much too, then told himself to stop. She'd made it plain enough he was wasting his time. He wondered if it was really because of her fiancé, or more to do with the fact that he didn't hunt, or do any of the other things she probably expected in a suitor. 'Well, I'd better go and see if I can commandeer the Ritz. That way, I might make it through my first twenty-four hours without being shown the turnstile.'

'And I'd better finish off with the old girl. Cheerio sir, and good luck.'

She tossed the spark plug into the air, caught it lightly and turned away to pick up a cleaning rag from the bench. Mike turned and pushed open the big door. Cold and dark rushed at him and he couldn't help looking back into the light and warmth for a moment before he shut the door.

7

The Ritz was not your average Yorkshire flea pit. To Mike it looked new and grand, with its pipe organ and a variety stage in front of the screen. The manager had boasted on the telephone that it was built to seat fifteen hundred customers but this morning nearly two thousand men and officers filled every plush seat, every carpeted stair and leant against every wall. The manager stood at the bottom of the wide sweeping staircase to the Circle, watching Army boots trample his prime quality Axminster with an expression close to physical pain, which he'd only managed to suppress for a few seconds whilst being thanked by Major-General Hobart for his contribution to the war effort.

The hubbub was tremendous. The order to attend had only come through over breakfast, occasioning a huge amount of rushing around arranging transport, cancelling training exercises and polishing of kit. Some of the men, noting the date, had assumed that an order to report to the cinema must be an April fool, but the idea of its being a prank fell flat when they heard Hobo was behind it. That was all they knew, so they were making the most of a rare morning indoors, in the warm, rather than being out on the freezing, sodden moors. The fact that the cinema manager was flanked by two groups of usherettes in far too much powder and lipstick for ten in the morning had added to the half-day holiday atmosphere.

Mike prowled the wings of the stage waiting for the GOC to finish briefing his senior officers. Hobo was radiating ferocity and it was easy to see the officers who thrived on his manner and the ones who wilted before it. Horley was there, dragged away from his latest test, looking as miserable as the day before. Mike still wasn't sure which group had the right idea about the CO. With a final emphatic nod, Hobo turned and came towards him. The men he turned his back on stood silent for a moment, then began to talk amongst themselves. One clapped another on the back and there were smiles, frowns and a general air that something had happened, that something was going to happen.

'Dixon?'

Mike felt the gimlet eye and straightened his back. The scar that ran from his hip up the back of his ribs pulled tight as he did so, like a rope taking strain. It didn't exactly hurt anymore, not like his leg, with its unpredictable aches and throbs, but it was there, a reminder. 'Sir?'

'Men ready?'

'All here, sir. Crammed in like sardines. So whenever you're ready.'

'No time like the present. Go and shut them up, will you?'

Mike headed for the centre of the stage as if it was an everyday matter for him to call two thousand men to order. He wished he had a gong or a klaxon and as he stepped forward and gazed out at the mass of khaki draped over the cinema's garish gilt and plush he felt his knees quiver. 'Get a grip, man,' he said to himself and, raising his arms like a policeman directing traffic, took a deep breath and bellowed: 'Quiet!'

The men in the stalls looked up and some broke off their conversations. But in the circle and up on the balconies the noise kept on. 'Quiet!' he shouted again, as loud as he possibly could. More men looked at the stage and fell silent, but still there was plenty of chatter up in the gods, where most of the men probably couldn't even see him. He glanced off to the side. Even in the darkness of the wings, he could see the glower behind the General's spectacles. His arms were folded and his eyebrows a solid blackthorn hedge. There was only one thing for it. He had no idea whether the CO would like it, but it was better than standing there all day. He took a deep breath, thrust two fingers of each hand into his mouth and gave a whistle that wouldn't have disgraced the Flying Scotsman in full steam. Silence fell as if someone had turned down the volume knob on a wireless set and the only sound was the sharp tap of Hobo's footsteps as he strode out on to the stage.

'Thank you, Dixon. Uncouth, but effective. Now, bugger off, would you?'

'Sir,' said Mike, retreating off-stage, unsure if he'd been praised or criticised. Behind him, Hobo planted himself, legs apart and arms folded and started. 'Now look here, I know you've all been wondering what this Division is all about. Some of you have trained under me before. Some of you haven't. Well, I have news for you. It's the news we've been waiting for, that really gives us something to do. More than something. Plenty. You have heard of the Lord Mayor's Show?'

The men stared at him, a wall of blank faces it seemed to Mike, watching from the wings. Hobo ploughed on. 'Big event in London. Lots of horses, pageantry and so forth. And of course they need people to go round after the parade to clear up the mess? Well, we're going to do the exact opposite. The Seventy Ninth is going to go round first and clear up before the parade. What I mean to say is, in our case the Lord Mayor's Show is the invasion of France and we're the ones who are going first to clear the way through the minefields and obstructions on the beaches so that the others can get ashore and peg out their claims inland. It won't be glamorous work, but it's important. Perhaps the most important job there is – and I've told General Brooke and the Prime Minister that the Seventy Ninth can do it. So we shall.'

A groundswell of chatter bubbled up immediately. Hobo held up his hand and it stopped. No whistle needed. 'How are we supposed to do this job? I'll tell you: we're going to do it by damned good training so that every man is capable of using his initiative to overcome any obstacle he meets along the way. We're going to need new weapons, new devices, ingenious ways nobody's ever thought of before to overcome every one of Jerry's defences. We need them in quantity and we need them fast. We don't have them yet and it's my job to get them in time for every man to be trained to use them.'

He paused again, as if even he was daunted by the task. Then he pushed on. 'Some of these weapons are in production, some are in the testing stage and some have yet to be invented. That's where you come in. We don't have the luxury of leaving everything to designers and the Ministry of Supply. We need the right ideas from people who understand armour and the job we have to do. That's why I'm setting up an open line of communication for any man with an idea to come direct to me. I don't want any of the "you're not paid to think" line in this Division. If you have a good idea that will help us destroy mines or blow up pill-boxes, or any suggestions for improving the equipment we already have, I want to hear it from the horse's mouth.

'Now, I'm going to set each unit to work on the task it's best fitted for, based on its previous training. Some of you will be on mine-clearing – with specially adapted mine-destroying tanks. Some of you will be trained to drive swimming tanks, working closely with the Navy. There shouldn't be any problem about that. We're all in this together and we'll sink or swim together. Whatever you do, I want you to remember that the Seventy-ninth Armoured Division is going to be in the vanguard when the Allies return to France and on our training and our initiative the whole success of the invasion may depend.'

He let this idea sink in. It sank in properly with Mike for the first time. 'Apart from the unstinting effort each one of us will be required to make to bring this Division into a state of readiness, there is one other thing we need to be conscious of at all times. That is secrecy. The weapons we will be using are totally new and their success depends on the Germans having no idea what is heading their way. They must carry on believing their Western Wall is impregnable until our tanks are moving across their minefields. Surprise is, in itself, one of our most crucial weapons. It costs nothing in terms of steel or man-power but, if lost, it can never be regained. So all your training will take place in remote areas, in conditions of absolute secrecy. None of the new weapons will be moved without being covered or disguised. Our tank harbours must never be visible from the air and, above all, none of you must speak of what you are doing to anyone outside the Division. Do I make myself clear? Good. Let's get on with it. There's a hell of a lot to do. Dismissed.'

As he turned and left the stage, Mike Dixon watched two thousand men begin to talk at once.

8

The next day found them in the East Riding addressing an equally bewildered audience, and the day after that the Killing Bottle wound its way up into the Cumbrian fells, a steep but not jagged range of hills covered in a velveteen blanket of sheep-cropped grass, hemmed loosely about with dry-stone walls. It was a grander, lonelier landscape than Mike's native Leicestershire wolds, with their neat arable fields, bluebell woods and ancient sandstone and granite outcrops.

'Now these chaps,' said Hobo, breaking into his daydream of home, 'are probably the most advanced in their training out of anyone in the Division. In fact, if we had to launch the Second Front tomorrow, the Fifth Tank Brigade is the only unit we'd have fully equipped to throw into the fight. Which is a pretty terrifying thought.'

'Why, sir? What is their equipment, exactly?'

Hobo looked out of the window. 'You'll see. I'm not saying they won't be useful, in the right circumstances. It's … well, you'll see.'

It was already dark when they reached Lowther Castle. The Brigadier led them to where his men were gathered on a cold hilltop and Hobo made the speech Mike was coming to know well by the glare of an arc-light run off a jeep battery. To his surprise, these men actually seemed to understand him from the off. He saw one or two nod with what looked like quiet satisfaction, and he heard one officer mutter to his neighbour, 'Thank God, finally somebody has an idea of what to do with us.'

When he finished, the men jogged off into the darkness. Mike was puzzled. As far as he knew, tanks weren't capable of fighting at night and it was pitch black up here, miles from anywhere. Still, one by one he heard the cough and rumble of engines starting up. As he waited for what would happen next he stared up at a sleek velvet sky foxed in places by clouds that drifted over the piercing stars. The moon was half-risen and its features seemed far clearer than last night in Rawdon, as if standing a few hundred feet up a fell had halved the distance between them. Suddenly both moon and stars were obliterated. Night lit up like the brightest whitest day. He swung around wildly looking for the source of the light, but the glare dazzled him, as though he was back on stage at the Ritz in Keighley with the spotlight full in his face.

Charlie Carrington was in what he was coming to think of as her usual pose, one foot on the running-board of the Humber, chin on top of the door. The mass of candlepower lit up the golden filaments of her hair where it swept under her cap, and her teeth shone white as a magazine advertisement for tooth powder. 'Impressive, isn't it?'

'What the hell is it?'

'Didn't he explain? It's the tanks. They have these giant lights on, instead of guns.'

She glanced to see if Hobo was in earshot, but he had walked forward with the Brigadier towards the line of tanks Mike's sore eyes could now make out advancing across the fell, each with a strange blazing eye mounted in place of the standard turret gun. There must have been a further order then because the lights began to flash. The silhouettes of the Major-General and the Brigade CO jerked crazily, like figures in an old magic lantern show, as Hobo thrust out an arm, clearly firing questions as he went.

Mike and Charlie turned away from the dazzling, flickering glare at the same moment and found themselves facing each other. The girl shut her eyes for a minute and then opened them wide. They were pale blue, fringed with long lashes.

'Makes you go all funny, doesn't it? I feel like I might fall over if I look right at them much longer.'

Mike felt exactly the same way. 'I expect that's the idea. Strobe has a very disorientating effect. It can cause fits.'

'Do you think it'll work, sir?'

'Seems a pretty crack-pot scheme. Might spread a bit of fear and confusion, I suppose. If it's a complete surprise. Certainly threw me.'

'Hmm, I'm not sure how easy it's going to be to keep it a secret. Even up here. One of the local ATS girls told me people can read their newspapers in the street in Penrith when this lot are on exercise.'

'How far's Penrith?'

'About ten miles as the crow flies.'

Mike burst out laughing.

'What's so bloody funny?'

He swung round to find the crazy jerking figure of a strobe-lit major-general right beside him.

'Honestly, sir?'

'Of course, "honestly", Dixon. Do you think we've time for anything else?'

Mike paused a moment before he went off the high board. 'Well, sir. Honestly, I think the idea's barmy. Surely its only possible use is in a night attack – and I don't imagine we're planning to invade at night, are we? We made a big enough balls-up of the last attempt in broad daylight. Even in a night attack I don't see why the enemy won't just shoot out all the lamps, then come back and finish off the job at first light.'

The clanking and grinding of a brigade of tanks lumbering across heather and gorse was almost deafening, but around the little group there lay an even more deafening silence. The General's face flashed white, disappeared, flashed white again like a stone gargoyle on a cathedral gutter. Charlie examined her toes, which appeared and disappeared three times a second. Each lightning flash seemed to last forever as she waited for the thunder to roll.

'I asked for honesty, man. Not bloody negativity. Of course, I know this Canal Defence Light isn't an all-purpose assault tank. I didn't design it. French came up with it originally. Still, that doesn't necessarily mean it's a non-starter. And the key thing is the men are already trained on it. Everywhere else, we're starting at zero. With men like you. Civilians. At least these chaps are keen to go out and do a job.'

Mike felt his face grow hot. 'I'm keen to do a job. Keen as anyone. Just give us the bloody tools. Decent tanks, decent guns, decent planning. I didn't ask to be a staff officer. Sack me if you want, sir. I'd sooner be in the ranks than on the general staff any day. Being a private soldier was good enough for my brother. And my father in the last lot.'

The General expelled a long huff of air. Mike fancied he could see the pale fog of breath flowing towards him through the ghostly light. He was still wondering which particular lousy posting they'd find for him when Hobart regained the power of speech.

'Don't be an ass, Dixon,' he bellowed. 'I know Dieppe was a disaster. Our job is to do better next time. We can't snap our fingers and expect the means to do it to arrive by magic. I'll sack you all right, if you turn out to be no use. Not before.'

The two men glared at each other. Mike licked his lips and was about to say more.

'Are you ready to go back, sir?'

Mike was surprised that the girl had the nerve to step between them, but the General didn't seem to notice. 'Yes, Charlie. I think we've seen enough for tonight. Take us back to Lowther. I have to go down to London in the morning. You two had better head back to Rawdon once you drop me at the airfield tomorrow. Dixon, get on and set up the rest of the briefings. I'll be back tomorrow night, so we'll start again first thing.'

They drove down off the hillside on to a narrow road lined with dry-stone walls. When they'd gone about a mile, the lights went out. It was as if someone had dropped a coal-scuttle over their heads. Utter blackness. Charlie braked hard and they sat until her pupils re-adjusted to the paltry pencil beams of the headlights. When she could, just barely, make out the road in front she sighed and put the Humber into gear.

She dropped them in front of the castle. When Hobo told her to be back at 06.30 she gave him her usual 'Right-o, sir' and disappeared. Mike wondered if she knew where she was going, whether she would get anything to eat or a decent place to sleep. Then he reasoned that if anyone could find her way around a strange castle in the black-out it was probably Charlie Carrington, whose confidence seemed to guide her like a compass. Hobo strode off without a word or a glance at him. He stood alone in the darkness for a minute. Then, having nowhere else to go, he followed the General inside.

9

At the airstrip next morning a Dakota sat idling its engines. The sun had come up and a layer of mist hung low over the field. Charlie bumped the car over the wet grass. A very tall thin officer was standing by the plane talking to a shorter well-built man in RAF blue, a curious-looking fellow with a flat open face and a shock of white hair that made it impossible to tell his age. When Hobo had gone to join them, Charlie turned to Mike.

'That's Jakub, see? The Polish pilot. With Colonel Burton. The Old Man loves arguing with him.'

'What about?'

'Oh, I don't know – French plays, music, politics. Jakub's far cleverer than me. Colonel Burton is too, of course. They say he took a First at Cambridge. History's his subject. When the General tries to have one of those conversations with me, we soon fall on stony ground. Unless it's about hunting. He was a great one for pig-sticking in his Indian days, you know. But when it comes to the arts, I'm afraid he rather loses me.'

'Literature and music not your strong suits at school?'

She laughed. 'I didn't have suits, strong or otherwise. My parents didn't believe in school. Not for girls. My education boiled down to a home-sick Belgian governess, riding lessons and six months in Switzerland being finished before I came out. I can *parlez-vous*, take a decent fence and curtsey. Apart from that I'm a complete nincompoop.'

He leaned forward. 'When you say you came out … you mean you were a debutante? Presented at court and all that?'

'Of course. Isn't everyone?'

He wasn't sure if she was teasing or not. If that was the world she came from, she was even further out of his league than he'd thought, fiancé or not. Though it hardly mattered. On present form he wouldn't be around long enough to ask her out again, any road. Gloomily, he slumped back and waited for Hobo to get into the aeroplane. When he did, Charlie trundled the Snipe round in a slow circle towards the edge of the airfield. 'Pity poor old Whitehall. They're in for it again today. Do you think they sound the air-raid sirens when they see him coming over the horizon?'

'Hmm, probably,' he murmured, and leaned back against the seat for the long undulating drive over the fells and dales to Rawdon. Soon he slept, the frantic last couple of days catching up with him. He only woke when the door slammed. Looking round groggily, he found that the car was parked in the broad high street of an old-fashioned market town. He had no idea where he was, so he got out and looked about for signs of Charlie Carrington. Finding none, he pulled out a pack of cigarettes and leaned on the bonnet, smoking and watching the town go about its business. Checking his wrist-watch he found it was two hours since they dropped off the CO. He realised he had missed breakfast. He had no idea how far they still were from Rawdon.

'Excuse me,' he said to a tweed-hatted matron carrying a wicker basket. She stopped, not unfriendly. 'What town is this?'

She looked surprised, then confused, then blushed and glanced around, as if looking for help. 'I'm not sure that I should, actually. I mean they do say "careless talk costs lives", don't they? If you don't *know* what town this is, I'm not sure I have any business telling you.'

She took a step back, holding her shopping basket defensively in front of her, as if he might really be a Nazi paratrooper in disguise and ready to shoot her at any moment.

'Lieutenant Dixon?'

He turned to see the driver approaching, swinging a paper bag, and smiling. 'I found us breakfast. A couple of buns. There were rumours in the queue that they even have raisins in.'

'Good work, Driver Carrington. Where are we, by the way? The natives aren't easy to crack.'

The woman in the hat blushed deeper but set her chin defiantly all the same.

'Skipton. Not far from home, but she's quite right not to tell you. How is she to know who you are?'

The woman shot a grateful glance at Charlie, stepped around them and hurried off.

'How do you know where we are, anyway?'

'My brilliant sense of direction, sir.' She smiled at him. If she'd noticed his use of her rank she gave no sign of it. 'Plus, I have a map. And I double-checked by looking in a telephone box on the way to the baker's. They haven't taken the addresses out of all of them yet. Tricks of the trade. Though I shouldn't be telling you, in case you are a Fifth Columnist.'

She slid back behind the wheel. Mike had his hand on the rear door but he changed his mind and climbed into the front passenger seat, moving the bag of precious buns. There was a moment of awkwardness, which he sought to cover by unscrewing the little ears on the bag and offering it to her. She pulled off her driving glove and he caught a whiff of damp leather and perspiration, not unpleasing, animal, before she pushed her hand into the bag and drew out a small, irregular bun. He reached into the bag and drew out its almost twin. His mouth watered as he bit into the bun. It was dry and crumbly, but sure enough, in the second mouthful he found a raisin, which gummed itself to one of his molars. He ran his tongue over it, relishing the sweet grapey flavour tinged with caramel where it had been toasted on the crust of the bun, sucking at his tooth until the last trace of raisin faded away. Charlie was munching hungrily and by the time they had both finished and were brushing away crumbs, the awkwardness of his coming to sit beside her had evaporated.

They left the town behind and Mike felt fully awake. He realised it was a fine spring day, the first of the year or at any rate the first he had been alive to. The road dipped and fell in front of them as they left the dales behind and he found himself suddenly, surprisingly, happy. The tyrant had been borne away into the clouds. There was nothing he could do to bring Rawdon closer or hold it further away. They would arrive when the road led them there, and until then he had nothing to do except sit next to a beautiful girl who had once curtsied to the king. There was a war on, and he was part of it, but for these few hours or minutes he could not wish his life different.

About five miles out of Skipton he heard engine noise that wasn't the Humber's straight six. It was something throatier that grew and deepened until a shadow fell over the windscreen and the noise became a roar.

The bomber passed over, the roar rising to a deafening boom as four great Merlins laboured along no more than two hundred feet above the ground. Mike and Charlie looked at each other, startled out of their peaceable silence.

'What was that?' asked Mike, when the roar had receded to a ringing in his ears.

'Lancaster,' said Charlie, without hesitation, her face pale and serious.

'Was — ' He corrected himself. 'Is your fiancé on fighters or bombers?'

'Bombers,' she said, as he'd known she would from the look on her face. 'But not Lancs. He flew — .' She fell into the same trap and hauled herself out. 'He flies Halifaxes. Seventy Six Squadron. Based at Linton-on-Ouse. Yorkshire, too, way over in the East Riding. Still, could have been worse.'

She stopped as they both realised it now was. They drove on in a silence that was nothing like before. He had to break it in the end. 'How long since he went missing?'

Maybe he was wrong to ask her about it. He was about to say something else, to try and change the subject when she said: 'Four weeks now. Nearly five. They'd just started going over there most nights, to different cities – Essen, Berlin, Hamburg. That night it was Nuremberg. Nobody saw his kite go down, but he didn't come back.'

'And there's been no news?'

'Not a thing. Nothing from the Red Cross to say any of the crew has turned up as a POW. I called the station a week ago to see if they'd heard anything, and they told me his two best friends have gone now too. One crashed on landing, on the way back from Dortmund. His undercarriage was shot up and he didn't know. The other one went down over Berlin. Four weeks ago they borrowed a car and came over here to console me about Bill. Now they're gone themselves.'

'It must be hard.'

She gave him a look that he couldn't read. 'It's … strange, more than anything. It really hit me when I heard those other boys had got the chop. Not just because I knew them, but because they were the ones who knew Bill best. If they're gone, all their memories of him have gone west too. All the things they did together, all the "Do you remember whens?" have gone now too. It makes it seem like maybe none of them ever really existed.'

She didn't look at him this time, just blinked a few times and shook her head.

'You don't know for sure that' – for some reason he didn't feel entitled to use the man's name – 'he's gone west though, do you? I mean, if nobody saw his crate go down, it's not certain. Sometimes it takes ages for news to come through about POWs. Or he might have come down in France or Holland and still be trying to get home. You don't know.'

'No. I don't. But that feels horrible. Some people say that they do know. That they feel it when someone they love dies. And I don't. I haven't. And I don't know what that means. Does it mean that he's not dead? Or does it mean he is, but I didn't really love him after all, because I don't feel it?'

'I'm sure it doesn't mean that.'

'Are you? I wish I was. I'm not sure I'd have made an especially good wife. Being in the ATS, it's hardly glamorous, these awful clothes and everything, but it's doing something, isn't it? I like having a job to do. Having a purpose. Sometimes, it even feels like a relief that Bill's not here, telling me how our life is going to be. When I catch myself thinking like that I feel awful, that I could be so utterly heartless.'

She swung the steering wheel and braked the Humber hard into a passing place. The car skidded on loose gravel, slid into the grass bank and stalled. Charlie sat still, blinking hard until she lost the struggle against tears. Her shoulders began to shake and she laid her head on the big steering wheel and sobbed.

Mike had no idea what he should do, but he had a very clear idea of what he wanted to do. He reached out and stroked her hair gently from the crown down to the neat little roll at the nape of her neck. She went quite still for a moment. Then she seemed to give way even more thoroughly to her sobs and he lifted his hand and repeated the motion. The texture of her hair was fine and silken and through it he could feel the shape of her skull. Both sensations were new and strange but he had the undeniable feeling that this was a topography he would come to know as well as he knew the shape and feel of his own body. At this realisation, he tried to pull his hand away. Here was a girl, weeping over her lost lover, and here was he, plotting to take the other man's place before his death was even a certainty. He despised himself. But he could not take his hand away.

Afterwards, when he went over the scene, as he did repeatedly, obsessively, he could never decide how long she had wept for and how long he had stroked her hair, before she turned her face to look at him. Crying had not turned her eyes pinched and red but huge and cloudy, with tears clumped on her eyelashes and streaked down her face. She seemed to him not less beautiful, but changed, blurred and almost other-worldly in her vulnerability. She shifted her head slightly so that his hand slipped on to her shoulder and, without his knowing quite how it happened, her head was against his chest and his arm was round her. She didn't cry any more. She was resting, like an animal that has been in pain and danger and has found a safe bolt-hole. He could feel the rise and fall of her breathing, whilst hardly daring to breathe himself in case he broke the spell and she moved away.

Too soon, though if it had lasted years it would have been too soon for him, she did. A van went past and that seemed to jolt her back to life. She raised her head and sat upright, wiping her eyes with the backs of her gloved hands. Mike fished in his pocket for a handkerchief and handed it to her. She wiped her eyes again, blew her nose, hunched up her shoulders and expelled a deep breath that was part-huff and part-sigh. She turned on the ignition and pressed the starter, but when she tried to move off she found the car was wedged against the bank. 'Oh Lord,' she said, 'Don't say I've pranged it. The Old Man'll murder me.' She went into reverse and eased gently away from the verge. There was a scar in the turf.

'I'll have a look,' he said and jumped out to inspect. The front wing had picked up a dent and a lot of mud, but he couldn't see any serious damage. He got back in.

'It should knock out,' he said. 'I could give you a hand if you like. I've done a bit of that sort of work, before the war.'

'I hope it does,' said Charlie, as she checked the road behind and pulled out, 'or I'll be the next one through the turnstile at Rawdon.'

At the thought of that, Mike lifted his hand to place it over hers on the gear lever. Just as he did so, she moved it to grip the wheel with both hands and, after a moment hovering in the space between them, his hand dropped back on to his own knee.

What they said was true. Howard Burton had taken a First at Cambridge. Not at one of the grand old places on the Backs. His was a self-effacing, red-brickish kind of college populated mainly by the sons of clergymen and products of the lesser public schools. The son of a country vicar himself, he'd toyed with the obvious idea of ordination before deciding against it, mainly because he was quietly unconvinced of the existence of the Almighty, which put rather a dent in the whole field. Instead he had found himself, the summer after going down, back at the Somerset school from which he'd set out only three years before. The stipend of an assistant history master with responsibility for coaching the Second XI had been tiny, but food and board were included, and anyway he had not been brought up to think that money was of any great importance.

He'd stayed there for a decade, living as quiet but absorbing a life as it might be possible to imagine. Teaching suited him. Two years after returning he was made assistant housemaster, with an almost imperceptible increase in his salary that was nevertheless just enough to allow him to propose marriage to the serious, clever undergraduette he'd passed cycling up and down Grange Road for several terms before he worked up the courage to flag her down and wangle an invitation to tea. After coming to live at the school, Mary taught flute and clarinet to the least unmusical boys. The following year, after their first daughter was born, he was made housemaster and at a stroke their family comprised not only the three of them but fifty boys as well. Burton was not a thrasher, preferring to believe that boys would behave as well as you encouraged them to behave, not as badly as you suspected they might. Generally they proved him right, exceptions being dealt with by the firm withdrawal of privileges such as Sunday tea with Mrs B, coupled with a subtly withering sarcasm in front of their fellows that hurt more than the cane or slipper and gave far less scope for either dumb or swaggering resistance.

It was a happy house. The boys liked Burton and, without glorying in it, he was aware of their affection. On taking the post, he had told himself that being buried deep in Somerset would leave him plenty of time to work his undergraduate thesis up into a book that would make his reputation as a historian. Yet it wasn't long before the hypnotic rhythms of 'term', cricket coaching, evenings in the village pub with the other masters, not to mention carving a little time out from school to devote to his growing family meant that his thesis was abandoned to a never-opened drawer. Had he looked for it, he'd have found it smelling of sweat and leather under a box of cricket balls that had gone out of shape. But by then, Burton hardly ever gave a thought to what his tutors at Cambridge had praised as his early promise. By then, he was more concerned with the early promise of others, and derived his greatest satisfaction from sending boys he'd stuffed with history up to his old college.

The war came as a horrible shock. Not that he didn't see it coming. No historian could follow the events of 1936 to 1939 in the newspapers without being aware of what was coming. But for someone who believed deeply in man's propensity for goodness, given the right encouragement, he found the failure of the great powers to stop a disruptive little oik like Hitler from tipping the whole of Europe into anarchy and disaster deeply, viscerally disappointing.

Burton had no personal desire to fight. However. The morning after three of his Upper Sixth cadged a lift into Frome to the recruiting office and joined up, he drove there himself in the lunch recess and did the same. He still felt a pang of guilt, sometimes, at the thought of Mary's face when he came home and told her what he'd done. But he couldn't, wouldn't, undo it and three and a half years later, the schoolmaster's life that had seemed so much his, so solid and immutable, felt as shimmeringly unreal as a half-remembered dream.

His military career had advanced surprisingly quickly but he was still not sure what had led to his appointment as GSO1 to General Hobart. He wasn't aware of having mortally offended anyone at the War Office, and so he could only think that it was either a random act of fate, or else someone had genuinely decided he was cut out for the job. At first, he'd thought it was going to be more than flesh and blood could stand. Mary had replied to his miserable letters, reminding him about a particularly bloody group of fourth-formers he'd had in '37 or '38. She urged him to wear down Hobo with the same mix of unshakeable steadiness and sweet reason that had eventually prevailed over the horrors of IVb. It wasn't easy advice to follow but, as with most of Mary's counsel, it was sound.

Nearly six months into the job, Burton felt he was on surer ground. Perhaps it was stoicism having its effect, or perhaps it was that his chief felt himself on surer ground too. Until the Army Council approved their charter, it was clear Hobo felt the Division might break up under him at any moment and trusted no one. Burton had attended enough meetings at the War Office by now to know Hobo considered the place a citadel stuffed to the battlements with his enemies. But today's meeting was the first since Brooke had delivered their charter and the General seemed buoyant.

'There's a great deal to do, Burton,' he said, as they were getting out of the plane at Hendon into a waiting car. 'But at least now we shall be able to get started properly. I don't believe anyone's ever had to develop so many types of machine in so short a time. But we need them. So we must find a way. It's going to take the imagination and initiative of young men to achieve it. Not hide-bound specimens from the old schools. Not fossils like Horley.'

'He's trying, sir.'

'Yes,' said the General. 'Very. Get shot of him, would you? There are plenty of crevices in the Army where creatures like Horley can hide. Not in my Division.'

Burton nodded. Horley was no great loss. The man was more of a bad influence than the General knew. It was finding better men than Horley that was the problem. The Army was an awfully big haystack and, even if you could spot the needle you wanted, fishing it out was by no means easy.

'New ADC's probably a non-starter too. Incredibly negative attitude. Do you know he had the gall to tell me yesterday that the only operational weapon in the Division is "barmy"? I think he's a bit windy too. After Dieppe probably. Battle-shock. We were testing Horley's mine-clearer the other day and the fellow damn near burrowed his way to Australia at the first bang.'

Burton's heart sank. This was much worse than the guillotining of Horley. He hadn't had chance yet to do more than exchange a couple of nods with the new man, but he had read his service record and been rather cheered by the contents. Dixon wasn't regular army, it was true, but hardly any of the young men were these days. Clearly, he wasn't of the officer class either, but in Burton's experience if any CO was willing to swap breeding for talent it was Hobo.

'That's a pity, sir. According to his file he was a promising Engineering student before he joined up. Loughborough College. There's a letter of recommendation from the top chap there that makes it pretty clear they were disappointed he didn't agree to go into a reserved occupation at Rolls-Royce or somewhere. I imagine it was that reference that landed him his commission. And what with all the new devices we've got to work up, I was hoping we might put his talents to pretty good use here.'

Burton held his breath. He'd learned that the key to influencing the General was not to confront him with counter-argument but to float an alternative idea as gently as possible, like a soap bubble, and hope it would hang in the air, weightless but intriguing, long enough to catch his interest.

Hobo was quiet for a minute. Then he said, 'It wouldn't be a bad thing to have a tame boffin on hand, I suppose. I expect we shall be dealing with the commercial firms and designers, as well as the Ministry of Supply and the PM's various experimental outfits. Would be good not to have to take their word for things all the time.' Then the bubble burst. 'Still, it'll only work if he gets the damn chip off his shoulder about Dieppe, or whatever it is that's eating him. You'd better sort him out, Burton. And fast. Or he'll have to go.'

'Sir,' murmured Burton, accepting responsibility for turning Lieutenant Dixon into a model staff officer forthwith. The thing about bubbles, he thought ruefully, was that when they popped in your face the soap could make your eyes sting.

Their meeting at the War Office began cordially enough. The officer in charge of procurement, Major-General Quiller, was a shortish, stoutish man, well upholstered in a uniform that screamed Savile Row. His hair was freshly barbered and brilliantined neatly over a large, square skull. The tracery of broken veins spreading like two pinkish-purple river systems across his jowls marked him out to Burton as an enthusiastic club man as surely as if he had been wearing his member's tie.

'Ah, Patrick,' he said, as Hobart and Burton were shown into his office, rather than one of the bigger meeting rooms. Burton noticed that his desk was clear, apart from a large silver ink-well in the shape of a ram's head, and a few regimental knick-knacks. Quiller was either a meticulously efficient organiser, or he didn't have a lot on. 'Good to see you. Got hold of another Division, I see. Monty certainly made something of those Desert Rats of yours. In the end. What's this lot called?'

Burton winced at that insulting 'In the end'. The story went that Hobo had been sacked from command of the Seventh Armoured Division in Egypt and sent home to kick his heels before being unceremoniously shunted on to the retired list. The Army scrap heap. Rumours as to why ranged from a supposed mutiny by officers who disliked the way his training regime interfered with their timetable of socials and polo matches in Alexandria to Hobo telling his commanding officer he was 'no bloody good'. Either way, he'd been given the heave-ho and now Montgomery had gone and beaten Rommel with his old mob and taken every bit of the glory. Burton glanced at the CO nervously. He seemed, for now, to be turning the other cheek.

'Hello, Freddie. Nobody's pinned a nickname on it as yet. We only received our charter a few days ago. Howard Burton, my G1. Major-General Quiller.'

Burton saluted, and got a languid acknowledgement, which turned into a wave towards a couple of straight-backed chairs. Quiller sank back into the leather-upholstered throne on his own side of the desk and looked pretty comfortable in it. There was no one else present, which seemed a bit odd. Meetings like this one were usually mob-handed affairs.

'Ah yes, your charter. Old Brooke sent me across a copy. Must be a bit of a disappointment. Not to be a front-line assault force, I mean. Still, everything's in short supply, as I know better than anyone, and at least they've found some kind of support job for your mob. Better than being broken up altogether.'

Burton, in the act of sitting down, resisted another glance at Hobo, who had laid his leather folio on the edge of Quiller's desk and was tugging at the zip. He extracted a copy of the charter and a stack of hand-written notes. When he spoke, Burton was relieved to hear he still had his temper on a leash. 'It's a good deal better than being broken up, Freddie. And it's an important kind of job, if you read the charter carefully.'

Quiller smiled, though for all the sincerity in it Burton felt he might as well not have bothered. 'Of course it is, my dear chap. I'm sure Brooke knows that if anyone can build something useful out of string and sealing wax it's you. But that's about all we shall have to give you, I'm afraid. Naturally, the bulk of our efforts on the procurement side will have to be devoted to the front-line divisions. Monty's going to need a mass of replacement equipment and men when he gets back from North Africa. Honestly, I'm not sure what we shall be able to do for your lot.'

Now it dawned on Burton why they'd been got in before the rest of the company. Quiller was trying to avoid a public stand-off, though if this was going to be his line he would need more than an oleaginous smirk to pull it off. As soon as Hobo spoke, Burton could tell that the mercury had begun to rise.

'Well, Freddie, I'm sorry to say that I think you have misunderstood the position. We may be a specialist division but there's nothing in our charter to suggest we're a second rate outfit without the same procurement priorities as any other division. If you'd like me to point you to the passages where the Chief of the Imperial General Staff sets out the crucial nature of the Seventy Ninth's task I'm more than happy to do it.'

Quiller's smile faded a little. His jowls sagged as the muscles slackened. 'That won't be necessary, Patrick. I told you, I've read the document.'

'Good, so if I run through a list of what we need you can explain how you're going to allocate the appropriate resources?'

'I don't see much point in … '

'Well, I do. Have you a stenographer here?'

'No.'

'Never mind. We can circulate a memo after the meeting. Burton, do the honours?'

'Sir,' said Burton, unscrewing his pen and opening his notebook in a hurry.

'Well then, as you know, because you've read our charter, the Seventy Ninth's vital specialist role,' he stressed the words heavily and Burton derived some small satisfaction from underlining them in his notebook, 'is to neutralise the German beach defences, using a swimming tank launched at sea and reaching the beach under its own propulsion; a mine-clearing tank; a tank doubling as an armoured personnel carrier and mobile mortar; and a tank with flame-throwing capability. For the last two, we believe we can make do with Churchills, even one of the older marks at a push. But for the Duplex Drive swimming tank, the Valentines we've been experimenting with to date are no damn good. They don't even have a main gun that fires high explosive. We need a better fighting tank, that's all. Shermans. That's the machine. The Churchill's too damn wide and heavy. It has to be Shermans.'

Major-General Quiller smiled again. This one was the sort of smile Burton imagined a greengrocer would adopt these days if you asked for a bunch of bananas, or a pineapple. 'You are aware the Sherman's an American tank, I suppose?'

Hobo snorted. 'Of course I know they're American. Don't you know the Yanks are on our side now? It's not as if I'm asking for German Tigers. Though if I could get 'em I'd certainly take 'em. They're fine machines. As for the mine-destroyers, we can't work with these dreadful old Matildas either. We need Churchills for those, too. If there was a silver lining to losing all our equipment at Calais and Dunkirk, at least we got shot of a load of antiques. I'm damned if the Seventy Ninth is going to turn into a museum for the last remnants of our ancient armour.'

While Hobo set out his shopping list, Quiller had been fiddling with a paperclip. Now he hooked it under his thumbnail and flicked it across his blotter. 'Well, you'd better make the most of them, because they're all you're going to get.'

Burton felt strongly that records of the ensuing skirmish should make clear that it was Quiller who fired the first real salvo. His memo certainly would. However, as a quondam history master he knew that the battlefield accounts of the victors are the ones that generally survive and he was by no means sure whether in the battle between Hobo and the War Office he would find himself to have been on the winning side. Nevertheless, he continued to take what notes might merit a place in the official record, until the exchanges became so rancorous that he stopped writing and silently, almost sorrowfully, screwed the lid back on his fountain pen.

As they left the War Office, Burton found himself wondering if the sand-bagging round the entrance might be as much to protect passers-by from the effects of blast from within as to protect those inside from the effects of blast from outside. Certainly his ears were ringing as if he'd just been through an air-raid.

'I suppose that could have gone better,' said Hobo as they walked slowly down the steps. Remorse had come upon him, as it usually did, almost as quickly as the tantrum that preceded it.

'Sir.'

'Me and my damned temper. Every time I go into one of those meetings I tell myself I'm going to keep it under control, bite my tongue and be the personification of reason. And every single time Quiller, or some other useless bum-sucker like Quiller, manages to be so aggravatingly stupid that I simply can't help speaking my mind.'

'It was … trying, sir.'

'Trying, Burton? You know what the problem is? I don't have charm. Not a jot of it. Never have had. Never will. Not that it's a quality I rate terribly highly, but it's what you need with those Whitehall types – smoothness, suavity, all that rot. I suppose he'll get the others in now and complain what a horror I am. Well, Brooke knew what he was letting himself in for when he put me in this job. He gave me the job of building an Armoured Division, and build it I damn well shall. Whether the War Office and the Ministry of Supply like it or not. What's the worst they can do? Get me the sack? Well, I'm used to that, at any rate.'

11

Remorse had soured into something fouler by the time Hobo arrived back at Rawdon. Dixon got the thick end of it when the CO discovered he hadn't yet completed the schedule for their Cook's tour of the Division. The impossibility of contacting commanders who had been out on exercises with their units all day was not accepted in mitigation.

'Good grief, man. I want to be on the road first thing in the morning. I don't know if you know Kipling, but the minute is certainly an unforgiving measure round here, and if I don't get sixty seconds' worth of distance run out of my officers, they don't last long. Other Divisions may have room for laggards and incompetents. Not mine. There's too much to do and too little time. Now get out and do your job, or I'll find someone who will.'

Mike made his chasing calls in a mood composed of equal parts misery and rage, banged the door of the officers' mess and threw himself violently into an armchair.

On the other side of the fire, Howard Burton flinched. A sheaf of thin blue paper was propped against his knee and a pipe smoked lazily in a pale green saucer on the arm of the chair. He really wasn't in the mood for any conversation besides the imaginary one he was trying to have with Mary. That was going badly enough. She had still not forgiven him for enlisting before his call-up came. His decision, or her reaction, had put up a barrier between them that three years apart had done nothing but reinforce. She considered the step he had suddenly seen as his duty as dereliction of his pre-existing duties to her, their three girls and the school. She rarely said as much, but her letters failed to hide her unhappiness, which he took as the rebuke she intended. She was teaching full-time now, perforce, and her letters were a litany of complaints about the petty politics in the staffroom, the deteriorating behaviour of the boys and her dislike of having to leave the girls in the care of a maid she considered unbearably slovenly. It pained him when she despised the school, tainting their happy life there. He was increasingly fearful that they might struggle to pick it up again when the war was finally over. He tried to write back in a way that would placate her, treading on eggshells. As a result, he knew his letters were strained and dull. Mary was a rigorous marker and he doubted she would award this one more than a C minus. Trying to press on, with Dixon glooming in the chair opposite, would probably condemn him to an even worse grade. 'No prizes for guessing where you've come from,' he said, without looking up.

Mike stood up again and felt his injured leg nag. He stuck it out straight and stamped the log in the fire basket down into the embers with a vicious kick. Sparks flew up and the ash glowed. 'No, sir,' he said. 'No prizes. Fact is, CO can't stand me.'

Burton looked up now, put his letter aside and screwed the top back on his fountain pen with a mild sigh. He picked up his pipe and set about relighting it. Clearly, the Old Man hadn't made his task any easier. He rarely did.

'Don't take it to heart, Dixon. You're not the first to have your ear chewed off. You certainly won't be the last.'

There was an eruption of laughter from the other end of the room, where the subalterns were playing billiards and Babington-Browne was attempting a trick shot with his cue behind his back. Mike shuddered at the noise. 'My face doesn't fit, you see. I'm not a tank man. I'm not even regular army.'

Burton glanced up from his pipe. 'I shouldn't worry about that too much. If you're good, he'll take to you eventually. If you're no good, it wouldn't matter if you were the Prince of Wales, you'd still be out on your ear. He's had a bad day, that's all. I've had my ration as well, don't worry. You might think of taking up a pipe. I find it soothing. Never used to smoke, but there we are. Needs must.'

Mike grunted and stared down into the fire, where his kick had stirred the fire into life and flame was beginning to lick hungrily round the log. 'Not sure it's worth the outlay. I've heard all about the turnstile at Rawdon station and I'm pretty sure I'm due to be the next one through it. Still, I shan't mind. So far as I can tell, it was the general staff that did for us at Dieppe so I'm not exactly keen on brass hats.' He looked up quickly. 'No offence, sir.'

'None taken,' said Burton, waving his pipe, 'though I'd have thought experiencing a disastrous landing first hand would make you keen to see things go better when we launch the invasion proper?'

Mike glanced up sharply and the older man detected a spark of interest behind the sulk. His schoolmasterly instincts prickled. The difficult ones were often the most rewarding in the end. Damaged he might be, disillusioned and hurt, but there was a potential there that was lacking from the square-headed types who jostled round the billiards table. Burton had also read the citation for his Military Cross. He noticed Dixon didn't wear the ribbon. Modesty? Or something else?

'Certainly couldn't go worse. Everything went wrong at Dieppe, as far as I could see. Not a single fucking thing went right.'

'They gave you a medal. Something must have gone right.'

Mike kicked the log again, so hard that sparks flew out of the grate and on to the hearth rug. Odd tufts on the bald, old sheepskin caught alight and glowed orange like incandescent filaments before greying and going out. A whiff of singed wool hung between the two men. Burton raised an eyebrow and messed with his pipe while he waited for an answer. 'No,' said Mike. 'Even that was a balls-up.' He bit his lip. Clearly hadn't meant to drop that out.

'Citation said you carried a wounded man under withering enemy fire and almost got him to safety at a cost of serious injury to yourself.'

'Didn't though, did I? Get him to safety. Got him killed instead. Every time I get a letter from my brother in his POW camp I think about Henry Peat. He'd be sending letters home now if it weren't for me.'

Burton sucked at his pipe and puffed a cloud of smoke. 'You know, Dixon, the thing about war is: things go wrong. "Things go wrong" is pretty much a definition of war. That's no reason not to plan, not to train. On the contrary, the better you plan and train, the better the men can cope when a battle inevitably turns into chaos. Sometimes you make a decision and it turns out to be the wrong one. Another day, it might have turned out right. In a game of chance the laws of probability cannot always rule in your favour. As a scientist, you must know that. I think you need to start looking at the thing from a different angle. Unless you're convinced that you alone ought to be infallible.'

Mike sat dumb for a minute before he shook his head. Burton ducked his chin in approval. 'Well, that's a relief. Last thing we need is anyone else round here thinking they're God. Talking of whom, you should be with the CO at these meetings in London. Then you'd know what we're up against. It'll be a miracle if we ever get a crack at Hitler. To do that, we first have to defeat the War Office, the Ministry of Supply and the massed battalions of the Civil Service.'

Mike glanced up. The eagerness of it reminded Burton of a sixth-former: 'Is it really that bad?'

Burton took another long draw on his pipe, then punctuated his reply with little puffs of smoke: 'I sometimes get the feeling the Civil Service really would rather lose the war than do a single thing against protocol. Everything has to go through the proper channels, nobody's nose must be put out of joint and they all seem more worried about their own careers than the fact that we have no decent tanks to fight in. The Old Man is a dose of salts. Problem is, no one particularly welcomes a dose of salts even when it's what they need – especially when it's what they need.'

'You can hardly blame them, the way he talks to people. Wouldn't he do better if he buttered them up a bit?'

Burton stretched out his long legs, stared at the ceiling and recited what sounded like a quotation: 'It's not only the good boys who help to win wars, it's the sneaks and stinkers as well.'

Mike looked puzzled. 'Who said that, sir? The Duke of Wellington? Lawrence of Arabia?'

Burton smiled. 'A little closer to home. I have it on good authority that Churchill said it when he was trying to persuade General Dill to bring Hobo back off the retired list. I had it from a chap on Dill's staff who was in the room at the time.'

'So he is a stinker then? I've been trying to make my mind up about him.'

Burton frowned. 'I don't know. He always reminds me, rather, of something from Henry James. *The Bostonians*, if memory serves. I can't remember exactly how James put it. It was something like: "The easiest way to divide the human race is into the people who take things hard and the people who take them easy." Hobo takes things damn hard. But at times like these we need people who do. There are precious few of them in Whitehall. Sadly, the sort of chaps who can't stomach him are the ones who are inclined to think things are rubbing along well enough as they are, or at least that it's too hard to change anything at this stage. Those "people who take things easy" again. The way they see it, tank production is up. Things are churning off the line. Why rock the boat? Even if the new tanks are already obsolete – too slow, not enough fire-power, with totally inadequate armour. We won't always be able to put superior numbers into every battle, as Monty's been able to do in Africa. The Old Man's right. We need better tanks.'

'So what do you think he'll do?'

Burton took the pipe out of his mouth and inspected the contents. What he saw seemed to dissatisfy him, because he frowned and put the thing down on its Spode saucer. 'Well, stinker or not, Churchill's on his side, thank God – there's another one in the "takes things hard" camp. He's spent half his life outside the pale because of it. If even he can't help, I wouldn't put it past Hobo to go direct to the Yanks, though that would cause an almighty row. I don't know yet, Dixon. It's certainly going to be interesting finding out. If you decide to hang around.'

12

Mike hung. Sometimes he felt it was by a thread and sometimes he wished himself in any other job in the Army. Hobo continued to be, by turns, foul and impressive, and occasionally both at once. But it was Horley who was next out through the turnstile. Other officers came in. Some of them went back out again sharpish. The ones who stayed were the ones who could stand being pounded at to train and train and train, on whatever decrepit equipment they were given. As the weeks went by, it became clear that Hobo's repeated doses of salts were starting to have an effect on the War Office's constipation. Ominous grumblings and indignant belches finally gave way to motion. New machines arrived, some of them direct from special departments that were not under Quiller's aegis. Some of the new equipment worked. Some of it explosively did not. Mike forced himself to ignore the ATS girl's advice to stand well back. At the trials, he stuck close to his General and clenched his fists not against the explosions, but against his body's weak and feeble reaction to them.

New units were joining the Division from all walks of army life too. It was still a thing of rags and tatters, but it was at least starting to look like a thing with a purpose, and a sense of momentum. There was little doubt that the forces of inertia were on the back foot. With him too. As spring fought its way into winter's Pennine strongholds, the light holding sway over the darkness a few minutes longer each day, Rawdon began to feel less gloomy and foreign. After all their travelling, there came a day when the Killing Bottle swung in through the tumbledown gate pillars and Mike found himself waiting for the soot-stained old hall to heave into view with a sensation that carried something of homecoming in it.

In the hospital the doctors had shown him exercises he could do to rebuild the strength in his wounded leg. He had taken no interest. Now he tried to remember what they'd said and adapt the exercises to the local terrain. The set he grew most keen on involved clambering repeatedly up and down hill between the hall and the farmyard. The leg definitely benefited, and if he sometimes ran into the girls from the motor-pool and took a breather in their little common room that didn't seem to hinder his recovery either.

At the beginning of May, he was hurrying in the General's wake on a tour of inspection when he heard a voice call out, 'Good God, Dixon?'

A stocky, rough-haired figure – a sort of Jack Russell terrier in human form – was leaning against the wheel-arch of a three-tonner parked at the roadside with his arms folded, giving him an appraising look. There was something of scorn in it. Something of conde-scension. Mike recognised both. He turned aside from the procession and put on a bland face. 'Hay-Wood. What are you doing here?'

The Jack Russell unfolded his arms and stuck his hands in his pockets before sauntering over. 'I might ask you the same thing. First you light out for the death or glory boys without telling a soul. Then we hear rumours you've been wounded in action. Then nothing. Not a word. What's your game these days?'

'Not much of one. Got posted as ADC to the commanding officer here. Some sadist's idea of a rest cure.'

'You? Driving a desk?' Hay-Wood gave a short, cool laugh. 'There we were feeling sorry for you, picturing you in your bathchair in some sanatorium with the rug tucked over your unmentionable injuries, when all the time you're swimming in gravy.'

Mike shook his head. 'If this is gravy, it's pretty hot stuff. You've not met him yet, I take it.'

'Only just got here. Half my lot's gone down to Suffolk for assault training. The rest of us are here to learn to drive Churchills. Bone up on radio comms. I've heard about him, though. Chap told me he's a right martinet. Duke of York type. Always marching his men to the top of the hill and marching them back down again. Sacks people at the drop of a hat too, I heard.'

Mike couldn't help grinning, even though the sword hung over his own head as much as anyone's. 'Hundreds. You'll need your wits about you. Anyway, what have you been doing since … ?' He felt slightly ashamed at the manner of his departure from the sappers. He'd packed his kit and left early the morning after he got his orders to report for commando training. Hadn't said a word to anyone besides the CO. Now it seemed a little childish. 'Seen action yet?'

Hay-Wood scuffed at some rock chippings with the toe of his boot. 'No, worse luck. I suppose you know we've transferred out of the Chemical Warfare Group for this. Spent a whole year mucking around with poison gas in Northern Ireland. You did well to give that a miss. Filthy stuff. If I never get another whiff of chlorine it'll be too soon. No more swimming baths for me. I'm right off the idea.'

'Well, there's no gas here. Nice clean bangs. That's all.'

'I suppose that's something. Though I can't for the life of me see why it's suddenly all the rage to shove sappers into tanks. We've been blowing things up pretty effectively for centuries without hiding behind steel plate.'

'Yes, well, the Old Man thinks the Royal Engineers should have been in armour a long time ago.'

'From what I hear, your Old Man thinks everything should be in armour. The joke going round the mess is that he won't eat his dinner unless it comes out of a tin can.'

Mike smiled. 'That's good. You should tell him that one – if you want a lecture. He hates it when people claim he's only interested in all-armoured assaults. Says it's the story his enemies have been spreading for years to try and get him put out to grass.'

Hay-Wood held his hands up. 'All right, old man. No need for the full communion service. But what about you? Now we're all here together, what's to stop you transferring back to the old mob? We could do with a decent mechanic on the strength if we're going to be going everywhere in tanks.'

Mike was surprised. Hay-Wood had been one of his chief tormentors in the officers' mess, forever taking off his northern accent and letting him know he wasn't the right sort. Now he was suggesting he come back. 'Yes,' said a bitter voice in his head. 'But only to do the dirty work. To be their mechanic.' He heard the voice, but found it didn't convince him. Something had changed in the relationship he bore to Hay-Wood, something like a change in the relative orbits of two planets. Hay-Wood was regular army, but Dixon had seen action. However big a disaster it had been, his experience in France meant he knew more about war now than his old mess-mates.

He gave the idea of going back to the Royal Engineers some thought. For the last two months he'd been dreaming of any other foxhole. Now he realised that he wasn't ready to leave. Did that mean he'd begun to believe in Hobo and his Lord Mayor's Show? He saw Hay-Wood was watching him with an appraising cock of the head, probably looking for a sign that the action Dixon had seen had sapped his nerve. Sapped it or snapped it. Pride he hadn't known he still possessed caused him to return the stare.

A dissonant chord made up of high indignation and deep anger from up ahead reminded him he was meant to be with the inspection party. Someone was in trouble. Hobo's entourage had formed a semi-circle behind him. The General was standing toe to toe with a private soldier in the middle of a rank held painfully to attention.

'What did you say, man?' shouted the General as Mike hurried up to the back of the claque.

'What's going on?' he mouthed to the officer next to him, who answered out of the corner of his mouth.

'Hobo asked him what he did in Civvy Street and the idiot told him. "Minded my own business."'

'Ouch!'

'Quite. Pin back your ears.'

The unlucky soldier swallowed, his Adam's apple bobbing, and prepared to repeat himself. His voice trembled but he got out, 'I said I minded me own business, sir. I kept a shop, see. Haberdasher's on Essex Road, sir. Now me old lady minds it on her own while I'm 'ere.'

Hobo, hands clasped behind his back, continued to give the man the concentrated attention of an eagle watching a vole for maybe five seconds, before he nodded sharply and said, 'Good man. You know, Napoleon meant it as an insult when he said the English were a nation of shopkeepers, but it's chaps like you, with small concerns to protect, who will really fight to stop the Hun in his tracks. Minding your own business. I like it. Hear that, Burton? This man was minding his own business, before Hitler stuck his oar in.'

'As were we all, sir.'

Hobo swung round to look at his right-hand man. 'Of course, you're not a career soldier either, are you Burton? I'd almost forgotten. Everyone's a civvy these days. Still, can't be helped. The only business we've got to mind now is how to pull off the invasion. Name?' The

85

gimlet eye was back on target and the once-and-future haberdasher flinched. 'Hipkiss, sir. Private Hipkiss.'

'Well, Hipkiss. Are you clear about our business?'

The hypnotised Hipkiss swallowed again and nodded, not daring to take his eyes off the commanding officer, until his sergeant at the end of the rank cleared his throat menacingly and he stammered out, 'Sir, yes, sir.'

'Good,' said Hobo, and turned to the officer at his side. 'I'll see the cookhouse now, Morris. Can tell a lot about a unit from the state of its cookhouse. Lead on, man. What are you waiting for?'

The inspection party wheeled and headed back past Captain Hay-Wood and his newly formed tank crew. Hay-Wood stood smartly to attention, but Mike could see a grin forming on his face as soon as the CO had gone past and, out of the corner of his eye, caught him tapping his watch and raising an imaginary pint mug to his lips. For reasons he couldn't fathom, Tiny Hay-Wood seemed to have decided to claim him as an old friend.

13

JUNE 1943, SOUTH WALES

The DC3 banked down over the long white cliffs of the Gower Peninsula. Dixon and Burton were in the tail, strapped against the metal fuselage. It was fiendishly cold and too noisy for speech. Up front, Mike could see Hobo in the co-pilot's seat, headphones jammed over his beret, jabbering away to the pilot. He gesticulated back in the exaggerated way Mike had noticed people do on planes when divided by noise and reconnected only by wires and headphones. As the plane lost height, he mapped in his mind the way they'd been criss-crossing the country for the past three months and reckoned they must be covering at least a thousand miles a week. His stomach told him they were descending fast, and a change in the engine noise preceded the bump, rumble and bump of the wheels hitting the deck. A series of jolts ran up his spine and he jerked sideways in his straps three or four times as Jakub squirted the brakes.

When the plane finally stopped, Dixon and Burton unstrapped themselves and stood up stiffly. Hobo was hooking his headphones up beside him. The Pole still wore his but had shoved one earpiece backwards, freeing one ear, so that he could hear what the control room was saying to him and still carry on his conversation with the general. He flicked switches on the panel in front of him as he talked. Hobo stood behind him, knuckles on his hips. Neither of them glanced at the men in the belly of the plane.

The door opened to let in a blaze of sunlight. Mike squeezed through the narrow doorway after Colonel Burton, rattled down the metal ladder and the two of them stretched their legs beside the tarmac. The scent of the warm grass, lush in mid-June, mingled with the smell of rubber from the plane's tyres and the hot oil stink of the engines. Mike looked up at the towers of cloud drifting lazily across a benign blue sky and found it hard to believe that he'd been frozen stiff up there a few minutes ago. Burton raised his field glasses and trained them on the water beyond the cliff edge.

'Flat as a mill-pond today,' he said, passing Mike his binoculars. 'God knows how these DD tanks would cope if it's rough.'

'Surely they'll choose calm weather for the crossing,' said Mike, peering through the eye-pieces at a sea that glittered sharp and blue.

'I take it you're not a sailor.'

'No, sir. Born in Leicestershire. Never sailed.'

'Hunting and shooting more your thing, eh?' Burton was teasing.

'Bit of poaching, sir. Rabbits mainly.'

'Fascinating, Dixon, I must say. You are a true English villein. Well, the English Channel may be a narrow stretch of sea, but she's no less unpredictable for all that. Even at this time of year you can't guarantee good weather for very long. Still, we shouldn't complain. You and I would probably be speaking Spanish if it wasn't for the weather in the Channel.'

'Sir?'

'The Armada, Dixon. 1588. If it hadn't been for a storm in the Bay of Biscay, history might have been very different.'

'That's your subject, isn't it sir? History?'

'It was once. And will be again one day, I hope. Though not if the only history on sale is that of the Thousand Year Reich.'

'At least maths and engineering are the same whichever side you're on.'

'You're all right then, Jack. Whoever wins.'

'I didn't mean that. It's just a comfort sometimes, when everything's so topsy-turvy, to know that whatever happens nothing can stop two plus two making four.'

'You're a strange cove. Besides, I'm sure if Herr Hitler decided that "four" was an answer devised by Jewish mathematicians to hoodwink the Aryan race you might find yourself under pressure to accept that two plus two made quite another number altogether. You wouldn't like that.'

'I don't suppose I should. Though it isn't as easy to rewrite the laws of science as it is to fake a bit of history. If Hitler decided two and two equalled six I'd like to see him try and machine a gun barrel to fit a shell. It wouldn't be long before his armaments industry ground to a halt. That's the difference. History's only stories, when it comes down to it. And you can always change a story. But maths, well, maths is the truth, isn't it? It seems to me dictators will always warp history to suit their purposes. The way I see it, history's mainly a long list of cock-ups, so a dictatorship has virtually no option but to rewrite history as propaganda. Otherwise it'd look ridiculous half the time. And you can't terrify people into submission if you look ridiculous, can you, sir?'

'I suppose not. I suppose having leaders who are ridiculous from time to time is a vital, if underrated, feature of living in a parliamentary democracy. I feel a little ridiculous myself now I know what a weak and feeble thing you consider history to be. But that's why we have to defeat Nazism, isn't it? To protect delicate flowers like literature and history from the vandals. Watch out.'

Hobo came clattering down the steps of the DC3, elbows pumping, quite forgetting that he had been the one holding things up. 'So, what time are they starting the launches, Burton?'

'Thirteen hundred, sir.'

Hobo looked from one to the other: 'Well, what are we waiting for? Is my car here?'

Mike had already spotted the big Snipe. 'I think that may be it over by the control building.'

As they started to walk, Burton briefed them on the plans for the day. 'We have a landing craft tank coming down the coast from Pembroke docks under naval escort. She has five Duplex Drives aboard and orders to launch them a thousand yards offshore. Once we've mastered that, we can try it over greater distances.'

Hobo nodded. 'We'll see what rate of launch they manage. It needs to be one every thirty seconds, no more, if they're going to keep in formation until they hit the shoreline. Shame we can't get more than four knots out of them. There we are. Tanks aren't speedboats.' He glared at Burton and Dixon, as if one of them might dispute the point. Neither of them did. 'I want you aboard one of the DDs, Dixon. You can report what's going on. From the horse's mouth.'

Burton cleared his throat, a sign Mike recognised by now as surprise. This was a new feature to the plan. 'Excellent idea, sir.' Burton was always at his most diplomatic when trying to talk Hobo out of something. 'But the landing craft will have left Pembroke docks some time ago. There's no way to get a man aboard now.'

'Nonsense, Burton. I'm sure they can let down a scrambling net and we can shoot him aboard before they launch the tanks. Navy must have a spare life jacket knocking about.'

Burton nodded, a bit doubtfully. 'Of course he's not been trained on the Davis breathing apparatus.'

'Don't be such an old woman, Howard. He'd only need that if he was down inside the tank. I want him standing on the turret with the commander, observing the thing from there. Besides, I'm sure Dixon has enough sense not to go getting drowned. Swim, Dixon?'

'Yes, sir.'

'There you are. Swims like a fish.'

An hour later, Mike found himself leaning out over the side of a motorboat, clutching with both hands at a web of heavy rope netting that reared up alongside, backed by a wall of rusty steel plate. The launch dropped away from under him and he hung by his arms, slamming his knuckles against the hull of the landing craft and scrabbling for a footing. There was a surge of engine noise as the launch made a fast turn away to avoid crushing him between the two boats and its wash soaked him to the waist. Faces peered down from a long way above and arms waved at him to start climbing. He saw no percentage in hanging around, banging against the hull, so he stuck the toes of his boots into the netting and grabbed at the stiff, rough loops above his head. The net sagged alarmingly under his weight and another wave soaked him before he scrambled out of the sea's reach.

Hands grabbed his arms as he reached the high gunwale and pulled him roughly up. He swung his leg over the top and sat there, panting. As he gulped air, he looked down and saw that the landing craft was less a ship than a rectangular open box. Apart from the wheelhouse at the stern the rest of the boat was nothing more than a sea-going tank harbour. Five tanks were secured to the deck with steel cables and each one was edged round with what looked like the cut-open bellows of a concertina. Their crews stood and sat around on the tanks. Some of the men had spotted his arrival and were staring up at him perched on the gunwale. Others were oblivious to being observed and sat with their backs against the wrinkled mass of canvas and rubber tubing, talking and smoking.

One of the sailors who had pulled him aboard led him along a narrow walk-way, down a set of steps and across to the wheelhouse. The tank commanders were all gathered there, and broke off their conversation as he walked in. He guessed they'd been debating who would give him his run ashore. He glanced round the group, so bulky in life jackets over their battledress that they virtually filled the narrow bridge.

'Wheelwright?'

The face in the tanker's beret was familiar, but not from here and not from now. Last time Mike had seen that face it had been under a riding hat, looking down on him from fifteen hands up. 'Bobby Mee?'

The other man burst out laughing at the shock on Dixon's face. 'Wheelwright, it is you! We were told there was a staff officer who needed a ride. Big-wig from Divisional HQ. Don't tell me they meant you?' He let out another laugh, and the others joined in, though it was clear they didn't quite get the joke. Mike hoped he wasn't blushing. 'It's my CO who's the big-wig – I'm just here to provide radio commentary on how things are going. From the horse's mouth.'

The other man shook his head. 'Well, now I know why they say stranger things happen at sea. Dixon here worked on my uncle's farm when we were boys. Uncle Fred always called him Wheelwright because that's what his grandfather was, the village wheelwright – undertaker too. This one used to wait outside the kitchen door for his half-crown like a faithful hound, didn't you, Wheelwright? And here he is, an officer on the Imperial General Staff. Well, they say war's a great leveller. What about that little brother of yours? Don't tell me he's Commander-in-Chief of the Household Cavalry.'

'Frank got put in the bag at Calais.'

Bobby Mee looked at his feet. One of the other tankers, the troop leader, cleared his throat. 'We'd better be getting on. Bobby, since you know General Hobart's aide you might as well take him with you. What are you, second off? That's probably as good a place as any to watch the show. Sort out the comms with your wireless operator so he's in contact with the GOC's launch. Oh, and can we get him a Mae West? Don't want to drown a brass hat if we can help it.'

Grabbing the proffered life jacket, he followed Bobby Mee out of the wheelhouse and across the deck to the tank standing second in line behind the landing craft's bow-ramp. Bobby vaulted up on to the back of its hull and turned and reached out his hand. He smiled, a bit sheepishly, and Mike realised he was embarrassed about blurting out all that stuff on the bridge. He grabbed the hand and scrambled up over the width of piled-up canvas. There was a narrow step welded on to the back of the turret and a kind of tiller. Mee climbed up on to the step and leaned over to peer down the open turret.

'We've got guests, Sid. Can you pass up a head-set and get ... ' he glanced over at Mike's badges of rank as if he still couldn't quite believe it, 'Lieutenant Dixon here a line to our lords and masters at Divisional HQ?'

Shortly after he was plugged into the intercom, an order came through to start up and the clattering roll of five tank engines added to the throb of the landing craft. The hiss of compressed air flooding into the rubber tubes was too faint to hear over all the other noise, but he could see the black tubes widening and unkinking as the air pressure rose, lifting the wrinkled canvas until it formed a smooth wall all around the hull. He couldn't help thinking aloud: 'Is it strong enough?'

Mee shrugged. 'We've had a few problems, even on the mere, which is flat as a cow-pat. Go too fast and the front begins to buckle. I usually send the gunner and co-driver down there to put their shoulders against it. We'll soon find out what it's like out here, won't we? Be funny, wouldn't it, if you and me – born as far from the coast as you can get – drowned at sea in a tank. God knows what the *Leicester Mercury* would make of that.'

'The *Leicester Mercury* wouldn't know anything about it. I suppose they'd call it a training accident and leave it at that. Any road up, let's try and keep out of the *Mercury*, shall we?'

Bobby Mee grinned. 'Any road, let's try.'

Down on the deck, the navy hands scurried around unhitching the hawsers that secured the tanks to the deck. The landing craft slowed to a stop and a couple of ratings ran forward to operate the bow-ramp. It went down with a squeal of slipping cables and a crash, sending a gout of water splashing up over the boat on either side. Spray hit Mike in the face and he found himself grinning. The first tank rolled forward slowly and edged its way down the ramp. Watching it, he could barely believe it wouldn't tip forward as if it were driving off a cliff. But it didn't. It sank, but steadily, the stain of water rising up the canvas until only the rim was visible above the lapping waves. Where it stopped, obeying Archimedes' rules on displacement as if he'd leapt from his bath only yesterday. Blue exhaust smoke billowed up over the top of the screen from the modified exhaust pipe, but the tank did not move forward.

'What's wrong?'

Mike's headphones crackled and he jumped at Hobo's voice. 'Not sure, sir.' He tapped Mee on the back of the leg. The command step was really too narrow for two men, but he needed to be able to see what was going on. He stuck out his hand and Mee grabbed it and pulled him up. Mee pointed at the rear of the tank. 'Don't think he can engage his propellers. No turbulence from the props.' He grabbed the turret for balance and dipped his chin to the mouth-piece. 'Think it's a problem changing from standard drive to propeller.'

Confirmation came over the radio a couple of minutes later and one of the accompanying naval launches went to rig up a tow. This was quickly done, but as the tug picked up speed it jerked too hard and pulled the Valentine over on to its beam. In an instant, the tank sank from view. Three men were left swimming, with the taut tow-cable pointing down between them like an arrow until the tug loosed the other end and it rushed down into the depths after its thirty-ton anchor. Mike held his breath, knowing there were two more men in the tank. After what seemed way too long, a head broke the surface, tore off its breathing gear and a face contorted with coughing. Another head came up a little way off and lay quiet in the water.

'That's all of them,' said Mee.

'Whole crew's accounted for, sir,' said Mike into the intercom, watching as a small naval launch rushed up to the coughing man and dragged him aboard.

'Good. Now try and keep yours afloat, would you? We're not made of tanks, you know.'

When the Navy had picked up the rest of the first crew, Mee ordered his driver to move off. The two Leicestershire men stood with their shoulders barged together on the narrow step. They watched the sea wash over the end of the steel ramp, which sagged a little as it took the tank's weight. Mike felt the platform tip forward as they drove off into the sea and clutched at the edge of the turret to steady himself. 'Just entering the water now,' he said, stating the bleeding obvious. It was a strange sensation, a bit like being on a canal boat in a lock when the water was being let out of the sluices. From being well above the surface, the sea was coming up to greet them second by second. As the water rose, he was grateful he was standing outside the tank. For the driver and wireless operator stuck inside, the tank was turning not into a boat but a submarine. At least he and Bobby Mee still had their heads above water.

'What's happening, Dixon?'

He jumped at the voice in his ear and realised he was holding his breath again. The tank seemed to have finished settling and the water, most of it, was still on the outside of the canvas screens. He could only just peer over the top of the canvas, though, and there was alarmingly little to choose between sea-level and eye-level. Odd waves slopped over the screens and ran down on to the tank hull. And it's almost calm today, thought Mike. There was a heavy clunk from down below and the Valentine began to move slowly forward.

'Driver's engaged the propellers. Seems all right,' said Mee.

'We've engaged the propeller drive, sir. Think we're off.'

'Looks like it. How are the screens holding up at the bow?'

Two of Mee's crew were already at the front with their backs pressed against the inside of the canvas. As he watched, Mike saw a good pail of water splash over the bow and down on to the men. One of them jumped away and shook himself. Then he must have seen the compressed air tube buckling because he pushed his hands against it and turned round, bracing his back along its length. Another bucketload poured on his head, but this time he didn't move.

'Dixon? You there?'

'Here, sir. All right so far. It doesn't look the strongest thing in the world, though. If the sea was running any higher ... Couldn't we reinforce with metal struts? We've got men with their shoulders against the air tubes and ... Christ!'

A bigger wave than any that had preceded it had swept over the boat's gunwale and water was running the length of the hull.

'Can you steer?' shouted Mee. 'I'm going to get them bailing.' He gestured at the long tiller lever, grabbed a steel helmet that was hanging from the turret and jumped down into water that came up over his boots.

'What's happening, Dixon?' came the voice in his ear again.

'Taking on quite a lot of water, sir. Need to start bailing. Any chance of fitting pumps for the future, do you think?'

'Just keep heading for shore, man. Tell whoever's steering to stop zigzagging. Keep bows to the waves or you'll sink.'

Mike grappled with the tiller, wishing he had had even one day's experience of sailing a boat in his life. Down on the hull, Bobby Mee and the two other crewmen were scooping up seawater in their steel helmets and tossing it back over the side, like so many chamber-pots being emptied out of the bedroom window.

Minute by nerve-wracking minute, land grew closer. Mike fought to keep the nose parallel with the line of the oncoming sea. Every wave seemed to try and push the bow sideways. When he wasn't quick enough to correct the steering, more waves rolled over the makeshift hull and once he heard a scream echo up from the inside of the tank. He leaned into the turret and spoke to the wireless operator. 'The hell was that?'

'Guessing Sid, Corporal Sidley, I mean, got a shock off the battery, sir. It's right by the driver's seat, and when the wet gets in … '

He fought the tiller even harder and counted every foot of headway they made. Finally, when they were protected by the curve of the land, Mee climbed back on to the control step and took over the steering. 'Now for a nice soft landing.'

Landfall came without warning and Mike clung to the turret to keep from falling backward off the step. There was another thunk from the gearbox, and they seemed to tread water for a minute while the tracks sought a footing. Just as he thought they'd have to switch back to propeller to drive them up on to the beach, the tank began to crawl forward with its familiar shuddering gait.

'We made it, sir,' he reported. The tank jerked and stopped. The engine roared and they rolled a few more inches before the tracks started to slip. Now they rocked and bounced on their springs without going anywhere.

'Damn it!' said Mee.

'What?'

'I think we're on some rocks. No grip.'

He told the driver to drop the screens. Mike heard the hiss of escaping air this time and in a couple of minutes the canvas sagged down over the hull like a heap of wet washing. He leaned against the turret, equally limp, the muscles in his arms quivering from the release of strain from fighting the steering. Mee was right. They had come to rest on an outcrop of rock pools. The tank rocked as Bobby jumped down off the step.

For the first time since they launched, Mike had time to turn and see how the other tanks had fared. All the way ashore, his headphones had been filled with the crackle of radio chatter. The third and fourth tanks had both launched successfully, but neither had been able to steer straight for shore. He could see them now, and they both seemed to be side-slipping across the bay. God knew where they'd land. Now it sounded as if the fifth tank had jammed in the bows of the landing craft. He could hear hammering and shouting down the intercom. The landing craft's ramp started to close slowly. It wouldn't go up all the way, not with a tank trapped in its jaws, but it rose halfway and the LCT turned slowly and headed back out to sea. The first DD sea trial was at an end.

Mike presumed Hobo would be furious at the fiasco, but when the CO hopped off the launch and waded ashore his mood was strangely good. 'Enjoy your sail, Dixon?'

'Bit hairy, sir. Wouldn't fancy it in a lumpy sea. Not unless we can strengthen the screen structure.'

'Let the workshop know what needs to be done. I think it'll be all right. Takes practice, that's all. Each commander and driver needs to have done six launches, both in daylight and by night. Give it a month and they'll be plopping out like Labrador pups.'

'You think so, sir?' said Burton, shaking out his wet trouser legs. 'It's an awful lot of launches. Especially at that rate.'

'They won't be at that rate, Burton. Thirty seconds apart, at most. Keep them at it and they'll soon get the hang. Your job is to keep on at Mountbatten to let us have enough LCTs and escorts. It's as much about the Navy knowing what we need them to do as it is about training our own men. We need to establish total confidence between the two services. When we get our Shermans and do a few mods, it'll go a lot better. Now, see how this tank has grounded on rocks. We need to train for any eventuality: rocks, sand, shingle, boggy ground. I want these men to have the initiative to handle any conditions that are thrown at them. We can't be sure where we're going to land exactly, so we'd better be ready for anything. Set up targets at the head of the beach so they can practise firing at enemy positions as soon as they get ashore. There's a great deal to do before we lose this range back to the RAF in October. It needs to be day and night, Burton. Day and night.'

'Yes, sir. Day and night it is.'

Burton was as good as his word and, though it was almost Midsummer's eve, night had fallen before the trials were called off for the day. Burton disappeared off to debrief his naval counterpart in Pembroke and the CO decided to ride back to the tank harbour on Bobby Mee's Valentine so that he could quiz the crew on what they had learnt.

Charlie was writing a letter against the steering wheel by the light of a small torch. Mike rapped on the window and said in a loud, stern voice, 'Watch that black-out, miss.' Charlie jumped and fumbled with the torch, which went off as she peered out to see who was there. When she recognised him she grinned with relief. 'Oh, it's you, Lieutenant Dixon. I thought I was in trouble with the local warden for a minute.'

He kept his face stern. 'You were showing a light, you know.'

'Oh Lord, could you really see it? I could hardly see the paper, so I thought it would be all right. It's just … it does get so crashingly dull waiting for you all. And mother says I'm terrible at writing, far worse than my brother … '

She realised he was teasing and she tailed off. 'Jump in, would you, sir? Or there won't be anything left to eat back at the camp. Where's the GOC?'

'Cadged a lift home on a tank. We're the rear-guard, you and I.' He climbed in the front, for the first time since their drive back from Lowther Castle months ago, and she turned the Snipe round and set off across the headland towards the camp.

'Good day?'

'Pretty hair-raising for the most part. But the Old Man seems to think it will get better.'

'Then I suppose it will.'

'You think he's all right, don't you?'

She shrugged, without taking her hands off the big steering wheel. 'He can be most awfully rude and impatient sometimes, when you're doing your level best. He's all right with me, most of the time, but I've heard him say such terrible things to people I'm surprised my hair hasn't developed a permanent wave. Mind you, some of the people he's torn a strip off have really seemed to deserve it. I have to bite my lip sometimes, quite hard, or else I'd burst out laughing. I say, what was that?'

'What was what?'

Charlie had stamped on the brakes and was peering through the windscreen. 'A light. Flashing.'

'Are you … ?' Then he saw it too.

'There!' she said, pointing at a light that flickered at irregular intervals somewhere ahead and to the left. The light disappeared again. A few moments later there was another, a long way off to the left, flashing in the same odd way.

'Somebody's signalling,' said Mike. 'That second light is either on the end of the headland or else out at sea.'

'I thought you'd finished for the night.'

'We have. Everyone's gone. At least I thought so. We'd better find out who it is. Can you see to drive without headlights for a bit?'

'I'm not sure. The track is pretty rutted here. If I use the ruts like tramlines we may be able to go part of the way without lights. I shall have to put them on when we reach the road or we'll soon be in a ditch.'

She put the car in gear and they moved off. He saw the set line of her jaw as she gripped the wheel, could sense her feeling through the steering column the lie of the tyres in the ruts of the grass track. The landward light flashed again, closer now, and lower down than they were.

'I think they're on the beach.'

'I think you're right.'

'Do you want me to go down there? It'll be easier driving on sand. I noticed earlier it was pretty hard-packed.'

'Can we get down?'

For answer, she swung the wheel sharply and the big car bumped up and down as the wheels came out of the ruts and broke through a bank of gorse. There was a tearing and scratching of snapping vegetation, then they were running on smooth sand and picking up speed.

'He wasn't joking, was he?' yelled Mike over the sound of the engine.

'Who?'

'Hobo, when he said you missed the hunting field.'

'No, sir. He wasn't joking.' And she changed gear as smoothly as he imagined she used to change from a canter to a full gallop.

The other light was flashing now, and Mike felt more and more convinced it was coming from someone out at sea. He'd seen the last of the naval escorts turn for home an hour since, and he had checked before the trial that there were no allied submarines in the area. Which meant it was either a merchantman or a German ship, maybe even a U-boat. He tried to judge how high above the surface of the water the light was. His hunch was that it sat quite low, which suggested a small boat or a submarine. 'We must be nearly on him,' he said, peering into the dark. He saw a movement, not thirty yards ahead.

'Put your lights on!' he shouted and as she did so something spun in the sand and moved away from them.

'It's a motorbike. He's off.'

She tried to coax more speed out of the Humber. The feeble headlights caught a plume of churning sand up ahead, but they did not seem to be able to gain on it. Suddenly, even the churning sand disappeared. They ran on straight for another hundred yards, but there was no sign. He looked over his shoulder and saw a light on the road, disappearing back towards town and the rest of Wales. 'Damn, he cut back up on to the road.'

Charlie braked heavily and they slid to a halt, a rain of sand flying over the bonnet and clouding their vision. 'Shall I go after him?'

The headlamp was already down to a pin-prick of light in the distance. Mike sighed. 'No point. He's well away.'

He stared out at the black sea, where there was no longer any flickering light to be seen.

They drove back to camp in deflated silence and Charlie stopped to let him out. 'What now, sir?'

'I'll report to the Old Man right away. Lord knows what he'll do. It's just what we've been dreading, that we couldn't keep things under wraps. Look, when I've broken the news here, I may need to let you know what's happening. Where are you billeted?'

'Two doors down from the pub in the village. I'll probably go in there for a quick drink after I go off duty. Calm the nerves. I'll see you there if you like.'

Mike nodded. 'I don't know how long I'll be. You realise you can't say anything to anybody about this, don't you?'

'I'm not a goose, sir. I never talk to anybody about work.'

14

It wasn't until just before last orders that Mike pushed open the door of the pub. Hobo had made him go over the story several times and, after deciding that there was little to be gained by raising a search party in the dark for a single unknown motorcycle, had sent a signal to MI5. Mike could imagine the flurry of activity in London as they tried to work out exactly where Linney Head was and how to get there fast. He stood inside the door and glanced around. It was a hot night and the fuggy pub smell of slopped beer, tobacco and stale uniforms was powerful and faintly repellent after the clean sea air. The saloon bar was thick with smoke, out of which loomed faces he recognised, crammed in beside the locals who were not about to be turfed out of their place by the army. Then, in an alcove tucked into the corner, he made out a shock of white hair thrown back in laughter, and opposite, a golden head, leaning forward.

'Anyone need a drink?' he said, over Jakub's shoulder.

Charlie looked up at him, little red spots high in her cheeks from the heat of the room and the drink she'd had.

'Scotch, please.' And she smiled at him, so nicely that he felt something inside him do a slow backflip.

He tore his gaze away and clapped the pilot on the shoulder. 'And you, Jakub? What's your poison?'

'A beer, if you're buying. It's Brain's – and we could all do with more brains.' He tapped his head with his fist and laughed at his own joke. He'd probably been in the pub all evening.

When he came back from the bar, Jakub stood up and went out, saying something about making room for the next pint. Mike pulled up a chair and handed Charlie her whisky. He noticed that her last glass was drained. Her eyes were bright and she leaned towards him until he could smell the Scotch on her breath: 'I haven't said anything, sir, about the lights. Not a word.'

'That's good, Charlie. And you can forget the "sir" in here. Name's Michael. Mike.'

'Mike,' she said, as if it was a word she'd never heard before. He wondered how many Scotches she'd had to calm her down after her gallop across the sands.

'MI5 is sending officers up straight away to investigate. So you'll need a clear head in the morning.'

She slumped back in her alcove, against the tall oak settle, with the air of a punctured balloon. 'Do you think I'm drunk? Because I'm not. I'm just … excited, I suppose.' She leant forward again. 'You don't know what it's like being a woman in this war. It's so damned boring most of the time. I mean, my job's more interesting than most of the things girls are allowed to do, but we never actually get a chance to do anything really to fight the Germans, do we? I so wanted to catch up with that bike tonight. Just think, if we'd caught a spy, it would have been … ' She stopped and smiled at a point behind Mike's head.

Jakub sat down in front of his fresh pint and glanced from Charlie to Mike. 'Not interrupting, am I? You two looked thick as thieves. It's not so fair, you know, when I've been charming her all the evening, for you to come in and win her away at the end.'

Charlie sat back in the shadows of the alcove again and Mike took a sup at his pint. 'Shop talk, I'm afraid, Jakub.'

'Oh, really? What has the Old Man been up to now? Who has he told to go to blazes this time? One of the old farts in Whitehall? Or Mountbatten, maybe?' He stopped and looked from one to the other, in mock horror. 'Not the King?'

Mike and Charlie both laughed. The first two were certainly not out of the question and, given the right circumstances …

'Nothing like that,' said Mike. In fact, the last few weeks he's been a bit less volcanic. Still impossibly demanding, but then there's a hell of a lot to do.'

'It didn't go well today?'

Mike shrugged, his face bare of information, as a bell rang and the landlord shouted, 'Last orders please, gentlemen. Mind my licence.'

Jakub jumped to his feet. 'One for the road?'

Mike and Charlie both shook their heads, but he was already in the scrum at the bar.

'He loves his English sayings, doesn't he?' said Mike. '"Thick as thieves", "One for the road".'

'He says he loves everything English.'

'Oh yes? I'll bet he says that to you.'

'Mike!'

It was the second time she had used his name, and he liked the sound of it, even piqued with indignation. 'I can warn him off if you like. If he's being a nuisance.'

'I can look after myself. He's only trying to have a bit of fun. He doesn't mean anything by it.'

'Men always mean something by it. Especially with a girl like you.'

The smile dropped from her face. 'What do you mean – a girl like me?' She looked down into her drink and then up at him, suddenly fierce. 'Are you saying I shouldn't be out drinking in a pub when my fiancé's missing? Perhaps you think I'm no better than I ought to be.'

'No. No. I didn't mean that. I meant … '

He was desperate to put things right, so desperate he had no time to come up with anything but the truth. 'I meant, a girl as beautiful as you.'

At that moment, Jakub came back with three glasses in his hand. 'Here,' he said, 'a toast. I wanted to do it in vodka, but they have none, so we have whisky. Still, a toast. To Hobo and all his Funnies. Here's to winning the war with crazy schemes!'

Mike and Charlie picked up their glasses and sipped, neither meeting the other's eye.

'What?' asked Jakub. 'What is wrong here? You were thick as thieves before. Now you're not talking?'

Charlie stood up. Mike thought she swayed a bit, but if she did she caught it quickly and steadied herself. 'Time for me to turn in.'

'But you have still some whisky!' said Jakub.

'I've had enough. I'm on duty tomorrow morning and I can't drive with a thick head.'

'Then I walk you back to your billet. It's not safe for a young lady in the dark streets all alone.'

'Jakub, it's only two doors away. I think I can manage that without attracting the attentions of the wrong sort.' Her tone was marked.

Mike stood up too. 'Charlie's right. It is time to turn in. I'll see her to the door. Night, Jakub.'

The Pole flung his arms out and tried to embrace them both. 'My children, was it something I said?'

Mike shook him off. 'Something I said, actually. But forget it. Stay and finish your drink.'

They pushed their way out of the bar and into the dark lobby. The pub was also an inn of sorts and Mike was billeted upstairs. The stairs were to the left and the blacked-out front door was to the right. Singing had started in the bar and Mike could hear a Polish accent leading the chorus. He wanted to tell her that he was sorry, to say something that would restore the easy confidence there had been between them down on the beach earlier. He had no idea how to go about it.

'Night then, sir,' she said, and pushed open the front door. A cool breeze blew in and he saw her shiver.

'Night,' he said, and watched her slip out into the black night, the door swinging back behind her. He climbed the stairs slowly, feeling the nag in his bad leg and a sudden rush of fatigue from a day that had started early on the east coast and was ending late on the west. He fumbled in his pocket for the key to his bedroom door and had to feel for the shape of the lock in the dark. As he found the keyhole and turned the key he heard a noise behind him, light footsteps, and a hand in his back pushing him into the room. For a moment he thought he was being attacked, that the unknown figure on the motorbike had somehow followed him, and then he smelled perfume and spun around. Hands framed his face and pulled it down until his lips met the corner of an eye, the soft brush of eyelashes. There was a giggle. Lips came up to meet his and he reached out his arms to pull a body against his.

For a moment, the shock of the contact was enough to hold them still. Then one kiss turned into another and another and he felt lips open beneath his. He kissed her deeper, moving one hand up into her hair, at the same time stepping back across the room and drawing her with him towards the bed. When the iron frame knocked against the back of his calves, he stopped and turned her, as if he were leading her in a foxtrot. He heard her give a little 'oh' of surprise. She broke off the kiss and the bed-springs jangled as she sat down on the edge of the mattress. He knelt in front of her and felt for her feet to undo the laces on her shoes. As he did so, she pushed her fingers through his hair. He unlaced her shoes and placed them to one side, ran his hands up her legs until he found the tops of her lisle stockings. She sighed and pulled his head up to kiss him again as he rolled down first one stocking and then the other.

He stood up and kicked off his own shoes and undid his belt. He saw her raise her hips and wriggle out of her skirt. Then she lay back on the eiderdown and waited for him.

His heart was pounding so fast and hard and his head felt so light that he feared he might black out. He tore off his battledress top and tie and lay down beside her in his shirt. She put a hand to his cheek and drew his face towards hers again. They kissed for what seemed both an age and no time at all before his hand slid down over her blouse and met the curve of her naked buttock. There was only one place on earth he could think of being – and in a moment he was there, inside her.

She gasped and kissed him fiercer than ever. He cupped her hair back from her face with his hands and tried to look into her eyes, but it was too dark. He could see nothing. So he abandoned himself to the sense of touch and held her tighter and moved in her deeper, until light exploded in his head and he heard her calling out in the darkness.

15

Two men were already in Hobo's office when Mike arrived at the camp next morning. One wore a pinstripe suit and the other a natty Prince of Wales Houndstooth. Soft felt hats hung on the hat-stand. Living in a world of khaki, they were the first suits he had seen for a long time and maybe that was why he found them sinister. He had knocked and entered as usual but had been told to wait outside until he was called for. A couple of straight-backed chapel chairs lined up by the door and he sat on one. He had been there only a minute or two when the door to the office opened. He stood up. One of the secret servicemen blocked the doorway.

'Be a good chap and fetch the ATS girl along, would you? We'll need to interrogate you both.'

Mike was still nodding as the door shut in his face. He turned and walked off down the corridor, looking for a clerk to send with a message to the motor pool, all the time thinking about how that word 'interrogate' held so much more menace than 'question' or 'interview' and wondering if it had been chosen deliberately. The word didn't feature in the instruction he gave to the clerk and nor did he indicate that the message came from him. He simply asked the clerk to convey that General Hobart wished to see Driver Carrington in his office at once, which he knew would be intimidating enough.

Returned to the chapel chairs, he could hear voices in the office, but they were too low to catch the words. He stared at the ceiling and wondered how she was feeling, and whether she would expect to find him here. In truth, he wasn't sure how he was feeling. He was afraid to interrogate himself. When he had been woken by sunlight streaming in through his bedroom window he had been conscious of nothing for a moment beyond a sense of great physical wellbeing. His very first thought had been, 'By God, I have slept well.' Then he remembered and opened his eyes and found he was alone.

He had no memory of her leaving, or even of falling asleep, but clearly he must have done, because it was morning and she was gone. The thought of her dressing in the dark and running the gauntlet of the pub's landlady and getting somehow back into her billet made him flinch with anxiety for her. More than that, he was filled with confusion. He knew lots of men who had casual wartime flings, but nothing about Charlie had suggested she was that kind of girl. At Rawdon, she had refused even to go out to the cinema with him in a group. He had done everything he could to conceal the fact that he was crazy about her. He'd never once imagined that she might feel the same. But did she? Or had she simply been looking for an anonymous release from the stresses of the war? Just because she thought he'd do for that didn't necessarily mean she liked him. He tried to think whether she had said anything as she pushed him into the bedroom, but if she had uttered a single word he had either not heard it or could not recall it now.

The sound of footsteps broke into his thoughts and he looked round. Her steps faltered for a second when she saw him. Then she steadied herself and came on, chin raised, looking band-box smart as ever, although the colour in her cheeks was a little higher than usual.

'Lieutenant Dixon.'

He stood. 'Take a pew. I'll let them know you're here.'

She sat down while he knocked at the door and waited, counter to his normal habit, to be told to come in. One of the London men opened the door with a 'What is it now?' look on his face.

'Driver Carrington's here.'

The man nodded and shut the door in his face again.

'Who's that?' asked Charlie.

'MI5, I think. Must have flown up, to get here so early. The Old Man and Burton have been in there a while. They're obviously taking it seriously.'

'Mmm,' she said, and that was all.

He stood, looking at the closed door. Then he sat back down. He crossed his arms, noticed she had done the same and uncrossed them. Then he didn't know what to do with them, never had arms seemed so unwieldy, so he crossed them again.

'For Christ's sake,' he said to himself. He tried to think of a normal, everyday remark to make, but everything he tried out in his head sounded either unutterably stupid or freighted with too much meaning. The idea of interrogation by MI5 began to seem much less excruciating than continuing to sit here like two schoolchildren waiting outside the head's office with no clear idea which of their misdemeanours had been found out.

Finally, the door opened again and Lieutenant-Colonel Burton came out, putting on his cap. 'Ah, Dixon. Charlie. You can go in now. I'm off to order some men around in tanks. It's all I'm fit for, apparently.'

The two of them were left beside the open door. He gestured for her to go first and their eyes met, accidentally, before they both looked away.

Hobo's office normally belonged to Linney Head's commanding officer. It was uncomfortably small for five people, especially when those five were a stony-faced major-general, two secret service officers and two people acutely embarrassed to be in each other's presence. You could have cut the atmosphere with a knife, though you would have had to brandish it carefully in such cramped quarters.

'Dixon, Carrington. These men are from the Intelligence Services. Colonel Robertson and, er … '

'Smythe,' said the doorkeeper, unconvincingly.

'Yes, quite so, Smythe. They need to know exactly what you saw down on the beach last night. As you know, secrecy of our operations here is absolutely paramount, so if there's any question of a security breach … '

' "If" being the operative word,' said Smythe.

Mike didn't know what to make of that. He sensed the girl turn to glance at him. He continued to look straight ahead.

'Now,' said the other man, the Colonel. 'What were you doing when you saw what you thought might be someone signalling?' He was looking at Mike.

'We were driving back to camp at the end of the exercise. Major-General Hobart had gone ahead with one of the tanks and Lieutenant-Colonel Burton had taken a jeep round the bay to debrief the Navy.'

'Everyone else involved had already gone?'

'Yes, we were the last.'

'And the lights you saw couldn't have been from vehicles or boats connected with the exercise?'

Mike shook his head. 'Only one tank had actually reached the beach. That had moved off to its harbour some time before – with the CO on board, as I said. The boats had gone back to Pembroke. Anyway, if it was someone connected with the exercise, why would they race off when we came up?'

'Where were you when you first saw the lights?'

'I saw them, sir,' said Charlie, 'just after we set off. I'd been parked behind a dune and I headed out along the track behind the beach, meaning to swing round and rejoin the road to town.'

'And what happened when you saw the lights?'

'I pointed them out to Lieutenant Dixon and he asked me to turn off my headlamps.'

'Which you did?'

'Sir.'

'And he saw them too, did he?'

'Not immediately,' said Mike. 'But after about half a minute I did, followed by an answering signal that seemed to come from the sea. It may have been Morse. I didn't make out the letters. Too surprised, I suppose.'

'Or too preoccupied.' This was Smythe.

'I beg your pardon?' said Mike, surprised again.

'I'm asking if the reason you were sitting in a staff car behind a sand dune with the lights off was entirely connected to the day's exercise.'

'I don't know what you're suggesting,' said Mike, aware that he was going red. A glance to his right told him Charlie's face was flaming too.

'I'm suggesting that you two were startled by someone entirely legitimately driving back to camp after the exercise. That you convinced yourselves it was a spy and went chasing around, what shall we say, somewhat hot-headedly?'

Mike risked a look at Hobo. He was watching through his black-rimmed spectacles with an expression that suggested he hadn't yet made up his mind whether this interpretation of events had merit. He appeared, for almost the first time since Mike had known him, to be unopinionated.

'That's utter rubbish!'

'Charlie,' said Hobo, in a warning tone, without taking his eyes off his aide.

'I'm sorry sir, but it's absolute bunkum. Lieutenant Dixon and I were on our way back to camp when we saw the light. That's when we turned out the headlamps and we only went to investigate because we thought someone was signalling out to sea. To suggest we were up to nonsense … it's insulting. I'm sorry sir, but it is.'

Mike glanced down at five feet two of bristling indignation. He had assumed she was blushing with embarrassment. He was wrong. The colour in her cheeks was anger, not shame. She was glaring at the men from MI5 with a ferocity she could only have learned from her boss, who said, 'That's enough Charlie, calm down. Colonel Robertson here, and Smythe, they're just doing their job, as they see it.'

'Well, why don't they ask us about the motorcycle? Why aren't they out looking for it, come to that? Taking casts of the tyre-tracks? Searching the village? Questioning people?'

'We are questioning people,' said Robertson. 'We're questioning you. And we'll do it our way, if you don't mind. Now, Lieutenant Dixon, if we accept that this person on the beach had nothing to do with your training exercise, how do you suggest they got there? Didn't you have the beach blocked off to civilians?'

'Yes, but the roadblock would have been dismantled, or at least unmanned once the last men left the area. The sentries probably hopped on the last truck back to camp.'

'So whoever it was may have been observing the sentry post and would have believed everyone had gone.'

'I imagine so, sir. He could have been watching our exercise from some concealed position. That's the danger. He might have been signalling details of what he'd seen to a U-boat. Which would be … ' he looked at the general.

'Catastrophic,' said Hobo. 'I've explained to Colonel Robertson the nature of our work here and why the element of surprise is so crucial. He's fully aware of the possible consequences, which is why we have to give MI5 every assistance. And respect their methods.'

'Thank you, General,' said Robertson. 'We have a pretty fair record of putting spies in the bag, actually. If there is a mischief-maker on the loose, there's a good chance we'll get on to them. As long as we don't have people blundering about like Robert Donat and Madeleine Carroll in *The Thirty Nine Steps* ... '

'Well, really,' said Charlie appealing to Mike for support. He stared straight ahead, like a good soldier.

'All right,' Smythe opened a notebook, 'let's assume there was someone signalling. And he did have a motorcycle. What can you tell us about it? The colour? The make? Estimate how powerful it was?'

Charlie looked at Mike again, and this time he met her eyes. They were miserable. 'Sorry, sir. It was about thirty yards ahead and churning up sand. Plus it was pitch black. Impossible to see anything clearly. But it must have been a fairly powerful machine to have outrun us like that. I was doing forty-five across the beach and he still got away from us.'

'And where did it go?'

'Back towards town. From there, who knows? Pembroke, Swansea, anywhere along the Gower.'

'Needle in a haystack, in other words,' said Robertson, uncrossing his ankles. 'For all we know, he could have been picked up from any one of the beaches along the coast and be back in Brest by now.' He stood up. 'We'll get men out looking for the machine. If we find it down near the coast, I'd fear the worst. If we don't find it, there's a good chance our man's still around. Or doesn't exist, except in some people's fevered imaginings. I almost hope for the latter.'

'Well ... '

Charlie was about to boil over again. Hobo held up his hand. 'I'm postponing any more training here until we can be sure we're not being watched. Burton's gone to stand them down. Dixon, have the plane ready to take us to Woodbridge in an hour. Driver Carrington, you can go back to Rawdon. Now get out, the pair of you.'

16

All the way back to Yorkshire the question that kept circling Charlie's brain was 'What on earth have I done?' The road through the Black Mountains was all but empty and as she drove through the bleak, deserted country she felt her banishment painfully acutely. So engrossed in self-interrogation was she that more than once she took the wrong turning. 'I'll say,' she told herself with heavy irony, as she put down the map and turned the car around, 'What was I thinking? Whatever made me do it? The whisky, obviously. And, oh God, I was so hopped up, by chasing that spy, or whoever he was. It was like hunting. It really was. The same feeling of the blood pumping, of being utterly alive, and not wanting the feeling to stop.' His body pressed against hers flashed into her mind and the shock of it made her shut her eyes to blank it out, even though it wasn't a visual memory but a memory of touch and taste and movement. Startled, she forced her eyes open again before she ran off the road. 'Damn it, Charlotte. You are such an idiot. What if you end up with a baby? Didn't give that a thought, did you?' She did sums in her head, not that she was sure when it was really safe and when it wasn't. Girls told such wildly differing stories, and you never knew how much was just gossip and wishful thinking. Lucky she was regular as clockwork. There should only be a few days to wait to find out if she was in that kind of trouble.

There was plenty of other trouble besides. Lieutenant Dixon – Mike – had been close enough to calling her a tart last night in the pub. Now he must be quite convinced of it. She'd hardly been able to look his way this morning and he'd seemed just as unwilling to meet her eye. No wonder that horrible Smythe person had got wind of something. His intuition had been right. It was only his timing that was off.

At the airstrip she had watched the Dakota gain height and shrink in size until it was smaller than a bird. When they climbed aboard together, the General, Colonel Burton and Dixon, it came as a relief from the acute awkwardness of the morning. But as they disappeared into the blue she had felt dismissed. Quite sent to Coventry – worse, Rawdon – and no knowing when she would see them again, or hear anything more about what was happening in the hunt for the man they'd chased along the beach.

Then there was Bill. It was more than three months now since he and his crew went missing. The last time she'd telephoned his squadron leader he'd sounded as if he was racking his brains to remember some event from ancient history. 'Nuremberg?' he'd said. 'March?' Then after a pause he'd said, 'I'm sorry, Miss ... er, we really don't expect to hear anything about a missing kite after this long. It may sound hard but I'm afraid it may be time to stop holding out for good news.' Only the day before, she'd written to Archie to ask him what she should do now. After all, Bill had been his friend at school. And Archie must have had to deal with this kind of thing when one of his tank crews went missing in the desert. Was it time to start believing that Bill was never coming back? Was it time to start getting on with her life? The letter wasn't even posted yet. It was still in the glove compartment and yet last night she'd acted as if her brother had already written back assuring her she was a free woman.

There was a lump in her stomach when she thought about Bill. She wasn't sure if it was guilt. Was it possible to feel guilt contingent on whether another person was alive or not? Questioning herself hard, she began to suspect it was something worse than guilt. She began to suspect it was a horrible kind of hope, the hope that Bill was not coming back. She was appalled at herself. But however hard she tried to shut her eyes on the memory, she couldn't deny that the way she'd felt in bed with Mike Dixon was very different, very much more potent and intoxicating, than she had ever felt with Bill.

17

AUGUST 1943, YORKSHIRE

Abandoning the range at Linney Head caused a massive logistical headache. First, Burton and Dixon had to scout and requisition a new training ground that met the CO's requirement of absolute remoteness and isolation. When they'd achieved this, identifying a Scottish sea-loch so remote it didn't even have a monster, they had to find low-loaders to transport all the DD tanks there from the South coast, travelling at night for added secrecy. Then they had to persuade the Navy to detach landing craft to Scotland for the duration of the training. Only once they'd established a basic camp on the shores of the loch could training recommence.

It was weeks before Dixon finally returned to Rawdon, tired, tanned and covered in midge-bites. He found Tiny Hay-Wood and his men had arrived back too, to train on the first of the obsolete Churchills to be stripped out and converted to Armoured Vehicles Royal Engineers. Mike found himself frogmarched to the Duke of Westmorland as soon as he came off duty. The pub was crowded. Mike had his back to the door of the saloon bar and was listening to one of Hay-Wood's best-worn stories when the sapper broke off and said, 'Oh I say, that's an absolute pip.'

He turned and came face to face with the girls from the motor pool. There was a brunette who looked pretty presentable too, out of uniform, but he was in no doubt which one of the trio Hay-Wood had been talking about. She was wearing a pale lovat sweater and a neat tweed skirt and her fair hair was not rolled in the usual way but held loosely in a clip at the nape of her neck. Mike was too busy looking at her to speak.

'Lieutenant Dixon,' said the brunette, 'we don't see you in here very often.'

Hay-Wood threw his arm round Mike's shoulders. 'You know these visions of loveliness, Mike? You might have said. Aren't you going to introduce them to one of your oldest friends?'

Mike had no desire to introduce Charlie to anyone, least of all to Tiny Hay-Wood but he said, 'Of course. Monica Stubbs, Charlotte Carrington and … '

'Deirdre,' said the third girl. 'Deirdre O'Neill.'

Mike nodded. 'And this is Captain Daniel Hay-Wood of the Royal Engineers.'

'Delighted to meet you, ladies. What are you drinking? Dixon here is in the chair, as punishment for his cowardly defection to the general staff.'

'Oh, hard luck, Lieutenant Dixon,' said the brunette, Monica. 'Three ports, large ones if you don't mind. We're celebrating.'

'Really, what's the party in aid of?' asked Hay-Wood, his arm still round Mike's neck.

'It's Charlie. She's had good news about her fiancé. He's alive. In a POW camp. Telegram came today. Show them, Charlie.'

Mike stared at Charlie, who had not said a word. She took a folded telegram out of her skirt pocket and shook it open. Monica snatched it from her and held it up. 'See? Can you believe it after all these months? No explanation of why it's taken so long for word to come back. Still, that's the bloody war for you, isn't it? Main thing is he's alive.'

Mike couldn't take his eyes off Charlie or force his face into the right expression. Tiny's arm was heavy round his neck and the sapper was bouncing on the balls of his feet. 'That's certainly a good excuse for a party. Calls for champagne really, if only the Hun hadn't cornered the market. Come on, Mike, what are you waiting for? These girls are fully entitled to paint Rawdon red tonight – and we're the ones to help them do it.'

Mike shrugged off his arm and turned away to the bar, shouldering his way between a couple of Hay-Wood's troop. He signalled to the landlord, who was serving down the other end, and dug in his battledress pocket for his cigarettes. As he dipped his head towards the flaring match, he felt a touch at his elbow.

'Light one for me?' Her hand was resting on his arm. The fingers were neat and slim and the nails cut short, slightly rounded. He noticed the pale rose glow under each nail and the ghostly semi-circle at the base of each one. He saw that one of the nails was broken off down to the quick and that there was oil ingrained there. 'Mike?'

He lifted his gaze to her face. They looked at each other for a few seconds. He had to look away. He knew he ought to say something, but no words would come. He still had the unlit cigarette between his lips. The match had gone out in his fingers. He took another cigarette out of the packet, struck a second match and lit them both. He handed one to her. 'Didn't realise you smoked.'

'I didn't realise I did either. Monica's been feeding them to me all day. Smoking's good for shock, she says. Calms the nerves.'

He nodded, and couldn't think what to say next.

'Yes, me duck. What can I get you?' It was the landlord's wife, called in from the rear sitting room to help deal with the crush.

'Oh, right. Three large ports, and two more pints of bitter please.'

When he turned back Charlie had gone, rejoining the little circle that included Tiny and the others, her back to him. As the landlady poured double measures of the thick ruby port into brandy glasses, Mike watched her turn her head to the side to blow a plume of smoke self-consciously up towards the ceiling. She pursed her lips around the cigarette and breathed in deeply. He had never seen anyone need a cigarette more. He kicked himself for not speaking to her. In the noise at the bar, he could have said anything and not been overheard. He should have asked her how she was feeling. Should have said something. He picked up the three port glasses and manoeuvred through the crowd, hunching his shoulders against knocks and bumps. 'Here we are,' he said, as cheerfully as he could, 'three large ports. Let me fetch our pints and we'll have a toast.' He came back a minute later with pint jugs for himself and Hay-Wood, who, showing commendable adaptability, now had his arm round the brunette.

'Quite right,' said Tiny. 'What's the name of this fiancé of yours, my dear, piss-poor correspondent that he is?'

'Bill,' said Charlie. 'Flight Lieutenant William Hartwell.'

'Well, then. A toast: to the bad penny who is Flight Lieutenant William Hartwell, turning up after all these months. A joy to the hearts of those who love him. A pain in the arse to those of us who think it's a crying shame his beautiful fiancée is already spoken for.'

'To Bill Hartwell,' chorused Monica and Deirdre, and Monica dug Tiny in the ribs with her elbow, crying, 'You are wicked, to say that.'

'What?' protested Tiny. 'It's true. The bloody RAF always gets their pick. They don't even have the decency to shove off and let someone else have a look in. I expect you're engaged to a Brylcreem boy too, are you?'

She dimpled up and shook her head. 'I'm not, as it happens.'

'Well, praise the Lord and pass the ammunition. I always say there has to be an exception to every rule. Isn't that so, Dixon?'

Nobody seemed to notice that Charlie and Mike had done no more than raise their glasses for a moment.

'No,' said Mike, dully.

'What? Poppycock. Everyone knows that there's an exception to every rule. I before E except after C and all that.'

'No,' said Mike. 'Not in maths. If there's an exception to the rule in maths, it means the rule is wrong. Finding a case in which a proof doesn't hold true just sends you back to the drawing board to find the flaw in the reasoning.'

'Lucky for me not everything comes down to pure maths, because this cracking girl here is definitely an exception to the rule that the Brylcreem boys get all the good stuff.' He gave the brunette a squeeze and she giggled and slipped her arm around his waist.

Mike glanced at Charlie. Hay-Wood's rule seemed pretty bomb-proof as far as she was concerned. No exception there. He tried to find it in himself to be glad that her fiancé was alive, even if he was in the bag.

He saw her raise her glass to her lips. She drained it and turned to put it on the table behind her. She had already stubbed out the cigarette. 'Look,' she said. 'Don't take this the wrong way. I think I'm going to go back. Feel a bit strange. It might be all the cigarettes. I'm not used to smoking. Think I need a walk in the night air. Clear my head.'

After a second's hesitation, Monica took her arm from round Tiny's waist. 'We'll come with you.'

The frizzy-haired girl picked up her gas mask holder from the back of a chair.

'No,' said Charlie. 'No, you deserve a decent night out. Stay. I'm not going to be fit for anything. Too much to think about. You stay and keep these chaps company. I'm ruining the numbers anyway.' She smiled vaguely in Mike's direction and turned and walked away. He watched the door close behind her. Deirdre, the frizzy-haired girl, looked at him with her head a little on one side and what she presumably thought was a coquettish smile on her flat face. Suddenly, he was part of a foursome.

''Scuse me,' he said, putting down his drink and gesturing towards the Gents. He pushed through the throng and, before the lavatories, ducked out through the side door. He hurried round the front of the pub and out on to the road that led back towards Rawdon Hall. There was a decent moon, a bomber's moon, he thought. Charlie was about twenty-five yards ahead, walking quite slowly with her arms hugged round her against the cool late summer night.

He ran after her. She didn't look round, and he didn't dare touch her so he slowed his pace and walked beside her, hands deep in his pockets. He didn't even glance across at her until they had gone another fifty yards in step. When he did he saw tears on her cheeks, shining in the moonlight. He put his hand on her arm and stopped. She tried to keep on walking but he held her arm fast and when she came back towards him he put his arms around her. She started to sob quietly, her arms drooping at her sides, resting her head against his lapel. 'I should be happy,' she whispered. 'But I'm not sure I am.'

'No?'

'This bloody war.'

'Yes,' he said, 'this bloody war.'

'Being separated like this, not knowing if he was alive. It makes you wonder. It makes you do things you'd never dream of otherwise.'

Mike's heart sank. 'Of course.'

'The other week. I don't want you to think I do that sort of thing all the time. Don't know what came over me. I think it was the excitement of chasing the motorbike along the beach – and I'd decided, that afternoon, waiting in the car, that Bill must have gone west after all. It'd been nearly five months. I've never heard of anyone getting good news after such a long time. That's why I was writing to my brother, asking him if he thought I should stop hoping any more. And I … I suppose I felt it was a weight lifted. I suppose I felt free again … and I just … '

'You don't have to explain,' he said. 'I'm of age. If a beautiful girl decides she wants to go to bed with me, I'm not the sort to complain. I never thought it was the type of thing you go in for regularly. Just figured it was a stroke of good luck on my part to be in the right place and so on.'

'It was more than that. If it hadn't been you – it wouldn't have been anybody else. I don't want you to think if you hadn't come into the pub that I'd have gone off with Jakub or one of the others.'

'That doesn't matter. Sometimes, with the war, one just … '

'No,' she said. She raised her face from his chest and looked at him. 'But … '

'But now there's Bill.' The name dropped from Mike's mouth like a stone.

She nodded. 'Maybe if it wasn't for the war, if he wasn't a POW … '

Mike held her away from him at arm's length. 'If it wasn't for the war, we'd never have met. I'd be a junior engineer lodging in dingy rooms in Derby or somewhere and you'd be … '

'Drinking too many cocktails at the Park Lane Hotel, bored out of my mind while Bill curried favour to get a safe seat.'

'I expect he'd have got one too.'

'I expect he would – and I'd have been an MP's wife, opening the village fête, listening to people complain about the state of their drains while they waited to see him.'

'Don't say you'd rather be here. Don't say Hitler did you a good turn.'

She looked at him steadily, the tears over now. 'I can't say that, can I? Not when he's stuck in a ghastly German prison.'

Mike thought of Frank in a POW camp, and the short, badly spelt, unconvincingly cheery letters he had received from him since

1940, written in pencil on standard forms, stamped here and there by both German and Allied censors. 'No,' he said. 'Of course not. The other night was just … '

'Exactly,' she said, gently shrugging herself free from his grip. 'It was just one of those … Can we forget it happened? Please?'

'Yes,' he said, knowing he was as likely to forget his mother's face, the little terrier that used to go everywhere with him and his brother, the moment he found out he'd won his scholarship to Loughborough College. 'Consider it forgotten.'

18

A week after the telegram from the War Office, a postcard arrived for Charlie. She was in the tack-room next to the stables that the ATS girls used as their mess. They'd made it liveable by stuffing balled-up rags into the broken panes of glass in the windows, white-washing the walls with a bucket of distemper sweet-talked out of the quartermaster and scrounging three decrepit old armchairs from the Hall. Charlie was curled up in the largest of them, dozing in front of the tiny servant's grate and its bare trowel-load of glowing coke when Monica brought the post. She banged through the door of the tack-room, filled with the uncontainable excitement of someone who has just read another person's mail. 'Charlie!' she said, then stopped and sniffed loudly. 'Charlie, for God's sake, it smells like you're cremating a horse in here.' Throwing the letters on the little deal card-table that served them as desk, dinner-table and dumping-ground, she man-handled the armchair, girl and all, a foot back from the fire. She put her hand to the side of the chair and pulled it back, stung. 'Ow! Charlie, you really are the limit. It's red-hot. Five more minutes and you'd have been a spontaneous combustion case. Like that character in Dickens – you know, Mr Whatsisname, in, oh, you know the book.'

Charlie uncurled herself like a cat, stretching all the way to her claws, and leaned over to look at the chair side. The leather was darker and glossier where the fire had scorched it, with a puckering of fine lines across its surface. She ran a hand lightly over it and yawned. 'I have no idea what you're talking about. You know I haven't read any of the books I ought to have read – and Dickens always sounds perfectly hideous. Anyway, no harm done. I quite liked the smell as the leather and the horsehair warmed up. I had a dream of hunting.'

Monica tutted and turned back to the table. 'If I hadn't come in, you'd have been dreaming of Guy Fawkes Night before much longer. Anyway, shut up about it – I came about something important.'

Charlie slumped back into the chair and yawned again, as rudely as she could. She liked their uncouth little den. Slouching there made a nice change from all the leaping to attention she had to do around the Old Man. 'What?'

'This!' Monica held out the postcard, address side up, as if the contents were entirely private and she hadn't read every word several times over. She did at least have the good grace to blush as Charlie took it from her.

It was a dull, cheap piece of card with a long German word printed on the front: **KRIEGSGEFANGENENPOST**. Charlie had no idea what it meant but she hated it on sight, massive and ugly, a marching file of merciless, black capitals. Without warning, her insides gave a great suck in on themselves at the thought of Bill stuck in a place where words like that held sway.

'Well?' asked Monica, impatient to discuss what she already knew. 'What does he say?'

She flipped it over, expecting to see the confident, sweeping writing in royal blue ink that had been his style ever since he was a schoolboy. Instead, the words were in pencil, in laboured upright capitals, and rather faint. She didn't recognise it as Bill's writing, even turned the card over again to check the name on the front. There it was, W HARTWELL, with his prisoner number and the mark of a stamp she guessed was the German censor. She turned again to the message on the reverse.

DEAR CHARLOTTE, EXPECT YOU'VE BEEN WONDERING
WHAT'S BECOME OF ME. NO GOOD I'M AFRAID. STILL,
THINGS ARE NOT TOO BAD HERE. EXTRA FOOD &
CIGARETTES WELCOME THOUGH. WOULD LIKE TO HAVE A
PHOTO OF YOU TOO IF YOU HAVE ONE – NOTHING MUCH
WORTH LOOKING AT HERE. LOVE FROM BILL

'Poor Bill,' she said. It was bad enough that he'd been shot down, bad enough that he'd been injured (he didn't say anything about that), but somehow worse that he had been deprived of his gold-nibbed Parker fountain pen, his royal blue ink and his heavy-laid cream paper. She knew it was absurd, but she felt he simply couldn't be himself, forced to write with a hard pencil on pulpy grey card, a German censor at his elbow. That must be why his writing had gone all stiff and what he said too. There wasn't a word on the card that couldn't have been written by any one of a hundred thousand prisoners of war. That was completely unlike Bill. To be ordinary, not to stand out from the crowd, was a thing he despised above almost all the other things he despised. She read it again. There was no more to be got out of it than before. 'Well, he's alive,' she said, handing the card over to Monica, who made a show of studying it, as if for the first time.

'And he wants a picture of you. That's romantic.'

Charlie bent down and poked at the fire with a piece of old metal fence-post that served as a poker. 'Haven't had a photo taken in ages. And since our house was all packed up to hand over to the Army, I'm not even sure where Mummy would have put the albums.'

'You could go into Leeds and have a studio one done. We could go together, you, me and Deirdre and have portraits done. And one of the three of us. As a souvenir.'

Charlie laughed. 'A souvenir? You make it sound as if we're here on holiday, great pals, having a lovely time, wish you were here.' She glanced up and saw that she'd hurt Monica's feelings. Her tone had been harsher than she intended. Defensive. Reluctant. She wasn't sure why. Then she realised. She hadn't felt guilty the morning after she went to bed with Mike Dixon. Not even when the telegram came. Somehow, being told by the War Office that Bill was alive hadn't seemed any more real than being told by the War Office that he was missing. Of course, she'd told Mike they couldn't go on. That hadn't stopped her thinking about him. She tried not to let on, to him or to anyone that she could hardly breathe if he was in the car, that she felt restless and jumpy, all nerve-endings, the whole time he was on the base, and flat as a pancake when he wasn't. But she couldn't hide it from herself. Any more than she could hide the fact that she felt herself instantly revolt against the idea of having her photograph taken and sent to Bill. And why was that? It took only a minute for her to identify the reason. Fear. Fear that it was true the camera never lied, and that he would be able to tell from her face what she had done.

The return letter couldn't be put off indefinitely. For a week she wrestled with the question of where to get a non-incriminating photograph. Finally, she wrote to her father. She had spent a leave with him in Scotland the previous summer and remembered him pulling out the old camera when they got back from fishing on the loch one morning with a serious pike. He'd done it rather ruefully, the two of them silently aware of who was missing from the picture: Archie, in North Africa with the Eighth Army; Cecilia, who had lately joined the Wrens and wasn't due for leave; and, least explicably and least regretted (by Charlie at least), her mother. Feeling an obligation to make up for the absences, she had gooned about, posing with the wickedly grinning pike in a variety of postures until her father had barked his rare laugh and called her a clot. Heaven knew if he'd ever got round to having them developed. Heaven knew if there was a good one among them. All she could be sure of was that when the pictures were taken she had not yet had an inkling of the existence of Lieutenant Michael Dixon.

Her father replied with the promptness of an old soldier, enclosing three snapshots and expressing his delight at the news that Bill was alive and safe, even though in the hands of the Boche. Two of the photos featured the pike, and were as foolish as she had feared. The third had been taken as they walked back up towards the house from the loch. She didn't remember it, but he must have stopped for a moment and called to her, clicked the shutter as she looked round. By some fluke he'd caught her quite in focus, smiling back at him with that protective affection she felt towards him even when her mother wasn't around. It had been a rare perfect Scottish morning, and the pale slanting sun had lit her hair and face in a way she couldn't help but admit showed her to her best advantage. She was wearing a favourite old Fair Isle sweater, and one of her father's jacquard handkerchiefs tied in a knot at her neck to keep off the breeze on the water. She found herself thinking how incredibly young she looked, and how thoughtlessly happy. And then there was nothing to be done except write a letter to Bill that that girl might have written.

19

Howard Burton found Dixon a puzzle. For the last few months he'd been convinced that the man had been recovering well from the trauma he'd suffered in France. Physically he seemed much stronger. His limp had gone and Burton never saw him now concealing his hands in his pockets when a tremor came into them, as he had in his early weeks at Rawdon. The anger, too, seemed to have left him and instead of that defiant boy's stare Burton had come to expect a grin and a dose of bubbling enthusiasm directed at solving whatever problem lay across their path.

Dixon was willing to put his shoulder to any wheel, but it had rapidly become clear that his forte was the engineering solution. While most people drift into a line of work almost aimlessly, there are a lucky few for whom it is absolutely clear what they should make their life's work. It was obvious to Burton that Dixon was a born engineer. His posting to the Seventy Ninth precisely as it was starting to develop a huge range of equipment was a lucky accident for all concerned. What raised it to the acme of serendipity was that in his commanding officer he had fallen in with a man who believed there was no substitute for talent. Hobo was delighted to discover that the awkward young officer who'd once tried to glare him out of countenance was able to stand beside him at a design engineer's drawing board and, more often than not, tell him what was wrong with their proposal, or what they were missing in terms of a solution.

True, even Dixon hadn't been able to make Hobo's wish for a jumping tank come true. The Old Man had been sure that with a steerable rocket at each corner, it should be possible to design a tank that could levitate over mine fields and obstacles. But neither the leading boffins, nor Dixon's ingenuity, could get the thing off the drawing board, let alone the ground. There were numerous other occasions, though, where his suggestions had made an important difference, and Burton was pleased that his early efforts to smooth relations between Hobo and the young lieutenant had proved worthwhile.

Now, annoyingly, something had gone wrong with Dixon. He'd been fine in Scotland, running around setting up the new training range. But almost as soon as he came back to Rawdon his mood seemed to change. At first, Burton thought he must be tired out and suggested he take leave, go home and see his family. This overture had been rejected with a degree of rudeness that shocked Burton and made him wonder if there was trouble there. He knew Dixon's brother was a prisoner of war because he often talked about him and it was clear they were very close. About the rest of the family he knew not a thing.

Maybe his sweetheart back home has thrown him over, he thought. He'd never heard Dixon talk about a girl though, and the only letters he'd seen him write were form-letters to his younger brother in Germany. For a while, he tried all his schoolmasterly tricks to get Dixon to open up, but the man remained taciturn and quick to anger. His sharpness more than once goaded Hobo into a full-scale tantrum. Luckily for Dixon, somewhere along the line the GOC had decided he was too valuable to sack.

'What's wrong with the boy?' he said to Burton in the Killing Bottle one day when Dixon had been particularly curmudgeonly. 'Can't you get to the bottom of it? It's as if someone's taken his puppy and drowned it in a sack.'

'Sorry, sir,' said Burton. 'I've done my level best, but I have no idea what's got into him.'

'Not good enough, Burton. What about you, Charlie? Any idea what's eating the fellow?'

Charlie shook her head and changed gear more clumsily than usual. She had an idea exactly what was eating Mike Dixon. Sadly, there was nothing she could do to help it.

20

At the end of November, Hobo called Dixon into his office. 'You're a scientist,' he said, tossing a sheaf of papers across the desk. 'What do you make of this?'

Mike was taken aback to see that the cover was stamped not only TOP SECRET but also BIGOT, the most secret classification of all. 'This is BIGOTed stuff, sir.'

'Yes, yes, Dixon. I asked you what you made of it, not to read out the labels to me.'

Mike opened the file. It was a report by a Professor J D Bernal. He glanced up at Hobo, who was glaring at him over steepled fingers with his usual intensity. Clearly, he was not prepared to wait long for an answer. The memo was headed: 'Report on the Geology of the Cotentin Peninsula, Normandy, as deduced by Desk Study'. The distribution list started with the Chief of Combined Ops and included General Brooke, the Prime Minister and, by far the least famous name in the list, Major-General Sir PCS Hobart. There were already a number of hand-written comments scrawled on the jacket of the report, the pithiest of which, in a flowing hand, read: '*No reconnaissance except at my* express *direction. WSC.*' He read the summary at the head of the memo and leafed through it quickly, stopping at various points to read more slowly or examine sketch maps with intricate keys.

'Well?'

Mike looked up from the last page. 'Seems very scholarly. He's certainly gone into it in some depth, with this stuff from Roman reports on fuel reserves in Gaul and pre-Norman history.'

'Yes, yes, it's very pretty, but where does it get us? It's all very well to say there were areas of peat on those beaches in Julius Caesar's day. We need to know if they're still there, and what their bearing capacity is. And I don't see how we can know that until we blasted well go and have a look.'

'He does say he's fairly confident that the geology of the beach at Brancaster is pretty similar to these beaches, sir.'

'"Fairly confident", Dixon? "Pretty similar"? We are building a complete siege train the like of which has never been seen before in military history and you think we should do all that, only to plonk our tanks down on the beach and cross our fingers that they don't bog? No. I know Winston is terrified of allowing any reconnaissance in case we give away the location of the invasion, but we can't take the risk that our armour goes ashore and immediately gets stuck. It'll be Dieppe all over again, magnified a thousand times. No, we need to know what the composition of those beaches is.'

'Sir.'

Hobart looked at him for a few seconds, pushed back his chair and shouted: 'Piddington!'

The clerk's head appeared round the door in an instant.

'I'm going to London. Dixon too. Call and set up a meeting with a Professor Bernal, you'll find him hunkered down at Combined Ops HQ. See if you can get the CIGS there too. Oh, and you might ask for Sir Malcolm Campbell as well.'

Piddington looked confused. 'Not the Bluebird chap?'

'Yes, Piddington, the Bluebird chap. He's an expert on the load-bearing capacity of sand, researched it all before his land-speed record attempts. Anything else you'd like to know?'

'No, sir. Seemed a bit odd, that's all.'

'Well, consider yourself enlightened. Now, any chance of jumping to it, or are we going to chit-chat all day?'

Piddington withdrew.

'Has Campbell seen the report? He's not on the circulation list.'

'Probably doesn't have clearance for it. But Bernal's obviously been talking to him, from what's in there. That's why I want you with me, to check his sums. These scientists love to put one over on the Army, make out we're all sawdust between the ears and should just accept their idea of what's good for us. I don't go along with all that. With the right people in the room, we can get to the bottom of what the potential difficulties are. Even so, I don't see how we can avoid reconnoitring the beaches. For the life of me I don't.' He pushed back his chair and stood up. 'We should have been on to this before, Dixon. Time's too short. God forbid we have to find different beaches. These aren't perfect, but they're the best there are. We have to find a way across them, peat or no peat.'

Mike looked down. The report was open at one of the map pages and he recognised the pointing finger of the Cherbourg peninsula. Under the Old Man's glittering eye, he'd focused on the narrow content, hardly considering the report's context. Now it dawned on him that he had just been made party to the most closely guarded secret in the Allied war effort, the precise location of the Second Front.

Entering a high-ceilinged room at Combined Ops HQ next day, Mike found himself reflected in a highly polished table about twenty feet long. There were eight or nine men already standing around it, some in uniform, others in civvies. He recognised General Brooke, Chief of the Imperial General Staff, and also the tall lean figure of the famous speed king, Sir Malcolm Campbell, whose aquiline nose could have been custom-built for its aerodynamic qualities.

'Ah, Patrick,' said Brooke, when he turned from his conversation and saw Hobo. Mike had seen photographs of Brooke in the newspapers and he had always reminded him of something he couldn't quite put his finger on. Now he realised what it was. In his heavy round spectacles, Brooke was the spit of E H Shepard's drawings of Owl in the Winnie the Pooh books.

'This is your show. Shall we get on with it? PM's in the House, but we may be able to see him later if it's really necessary.'

Brooke took the head of the table. Hobo sat to his left and motioned Dixon to the chair next to him. There were far more senior officers milling around and Mike felt it looked presumptuous, sitting so close to the head of the table, but Hobo's gesture was unequivocal. He sat. The civilians took the seats opposite. It was always this way at meetings between army personnel and civil servants or men from commercial firms. Always this taking of sides.

Hobo opened the file and took out Professor Bernal's report. An intense and lively looking man, with a heavily-crumpled shirt collar and an unruly shock of thick hair that stood out on either side of his face, opened his own copy and looked up expectantly. This must be the professor. But Hobo spoke to General Brooke as if they were the only two present. 'The problem we have to solve is this question of the bearing capacity of the beaches. It seems to me the Professor's research is all very fine, but it doesn't give us the answer. It merely begs the question.'

One of the civilians, a round-faced man whose brilliantined hair gave his head the appearance of having been polished like a ball bearing, put his hand up at this. 'If I may, General Hobart. Before we discuss Professor Bernal's report in any detail, I propose that we hear from Sir Malcolm Campbell. Sir Malcolm has been providing expert assistance to Combined Ops on this matter but does not need to stay for the remainder of the discussion. If we can deal with his specific expertise first, we needn't take up any more of his valuable time.'

Hobo glared at the man from the ministry. He's right, thought Mike, Campbell isn't security-cleared for this. Hobo sighed, a touch pointedly. 'All right, Sir Malcolm. We'd better take you first then. We all know, of course, your achievements regarding the land-speed record. My understanding is that you've made a study of the bearing capacity of various types of ground. What we're interested in is sand. Unfortunately, we're not talking about driving across it in some super-light racing machine. We're talking about tanks. What do you know about that?'

He laid down his challenge and Campbell, who had taken the seat beside the scientist, took a deep breath up that beak of a nose and said, 'Well, General, Professor Bernal has been kind enough to give me figures on the size and weight of these tanks of yours. Obviously, I don't know the exact composition of the sand we're talking about, and sand does vary quite a bit, but from the research I did before the war, in Daytona, Florida, I'd say so long as you have fourteen inches of sand over any potentially bogging sub-stratum, clay, peat or whatever, you should be all right even with the heaviest battle tanks.'

'And if there's less?'

'Less than a foot of good sand and there's a risk of bogging wheeled vehicles, especially if they follow in each other's tracks. It would be best for them to mount their assault across a wide front, rather than up a narrow lane. Though I understand the presence of mine-fields may preclude that. The difficulty, of course, is that you can have sufficient depth in some parts and then in others the composition changes. It's not so bad on dried-up lake beds and so forth, but sand on a beach, that's a different thing. You're dealing with erosion by the sea, human activity, natural geological variation over the area, seasonal action of tides and so forth. That's why I never did my record attempts on beaches. Sand, certainly. Beaches, no. Too variable.'

Hobo nodded grimly. 'Do you have your calculations with you? This idea of fourteen inches is pretty crucial.'

Campbell opened a leather case in front of him and picked out a slim set of papers. 'Sage, that's to say Professor Bernal, has already seen my reasoning. He didn't raise any objections to the principles or my calculations.'

'That's as maybe. But I very much doubt Professor Bernal will be driving a tank over any beaches himself, so perhaps it doesn't seem so important to him as it is to us tank men.'

Campbell raised a haughty eyebrow. 'You do know, I suppose, that the Professor here is reckoned to be one of our most brilliant minds in a range of scientific fields. I should really think that if he's happy with my calculations there can be no objection to them from a merely military point of view.'

Bernal smiled at this, but Hobo held out his hand for the papers and, when Campbell passed them across, waved them to Dixon. 'You'd be surprised at how often the most brilliant minds overlook something that is plain as the nose on your face to us mere military types. Dixon here will be in touch if he has any queries. Is that all you had in mind for me to ask Sir Malcolm, Mr … ?'

'Galvin,' said the shiny-headed man. 'Yes, I think that was about it.'

'If no one has anything else, I think we can release Sir Malcolm.'

Campbell re-fastened his portfolio and stood, a little self-consciously. Brooke stood too and came over to shake his hand. He led him to the door and came back, frowning. 'You don't have to be so damn brusque, Patrick. Man came here to help.'

'Then why wasn't he given security clearance so we could discuss the issue with him fully?'

Galvin coughed. 'There's a bit of a question mark, actually. Some suggestion that he used to be a friend of Mosley's. Under the circumstances, we couldn't take the risk of letting him know any more than we had to.'

'They gave him a knighthood, for God's sake. Now you're saying he has fascist sympathies?'

Galvin wriggled. 'There's some evidence he once drove Bluebird with the flag of an organisation associated with the British Union of Fascists painted on the side. Who knows if he even knew what it was? Still, can't be too careful.'

'Quite. No problem with Bernal here is there, or we've all had a wasted journey?'

Bernal leaned back in his chair and gave Hobo a long look. Mike was surprised to see that he didn't seem intimidated by the old man. There was a spark of amusement in his eye. Galvin was indignant. 'Professor Bernal is Chief Scientific Advisor to the Chief of Combined Operations. Lord Mountbatten placed the utmost confidence in him and he has the highest security clearance. The Professor has a wide remit to research the data all services will require to ensure safe landings in France.'

'Splendid,' said Hobo. 'Well, Bernal, we've all read your report. What I want to know is: can you be sure our tanks won't bog on these beaches?'

'Obviously,' said the Professor, leaning forward and looking round the room, 'from a scientific point of view, it's impossible to be categorical on the point. Ideally, of course, we would like to have samples of material from the actual beaches. I understand that's not practicable, therefore our findings are necessarily deductions from the documentary and photographic information available to us. Having said that, I believe we can be reasonably confident that large areas of the beaches will prove suitable for our purposes.'

'I suppose you wouldn't care to speculate which areas, from a scientific point of view, those are likely to be?'

'I'm sorry?' There was a slight lift to the scientist's accent that struck Mike, and it wasn't until that 'sorry' that he placed the accent as Irish. From deep down, way back before – he guessed – an English public school, but definitely Irish. He wondered whether Hobo would spot it, and whether he would be rude about it if he did. He seemed in a mood to be gratuitously rude to everyone. Whitehall definitely brought out the worst in him.

'It seems to me, Professor, that your report does no more than propose we send the entire British Expeditionary Force (not to mention the combined forces of the US and Canada) to carry out field-testing of your theories. I can see you'll have material for a very learned paper if this experiment proves that the beaches of Normandy are, in the event, unsuitable to bear a significant weight of armour, but it won't do much for our war effort.'

'Patrick, there's no need for sarcasm,' said Brooke. 'The Professor's only working within the constraints placed upon us all. Professor Bernal, I understand you have identified a beach here in England with similar characteristics to the ones in question.'

'Yes,' said the scientist. 'From a geological point of view, the beaches in question appear very similar in composition to some of the north Norfolk beaches, Brancaster in particular. And we have of course taken extensive samples there to look at bearing capacity.'

'And is there peat or clay at Brancaster?'

'There is. In limited patches. A particularly heavy blue clay in places, which would definitely cause problems for heavy armour. Our interpretation of the photo-reconnaissance of Normandy shows patches on the French beaches that appear very similar.'

'But you don't know for sure what those patches are?'

'No. We do know the Romans recorded fuel reserves of peat in these areas two thousand years ago. So it's likely to be peat or clay. No reason why it shouldn't be both. I holidayed in Arromanches in 1935 and the water was quite turbid, consistent with there being peat suspended in it. My copy of *Le Guide Bleu* from that trip refers to the local peasants collecting "gourban" from the shore line. "Gourban" is a kind of peat.'

Hobo had allowed Brooke to take over the questioning. Now he broke in, 'You cannot seriously expect us to base our preparations for an invasion of north-western Europe on some mouldy historical facts you dug up in the British Museum coupled with your holiday reminiscences and a note in a ten-year-old tourist guide. Sir,' he turned to Brooke, 'we simply have to reconnoitre these beaches. To plan an invasion without knowing what the ground conditions are would be, well … it's madness. If there is soft ground, I'm confident we'll find a way of getting over it. But we have to know in advance what we're dealing with. To go in blind is sheer irresponsibility. It could cost us the war.'

Brooke held up his hand. 'I take your point, Patrick, but you know the PM's view of physical reconnaissance. Those beaches are already heavily guarded. It would be an utter disaster to have to change the thrust of the invasion now, because Jerry had wind of our intentions. That could cost us the war too. I can go to him, but I can't guarantee he'll see the force of the argument.'

'Let me come and convince him.'

Brooke gave Hobo a wary glance. 'I'm not sure that's a good idea. It'll take careful handling, not a bull at a gate.'

Mike had been looking over at Hobo's copy of the Professor's report, which was open at a page showing photographs of one of the Normandy beaches and, for comparison, the beach at Brancaster. An idea came to him, and a second later he found he'd said, 'We could always reconnoitre Brancaster first.'

Hobo swung round sharply. 'I've already told you, we're not invading bloody Norfolk!'

Mike quailed, but pressed on. 'No, sir. Not for its geological properties. As a trial run. To see if it can be done without detection. We could set up a whole lot of sentries on the beach, mines and defences too. Send men in from the sea to reconnoitre it as if it were under enemy control. See if they can get in and out without being spotted. If we get it off pat in Norfolk, maybe the PM will let us try it in Normandy.'

The two generals looked at him. Brooke nodded first. 'It's not a bad idea.'

Bernal scratched his head. 'It's not. Certainly, I would be a lot happier if we had proper samples from the actual beaches to analyse.'

Hobo scowled. 'It'll take time we don't have. I'd rather put the effort into organising the real thing than a trial run.'

'No,' said Brooke. 'I think your chap's right. We have a better chance of getting the go-ahead for the real thing if we prove it can work first. You've seen the PM's note on Professor Bernal's report. It won't take long to set up a trial at Brancaster. All you need is a couple of commando and a suitable boat.'

'Sir?'

Hobo looked less than thrilled at the possibility of a second idea from his ADC. 'What now, Dixon?'

'I'd like to volunteer, sir. To do the reconnaissance.'

21

DECEMBER 1943, NORFOLK

Looking out at Brancaster beach from the top of the low dunes on a bright, freezing December day Mike Dixon could imagine how strikingly beautiful it must have been before the war. It was as wide as the horizon and at low tide the sands seemed to stretch away forever. What must forever have been a pure and empty landscape was ruined now by the ugly works of belligerent man. He couldn't help feeling partly responsible. Even before his bright idea in the conference room at Richmond Terrace, Brancaster would have been on a defensive footing, with barbed wire in great loops across the sand and pill-boxes at intervals. Because of him, these had been supplemented with the panoply of beach defences copied from reconnaissance photographs of the Germans' Atlantic Wall and made in Hobo's workshops. A large number of the V-shaped metal gates known as Element C were set to be submerged from half-tide. Hedgehogs welded together out of steel girders had been strewn about the beach as if a giant had been playing jacks there. Innumerable concrete and wooden posts were driven into the sand and the whole place seeded with an unhealthy quantity of mines.

It hadn't been easy persuading Hobo to let him go on the recce and, looking out at the cold waves, Mike couldn't help wondering if he was up to it. What if he froze like he had in the gulley at Dieppe? At his medical, the somewhat bored MO expressed himself satisfied and Mike realised that, for all that the scars on his body were still rather new and surprising, nine months running after Hobo had made him fit again. A couple of weeks training in a swimming baths in Ipswich seemed to confirm that the leg he had grown accustomed to thinking of as 'bad' was now hardly less good than the other. That made him wonder if the pains he still felt in it sometimes were in the leg at all. It wasn't a comforting thought, but it was too late to back out now.

His next anxiety concerned the commando who was to be seconded to the operation as his oppo. He hoped it would be a stranger, but when the truck drew up at the head of the beach the bulky figure that jumped down off the tailboard was instantly familiar. Mike's heart sank. Bruce Ogden-Smith had been one of Henry Peat's best mates. Not only that, he'd been one of the men who'd lifted Henry off him and carried him to the boats. He swallowed and forced himself to meet the big sergeant's eye. 'Bruce … '

'Long time no see, sir. You look better than the last time, too.'

Mike nodded. 'I didn't have a chance to say anything at … at the time. I owe you … '

The sergeant waved the words away. 'You don't owe me. We had a chance to grab you, so we did. That's all there is to it. We'd have grabbed Henry too if there'd been anything left worth grabbing.'

Mike felt his cheeks burn. The question he lived with every day presented itself yet again. Should he have left the man behind? If he had, maybe Henry'd still be alive. And the supplementary question, even harder to un-think once it had been thought: was the real reason he'd hoisted Henry on to his back to protect his own skin as he crossed the killing ground? He was used to those two scurrying round his brain like rats in a grain bin. Now they were joined by a third question. What did Bruce and the others think about it?

If Ogden-Smith thought anything about it he gave no indication and was now examining the beach defences through a pair of binoculars. He passed the glasses to Dixon, who took them and started to scan the beach below the high-water mark. He watched a series of long breakers roll into shore and saw how rapidly the tide advanced up the seemingly endless beach.

'We shan't have too long in any one spot,' he said. 'And we can't go above the high-water mark or we'll leave footprints.'

'Do you think the sentries'll come down below the tide line?'

'I hope so. We need them to show us where the mines are.'

'Let's hope they're ordinary Tommies, not anyone special.'

'There will be one or two irregulars on the strength. Hobo's coming down and I heard the Professor is too – Bernal, egghead from Combined Ops. The Great Sage, they call him, because he's reckoned to know just about everything there is. He doesn't believe we can get the samples, even using Malcolm Campbell's new silent digger, without being potted.'

'Man of little faith, is he? Be nice to prove there's a thing he doesn't know then. See if we can get our stuff from right under his nose.'

Mike couldn't help laughing. 'Hobo would enjoy that.'

They ate an early lunch and drove over to Wells harbour. A flat-bottomed hydrological survey vessel was tied up to the harbour wall, rising and falling with the swell. They climbed down the metal ladder set into the wall and jumped aboard. The boat's commander shook hands and showed them to a small cabin, most of which was taken up with their gear: water-proofed canvas suits, to be worn over sweaters and trousers, that sealed at the ankles and round their necks, a string of twelve aluminium sample tubes strung on bandoliers, underwater writing pad and pencil to be strapped to the relevant arm, revolver, trowel, Campbell's specially made spring-loaded auger designed to produce a fourteen inch sample, sounding lead, compass and torch.

'Enough baggage for you chaps?' he said. 'Sooner you than me, trying to swim a mile in the North Sea festooned with that lot.'

Dixon and Ogden-Smith set about checking their kit and water-proofing whatever they could. Ogden-Smith sealed his torch inside an army-issue condom, knotting the end.

'We should take more of these to put the soil samples in,' he said. 'In case the threads on these aluminium tubes aren't fully water-proof.'

'We can try,' said Mike. 'Do you think the Army designed them to take fourteen inches?'

'Don't know about you, but they're no good to me otherwise.'

Mike laughed. 'I haven't missed you, Bruce. Haven't missed you a bit.'

'Except you clearly were missing the old mob or you wouldn't be putting yourself up for this business. I mean to say, if it comes off all right tonight, we must be prime candidates for the main event, mustn't we?'

Mike nodded doubtfully. If things went well tonight, it would be logical for the same team to carry out the reconnaissance in Normandy, yet Hobo was dead set against him going into enemy territory. The question was still unresolved. He'd carried the day so far by playing on one of Hobo's favourite themes, the importance of using the best-qualified man for the job. All he had to do now was to prove the job was a good 'un. Of course, if he disgraced himself in some way he'd be off the main reconnaissance and probably out of the Division before morning.

They finished sorting their kit and went up on deck. The weak mid-winter sun had disappeared over the horizon and the light was fading into a grey sea.

They found Wilmott, the captain, on the boat's small bridge, hunched inside his duffel coat. 'We cast off at 18.00,' he said. 'It'll be thoroughly dark by then and there's no moon. I aim to set you down off Brancaster shortly before high tide. You swim in, do your stuff and swim back with the out-going tide. Unless you get yourselves arrested. Don't forget to radio and let us know, either way. This is a hell of a tub to sit around on in a North Sea swell.'

Mugs of hot stew appeared and were despatched. The boat cast off its mooring and headed slowly out into the darkness. Dixon and Ogden-Smith stood on the bridge in their greatcoats, feeling the buck and smash of the waves against the hull when they left the shelter of the harbour behind. The helmsman strained to keep the boat on course as her blunt bow was knocked sideways by each wave.

'Lousy throttle-control on these things,' shouted Wilmott in Mike's ear. 'Designed for survey work in calm water, not tooling around in a rough sea in the middle of winter.'

Mike nodded and clutched one of the pillars, his attempt at leaning casually having just led to him smacking his head against the cold steel bridge housing. He was almost beginning to look forward to being in the water, stretching out stroke by stroke towards that wide beach. 'Think we'll go below and get set up,' he shouted.

Wilmott smiled: 'See you shortly.'

The two men crowded down the narrow stairwell. At first it seemed an improvement, until they realised the motion of the boat was magnified down here and Mike understood why Wilmott had smiled. The next moment he sensed a strange echo of memory and couldn't trace it at once. Then he was swept back to the wallowing landing craft at Dieppe, and felt the old tremor start up in his fingers. A stab of fear under his ribs taunted him. He swore at himself and shrugged off his coat, trying to shrug off the tremor with it as he dragged his arms out of the sleeves. Ogden-Smith was already climbing into his swimming suit, pulling the stiff canvas up over his trousers and sweater. He left off the hood, slung the bandolier of metal tubes across his chest and set about strapping the underwater writing tablet to his right arm.

'You look like a Mexican bandit who's stumbled into a Jules Verne novel,' said Mike, feeling a bit better as he pulled on his own suit.

'False moustache is about all that's missing from this lot,' said the sergeant, looking for somewhere to stow his revolver in its oilcloth bag.

He shoved a trowel down one of his seaboots and found a pocket for the compass and torch. There was still Campbell's spring-loaded auger, about the size of a bicycle pump. This he fastened on to his back with a belt. It occurred to him as he did so that at least it gave him a little extra back-bone, and he found himself smiling at his own joke.

'Going up on deck,' said Ogden-Smith. 'Before I get a second look at that stew.'

'Right behind you,' said Mike.

It was only just after seven when they slipped over the side of the pilotage boat, but the freezing cold water and the moonless sky made it feel like dead of night. They'd agreed the boat shouldn't come closer than a mile offshore lest its engine be heard from the beach. The noise of it was soon lost behind them and they were alone in the darkness with only icy waves splashing into them and their own laboured breathing for company. Mike was immediately aware of the difficulty of keeping a course towards a blacked-out shore on a moonless night. As long wave after long wave surfed up behind, it was almost impossible to be sure they were swimming straight towards land, or calculate how the currents might be sweeping them off course. All they could do was keep together, consult their compasses from time to time and hope.

It seemed a cold age before Mike heard the sound of surf breaking on a shore. He lifted his head as far above the surface as he could and cast around for any sign of a light. A wave broke over his face and he coughed and suppressed the sound. He flung his head back to clear the salt water from his eyes and peered into the darkness again, treading water. Finally he saw the tiny red glow of a cigarette end a few hundred yards to their left. Ogden-Smith was ahead of him and Mike stretched out his stroke to catch up. When he was on the sergeant's shoulder, he said quietly, 'Sentry, to our left.'

Ogden-Smith paused in his stroke and scanned the shore. He turned his head. 'Got him.' He swallowed seawater as he spoke, and spluttered, 'Current's carried us down. Want to swim up or crawl along the beach?'

Mike pointed straight ahead. They pushed on, sliding their arms into the water with the minimum of splash until the tide picked them up and swept them in with a rush. Mike's boot hit bottom and he was relieved to find it sand, not crunching pebbles. He turned his head and sensed rather than saw the bulk of the man beside him. Keeping low, they squirmed through the surf and lay at the edge of the water like two bits of driftwood. Gradually, their eyes grew accustomed to the faint starlight and the beach began to resolve into logical shapes. Steel and wooden defences had a different density to them than the spaces between and there was more than one wavering spot of red light. There was also an engine running and, turning his head to and fro to locate the sound, Mike finally made out the outline of a truck. It had to be on the track leading down to the beach and now he knew exactly where they were. Ogden-Smith was at his shoulder. 'We're west of the access road. See, there's a lorry on it.'

'Bet that's where the brass hats are. Keeping warm.'

'Let's work our way over there. Take samples and mark gradients as we go.'

For the next hour they slid silently over the sand like seals, sweeping the ground gently for buried mines. The speed king's auger worked well, though it needed easing up and down gently a few times after each go to expel sand trapped in the mechanism and prevent it jamming or scraping. When Dixon had a sample, Ogden-Smith took a note of their position and unscrewed the cap off one of the aluminium tubes, careful to cover the phosphorescent number on the end in case it glowed too brightly. He fitted one of his army prophylactics over the neck of the tube and Dixon discharged the auger into it. The first time, the sergeant tried to tie a knot in the end of the rubber, but his fingers were too clumsy with cold and next time he just screwed the cap hard back over the whole thing.

After each reading or sample, they lay still and watched those who were supposed to be watching for them. There was a little knot of men around the truck and soon they were close enough to hear the rumble of voices. Dixon tried to spot the ram-rod posture of the GOC, but he was soon convinced that Hobo wasn't part of the gathering. He wouldn't have had that engine running, for a start. And, since it continued to run, he concluded he couldn't even be within earshot. He lay quiet and watched, and saw something that made him put his hand out to touch Ogden-Smith's arm. One of the figures had reached up and run his fingers through a fat mop of hair.

'It's Sage.'

'Who?'

'The Professor. Bernal.'

'Doubting Thomas?'

'That's him.'

'What shall we do?'

151

'Let's see how close we can get. Do more sampling. If he does anything worth noting, write it down.'

They crept forward. Soon they could hear the various conversations going on around the truck. The driver and his mate were complaining about the cold and what a sheer bloody waste of time it all was. Bernal was engaged in deep debate with Howard Burton on some aspect of medieval architecture as found in the churches of East Anglia. The old history master sounded more animated than Mike had ever heard him, but he wasn't sure he had the upper hand in the argument. Sage seemed to know his onions. They worked away filling their tubes with samples and their note pads with facts and figures. Not least among these were notes of the precise times when Professor Bernal blew his nose, disappeared round the far side of the truck to urinate, and reluctantly conceded to Burton the superiority of the lantern in Ely Cathedral to the spire at Salisbury. The last tube filled, Ogden-Smith asked a question with his eyebrows. Dixon considered for a moment and answered it by standing up. The sergeant scrambled to his feet too and they strolled up to the truck.

'Evening, Professor.'

The scientist swung round and a soldier who had been leaning on the bonnet of the truck grabbed at his rifle and brought it to bear. Dixon and Ogden-Smith put their hands up rapidly. Burton spoke sharply to the sentry: 'Put it down, man. They're ours. And it's a good job they are, or you'd be lying in the sand with your throat cut.'

'As would we, Colonel. As would we.' This was the professor, who put out his hand to shake Dixon's. 'Well, I said it couldn't be done, and you've proved me wrong. Good show. Did you get samples, or have you just been eavesdropping?'

'Both, sir. We've got everything we came for – and a lecture on Norman and mediaeval architecture thrown in. Bruce is about ready to take his degree in it.'

'I'm about ready for some hot cocoa and a blanket, sir, actually. Do we have to swim back out to that ruddy boat?'

Mike nodded. 'We should. Prove it can be done.'

'Nonsense,' said Bernal. 'I've seen enough. The PM is expecting a report as soon as we can get it to him. I'm going straight back to London. Come down with me and we'll go and see Lord Cherwell together. The sooner we get on with the real recce the better.'

Burton agreed. 'Better do as the Professor says, Dixon. I'll debrief General Hobart. He's at the other end of the beach.'

Standing around, Mike had started to shiver. He couldn't control the trembling, but he didn't mind. He knew it was only from the cold. He grinned, as much from relief that he'd been able to do the job without succumbing to the panic that had taken him over at Dieppe as at finding they didn't need to swim back out into the freezing North Sea. When he went to speak, his voice came out through chattering teeth.

'Th-thanks, sir. C-Could you radio the pilotage party and tell them they can go home? Oh, and let them know it's not because we got pinched, would you?'

'I'll do that, Dixon. There are blankets in the back of the truck. I should get out of that gear and warm up. Don't want you dying of pneumonia on the dress rehearsal.'

22

DECEMBER 1943, OXFORDSHIRE

The Killing Bottle slowed and came to a stop alongside a grass verge. Charlie turned to her passengers. 'Here you are, sir. Safe home for Christmas.'

'Thank you, Charlie. Step in and say hello to my wife, won't you? It's a long drive back to Yorkshire. Might as well take a bit of a break.'

Charlie recovered first from this unexpected display of consideration and climbed out to open the rear door. Mike got out on the other side and looked up at the house the Old Man called home. It was a stone village house of quite remarkable antiquity, sitting right in the main street of a village about half an hour north of Oxford. If you had wanted a house that symbolised England in all its long-established peaceful domesticity, you would have gone a long way to find a better. The ancient stone steps leading to the front door were cracked and worn from centuries of comings and goings and the flower borders to either side had recently given up their railings for the war effort, the blackened iron stumps sticking out of their stone bedding like teeth in an old tramp's jaw. A massive Gothic front door, where the three of them now waited in the gathering winter dusk for a response to Hobo's determined bell-ringing, sat within a stone surround, terminating in two carved bosses that the ages had worn away to mere featureless knobs. The stone itself was a kind of soft limestone that glowed like honeycomb even in the weak sunshine of a winter's afternoon.

Dixon came from brick country, hard red machine-made bricks of the Industrial Revolution that formed themselves into workmanlike hard-edged houses. There were no houses like this round his way. Yet it didn't seem so grand that he found himself inclined to hate it.

Rather it moved something in him that he hardly knew what to call, some instinct of protection.

'Pretty old house, sir,' said Charlie, by way of conversation.

'What? Oh yes. Horribly run down when we took it on, been in farming hands for a long time, so nothing had been done in aeons. Course I've hardly been here lately, but Dorrie has worked a woman's magic on it.'

As he said her name, she opened the door. 'Patrick! I didn't dare hope you might really make it today. This is wonderful. Come in. Come in, and your friends too.'

Mike smiled at being taken for one of the Hobo's friends. Husband and wife embraced in the doorway and Mike heard him say, 'Darling woman,' in a tone far different than any he'd heard in the last nine months.

He glanced across at Charlie and saw a strange look on her face. Her lips were twisted in an odd smile and her eyes seemed to glitter. Then Hobo remembered them. 'Come on in, you two, it's hard enough to keep any heat in this place without letting it all fly out the door.'

The cross-passage inside was just wide enough for the two pairs to stand and exchange introductions. Dorothea Hobart was not at all what Mike Dixon had had in mind. Foolishly, he now saw, he had imagined Hobo's wife as a female version of his commander – elderly, stern and dowdy. Instead he was faced with a woman in, he guessed, her mid-forties, dressed as attractively as the clothing ration would allow and with an evident natural charm and ease of manner that Hobo was entirely missing.

When they had all shaken hands, she led them into a sitting room where a small coke fire was burning in a huge open fireplace under a wide old oak lintel. She helped her husband out of his greatcoat and Mike reluctantly shed his own, only to find the room surprisingly warm. Hobo stood with his back to the fire and beamed at his wife. 'So, where is she? Surely term has finished by now.'

'She's been home a week. We were making mince pies when you rang the bell – of course, the mincemeat is mainly apple these days, at least that's something we're not short of in this house. I'll go and get her. Tea, everyone?'

'Lovely. Is there anything I can do to help?'

'No, no, Charlie, isn't it? You've driven a long way and have further to go. Unless the two of you would prefer to stay over and go on tomorrow? Yorkshire's an awfully long drive, especially this time of year. It would only take two ticks to air the beds.'

'Oh, don't mollycoddle them, woman. They're in the army and driving is Charlie's passion. She'd drive all night if you let her. Now, where's that daughter of mine?'

Mike and Charlie glanced at each other again. Here was another surprise. Neither of them had guessed at the existence of Hobo offspring. He was moving away from the fire towards the door when it opened and in flew a girl of thirteen or fourteen. 'Daddy!' she cried and flung her arms around the General's waist. 'Mummy said you probably wouldn't be here until Christmas Eve. Oh, what a marvellous Pa you are. Isn't he a marvellous old thing, Mummy?'

Dorothea smiled. 'He is quite the most marvellous old thing, darling. Now put him down, you have three whole days to spoil and pet him before he has to go back to being beastly to Hitler. In the meantime, take care not to dispel all his military mystique in front of his staff.'

Too late. When they took to the road again after copious tea and mince pies hot from the kitchen range, it was with a warmth inside that owed as much to the surprising felicity of the Hobart domestic scene as to the food and drink. Lady Hobart showed them out into the darkness that had fallen since they drove up and Mike waited for her to close the front door before he crossed in front of the car and climbed into the front passenger seat. He gave a laugh and said, 'That was a turn-up for the book.'

'Wasn't it just?'

'Fancy old Hobo having a family like that. Stupid, I know, I always assumed that if he was so damn keen on fighting this war twenty-four hours a day it must mean he didn't have much to go home to.'

'At least we know what he's fighting for now. It's not only professional pride, or an intellectual challenge. He has as much to lose as anyone.'

'More than you or I.'

She took her eyes off the road for a moment to look at him, and changed gear more jerkily than usual. 'Yes. More than you or I.'

'I mean, if I go, obviously it'll be bad for my parents, but I don't have a wife and child depending on me. If anyone has to go, better that it's me than a married man with children.'

'Mike,' he noticed she used his Christian name again, the first time it had been anything other than "Lieutenant Dixon" or "Sir" since Linney Head, 'you're not going anywhere.'

'Well, as it happens, I am.'

Now she took her eyes off the road for longer. 'Where?'

'Oh, you know, I can't really say. It's just that I've sort of asked to go back to the shop-floor for a while. Only thing is, I may finish up a complete write-off. But it doesn't seem to matter so much, does it, when you see the home life of our own dear GOC, I mean? It reminds you what it's all for.'

'Of course it matters, you great ass.'

Mike looked at her, surprised by her tone.

'One day, you'll have a wife and child like that. Hordes of children probably. Draped from every limb. Don't throw your chances away just because you feel like running for your picture in the papers.'

'No danger of that, I'm afraid. If this thing doesn't come off, there won't be any headlines.' No, he thought. If I come up short, that'll be the last anyone hears. Anyone except the Gestapo. 'Thing is, I wondered, if I should go west, whether you could bear to go and see my people. They think I'm safe in a desk job, you see. And this business is so hush-hush I'm not sure what the official story will be. You could at least tell them, tell them it was my own fool idea anyway. Is that too big a favour to ask?'

She was silent for a while, staring straight out through the windscreen. Then she said, 'I think maybe it is, yes.'

Mike felt a flare of anger. Did she really think his family so far beneath her that the idea of spending half an hour in his mother's front parlour was too horrible to contemplate? 'I'm sorry,' he said. 'It was wrong of me to ask. I expect the CO will write something or other to them.'

Charlie went on in a rush, as if she'd not heard him, 'You know what they'd think, of course? If I were to go.'

'What?'

'That I was in love with you. And that you'd sent me so that they could comfort me, not the other way round.'

'Why would they think that?'

She did her habitual thing of shrugging without taking her hands off the wheel or her eyes off the road. 'I went to see Bill's mother, you know. When he'd been missing for a while. *She* seemed to think she ought to comfort me. Though it was plain as a pikestaff that her grief was so much worse than mine. It was awful, seeing someone feeling what I ought to be feeling, when I couldn't feel it that way myself.'

He flinched at 'Bill'. Why the hell did she have to bring him up? He hardly listened to the rest of what she was saying. When she stopped, there was silence. He supposed he had to say something so he said, 'I understand.'

'Do you?'

Suddenly he felt thoroughly irritated. He'd had enough of it. She was far too superior to do this bit of a favour for him and that was that. Fine. Drop it. Except she couldn't drop it, could she? Insisted that he understand why, didn't she? Even though the reason she gave was a load of cock and bull. How like a woman, always wanting to take the high ground, even when she didn't deserve it. He sighed, and tried to come up with a reply that would persuade her to let the whole stupid thing drop. 'Yes, I mean, I wouldn't want to put you through all that again. Especially as we're not … I mean, especially as it would all be a misunderstanding. I can quite see how embarrassing it would be if my mother … though I honestly don't see why she should think that. It's not as if I've written to her about you or anything.'

'But that's exactly why she would think it. If I were to turn up out of the blue. Don't you see?'

'No, I can't say I do. You see, my mother's not at all … ' He was going to say, 'like Bill Hartwell's, fainting on a chaise longue in her drawing room,' but then he pictured his mother, in her old yellow bib apron, scrubbing clothes with carbolic soap in the big pot sink, her arms red from the hot water. Imagined her looking out the kitchen window to see a society blonde in uniform walking up the brick path, past his father's sweet peas. What in hell had he been thinking, even suggesting it?

'Your mother's not at all what?'

'Not at all like you, or anyone you know,' he thought. But said, 'Oh, you know … she's not the fanciful type. She doesn't generally go round imagining things that aren't true … '

'And what about things that are?' She spoke very softly and he didn't catch her drift for a moment. They drove on in silence while he puzzled over her remark. Then her possible meaning lit up in his head like a flare going off and he turned to look at her. They had come into a town now and she was in the act of changing down through the gears. 'Banbury Cross,' she said, and nodded at the monument they had slowed down to drive round.

'What?' he said, confused as all hell.

'"Ride a cock horse to Banbury Cross, To see a fine lady on a white horse, With rings on her fingers and bells on her toes, She shall have music wherever she goes." The nursery rhyme. Remember?'

'Yes and Dr Foster went to Gloucester in a shower of rain. Don't change the bloody subject!'

She looked at him, shocked.

'Look, pull over, will you? For God's sake, just stop.'

She checked her mirror and braked to a halt in front of a hotel built out of the same honey-coloured stone as Hobo's house. 'Do you want to get a drink?'

'Damn right!' He didn't quite know why he was angry, but as he got out he slammed the door so that the big Humber rocked. He crossed the pavement and went into the bar of the old coaching inn without checking if she was following. He had his cigarettes out of his pocket and was about to light one when he was conscious of her at his elbow. 'Want one?' he said, holding out the pack. She shook her head. 'Drink?'

Shook it again. 'Driving.'

He thought about this as he lit his cigarette. In little more than a week he would be crawling ashore on an enemy coast, with a good chance of not coming back. He had told himself it didn't matter, since he couldn't have the girl he loved, and couldn't see his way to loving any other. And now this. He came to a decision. 'You wouldn't have to drive if we stopped and went on in the morning.'

'No,' she said, not looking at him. 'I suppose not.'

Without another word, he went out of the bar. When he came back she was sitting at a table in the corner, with a glass in front of her. 'What have you got there?'

'Dandelion and burdock.'

'Filthy stuff. Wouldn't you rather have a Scotch?'

'I would, but … '

'No need for buts, I've taken a room.'

He looked straight at her, their eyes met and he saw the colour rise in her cheeks and her throat. His own heart was beating wildly and he didn't dare take his hands out of his pockets in case they were trembling. Neither of them moved for what seemed like a long time. She pushed the half-empty glass away from her and said, 'Better get us both a whisky then.'

They drank two each, the second only because neither of them was brave enough to initiate the final step towards the stairs. They kept away from the subject of his 'wildcat thing'. Self-consciously, they talked of Christmas. She told him she was going on leave directly she had returned him to Rawdon, off to London to spend her seventy-two hour pass with her family. 'What about you? Going home?'

'Not with this show on. The truth is … ' The truth was Mike hadn't been home since May 1940. Hadn't seen or spoken to his parents since the day he joined up, which was the same day they'd had the telegram about Frank. It had been a Sunday and they were having dinner when the boy knocked. His mother went to the door and came back to the table with the wire in her hand. She put her hand on his father's shoulder and he took it from her and opened it. When he'd read it, he passed it back to her but his eyes were on Mike.

'Seventeen years old,' he said. 'Seventeen years old, and now missing, presumed taken prisoner. Lad shouldn't even be in the army yet. Only joined up because some others were too busy to do what was right. Hanging back when decent folk were taking a step forward to volunteer.'

Mike had stood up, pulled the jacket off the back of his chair and walked out of the back door. He could hear his mother crying as he went down the path.

The Army must have sent them another telegram when he was wounded because he'd received a letter from his mother in the hospital.

'Dear Michael,' it read, in her painstaking printing. 'Your Dad and me are greaved to hear you have been hurt. Is it bad, son? The wire didn't say much. If you send me word, I will come. Your loving Mam.'

The hospital had been on the South Downs. At that stage Mike had been too ill to have a clear idea exactly where he was. All he knew was that to expect her to come to him was too much to ask. His mother had been to Nottingham once, but never, to his knowledge, further south than Derby. As a girl she had ridden a bicycle, but had given it up forever when his father had tried to teach her to use one with gears. Since then, her world had been confined to the places she could walk to, and populated wholly by people she knew.

He was too sick to write himself. A nurse did that for him, though even as he dictated the letter he knew it would hurt them again to see a stranger's writing instead of his. Knew it would widen the distance between them even more. But he was too weak to hold a pen – and he feared that if he didn't reply at once his mother would set out on a journey that was beyond her.

'Dear Mam and Dad,' went the letter, 'no need to worry. I am in good hands and on the mend.' He wasn't sure that either was true, but all the same. A griping pain in his belly made him gasp and the nurse, whom he only realised later had been pretty, squeezed his hand where it lay clenched on the sheet. 'We can do this later.'

'No. I want to get it off. What have you put so far?'

She read it over and he nodded stiffly, back rigid, fending off the pain.

'I will soon be up and about again. Don't try to travel. Trains are in a mess. Please send my address here to Frank so he can write. And his to me, as I have lost it. Sorry. Hope you are both keeping well. Your ... ' He hesitated – loving, obedient – hardly their view of him. 'Your son, Michael.'

'Shall I read the whole thing back?' said the nurse, then looked up and saw that his eyes were closed again. She put a hand on his arm. 'You'd better give me the address, for the envelope. I'll post it for you on my way home.'

'Seventy-Nine Forest Street,' he murmured. The house he was born in, his mother too. Her father's house with the wheelwright's shop in the back yard, where he and Frank had played cricket using long triangular off-cuts of wood as bats. Elm, not willow, from the coffins his grandfather made, more often than wheels. And a ball of tight-wound rags from his mother's rug-making to bowl with. 'Shepshed, Leicestershire.' Home. Then he fell asleep.

Why had he thought of that now? Why had it occurred to him to ask Charlie to go and see them if ... Maybe she was right. Maybe he had wanted them to know that a girl like that had cared about him. As if that would make them think better of him somehow.

'Let's go up, shall we?'

'I'll just fetch my bag.'

He collected the key, signed the register as Mr & Mrs Dixon and couldn't help thinking of his parents again as he wrote the words. Outside, he heard an engine start and, looking out, saw the Snipe move off. He held his breath until she turned in through the carriage arch. Two minutes later she walked back in with her bag, looking perfectly collected despite the Scotch.

'Darling,' he said, for the porter's benefit, but finding he liked the sound of it, 'Let me take that.'

'Thank you, darling,' she said, with a glint of a smile and handed it over.

'Will you and Mrs Dixon be requiring breakfast, sir?' asked the porter, entering into the spirit of the thing.

'Very early, if that's possible. We shall be leaving by,' he looked at his watch, 'six thirty.' He was conscious that he ought to be back at HQ at the normal time in case Hobo should think of a reason to telephone, as he almost certainly would.

'I'll ask the kitchen to leave something out on a tray under a cloth in that case. You'll have to help yourselves.'

'Should I pay the bill now?'

'If you would. Pound and four shillings, including for the breakfast.'

Mike laid a pound note and coins on the desk as Charlie stood calm beside him.

'Thank you, sir. Night then.'

'Goodnight,' said Charlie and they walked up the broad old stair of the inn together, her hand on the crook of his arm, for all the world like an ordinary married couple breaking their ordinary journey in an ordinary English market town. The carpet on the landing was worn threadbare and he fought a longish battle with the awkward door before it surrendered and gave in upon a dingy room that smelled powerfully of stale smoke. Charlie crossed to the pale shadow of the window and drew the black-out curtains. Mike turned on a lamp, which threw a weak yellowish light across the scene. The room was cold. There was an electric fire with a meter and he knelt down to feed it a couple of shillings. When he stood up again, she was pulling aside the nubbed candlewick bedspread. She ran her hand over the sheet. 'Brrr! Freezing.'

The space between them seemed for a moment unbridgeable, gelid and filled with particularly English embarrassment. With two determined steps he crossed it and put his arms round her. The last time he'd done it, in Rawdon, she had been crying and her arms had hung at her sides. Now he felt her hands slip inside his greatcoat and press against his back.

'Hmmm. Warm,' she said.

He pulled the two sides of the coat out and round them both and dipped his head to kiss her. The touch of his lips on hers was a shock and yet already wonderfully familiar. After a minute or two he broke off and looked at her. Just to be sure of what he thought he knew. She looked back, unblinking, for long enough to settle the point. Then they went to bed.

The first time came to an end in shuddering relief that what had happened at Linney Head had not been a fluke or grown exaggerated in their memories to something unreal and unrepeatable.

They slept for a while.

He wasn't sure if he woke first, or if she did. He had no idea what time it was. As his consciousness gathered, he felt a silken soft weight pressed against his back. It stirred as he stirred and he felt a leg move gently against his. He rolled on to his stomach and on to his opposite side so that he was facing her in the bed. He could see nothing in the dense dark of the black-out, but he could hear her even breathing. He wasn't sure if she was awake, but he moved toward the warmth of her until he felt her breath on his lips and he kissed her as gently as he knew how.

For a moment the lips he met were soft and slack. Then he felt them stir into response and a hand slid up his arm, ran along his collar bone and cupped his face. Her fingers stroked the creases at the corner of his eye, and he felt, maybe for the first time ever, how a touch, just a touch, could communicate the full meaning of love. He pulled her close and they turned into one another for a second time.

Afterwards, they lay on their backs in silence, each listening for the other's breathing to return to the unfeignable regularity of sleep. But Mike was far from sleep now, too conscious that even the longest night of the year must come to an end at last and that, when it did, they would be just one morning's journey away from parting. He had to know the time, calculate how many more hours and minutes he had of her before that parting. He dragged his arm out from under the covers and held it close to his face, trying to make out the dim fluorescence on the hands of his wristwatch.

'What time is it?' she whispered.

'You're awake.'

'Shall I turn on the light?'

'No need. I can see, it's a little before three.' He let his arm drop to his side. 'We shall have to be up before six.'

'I know.'

'We ought to get some sleep.'

'Yes, we ought.'

They both lay silent. Mike closed his eyes, but they floated open again and he stared into the darkness, unable to get over the miraculous fact of her beside him in the bed. Somewhere in the inn, a clock chimed the hour.

'Mike?'

'Yes?'

'When are you going on this thing?'

'I can't, you know, I can't really say.'

'Will you be gone when I come back from Christmas?'

He didn't answer at once.

'Mike?'

'Yes.'

'Will you?'

'Yes.'

'Oh,' she said, and it came out partly a sigh and partly a moan. He felt for her hand and took it in his, lacing their fingers. 'You mustn't worry.'

'Mustn't I?'

'No. It won't do either of us any good. I've said it's a wildcat kind of a thing, but I shouldn't be doing it unless I thought I could pull it off. We've already had a dress rehearsal and that went off according to the programme, so there's really no reason this shouldn't too. And if it does come off, it could be an important step towards ending the war, towards bringing … Bill … and all those other chaps home.'

'Do you know how we met, Bill and me?' she spoke almost dreamily.

'No.' He didn't want to know. He cursed himself for conjuring him into bed with them.

'He was my brother's best friend at Shrewsbury. I was the classic little sister, hanging about when Archie brought his glamorous friend down in the holidays. God, I was jealous of him, being allowed to go away to school. It was so bloody unfair. I suppose that was partly why

167

I made up to Bill. To show Archie I could make his friend like me better than him. Fifteen, when he first kissed me. He was eighteen. Head of house, captain of rowing. I was dumb with admiration. He came out hunting and even though he wasn't an experienced rider, he threw himself at every fence, every hedge. Kept up with me stride for stride. It was the most exciting day of my life.'

'You fell in love with him.'

'He went up to Oxford. They both did.' She carried on as if she hadn't heard him. Certainly hadn't heard the way he made it sound like a reproach. 'Bill joined the Union, went all out for his blue. I was still stuck at home. Archie dropped him after a bit, or was dropped. He never would tell me why. Now I think it must have been because Bill was going with other girls. I went to Oxford on the train to see him one weekend and when we were out we met this girl from one of the women's colleges. She was tremendously smart and condescending. I was only seventeen, thick as a plank, but it didn't take a genius to see that he'd been with her. Of course, I didn't really know what that meant. I only knew about kissing, really.'

'Didn't you confront him about it?'

She sighed. 'Bill isn't the kind of person you can confront. He'd have turned the whole thing into a Union debate and gone on and on until he'd won. I thought I was being terribly grown up, not letting it matter to me. Now I think maybe it didn't matter because I wasn't actually in love with him.'

'But you thought you were.'

'I was seventeen. Show me a seventeen-year-old girl who doesn't want to believe herself in love. I was eighteen when he proposed. The morning of the Boat Race. I went to see him off and he looked so dashing in his white shirt with dark blue silk facings. I stood on the tideway at Putney as they carried the boat down to the water. Then he came jogging back up and threw a little square box at me. "Look after this for me, would you?" he said. I said, "What is it?" He said, "Look and see." So I did. And it was a ring. A quite beautiful one. Diamonds and a sapphire. Oxford colours. I was so surprised. My mouth dropped open. I must have looked an idiot.'

Mike imagined an excited eighteen-year-old Charlie, standing by the sparkling river on a spring morning in a London not yet made drab and dusty by war. He pictured the young Corinthian, fair-haired, no doubt, like the best Hitler Youth, showing off his expensively fed, expensively trained frame in his Oxford jersey. Entitled to his day on the river in front of the whole of London just as his privilege entitled him to every prize English society could bestow, including the best girl. So many prizes laid out before him he didn't value any of them. Mike doubted he'd ever hated anyone more than he hated Bill Hartwell.

'"Will you wear it," he said, "if we win?" My head was all scrambled. I couldn't get any words to come out. I just nodded. "Better go and beat Cambridge!" he said. And they did. So what could I do?'

'You said yes.'

'I'm not sure he ever asked me properly. You can imagine the kerfuffle after the race. There was champagne, a dinner at the Café Royal. All the chaps had girls along. It was about my first grown-up affair. I wasn't even "out". He hardly paid me any attention all night. What with the songs and the speeches. They all went off into a scrum at one point, the crew. Do you know what?' She laughed and played with his hand, which lay slack in hers. 'I'd almost forgotten. I was so fed up I actually went and threw his damn ring into the middle of his gang of yahoos. Thank God it was a decent size or no one might have noticed. Someone spotted it and gave it back to him. He came over and said, "What the devil did you do that for?" Put it back on my finger and rushed away again to rejoin the crew.' She laughed again, then stopped. 'It was all rather a foregone conclusion after that. He was about to start reading for the Bar when Hitler marched into Poland. We talked about getting married a few times, after he joined the Air Force, but the moment never seemed right.'

She stopped talking and they lay still, even her fingers had stopped moving. It was as if she had come to the end of what was known. Mike waited for her to go on. Every word had made him feel worse. The picture she'd painted was all too bitterly familiar. How could he compete with a rich, confident bastard who rowed for Oxford and saw as a completely natural thing his progress through the Inns of Court and the House of Commons? Even his faithlessness wasn't held against him. His mouth was dry as dust, so he swallowed and said, 'What are you going to do?'

'I don't know,' she whispered. 'He sounds so different now, in his letters … Not the Bill I used to know. And I don't know if that's a good thing. Or a bad. He seems to, well, he seems to need me for the first time ever. Before, it was always like he was carving out a little chunk of time for me that he could hardly spare. Like throwing a titbit of meat to a dog. Now, I suppose now he has more time than he knows what to do with.'

'So you don't think you were really in love with the old Bill, but you might be in love with the new one?' The words flowed through his veins like the poison from a snake bite, breaking down his blood. His heart seemed to slow and he wondered if it would actually stop before she answered.

'Stupid,' she said thickly, and he realised with a jolt that she was crying. She pulled her fingers out of his and her elbow knocked his side as she wiped at her eyes. A drop of wetness flicked on to his shoulder. 'Why am I so bloody stupid?'

He couldn't bear to ask whether she meant for loving Bill Hartwell or for going to bed with him, so he just reached out and stroked her hair, in case it was the last time he had the chance to do it.

23

The Savoy seemed like a film set or a dream after her tiny shared room in a farm labourer's cottage in Rawdon. She had grown used to a mattress stuffed with prickly horsehair, not luxuriously quilted springing. Army blankets, not fine linen. She ran her finger absently down a line of stitching on the satin coverlet that lay in slippery disarray over the huge bed in her mother's suite and sighed, 'Seems a bit odd, that's all.'

'What does, darling?'

Charlie hesitated. Telling her mother she was missing her Yorkshire billet would attract nothing but derision. She tried a more moderate line. 'Spending Christmas in a hotel, when we have a perfectly good house in town. It's the first time the family's been together in simply ages and now we're bound to be surrounded by all sorts of ghastly acquaintances.'

Her mother turned round from the dressing table, where she was putting on her face. 'Charlotte, you don't really expect me to try and conjure up Christmas dinner, with no cook or servants, in a house that's been in mothballs for four years?' She waved the powder-puff she was poised to dab at her nose and a cloud of powder floated down towards the carpet. Charlie tried to picture her mother in the basement kitchen at Eaton Place, hot and bothered, in an apron, wrestling with the range or peeling potatoes. The absurdity made her giggle.

'What's so amusing?'

Charlie picked at the stitching some more. 'Oh, nothing.'

'Look, darling, why don't you run along and put on a nice dress instead of that ghastly uniform? Do something about your hair … if you're quick maybe Giovanni would have time to put a wave in it, or at least give it a decent trim. Shall I call down for you? I'm sure he'll squeeze you in if I tell him it's an emergency. And, quite frankly, for once I wouldn't be fibbing.'

Charlie looked at her mother. Lit from the side by a peach silk lamp on the dressing table she looked remarkably beautiful and a fraction (more than half, certainly less than three quarters) of her age. She was in an eau de nil satin slip and her shoulders were plump and creamy without any sign of sag or wrinkle, or of the privations of rationing. Her blond hair was perfectly dyed and perfectly pinned in a chignon at the nape of her neck. Unlike her daughter's, there were no dark circles of fatigue around her eyes.

The evening dress hanging from the picture rail was a gown Charlie vaguely recognised from before the war. It had come from a grand couturier, though now it had a different neckline and chiffon sleeves. The straitening circumstances of war hardly seemed to touch her mother at all. She always seemed to know a dear little man, or a clever little woman, who could fix things up perfectly so that she should not be put out by the difficulties that afflicted everyone else. Charlie pressed on. 'What I don't understand is why the house is still closed up anyway. I mean, you're here in London almost all the time. And now Cec is working in St James's surely it'd make more sense to open Eaton Place than for her to be in digs in Chelsea and you to live in a hotel.'

'No, darling, it makes much more sense for me to be here. So much less trouble than having a house to run. Especially as I'm busy most of the time with my committees. Cecilia is quite happy slumming it with her pals in the King's Road. It's a foetid little coal-hole, but that's what the young like, isn't it? To strike out and fend for themselves.'

Charlie supposed that might be right, if the alternative was being under Veronica's controlling thumb.

'But what about Papa? Wouldn't he rather be in his own house when he's in town?'

'Nonsense. He's hardly ever in London these days. When he is, he's happy as larry at Bellamy's. Always plenty of old soldiers to talk to. Anyway he'll be here for dinner. And at lunch tomorrow.'

'Surely he's staying here with us over Christmas?'

Her mother had put down the powder-puff and was working a little brush across a solid block of mascara that she had wetted with a licked finger. Now she lifted the brush and started to work on highlighting her arched and plucked brows. Charlie saw her mother's eyes flick from their task to stare straight into the mirror for a moment. There was something odd about the look she gave herself. Then it was gone and she put down the mascara and turned round to face Charlie. Having only one eyebrow done gave her a faintly sinister expression. 'Charlotte, I know you think I live a life of utter idleness and self-indulgence, but actually I am considerably pushed, what with the evacuee committee and my nurses, and all sorts of people coming and going through London the whole time. I can't always be altering my arrangements just because your father decides to descend from Scotland. You seem to think you're the only one doing anything useful, rushing about the country with your mad-eyed General in tow, but really it's hardly fair.'

'He's not mad-eyed.'

Her mother turned back to her mirror. 'So you say, but I was talking to Freddie Quiller last night and he maintains the man's an absolute menace. Famous for it, apparently.'

Charlie felt her temper start to rise, like it always did. 'He is not a menace. He's just trying to get the War Office to do its job and

173

get us the equipment we need. Anyway, Freddie Quiller shouldn't be talking about him. To you or to anyone. Hasn't he heard of the Official Secrets Act?'

'Oh Charlie, don't be a prig. If there's one thing I can't abide it's a prig. Freddie's a dear friend, and he knows you work for old Hobo so he's bound to say the odd word about him. He has to deal with him, after all, when he comes in throwing his weight about at the Ministry. Flatly refuses to wait his turn for anything, Freddie says. Always trying to barge to the front of the queue.'

'That's because we haven't got enough ... '

Charlie bit her lip. She knew her mother's love of gossip too well. Anything she said would be doing the rounds of London cocktail parties seconds after the words were out of her mouth. She picked up her ghastly ATS jacket, slid off the bed and headed for the door. 'I'll see you at dinner,' she said, with a familiar sense of having been bested by a steelier will. The longer she was out in the world, doing a job she thought she was not bad at, the more she felt it should be easier to stand up to her mother. But, as always, it had taken only a few minutes for her to feel the old merciless order re-established.

Her mother, who was now smiling glassily while she applied rouge to the apples of her cheeks, darted a look at Charlie through the mirror. She was prepared to let her vanquished opponent leave the arena, but not without a parting shot. 'All right, darling. But please try and do something about your appearance, would you? I know you're somewhat in purdah with Bill in a POW camp. Still, there's no need to turn into a total frump. It is Christmas Eve, war or no war.'

When they gathered for drinks, Charlie watched her mother, from a distance, at the centre of a circle of attentive men. Her father was not among them. She spotted him at the bar, one of the few in evening dress rather than uniform. He looked smaller and older than when she had last seen him. When he moved to greet someone his limp seemed more pronounced, as though the artificial leg he'd had since Passchendaele had ceased to fit. She couldn't decide if this was because the leg had worn down and become too short for him or because he had worn down and become too short for it.

'So much for a quiet family Christmas, eh?'

The voice in her ear was deep and familiar and she hadn't heard it for over a year.

'Archie!' She flung her arms round her brother and he crushed her in a bear-hug so hard that his uniform buttons dug into her chest. 'When did you get back? I haven't seen you for such ages. Let me look at you.' She held him at arm's length. 'My God, you're brown as a nut!'

'We sailed into Southampton three days ago. Since then it's been bedlam, getting the tanks on to transporters. Dealing with all the compassionate leave applications. You wouldn't believe how many chaps' wives have made off with another while we've been in Libya. Made me very grateful not to be a married man, I can tell you. I finally got away this morning and I don't have to report back until the New Year.'

'Arch, that's marvellous. Nobody was sure if you were even going to make it for Christmas, and now you're here for a whole week. Oh, it is going to be a happy Christmas after all.'

They were beaming at each other, like the old friends and partners in crime they'd always been, when their happiness was broken in on by a shrill cry, 'Archie, darling!'

Charlie saw at once that her mother's meticulous preparation for tonight had paid off. She looked magnificent.

'Mother, you look younger than ever. How do you do it?' Archie was right. The other wives, most of them mothers of fighting sons, wore their cares upon their faces, which only made the contrast with Veronica Carrington's untroubled radiance all the more marked.

'Oh, don't tease, darling. I haven't a moment to spend on myself these days. But what about you? Black as an Arab and thin as a whip. What has the Army been feeding you on?'

'Bully beef and dates mostly. I'm looking forward to decent English tack.'

'Well, don't expect too much. Even the Savoy is struggling to make ends meet these days. I heard a rumour that unless there's an invasion next year their cellars will be out of Champagne by next Christmas.'

'My God, no wonder Churchill is keen to give the Yanks their Second Front. I never realised things were so serious.'

'There you go again, teasing. I don't know when you became so sarcastic. You were never sarcastic as a boy. I suppose this is what comes of spending so much time cooped up in a tank with God knows who.'

'The lower orders, mother, I'm afraid to say. Still, we do maintain a rigid hierarchy, you know. As tank commander, I sit on top of the gunner and he sits on top of the driver. It's all perfectly done according to the rules of an ordered society.'

'Oh, do stop it, Archie. Someone will hear you and think you've turned communist or something dreadful. Now, there's Freddie. I do just need to have a word before dinner.' She squeezed his arm with a white gloved hand and floated away. Archie watched her go, trailing clouds of chiffon. 'The old girl's looking good.'

'Isn't she?' said Charlie. 'And not a moment to spend on herself these days.'

He laughed. 'Sarcasm seems to be spreading through this family like a rash. Where's Cec? Surely sweet Cecilia can't be infected. She's not been rubbing up against the lower orders, has she?'

'I doubt it. Her office is in St James's and she works for a Colonel, so she should be safe enough. I don't think she's here yet. She had a late shift. Mother insisted she should just tell them she was needed at the Savoy, but Cec wouldn't do it.'

'Course not. Girl's never had a black mark in her life.'

A waiter went past with a tray of champagne cocktails and Archie swiped two. Charlie swiped two more and clinked hers against his.

'Dolt! I was getting one for you.'

Charlie giggled. 'I know, but now you have two and I have two. What went wrong, do you suppose, between you, the great Oxford scholar, and Saint Cecilia, to cause me, the dolt?'

He looked at her over the rim of his glass. 'Is that a serious question?'

'Yes.'

'Then I shall give it a serious answer. Which is that you are not a dolt, Charlotte. You have simply had the misfortune to remain uneducated. Happily, what you lack in erudition, you make up for in beauty and guts, which in my book are much more useful. Cheers.'

'Merry Christmas!'

They each drained one cocktail and put the two empty glasses down on a side table.

'Shall we circulate?'

'Let's do. But let's not talk to anyone unless it's Cec or Papa. I haven't seen you for a year. I'm not ready to share.'

'Suits me. Anyway, I wanted to ask you, what news of Bill?'

Charlie looked down into her remaining champagne cocktail. Bubbles were feasting on the sugar lump in the bottom of the glass.

'You know he's in a POW camp?'

'I heard. Where?'

'East Prussia, wherever that is. Being uneducated, I don't have the foggiest clue.'

Archie leant down and brushed an imaginary chip off the shoulder of her evening dress. 'Does he write?'

'Whenever they let him. On those awful printed forms. Have you seen them? And everything's read of course, by both sides. It's horrible. I never know what to write.'

'Poor Bill, he's the last person you could think of as a POW. I bet he's champing like hell. Still, at least he's got you, waiting for him. At least you haven't hooked off with some Yank or Pole, like half the wives in my squadron.'

Charlie found it suddenly impossible to raise her eyes from the streams of bubbles swimming up through the wine, like fish rising to the fly. He knew her too well. If he saw her face, he'd be sure to guess the truth. She took a gulp at the champagne. 'But you said yourself, "Thank God I'm not a married man." All that sort of thing seems pretty hopeless now. Even our parents don't seem to be able to manage it anymore. Look at them – are they even still married? Or have they split up without us even noticing? We're all so busy with our own little bits of the war. You know Papa's staying at his club?'

Archie frowned. 'No, I didn't. I hadn't thought about them. They seem ... Christ, Charlie, don't try and distract me on to yet another thing I haven't got a grip of. We were talking about Bill. You're not thinking of throwing him over are you?'

Charlie put off answering by taking another deep swallow of her cocktail. At this rate she'd be tight before the fish course. When she shook her head, she wasn't sure if she was saying 'no' or merely shaking off his question, but it must have looked more definite than it felt because he said, 'Good. Because I've seen what it does to men when they get a "Dear John" at the front, and I daresay it's the same in a camp. Total bloody impotence. That's the worst of it. There's nothing they can do. Some go crazy. Some go quiet and let it eat away at them. Some go AWOL. I've had to deal with one today who skipped as soon as we landed, off to sort out his old lady and the filthy sod who'd got his feet under my man's kitchen table. Really good sergeant I can ill-afford to lose, and now he's up on a charge of desertion. I shall try and get him off it, but it's hardly likely I shall manage it. Good God, is that Cec? What the hell happened? She's gone and turned into a fully-grown woman.'

When dinner was announced, their mother took Archie from her at the door to the River Room and made an entrance with him. She looked almost as if she expected applause. Charlie turned back to wait for her father and sister. Cec had her hand through his arm on his limping side and Charlie could see he was making an effort not to show his handicap. Cec was in a midnight blue satin dress that set off her pale skin and dark brown hair. She was slender as a sapling and still more a girl than a woman, whatever her brother thought. 'We're so unlike,' thought Charlie. 'She's so sensible, always looking before she leaps. I'm such a bloody bull in a china shop. We don't even look the faintest bit like sisters. She'd never let herself get into my kind of mess in a month of Sundays.' Yet she wasn't jealous. It was impossible to be jealous of someone so hesitant and innocent. It would have been like being jealous of Bambi. She embraced the two of them together as they came up to her. 'Darlings! Happy Christmas.'

'Charlotte, here you are at last.' Her father kissed her cheek. 'I saw you across the bar, talking to Archie, but there was far too appalling a crush to try and reach you. It was wonderful to see the two of you together, laughing like that.'

'Were we?'

'Yes, it looked marvellous. We'd have thought nothing of it, would we, a few years ago? Now, to have you all together for Christmas seems almost too miraculous.'

'I suppose it does.'

'If only Bill were here, the family would be complete. Have you heard from him?'

'Yes. He's, well, he's getting on with it. There's nothing else he can do, is there?'

'Probably running Oxford Union Society debates and a camp parliament, if I know Bill.'

'I don't know. He can't say much in his letters.'

'Of course not. Damn shame. Anyway, have you seen this gorgeous creature claiming to be Cecilia? Not that she was ever an ugly duckling, but all the same. I haven't seen her in six months and I swear it's not the same girl.'

'Papa, will you stop saying that sort of thing? It makes me want to die of embarrassment.'

'He does have a point, Cec. You look terrific. Where did you get that dress?'

'It's one of Mummy's. She decided the colour didn't suit her, so she gave it to me and I had it altered.'

'Bet you had to have it taken in about a yard. You've the tiniest waist I've ever seen. I reckon I could get my hands right round it.'

'Shh! Don't tell Mummy. She hates the idea that anyone's thinner than she is. I told her I just changed the neckline and the hem.'

Charlie laughed: 'Cecilia Carrington, you are definitely heading for sainthood. Just for that, I shall let you sit next to Archie at dinner.

So long as I can have Papa on one side, I'll take my chances with the rest.'

If she'd known that her fit of generosity was going to lead to her sitting next to Freddie Quiller, she would have thought twice about it. More than twice, probably. She'd never met Major-General Quiller, but she'd heard some very rude things said about him in the back of the Killing Bottle. Within ten minutes of meeting him, she concluded they were all true.

'Thing is, Charlotte,' he was saying as the waiters cleared the soup plates, 'the last thing we need at a time like this is some damned fellow rocking the boat. We're all doing our level best under impossible circumstances and if one chap keeps on standing up and saying it's not good enough and demanding his equipment before anyone else gets a look-in, well it just won't do. Bad for morale, you see.'

'But what if it isn't good enough?'

'I'm not with you, my dear.'

'What if your best isn't good enough? What if the men at the front, men like Archie, never get equipped with tanks that are a match for Tigers? Don't you think that will be bad for morale? Or is it only morale in Whitehall that matters?'

Quiller's face flushed and his chins quivered. Charlie knew she'd been unforgivably rude, but she wasn't about to hear Hobo rubbished without retaliating. She crumbled a dry bread roll on her side plate to smithereens, while Freddie Quiller fought with his emotions. Eventually he mastered them and gargled a kind of laugh. 'After what men like your brother have accomplished in Libya, maybe Rommel has gone running back to Berlin asking to swap his Tigers for Cromwells.'

This seemed to Charlie such a completely stupid remark that she called on Cecilian reserves of patience and bit her tongue to forestall another rude reply. Quiller ploughed on. 'Archie's in the Sherwood Rangers, isn't he? Fine regiment. Wonderful tradition. Though even they are having to accept the kind of replacements they never would have taken into the regiment before. I don't just mean men who aren't regular soldiers. Men who don't hunt. Chaps from the minor public schools. It's never easy, that kind of thing. So much better for cohesion in a regiment when the other officers are the sorts of chaps you naturally get on with. It's a crying shame, but there it is. Needs must, I suppose.'

Charlie thought of Mike and his 'wildcat thing'. He didn't hunt and he hadn't been to even a minor public school. As far as she could make out, his school had been a sort of technical institute training engineers for the big industrial concerns. That didn't matter to Hobo, who was far keener on men with ideas than on maintaining tradition, but a man like Freddie Quiller would never consider Mike Dixon good enough to be an officer in a decent regiment. And, all the time, Mike was off risking his life while fat Freddie Quiller sat in a hotel dining room waiting to be fed Dover sole.

She stood up abruptly and her napkin slid to the floor. Quiller stared at her in surprise. 'Sorry. Need some air.' She pushed her way between the close-packed gilt chairs and burst through the heavily-curtained doors on to the river balcony. The doors swung efficiently to behind her and the cold took her breath away after the heat of the crowded room. The complete darkness was almost as much of a shock. She walked forward, hands outstretched until she touched the stone parapet. The Thames ghosted along below, but she could hardly make it out until the moon edged from behind a cloud and the grey black waters glinted a blued steel reflection. Beyond the river lay Lambeth and the whole of South London and yet for all she could see of it she might have been on a clifftop looking out over a great blank ocean. She shivered and hugged herself, freezing but not wanting to go back inside to hateful Freddie. What a hash she was making of tonight. Of everything. If only she knew where Mike was, and what he was doing.

Behind her, the music surged. A wedge of yellow light shone briefly and went out. She couldn't see who had come outside. Please God don't let it be Freddie Quiller, she thought. Or Mother.

'Charlie?'

'Oh, Archie.' She turned and hugged him. He felt thin and strong as steel, but warmer. 'It's all such a bloody mess.'

'You can say that again. As soon as you dashed off and left Quiller alone, Mother dropped me like a stone to go and sit by him. It just occurred to me: you don't suppose they can be having some kind of grotesque affair, do you?'

Charlie stood still for a moment. Then she started to laugh. 'Well done, Arch. There was I thinking tonight couldn't possibly get any worse and you go and put the tin lid on it. Come on, let's get another drink. Don't know about you but I'm nowhere near tight enough for this.'

24

New Year's Eve was not quite the moonless night for which the mission had originally been slated. The date was Churchill's choice. 'Carousing' was his reasoning. On New Year's Eve, he said, the German sentries would be determined on carousing and thus distracted by drink and local girls. They crossed the Channel in a motor torpedo boat. It bashed through the winter swell until they were three miles off the French coast, sticking within its regular patrol route, in case the Germans had some way of tracking it. They clambered over the side and dropped down into the same hydrological vessel they'd used in Norfolk. Commander Wilmott greeted Dixon and Ogden-Smith with a friendly handshake.

The MTB tore off and the pilotage party made its painfully lumpy way towards the beach. Wilmott put down his glasses at one point and chuckled. 'Glad we didn't bother waiting for the dark of the moon.'

'Why?'

'Because they've got the bloody lighthouse switched on at Luc-sur-Mer. Damn sight brighter than the moon. You'll need to keep your heads down.'

Mike looked out and saw the sweep of the light from the shore. He started to count the number of seconds between each recurrence of the beam. He glanced at Ogden-Smith. 'Got it, Bruce?'

'Got it. It's a bit like skipping. Just have to get into the rhythm.'

They went below and clambered into all their kit. The sea was much rougher than it had been off Brancaster and they bounced around the cabin, colliding with the walls and each other, already feeling pretty sick. There was one extra piece of kit than there had been in Norfolk, a bottle containing two capsules. It slid across the table. Mike caught it up and read the label. He unscrewed the cap and offered the bottle to Bruce.

'What is it?'

'Suicide pill.'

'No fear.'

'Better take them with us. We can't afford to get pinched.'

'We won't get pinched.'

'Things might go wrong. It's a war. Things do.'

'We'll be all right. Just do for me what you did for Henry. And I'll return the favour.'

Mike felt ice form in his guts. Looking at the bottle in his hand, there seemed no point in not telling the truth. 'I didn't do Henry any favours. If I'd left him to be captured, he might still be alive.'

Ogden-Smith shook his head. 'Didn't you hear? About the Commando Order? Hitler was so pissed off about the raid, he issued orders that all captured commandos be shot as spies. Henry had had it, either way. You were the only chance he had. Poor sod.'

Mike rattled the pills. Could it be true? If it was, did it change anything? It didn't change the fact that he was only still alive because Henry Peat had taken a back full of lead for him. He still wasn't certain if he'd been trying to save Henry, or only himself. However many times he re-lived the events of that morning, waking, sleeping, every state in between, it was never any clearer than it had been the first time. The deafening racket of panic in his head was never any less. He'd read in the papers the accounts of decorated soldiers who had done extraordinary things in battle. To a man, they described seeing things in slow motion, knowing what they had to do. It had been nothing like that with him. Going back for Henry had been a random, instinctual act. That terrified him – because he didn't trust his instincts. What if they took over again tonight and he messed everything up? He'd been all right at Brancaster. But that was just a dress rehearsal. On home turf. This was the real thing. And the whole of the invasion planning depended upon it going right.

He glanced across at Ogden-Smith, who was still adjusting the straps on his gear. Not only the invasion, but another good man, as strong and sound as Henry Peat, whose life depended on him keeping his head. Slowly, he screwed the lid back on the bottle. He stood it on the table and gestured to the ladder. 'Shall we?'

A mile from shore, Wilmott cut the engine. He came out of the deckhouse to see them over the side. 'We'll wait at the rendezvous. If you're not there by first light, we'll have to leave you to it. So don't mess about. There's good chaps.'

They slipped over the side and Mike tried not to cry out as the freezing water enveloped him and rushed into his boots. He moved his arms and legs in extravagant swimming gestures to fight the shock of the cold and could hear Ogden-Smith coughing and spitting as he did the same. The wind was blowing up the Channel, whipping the tops off the waves into their faces. Swimming was heavy going. He tried to focus on the lighthouse, and was soon conscious that they were being swept down past the point where they had hoped to make landfall. He willed himself to swim faster even though his sodden boots weighed like lead and he could feel an ache spreading in his bad leg. He concentrated on slicing the water with his arms, counting his strokes in batches of ten as if he were back pulling cabbage plants on Fred Mee's farm. Long after he'd lost count of how many batches of strokes he'd done, he finally struck bottom. Ogden-Smith came up behind and they lay in the surf for a minute or two, panting like dogs.

Mike was scared at how exhausted he was. He had no idea if he'd have the strength to swim back to the rendezvous point. From the village came the sound of music and a ragged burst of singing. Hard to tell if it was French or German – probably both. Yellow light gushed out of a doorway and the music blared. The door shut and muffled it. Looked like the PM had been right about the carousing.

As soon as he had the strength, Mike stood up and began to stumble down the beach. He aimed for a trot, but his legs were so numb with cold that it was more of a drunken shamble. Ogden-Smith followed and they jogged along the wet sand. After a couple of hundred yards, the sea-water squelching in his boots had warmed up and he felt a bit better. Ten minutes later, he dropped to his knees and clawed at the belt round his waist, loosening it enough to free the auger from his back. Ogden-Smith knelt beside him. He pushed aside a pile of seaweed and tapped at a dark patch in the sand with his trowel. 'Here. I reckon this is Sage's peat.'

Mike looked over his shoulder. The light was scouring inland. He stood and pushed the auger into the ground. He shot the spring, wincing at the noise. The sergeant unscrewed the first of his aluminium tubes and Mike released the sample into it with a wet thump. Ogden-Smith took a compass bearing and marked the position on his writing tablet.

They scuttled across the beach. The temptation was to take samples close together and get out quick. Mike fought it. Though he could hear Ogden-Smith's teeth chattering and his fingers were numb, he knew it was crucial to do the job right. After surveying the mid-section of the beach they crawled up towards the high-water mark. Mike was easing the spring in the auger when he felt a tap on the arm. He glanced over to see Bruce pointing urgently, the whites of his eyes showing, wide with alarm. He looked up and saw a sentry coming right towards them, spot-lit by the lighthouse beam. His field grey overcoat shone silver in the glare, buttons winking like jet ornaments. He was no more than ten feet away and, if not for the blinding light shining right in his face, must have seen them already.

Mike dropped on to the wet sand and wished it was a nice, dry dune he could dig himself into. Instead it was smooth, hard as cement and horribly revealing. He put his hand down his boot for his revolver in its oilcloth bag. Had he time to unwrap it? Would it fire? He tried to work out if the tide had turned yet. How many yards they had to run. How long it would take the rest of the guard hut to pile out when they heard gun-shots. As his head spun with multiple calculations, he felt his heartbeat start to gallop. He clenched his fists and forced himself to breathe. It was not going to happen again. He was not going to let Bruce down the way he had Henry. He had made the decision to leave the poison pills on the boat. They could not be taken up. It was his job to get them out of this.

The beam from the lighthouse was turning, turning, so that in another few seconds it would no longer be shining in the sentry's eyes. When the toe-cap of the man's boot landed so close it flicked sand on to Mike's hand he turned his head to look at Bruce again. The sergeant's right hand was spread out next to his head, covering something that glinted dully. His lips were pulled back, teeth clenched, in the snarl of a predator ready to strike. The sentry took another slow stride and still did not see them. Mike put out his hand and closed it over Bruce's wrist, willing him not to make a move with the knife unless they were discovered. The soldier's next footstep came down three inches from his head. The man had only to look down. Instead, he put a hand up and rubbed his sleeve across his eyes, grunting as he did so, and Mike realised that even though the light had passed over it had left him blinded. The CDL tanks on the fells at Lowther leapt to mind. He remembered blinking helplessly to disperse the multi-coloured dots the mass of candle-power had burned on to his retinas. Maybe those tanks will work after all, he thought, as the German's foot lifted again. The next step would take him past, just. The slightest noise or movement would still make him turn. They lay like dead men, dead men with pounding hearts, as the foot lifted and came down again a yard off.

When the sentry was fifteen yards off, they squirmed down the beach, watching all the time for the moment when he would turn and re-trace his steps. Mike hoped fervently that when he did so the light wasn't spread out in front of him and he didn't spot their retreating spoor in the wet sand. They waited a quarter of an hour, by which time they were almost paralysed with cold. Ogden-Smith's teeth had unclenched and begun to chatter again. There was no sign of the sentry. He looked at his watch. They had to work fast now if they were going to get what they'd come for. He headed back up the beach.

When they each had eight full tubes, he signalled it was time to go. The tide had come in, which meant further to swim but at least their tracks would be covered. They waded as far out as they could, gasping at water that seemed more freezing than before, then set off swimming, trying to make their strokes as soundless as possible. With the lighthouse behind them now, it was harder to judge when to duck under the beam. He tensed every time the water around him lit up, holding his breath for a shout or the whistle of a bullet.

The light wasn't their only problem. The sand-filled bandoliers were much heavier than he'd expected. He cursed his lack of thoroughness at not insisting on swimming back to the boat off Brancaster. If they had, they would have realised how damn near impossible it was to swim a mile loaded down with a girdle of sand-bags. Too damn full of ourselves over sneaking up on Sage, he thought, as he swallowed another wave and kicked with all his strength just to stay afloat. His bad leg had already been pretty shot on the way in. It was hurting again like a bloody bastard and he bit his lip against the pain till the salt-sting told him he'd drawn blood.

The beach was separated from the open sea by a line of tall breakers. Ogden-Smith was a little ahead and Mike watched him change his stroke to a vigorous crawl as he attacked the breakers. He ploughed forward, kicking strongly. A minute later he bobbed upright and fell back to the beach side of the waves.

Mike swam ahead and gave it everything as he hit the leading edge of the surf. Water smashed over his head as he thrashed his arms and legs as hard as he could. Then he felt an incoming wave catch at the bulk round his waist and push him upright like a cork. He slammed up through the wave as it carried him back and dumped him in calm water. He looked round. A head bobbed a few feet away. 'Not exactly a piece of —' he swallowed a wave and spat it back out, 'cake, this.'

'Not exactly.'

'Another go?'

'Nothing else.' Bruce's head disappeared under water. He came up again. 'Nothing else on the calendar.'

They swam forward, matching strokes, as if the two of them together could combine forces against the power of the sea. They entered the wall of surf at about the same time and were beaten back within seconds of each other. Mike trod water with one leg only, the other bent up under him in a spasm of pain. Somewhere beyond the breakers, a boat was waiting for them. 'Can't dump the —' he spat water, 'the tubes. Might wash ashore.'

Bruce grunted. 'Could dump the samples.'

'And have to come back again? Don't fancy that.' He trod more water. 'Need to work out these breakers. Wait till they're most confused and swim like hell.' A wave caught him and he fought for breath. 'Like the lighthouse. A pattern.'

They hung in the water, treading away, watching the waves. For a while it seemed hopeless. A burst of singing erupted from behind them, more concerted than before, as if several parties had joined together. Mike ignored the noise, concentrating on the wave pattern, until finally he saw a spot in the line of surf where a peak and trough intermittently but consistently arrived together and contrived to cancel each other out. When they did they created a momentary channel, a possible passage to open water. He sent up a silent hail to the gods of mathematics, then flung the water out of his face with a shake of the head and whispered urgently, 'On my signal.'

He waited for the two lucky waves to repeat themselves and as he saw them form to left and right he hissed, 'Now!' He launched forward, swimming as he had never swum before in his life, conscious that there would certainly not be enough strength for another effort after this. He felt the waves clutch and drag at him, his leg was on fire, but it was a blaze that drove him on. Water flooded his nose and mouth and he forgot about breathing, determined at all costs not to be turned on his back. There was one great slam against his chest and he thought he was gone, but something made him refuse to give in, some little word that pulsed in his brain, and that word was: 'Charlie'. Then he was conscious that his arms and legs were churning along on the surface and the water was calmer. He raised his head and was finally able to take a breath. He flung the water out of his face and looked around frantically. It was pitch black and for a moment he could hear nothing but his tortured breathing in his ears. Then he heard a shout behind him. He turned back wearily towards the breakers, searching the white water for a sign of Bruce. Nothing. Fear gripped him that he had heard the man's drowning cry.

It came again, not from the breakers but from the calmer water a few yards away. Not the cry of a drowning man. A shout. He swam towards it and when it came again he made it out.

'Happy New Year, Mike! We did it.'

Rage boiled through him at the bloody great knuckle-headed idiot treading water still within earshot of the enemy. 'Swim, you bugger! Or do you want to get us caught?' he hissed.

'Sorry,' came the whispered reply. 'Swim it is.'

The sea was rougher beyond the breakers. As they pulled away from the shore, it was hard to be sure that they were pointing the right way. The probability of a low flat-bottomed boat spotting two dark heads in a choppy sea on a cloudy night seemed slimmer and slimmer the further they swam. There were still about four hours to first light. Mike wasn't sure they could keep their heads above water until they could make contact. Wasn't sure he could, at any rate. His leg was agony now. He'd forgotten about it during the crisis on the beach and swimming through the breakers. Now every kick sent a thumping great spear of pain through his thigh. He clamped his teeth together and tried to focus on what he had to swim home for. There was a girl, who wasn't maybe even his girl. But she was the one he wanted, at any rate. Knowing that was knowing something. There was his brother, who wasn't at home, but would be one day if jobs like this one came off. There was even Hobo, who would be left in a hell of a jam if they didn't make it back, not knowing if the whole invasion had been compromised, and probably taking the blame from all sides for his damn fool idea.

Somehow, he kept moving. Little by little, they worked their way to what they hoped was roughly the right spot, before pulling out their torches. Using the lighthouse as a back-marker, they shone the wavering directional beams out towards home. It seemed a pathetic gesture, the more so when they had been shining them into the empty blackness for the best part of an hour.

Out in the darkness, they heard an engine. Felt as much as heard it, vibrating through the water. Mike thrashed around, searching desperately for the silhouette of a superstructure against the dim horizon. It could easily be a French fishing boat, or a German E-boat returning from patrol. He dipped his torch under the water. Bruce did the same. Then he heard the hull slapping uncomfortably, hard and flat, against the waves and a minute later the unmistakable square outline of the survey vessel was visible against the dark grey sky. He thrust his hand up and waved his torch for all he was worth. A short while later the boat was bumping up against them and hands reached down and hauled him up by the webbing straps on his bandolier. He was enormously grateful to those hands, because he knew he couldn't have climbed aboard on his own. Seconds later, Ogden-Smith lay hiccupping beside him and the boat turned to seek its own rendezvous. Commander Wilmott stood over them as the engine picked up speed. 'God, that was tricky. I wasn't at all sure we were going to spot you. Did you get everything?'

Mike was still panting and could hardly speak. 'Think so. Most of it, anyway.' Then he rolled on his side and was heartily sick.

'Get them below,' said Wilmott, ignoring the slick of vomit on his deck. Mike felt hands pull him into a sitting position and wrap a blanket round him. His arms and legs seemed to belong to someone else entirely. He was virtually carried to the companionway and pushed down the stairs. He landed at the bottom in a heap. Another body dropped down after him. Mugs of cocoa appeared and the two of them sat knee to knee, cocooned in blankets and cradling the miraculously hot liquid, wondering if they were really still alive.

Halfway down the cocoa, Mike felt the warmth seeping back through his body enough to reach out his mug and clink it against Bruce's. The sergeant's eyes opened a crack. 'What?'

'Just wanted to say: Happy New Year, Bruce. Here's to 1944.'

'Didn't we already do that?'

'Yes, Bruce. But there's a time and a place.'

Ogden-Smith grunted and fell asleep where he sat.

No sooner had Mike closed his own eyes than he felt himself shaken awake. He forced his salt-crusted eyelids open to find Commander Wilmott standing over him. It took a minute or two to realise what he was saying. 'Time to transfer on to the MTB, old chap. She'll get you into the Solent faster than we can. Less chance of running into an E-boat patrol too.'

Mike blinked and tried to stand. Found he didn't have the strength for it. Wilmott put a hand under his elbow and pulled him to his feet. Ogden-Smith was still slumped opposite. Mike leaned over and pushed at his shoulder. His head lolled and stirred. 'Gerroff.'

'Time to go, Bruce.'

He shook his shoulder hard now. The canvas suit was still wet under the blanket. All they'd taken off before falling asleep were the bandoliers. Mike dragged these up off the table and threw them over his shoulder. 'On your feet, Sergeant. Time to go.'

Ogden-Smith woke finally at the clang of the aluminium tubes banging together. The blanket slipped from his shoulders and he held on to the cabin table and pulled himself up, delivering himself of a titanic yawn as he did so. 'No rest for the bleeding wicked, is there?' he mumbled, once his jaws had re-located.

'Not if we want a quick run home and a chance to get out of this wet kit. Got everything you came with?'

The sergeant patted himself down. 'Think so. Revolver. Compass. Torch I think I dropped on the deck. Just … Hang on. Trowel? Did you pick up my trowel?'

'No. I had the auger.' He felt round his back. 'Still do. God knows how I slept with that there. You had the trowel.'

'Shit.' Ogden-Smith shoved his hands down his boots. 'It's not there now.'

'Could easily have fallen out when we were swimming. Do you remember putting it back down your boot before we set off?'

The sergeant rubbed his hands up and down his face, trying to think through his exhaustion. 'To tell the truth, I don't. I had it when we were digging … then that Jerry sentry came up. I'm not sure I had it after that. The other areas we took samples were wetter, lower down and we didn't need the trowel. Christ on a bike, sir. I think I left it on the beach.'

The elation that had been going a little way to countering his exhaustion fell away completely and he almost slumped back down on the bench. Rather than an unqualified success, he would have to report that they had left behind evidence of their presence from which the Germans might be able to deduce the Allies' invasion plans. Exactly the thing the PM had been so anxious to avoid when he forbade this type of reconnaissance. Bruce's eyes were searching his face for the anxiety he was clearly feeling himself. 'Oh well, nothing to be done about it now,' he said. 'Better get back and report to the Old Man as soon as we can. There's a good chance the trowel will be carried out by the tide anyway.'

'And if it isn't?'

'If it isn't, we have to hope the Germans don't spot it. If they do, we have to hope they don't realise it was ours. It had been stripped of identification marks. It was just a trowel. And the locals have been digging peat on those beaches for two thousand years or so. Remember?'

The sergeant nodded and his face lifted a little. Mike was glad to have taken some of the weight off his shoulders but he didn't feel any better. He was responsible for the mission and he was the one who would have to explain to Hobo what had happened.

They tackled the steps to the deck, where they found a flat grey morning and their punt banging around against the steeper hull of a motor torpedo boat. Both crews were struggling to keep the two craft together, but apart, with ropes and fenders. Wilmott was anxious to transfer them so that the boats could go their separate ways before they did each other a mischief. They found themselves pushed and pulled up rope ladders on to the higher deck of the MTB. There, another naval officer took them below to get into dry clothes. They towelled down with their backs to each other, too tired and deflated to speak, and pulled on the thick naval sweaters, trousers and sea-boots laid out for them. That was better. Better still was a fantastic smell of frying bacon and soon they were seated before huge mugs of tea and fry-ups that tasted better than any food in the history of the world.

Two hours later they were in Southampton Water. Hobo was waiting for them on the quay with Sage. In the harbour-master's office, Dixon handed over the sample tubes and the water-proof tablets covered in chinagraph scrawl. Then he took a deep breath and confessed to the missing trowel. He fully expected the Old Man to explode. In fact, Hobo merely glanced at the Professor and walked away, his hands behind his back, to look out over the busy harbour. After a long pause, he said, 'How many miles of beach are there, between the Pas de Calais and, say, St Malo, Professor?'

Bernal scratched his head. 'Three fifty, maybe four hundred? I'd have to check, but something of that order.'

'Could you do that? In the meantime, Dixon, get on to the Air Force and tell them we need to borrow a bomber tonight. One with a damned accurate bomb-aimer and a pilot who can fly low and straight. Then get on to Ordnance and order up a couple of crates of unmarked trowels.'

'Sir?' said Mike, wondering if extreme tiredness had finally robbed him of his reason.

Hobo allowed his irritation to show for the first time. 'Oh, dammit, Dixon, bugger off and get some sleep, would you? I'll put someone else on sorting this out. By the time you wake up, there'll be a trowel on every beach in Northern France. Let the Germans make what they can of that. Eh, Sage? Let's see what they make of that.'

The Professor laughed and gathered up the tubes of precious samples, shaking his head. 'I'll give you this much, General. If hare-brained schemes are what it's going to take to win this war, I think the Germans are in danger of being seriously out-gunned and out-manoeuvred.'

25

JANUARY 1944, SUFFOLK

It was nearly a week before Dixon was pronounced fit. When they let him go, he was disappointed to find himself ordered to Hobo's HQ in Suffolk, rather than Rawdon. There was nothing to be done about it. At Hurt's Hall he found Howard Burton up to his neck, organising the biggest show so far of what some wits had taken to calling Hobo's Menagerie. The Old Man was in a fever of anticipation because the show was for Brooke and General Eisenhower, the American who had been appointed Supreme Commander Allied Forces just before Christmas. Hobo was determined they should not leave Suffolk lacking any scintilla of information about the Funnies that they might conceivably need.

Burton told Dixon, with something like nostalgia, that the preparations put him in mind of a particularly frantic School Open Day, where every class-room must be filled with ant colonies in glass cases, chemistry experiments designed to create satisfying whiffs and bangs and the First Fifteen ready to rampage down the wing against a carefully-chosen, slightly weaker opponent. Patiently and thoroughly, he was commissioning sand tables with models of every device in miniature action, blackboards written up with technical specifications, pages of statistics from trials, cine films of training exercises. Those were only the pre-lunch exhibits. After lunch – and he had already prevailed on Hobo to lay on the best spread possible for once – a collection of Crocodiles, Crabs, Arks and AVREs would be standing ready across the low Suffolk landscape to show their paces, with the finale entrusted to a troop of DD tanks poised to waddle down into Fritton Decoy and swim like ducks on a pond. There was even a brand new Funny they'd been working on full-tilt since Sage's tests on the samples confirmed the presence of patches of sticky blue clay on the French beaches – a tank with a reel made of coir matting and scaffold poles on a kind of spindle mounted in front of the turret. Crazy-looking as the rest and nick-named Bobbin.

All leave was cancelled until the big day. Hobo showed no sign of visiting Yorkshire until it was over. Mike had to face the fact that he would not see Rawdon for weeks. Once or twice, he sat down to write to Charlie. Something always stopped him. She was still engaged to Hartwell, after all. And what had she meant, when she cried and called herself stupid? Stupid for going to bed with him again, most likely.

The officers' mess was already two thirds full when Dixon walked in at 06.30 on the big day. Most of the men had fallen into bed only a few hours earlier, and there was a powerful sense of 'examination in progress' about the place. No one wanted to be the man who let the side down. Burton, who was staying behind to handle last minute crises, had told him to meet the GOC in front of the house at 07.00. He was out there in the slowly gathering light ten minutes early, so as not to be accused of 'cutting it fine'. At 06.52, a staff car pulled up beside him. He stared at it dully. It was not the car Hobo generally used in Suffolk. The driver cut the engine and climbed out. 'Lieutenant Dixon. No, hang on, it's Captain Dixon these days, I see. Congratulations on the extra pip. And Happy New Year. It's been long time no see, sir.' ATS Driver Carrington gave him a smart salute and, though he returned it with a straight face, inside his heart was bouncing off the walls of his chest like a well-struck billiard ball. Before he could think what to say, he heard footsteps on the gravel behind him and she saluted again. 'Morning, sir.'

'Ah, Charlie,' said General Hobart. 'Splendid. Safe pair of hands is what we need today. I knew you were the one for the job. Managed to fit some sleep in after your long drive?'

'Sir,' she said. 'It's a pretty straight run down on the Great North Road. They found me a bunk in the Attery here and I went out like a light.'

'Good girl. Let's be off, shall we? Better not keep the big-wigs waiting.'

Charlie made good time to Ipswich station, though Mike was quite sure she had never been there before. Field Marshal Brooke's private train drew in just before nine. The two senior officers stepped down looking fresh as daisies, considering that they carried the burden of the Allied war effort on their shoulders.

'It was a good idea of Winston's, to give old Brooke that train for his birthday,' said Hobo to Dixon as the two men walked along the platform towards them. 'Makes up a bit for the diabolical hours he makes him keep.'

Cordial greetings and salutes were exchanged, before the four of them climbed into the Humber, leaving the rest of the entourage to dispose of themselves among the other staff cars that had driven out from HQ in their wake.

'Your bright idea worked out then, Dixon,' said Brooke as they drove out of the town.

'My bright idea, sir?'

'Beach reconnaissance. I hear you carried it off neatly at Brancaster and then popped over to France for Hogmanay and brought back the goods from under Jerry's nose. Sage speaks highly of your initiative.'

The driver muffed a gear change. Three generals swayed and Hobo scowled at the back of her head.

'Thank you, sir.' Mike was surprised that his exploits should attract such notice. 'I ... well, it went off fairly smoothly in the end. The odd minor hiccup.'

'You mean the trowels?' Brooke laughed. 'Yes, I understand Bomber Command is convinced that the Army is quite barmy since we asked them to send a Lysander to bombard the beaches of northern France with garden trowels. Still, I don't suppose the bomber crew was all that unhappy to have traded the flak over Berlin or Hamburg for that run.'

Eisenhower, a big man with a surprisingly gentle and innocent-looking face, looked from one British general to the other in bemusement. Hobo glared at Brooke, clearly annoyed that the CIGS was making the Seventy Ninth out to be a load of crackpots. What he needed was for Eisenhower to take the Funnies seriously. 'General,' he said, 'we've laid on a very busy programme for you today. There's a great deal to explain and get through. As I'm sure you know, we've been tasked to solve this problem of the Atlantic Wall. The obstacle posed by mines and the need for a great number of demolitions, given the thickness of the concrete defences, could have a tremendous delaying effect on our advance. Without armoured support right in the van of the attack, we should be asking the infantry to do the impossible. I don't believe in asking the impossible. The bloody difficult, yes. Any properly trained soldier should be prepared for the bloody difficult. But the impossible, no.' He shook his head emphatically. 'So, we've been working on devices that can land in the very forefront of the assault and clear lanes rapidly through the beach defences to shoot the conventional armour and infantry through to their objectives inland. They may look, some of them, a little unlikely. But they are all tried and tested – and with crews trained to deploy them with initiative, to be prepared for wherever they may land and whatever obstacles they may encounter, I believe they will offer invaluable, in fact, sir, I'd go so far as to say, indispensable support to our conventional forces. Be they British, Canadian or American.'

He paused, only to fix Eisenhower with his most intense of stares, to see if a man who had never commanded a unit in battle was capable of understanding the critical importance of what he was being told. Mike thought Eisenhower took it well, given that he had never been exposed to one of Hobo's lectures before. With hardly a flinch from the aquiline stare, the Supreme Commander Allied Forces nodded his big baby's head and said: 'I'm all eyes and ears, General. All eyes and ears.'

Hobo gave a curt nod to show that he was satisfied with this and, without any seeming pause for breath, proceeded to explain his proposed assault organisation in minute detail all the way back to Hurt's Hall. While Brooke and Eisenhower had no choice but to give every indication of close attention, Mike was able to sit back whenever his commanding officer leaned forward to emphasise a point. By turning his face very slightly to the side, he could see just a sliver of Charlie Carrington. Not her whole face, but an ear, the start of her cheek, the roll of pale gold hair disappearing under her cap. He gripped the edge of the seat with his fingers, to prevent them reaching out and touching that hair. She pulled up to a T-junction and looked first to right and then to left. As her head came left their eyes met before she looked straight ahead again and engaged first gear. He watched her cheek suffuse with pink and as they straightened out of the turn she mucked up another gear change, from first to second, almost shooting Hobo on to the floor.

'Charlie, for Christ's sake!' he snapped, grabbing the door handle.

'Awfully sorry, sir,' she said, and Mike couldn't help smiling as the cheek turned crimson.

When they reached Divisional HQ, Charlie jumped out and held open the back door for the VIPs. Mike caught side-on the hard stare Hobo gave her as he followed Brooke and Eisenhower towards the house.

'That was your fault,' she hissed.

'I don't see how,' he said, under his breath. 'Will you be here tonight?'

'Depends on whether I get the sack.'

'Better keep your mind on your job from now on.'

'And to think I was worried about you,' she said, and slammed the car door shut.

Hobo's head started to swivel back their way and Mike hurried to catch up. He looked back once and she was still standing by the Humber, watching him go with an expression that was unguarded for the half-second before she saw him looking. Then she turned away. Even so, that half-second was enough for him to see that whatever had been going on between them before Christmas was still going on now.

Maybe Mike Dixon was less than objective that day, but it seemed to him that Hobo's sales pitch for the Funnies fell on fertile ground. Brooke and Eisenhower both appeared interested and enthusiastic, no matter how crazy-looking the device under scrutiny. Most of the demonstrations went off according to the plan. Even the brand-new Bobbins unspooled their reels of coir matting over patches of specially prepared mud relatively smoothly, and not at all as if they'd only been dreamt up three weeks before.

Just before dusk, they reached the Duplex Drive tanks. Brooke had already been for a drive in one, so he stood back and let the American climb aboard.

'Pray it doesn't sink, Patrick,' he said, cheerfully, as they stood together at the top of the bank.

'It won't, sir. Although we do have frogmen lurking in the reeds, just in case.'

Eisenhower, standing with the tank commander, gradually disappeared from view along with the upper half of the tank. It occurred to

Mike that with the screens up the thing resembled nothing so much as a huge tin of Spam, which now trundled towards the water's edge and angled down the bank. Though he had seen it many times by now, it still seemed unnatural to watch thirty tons of Spam drive into a lake and expect it to float. He held his breath, as he always did, while the water crept up the screens until there was no more than eighteen inches of freeboard. Then the tank's gait changed and the thing was no longer driving but swimming.

He breathed out. Brooke and Hobo simultaneously did the same. They stood watching as the Sherman made a cumbersome circumnavigation of the mere.

'Think he's enjoying himself?' asked Hobo.

'Don't suppose he's had so much fun in ages,' said Brooke. 'Nothing like defying the laws of gravity to cheer a fellow up, you know. He's a very genial chap, Ike. I'll say that for him.'

Eisenhower was delivered safely ashore, stepping down over the screens that collapsed like wrinkled stockings round the tank's ankles at the release of the compressed air tubes. He was beaming broadly as he clambered up the muddy bank. 'Well, gentlemen,' he said, 'that was just a fine trip. I'm not sure I'd like to try it in a rough sea, but a fine trip all the same.'

'We've tested it in seas running at up to three feet, sir. Any more than that and things get a bit iffy. But we shall be aiming for relatively calm weather for Overlord.'

'That's the plan. But you know the British Channel better than I do. They tell me it can be rough just about any time of year.'

'That's true, sir. Of course, if necessary, we can launch closer into shore. I believe the unique advantages of the swimming tank – the advantage of surprise, first and foremost – should not be underestimated.'

'I have no intention of underestimating them. In fact, I'm going to order five hundred Shermans converted to Duplex Drive straightaway. Can you supply them? And provide men to train American units on how to operate them?'

Hobo beamed, but shook his head. 'Our pleasure to provide the training, sir. I wish I could promise you the tanks as well, but I'm pushing as hard as I can to get enough converted to DD in time for the invasion for our own forces. What if I were to send one of my best men over from Birmingham with the blueprints? Could you get the things manufactured in Pittsburgh?'

'I'm sure of it. Put one of your guys on a plane to the States with the plans and we'll go into the DD business for ourselves.'

'That's splendid, sir. By God, we envy your capacity for production. And the other devices? I believe the Crab flail and the AVRE with the spigot mortar are both going to prove crucial in clearing mines and obstacles. They are mounted on Churchills at the moment, but I'm sure they could be adapted to suit an American tank if need be.'

'Well, I shall certainly be sending my force commanders down to take a look at what you've done here – I'm sure you understand that I have to give them some leeway over how they plan their assaults. As you can imagine, we have our own ways of doing things. For example, I know our demolition engineers prefer to work with armoured bulldozers. I'm not sure you'll get those guys to hole up inside a tank.'

Hobo's face clouded over. 'Problem is, a bulldozer doesn't provide a fraction of the protection for your sappers that a tank can – and, as far as I'm aware, it can't fire back. With respect, sir, I'm not sure your commanders have fully appreciated the weight of fire they're likely to come under on these beaches. An AVRE will by no means be a comfortable place to be but, as you saw earlier, it can obliterate pretty much any kind of threat from eighty yards and it ensures a decent chance of getting your men into position close to the beach obstacles. You're going to need those men to punch holes in the wall for the infantry to move up through. Lose your sappers and you may lose the beach-head.'

'Yes, well, Patrick,' said Brooke, moving in between them, conscious that Hobo was beginning to hector the Supreme Commander, 'I'm sure General Eisenhower will be making some pretty strong recommendations to his commanders. After all, there's plenty here for them to pick and choose.'

'Pick and choose?' repeated Hobo, in the tone of a man who does not believe his ears. 'I honestly don't think it's a question of pick and choose, sir. It's not the menu at a Lyon's Corner House. Every one of these devices has been developed to address a specific problem, problems which are likely to be found on every one of the invasion beaches. Unless they're used properly – I mean, comprehensively – they won't be used to their full potential. That will cost lives, it will cost time, and it may mean we don't get off the beaches at all.' He stood with his arms folded, the personification of belligerence, toe to toe with the man who had put him into his job. Mike winced. Brooke blinked, owlishly, behind his large spectacles and jabbed his finger at his Major-General. 'You are the bitter end sometimes, Patrick. It's a good job we know each other so well, and that you've done such wonders building this division because anyone who had less respect for you than I do would find you quite unbearable. Whether you like it or not, you cannot force these devices of yours on to the American commanders. We can offer, we can advise, but we cannot insist. Is that clear?'

To Mike's great relief, Eisenhower came to the rescue before General Hobart had the chance either to abase himself or, just as likely, become even more insubordinate.

'Well sir, I must say I think that what you've achieved here in less than a year is remarkable. Ingenious and remarkable. Not only the devices themselves but the pitch to which you have trained the men and the way you've instilled in them the importance of cooperation between the different services. That alone is heartening to see, because Overlord is going to be the ultimate combined op – and you can rest assured that I will make it very clear to everyone under my command that they should give the specialised armour you have developed here the most serious consideration for inclusion in their assault plans.'

The American smiled and stuck out his hand for Hobo to shake. Hobo looked at it for a moment, as if he didn't know what it was, then realised that what it was was the end of the matter. He put his own hand out to grip Ike's, almost in resignation, and they shook.

Brooke was adamant that General Hobart should not be kept from his valuable work by the tiresome obligation to accompany his visitors back to the station. The task fell instead to Dixon and no sooner had they turned out of the driveway than Brooke said to Eisenhower, 'He's quite impossible, I'm afraid. A genius, in his way, and I'm delighted we found him a job so suited to his talents – but, as you see, he's quite unhouse-trained.'

Mike, who had sat in the front to give the two senior men a semblance of privacy, held as still as he could, caught between wounded loyalty and the urge to laugh. Eisenhower stretched out his legs and said, 'Well, I have to tell you, I liked him. I liked him a lot. In the United States, we're maybe more used to men who speak their minds than you are over this side of the pond. We haven't had so long to become civilised as you, so the rough diamond is a more common type with us. If I may speak plain, some of my officers find it a little hard going with a few of your grander type of men. They find them a little – is 'languid' the word I want? Nothing languid about that guy. No, sir.'

Brooke gave a hoot of laughter. 'You're quite right. Of all the criticisms I've heard levelled against Hobo over the years, excessive languor has not been one. Perhaps, you know, it would have been better for him if he'd been born in the New World rather than the Old. His complete inability to tell anything besides the unvarnished truth – even to his superiors – might have made him more popular in the land of George Washington than it ever has here. Sadly, it has been Hobo's fate, at least up until now, to be what we would call (I don't know if you have the same phrase) a prophet without honour in his own country. The truth is, the Germans took more notice of his ideas on tank deployment before the war than we did. Blast them! Rumour has it that General Guderian read his papers on mobile armoured tactics with great interest and, if you think about it, the Panzer offensive through the Ardennes that did for Belgium and France was pretty much text-book Hobo. Sadly, it's not exactly the sort of thing that redounds to his credit.'

Brooke paused. Glancing in the driver's mirror, Mike saw him look out of the window, almost wistfully. He blinked slowly. 'Still, I'm glad we found a place for him where his ideas can be of real use at last. He's a wonderful trainer of men, you know. The ones he doesn't sack or scare to death. You really would do well to encourage the use of his devices where you can. I'm pretty sure his men won't let your chaps down.'

Mike smiled to himself at the Chief of Staff's appeal to Eisenhower, incomparable in its subtlety to Hobo's harsh words and harsher stare. Ike responded with a parry of equal deftness and, by the time they drew up at the station, Mike was conscious that he had been privy to a master class in high-level military diplomacy. He got them away into their train with little more talk, sensing that they were as exhausted by their day as everyone else.

Back at the car, he swung himself into the front passenger seat and said, 'Home, James, and don't spare the horses.' He looked across at Charlie, who looked back at him squarely for the first time since 6.52 that morning. 'Actually, scrub that, James. Just get us out of Ipswich, and pull over at the first opportunity. I can't wait much longer to kiss you.'

'Sir,' said Charlie, and moved off slowly, as if he'd given her an entirely conventional order. Only when she took her hand off the wheel to change from second to third and his fingers closed over hers on the gear lever did she give way to a smile. They drove in silence through the darkened town, the only sounds in Mike's ears the steady thrum of the Humber's engine and the pulsing of his blood. Ipswich seemed much bigger than it had any right to be and he began to wonder if they would ever come to the end of it. Then all at once they did and were out in the Suffolk countryside again. They drove on for a mile or two, at the usual terrifying speed, before the neutered headlights picked out a large flat stone with half a dozen milk churns balanced on it at the side of the road. Charlie braked hard and reversed fast into the farm track that led away into the fields beside the churns. She switched off the engine and the headlights.

'Charl—' She put a finger to her lips, listening for something. They sat there for a minute before two sets of headlamps came snaking along the road behind them, went past and snaked on, their rear lamps fading cigarette ends in the night. 'The other staff cars were behind us. We can't be too long, or they'll wonder where we've got to.'

'You should have been a commando, you know. You have quite a talent for this cloak and dagger stuff.'

'Should have been born a man, at least. Much more fun. I make a pretty rotten girl.'

'Oh, I don't know,' he said. 'I'm not sure I'd be so keen to do this if you were a chap,' and he cupped his hands on either side of her face and kissed her. It started prettily enough. Then her lips parted and her tongue flickered against his. A long throb ran through him and he pulled her tighter against him. She was half out of her seat and his knee was jammed up against the gear stick. Still he dragged her closer and kissed her like there was nothing else in the world worth doing.

Finally, even the longest kiss ends. Finally, he ran his fingers down her neck and planted a little kiss there too. His hand dropped to where her naked breast should have been. Instead he encountered wool serge and a tin pocket button. He sighed and sat back. 'I hate this bloody war sometimes.'

'Only sometimes?' she said.

He grinned, sheepishly. 'Well, I hate it when it stops me getting at you.'

'But not when it gives you the chance to rush about like the Scarlet Pimpernel, dropping behind enemy lines and doing your level best to get yourself killed?'

'I was doing my level best not to get myself killed, if you want to know about it. Anyway, when I put myself up for that thing I didn't think it particularly mattered. It was after we'd agreed to forget all about what happened in Wales. I didn't exactly think I had a lot to come back for. But things looked a bit different after … I mean, when it came to it. Anyway, here I am. Safely back behind my desk.'

'For good?'

'Hobo's made me give my word I won't go volunteering for anything else, at least until the Second Front's under way. Says he doesn't have time to train up another ADC.'

'Good old Hobo. Christmas was a nightmare. New Year's Eve was worse. Everybody celebrating like idiots and I didn't even know if you were alive.'

He could hardly see her in the darkness, but he heard a break in her voice, and felt the warmth of her breath on his cheek. The car was suffused with the delicious scent of her and he could barely believe she was really there, within reach, for the first time in weeks. He knew they had only a few minutes, yet still found himself saying: 'What about Bill? Have you thought about what you're going to do about Bill?'

She said nothing for a minute and then, 'I can't break it off on one of those terrible letter forms they make you use. Not when he's going to know every word's already been read by their censors – and ours. It's too humiliating.'

'But what if you were planning to marry someone else? You'd have to tell him then, wouldn't you?'

As soon as the words were out, he was conscious that it was a pretty pustulent proposal, so he was hardly surprised when she turned her head away.

'But I'm not planning to marry anyone else,' she said, to the cold, black glass of the side window.

Mike swallowed a stone. 'You mean you want to ditch me, as well as Bill?'

She swung back to face him. 'No, I don't want to ditch you. My God, I'd give anything to go to bed with you right now. But I just can't leap straight out of one promise into another when we have no idea how long the war's going to go on. It's too hard, Mike, to be always dreaming of a future that might never happen. Don't you see? I'm exhausted by it.'

He didn't see. 'It's because I'm not good enough for you, isn't it? Oh, good enough to go to bed with. But not the type you'd want to be seen out with in public. Not the sort of chap you can take home to Mama and Papa and say: "This is the man I'm going to marry."'

'Don't be a fool, Mike.'

The coldness in her voice goaded him. 'But I am a fool, aren't I? To think a girl like you'd ever want more than a hole-in-the-corner affair with someone like me. Of course you're not going to write and tell the soon-to-be Right Honourable William Hartwell MP that you're throwing him over for a chap like me.'

'You're being stupid. I can't talk to you if you're going to be like this.' She started the engine, switched on the lights and turned on to the main road. They drove in silence until they reached the gates of Divisional HQ. He was still angry, but he couldn't bear the silence to last until he had to get out. As they came up the drive he reached over and laid his hand over her gloved one on the gear lever. Her fingers twitched slightly, but she didn't try and shake him off.

'It's not a hopeless case, is it? You and me.'

She gave him about a third of a grin. 'Not altogether hopeless. Where there's life, and all that. What does Colonel Burton say? *Dum spiro spero.*'

Mike knew Howard Burton's favourite Latin tag as well as Charlie. 'While I breathe, I hope.'

'That's it. Let's just keep breathing, shall we? Keep breathing, keep hoping. And one day maybe the war'll be over and everything'll be able to go back to normal.'

It wasn't what he'd hoped for. Given the gulf in their backgrounds, 'normal' wasn't the status quo he wanted to see restored. But it was a thread, a line, and he wasn't too proud to grab on to it.

26

Eisenhower was true to his word when he promised to send his generals to look at the Funnies. The trouble was, they didn't seem to like them much or understand them. One commander guffawed at the Bobbin when it unreeled its carpet across a patch of East Anglian mud and the others could not see the point of the CDL light at all. Dixon was incensed to hear them laughing as they stood watching from the sidelines, quite forgetting that he'd been equally sceptical when he'd first seen them for himself. The one thing they really liked the look of was the flame-throwing tank known as Crocodile, which aggravated Hobo, as it was still in development, with various kinks to be ironed out and, try as he might, he could see no way of having it ready in large numbers before D-Day. Dixon couldn't help thinking that the Funnies just weren't 'Hollywood' enough to attract the Americans. Something about their home-made look, their rude ingenuity, their lack of glamour didn't appeal to the Yanks. In the movie reel that ran in every American head, a scene where their heroic GIs ground slowly up a beach in a cloud of flying sand behind an old tank thrashing chains at the ground like a chaotic street-sweeping machine simply did not play. 'Not enough Hollywood,' thought Mike. 'Too much Ealing Studios.' That was why they liked the Crocodile, its spout of burning flame roaring through the air and flaying its target a hundred yards away. 'Whoa,' said one of the senior officers, when he saw it. 'Whip-crackaway! I could use some of those babies.'

It was the rejection of the Armoured Vehicle for the engineers that exasperated Hobo most. Maybe it was because he was not only a tank man but had also once been a sapper that he could not understand the American generals' refusal to contemplate putting their demolition engineers behind armour.

'Don't they see?' he said to Mike, after yet another breezy American assertion that their guys would make it inland much quicker with their gear in light boats, supported by high-speed armoured 'dozers. 'They keep telling me their men have guts, as if guts are a substitute for armour-plating. The Canadians had plenty of guts at Dieppe. That didn't stop their assault being destroyed in an hour and a half when they couldn't get off the beach, did it?'

'No, sir.'

'They just don't seem to realise the tremendous delaying power there is in mines and obstacles. If their rubber boats get hit, as they are bound to be, the best part of their sappers will go up on their own explosives, and they'll have no one to clear the way for the armour and infantry.'

'No Lord Mayor's Show,' said Mike, thinking aloud.

'Eh?' said Hobo. 'What? Oh. No. No Lord Mayor's Show and no ticker-tape parade down Fifth Avenue either. Blasted Yanks! Still, we can't do the invasion without them, so there's nothing to be done except keep on bashing down their doors. Putting these shows on for Bradley, Marshall and the others. I don't care if we turn into a concert party doing ten shows a week, so long as we get the right notices in the end. We need to be at their training exercises too, so we can see how they plan to solve these problems of mine and obstacle clearance. Maybe then I shall get the chance to point out the flaws in their thinking. I hope to God it won't be too late.'

'I bet they'll love that,' said Mike, only to himself.

The Americans' final pre-invasion exercises weren't slated until April. Until then, the exhausting days ran on without let-up. The invention phase of the Division was just about over now, slightly to

Mike's disappointment, and the spotlight moved on to the equally intense difficulties of producing the necessary quantity of machines and training men to use them in the face of a pressing but secret deadline. Hobo continued to be at war with the War Office quite as much as with the Germans and, though he now had the clear and unequivocal backing of Brooke and the PM, people like Freddie Quiller seemed to be even more obstructive than ever.

Extreme tiredness had become such a normal state it wasn't worth remarking. Mike was snatching a nap in the officers' mess at Rawdon one Sunday afternoon when he was shaken awake. Opening his eyes, he found Babington-Browne grinning down at him as if he'd just been told the greatest joke. 'Wakey, wakey, Captain Dixon.' He tried to gather his thoughts. 'There's an extraordinary little chap asking for you. Tiny fellow. Very strange way of talking. Reckons he's your father.'

Mike sat up in a hurry.

'Piddington was about to see him off the premises. I thought I'd better check with you first. Just in case.'

'Where is he?'

'Waiting in the hall.'

Mike got to his feet, still unsteady with sleep, and rubbed his face. When Babington-Browne moved to follow him out of the mess, he turned and with a look told him to stay put. He shut the door on his way out for extra emphasis. The long corridor leading to the entrance hall was gloomy at the best of times, and more so in the fading light of a March afternoon so that Mike knew he would be nothing more than a silhouette to anyone waiting in the hall. By contrast, an old mullioned window halfway up the staircase illuminated the flag-stones below and in the middle of a patch of faintly pinkish light stood a small man in dark jacket and trousers, holding a check cap that he was moving nervously between his fingers.

'Dad?' Mike's heart thudded against the walls of his chest as he tried to guess what drastic circumstances could have led his father to make the trip all the way to Rawdon. 'It's not Mam, is it?'

His father shook his head and took one hand off his cap to hold it out to his son. Mike grasped it and was shocked at how small and thin it was, only the palm tough and calloused as he remembered. Then he looked his father in the eyes and saw them wet with tears. His stomach turned to water. 'Not Frank?'

'No, lad. Frank's all right. Far as we know. No, I'm an old fool. It was seeing you, after all this time. Four years, nearly. You've not been home once.'

'No. Sorry. It's been … '

'Your mam's missed you.'

'I thought you didn't … '

'We were upset, son. Over Frank. He were the babby. You know your mam were always soft on him. We never meant you to … ' He waved four years away with his cap. 'Your mam wanted to come and see you when you were in the hospital down south, but it would have been too much for her, you know.'

'I know. I wrote and said not to.'

'Any road, you look all right now. Fit for owt, by the looks of it. And a captain these days.'

Mike touched the crown on his collar self-consciously. He'd never thought to let them know about his promotion. Hadn't supposed it would make any difference. 'Look, do you want a cup of tea? We can go to the … ' he thought of the officers' mess, and thought again. 'We can go to the kitchens. See if there's any chance of lardy cake. There sometimes is on a Sunday.'

His father shook his head, doubtfully. 'I don't want to cause you any awkwardness, son, turning up here like this. It's just there's something your mam and me need you to do, and it isn't the sort of thing we could explain in a letter. You know we're not great ones for writing.'

Looking at him, Mike saw that he had aged much more than four years since the day the news had come about Frank and he had slammed out of the kitchen, burning with anger and shame. His father had always been wiry. Now he seemed not much more than skin over bone, his cheeks hollow and his hair grey where it had been black and shiny as a bird's wing. Babington-Browne was right. He was tiny. But had never seemed so before. Mike wondered how his mother had altered in four years and realised how little he'd thought about the pair of them. He felt a sudden longing to see her again too, and he meant it when he said, 'I'm glad to see you, Dad. Let's go and get that tea and you can tell me all about this whatever it is.'

Avoiding any further encounter with Babington-Browne, he led the way out of the front door and round the back of the hall to the kitchen door. Within a minute or two they were seated at the long scrubbed wooden table with mugs of strong tea and a slice each of glistening lardy cake. The cooks had the old black range stoked up, ready to cook the evening meal, and Mike was glad to see his father more at ease than he had been standing in the hall. 'Well, then?'

His father took a deep swig of hot tea and swallowed it. 'It's our Beattie. She's gone off with an Eyetie.'

Mike laughed. He couldn't help it. 'An Eyetie? Where on earth would Beattie find an Eyetie?'

'On Freddie Mee's farm, that's where. There's a POW camp near Ellistown and they let them out to help with the harvest and picking the cabbage plants. She met him there – Giuseppe or Giovanni, summat like that – and now he's turned her head and she's on about wanting to marry him.'

'What about Frank?'

'What about Frank indeed? I tell you, Michael, I've known that gel all her life and I never thought there was any wickedness in her. Not like this. Sad to say, if she's not careful she'll find her sen tarred and feathered. The feeling in the village is that strong.'

'Frank wouldn't want that.'

'Frank knows nowt about it. That's why I'm here. She says she owes it to him to write and tell him she's in love with Garibaldi but your mam and me think, if he has to hear it, it'd be better coming from you. He always listened to you, Michael. You're his brother. You'll know how to break it to him.'

When his father had gone, heading off into the darkness on a borrowed Brough Superior despite Mike's offer to find him a bed for the night at the Duke of Westmorland, Mike sat down to write a letter to his brother. He pulled out one of the forms issued by the Red Cross and slowly wrote the address details on the front, buying time before he had to turn it over and begin.

'Dear Frank,' he wrote. Then he thought back to that night in the car with Charlie, when he'd got back from France and had been pushing her to break it off with Bill. Now he knew what she meant about how impossible it was to write this sort of stuff. He'd been angry with her, convinced she was playing a game with him. If he was honest, he'd been angry with her ever since. Work had kept them apart most of the time, but he'd not sought her out even when they were in the same place for a day or two. He'd seen her look at him questioningly a few times when she'd been driving them. You're a self-centred bastard, Dixon, he thought. Never look at things from anyone else's point of view unless you're absolutely forced to it, do you?

Back to the letter. There was nothing else for it. He chewed his pen for a bit, decided on an unvarnished approach. Neither he nor Frank were ones for pretty language, so: 'Dear Frank, Hope this finds you well. Bad news from home, I'm afraid. Beattie has gone off with someone else. She wanted to write and tell you herself, but Mam and Dad thought it might be easier coming from me. God knows why. I hope you aren't too cut up about it. Look on the bright side – there are lots more girls here waiting for you to come home – and most of them don't smell of cow shit! Keep your chin up. I'll be seeing you soon I hope, Your loving brother, Mike'. He thought it best not to mention that Beattie's new lover was Italian. For one thing he didn't want to give the German censor the satisfaction of thinking that English girls were vulnerable to the charms of Axis soldiers. He didn't know if it was right to try and make a joke of things, but Frank always loved a joke and he didn't see how it could make things worse. He read it through one more time, stood up and put it in his pocket. The village post-box was set into the wall of the pub and he might as well go and post it before he had second thoughts.

27

APRIL 1944, DEVON

Exercise Tiger was the final and biggest pre-invasion drill, a full-scale beach landing on the Devon coast in the last week of April. It wasn't too hard for General Hobart to wangle himself an invitation, although it did come at the price of a promise to Field Marshal Brooke that he would do his level best to be tactful about what he saw.

On the first morning of the exercise, Charlie collected them from their billet at 05.30 to deliver them to the observation post on the landing beach. It was still dark, but the sky was altering to the colourless grey of pre-dawn. Hobo looked at his watch. 'Damned quiet, Dixon. Naval bombardment should have started by now.'

When they reached the OP where their American liaison officer was waiting Hobo wasted no time on greetings: 'Where's the naval bombardment, Major? It was due to go in at 05.00.'

Mike guessed Major Pete Corlett was in his early thirties. Lean and tall, just returned from supervising amphibious landings in the Pacific. His uniform hung a little loose on him and there was a yellowish cast to his tan that made Mike wonder if he'd been sick with some tropical ailment.

'H-hour's been put back an hour, sir. There was roughish weather out there last night and the back of the convoy's lagging a little behind.'

'What's the significance of that white tape?' Hobo was peering at the beach through field glasses. Now he handed them to Mike. About halfway between the sea's edge and the high-water mark a white ribbon, staked at intervals, ran right across the beach.

'You know it's a live firing exercise? The defenders are tasked with laying down fire as far as that line and no further.'

'I see. And what about mines?'

'Well, they have maps of the minefields – both the Navy and the beach engineers.'

'They're working together, are they?'

'In a manner of speaking, sir, yes.'

Hobo balked at this. 'I don't care for manners of speaking, Major. Are they working together on mine clearance as a co-ordinated force? Or are they not?'

The Major pushed back his cap and scratched at the isolate tuft of remaining hair on the crown of his head. Mike was put in mind of Stan Laurel and tried not to smile.

'The way it works is the Navy takes responsibility for all obstacles and mines below the high-water mark and the beach engineer corps is in charge of anything above high water.'

Hobo's eyebrows shot up and rippled over the rims of his spectacles. 'That's the way it works, is it?'

'That's the way it's been carved up, sir.'

'But what if you disembark well below high water? Are the beach engineers going to sit around in deck-chairs waiting for the Navy to clear all the mines until they reach dry sand? Does your Navy have armoured bulldozers or landing craft with mine-clearing ploughs attached?'

Corlett looked a bit sheepish. 'No sir, they'll be pretty much clearing by hand. The engineers have tankdozers of course, and unarmoured Caterpillars. Their kit's mainly in light boats. And the Navy, I'm not exactly sure what special equipment they have in theatre. They … '

'Madness!'

The American looked as if he wasn't quite used to being charged with insanity. 'I'm sorry, sir.'

'It's complete madness, Major. Your sappers will be horribly vulnerable. All available manpower needs to be engaged in the demolition task as soon as they hit the beach. Flexibility, adaptability, initiative, that's what you need. Not rigid lines of demarcation. How much training have they done together, the Navy and the Army, to co-ordinate this absurd tag match?'

Corlett frowned. 'Very little, I'm afraid, sir. I just got here ten days ago. I'm to co-ordinate the training for this demolition task between now and D-Day using the expertise we've gained doing landings on defended shores in the Pacific, but … '

'And who was in charge of training before you?'

'Before me, sir, no one, I believe. Not in the European theatre. Not on this question of amphibious obstacle clearance specifically. I mean, there's been a lot of discussion of how it should be done, some work on mechanical devices and the like. Nothing's come of it so far though – so what it comes down to is the Navy and the Engineer Corps … '

Hobo interrupted him. 'I hope you've plenty of men, Major, because you're sure as hell going to lose a lot of them.'

The American looked grim. 'I'm afraid you may be right, sir. My problem is getting anyone to listen.'

'But you're the expert, man. That's why they've put you into the job, isn't it? Because you've already been working on the problem in the Pacific.'

'That's true. If it was only the Army I had to deal with, it might not be so bad, but you know what the US Navy's view of experts is.'

'I don't, Major. Enlighten me.'

'Well, sir, the US Navy's definition of an expert is, if you'll pardon the language, "a son of a bitch from outta town".'

Hobo glared at him for a moment, threw back his head and let out a barking laugh: 'That's good. Oh, that's very good. You know, I think the US Navy and the British Army Council might have a good deal in common. You must come and see us, Major. We're putting together a loading plan, so we have the right men and vehicles in exactly the right order for disembarkation on to every sector of beach. We've been training to meet this problem of breaching the Atlantic Wall for over a year now. If there's anything we can do to improve your men's chances with our (if you'll pardon the expression) "expertise" I'll be more than happy to share it with you.'

Corlett stuck out his hand and Hobo shook it.

'Offer's much appreciated. It sure is.'

As he finished speaking, there was a flash over his shoulder, out to sea, and a second later the air was filled with a whistle and a booming crash. 'There she goes, sir,' the American shouted, pointing to another series of flashes that transformed themselves seconds later into explosions on the beach in front of them. Mike's whole body vibrated and he began to sweat. He wondered if he'd ever be able to take the crash of big guns without his mind careering back to Dieppe.

'About time too,' yelled Hobo happily, as a trickle of dust poured from the roof of the hut on to his greatcoat. The guns seemed to have no effect on him at all.

Mike held his wrist still by a great effort of will and looked at his watch. Hobo raised his binoculars. The light was gathering strength now and they could already see the battleships and troop-carriers and, in front of them, a mass of landing craft heading towards the shore. He checked his watch again. The troop transports weren't quick – the men joked that LST stood for Large Slow-moving Target – but he couldn't see how it was going to take them another hour and a half to make landfall. Just as he'd formulated the thought, Hobo yelled at the American, 'Are you sure H-hour's been delayed? If I had to judge, I'd say those landing craft are going to beach dead on 06.30.'

Corlett bellowed back: 'Order came through about 03.30. Navy must have seen it, seeing as they delayed their bombardment. Only question is … '

'Whether the troop carriers got the signal.'

Corlett nodded. 'Guess we'll soon see about that.'

Shells from the great naval guns continued to track across the sky, grey slugs growing rapidly to the size of cars before they smashed down, throwing up sand and sod and concrete debris in a relentless man-made earthquake. The concrete shuddered under their feet and the air filled with dust, making them cough.

The first landing craft hit the shore at 06.27. Through his field glasses Mike saw the ramp drop and the first men jump down into the surf. One or two tripped and fell as they landed, picked themselves up, or were hauled up by their comrades, and waded ashore. The first infantrymen were followed by a tank, the outline of a Sherman that he had come to know so well, gingerly moving forward down the ramp, tipping and slithering into the water. He knew the crew would be praying the seawater wouldn't swamp the engine. The tank paused for a moment and then started to crawl up the beach. Immediately, soldiers took cover behind it. More landing craft reached the edge of the surf and lowered their ramps. Men and tanks spilled out all along the wide strand until the white surf at the sea's edge was hidden behind a dark wall of ordnance and running figures. For all his knowledge of the invasion plans, Mike couldn't help being impressed. This is how it'll be in Normandy, he thought. Man at his most irresistible. Chin up, Frank. We're on our way.

The first Sherman, with its little gaggle of followers, was heading steadily up the beach, seeming to suffer no problems with the going underfoot, when it disappeared in a cloud of sand and a rain of fragments. For a moment, he thought it must have hit a mine. Then he heard a deep boom out at sea and saw another shell speeding in towards the beach. He looked back to where the tank had been. As the dust cleared there was just a dark tangle on the sand. Nothing moved near it.

'Goddamit, man!' shouted Hobo, lowering his field glasses. 'They need to call off the bombardment. It's clear no one's told the assault force about the delay. They're getting chewed to pieces.' He snatched up a field telephone. 'Get me Field HQ.'

It took an age to get through, but far less time for Hobo to communicate his message. Corlett blanched under his tan at the sheer violence of the tone and language. Shells continued to smash down into the confusion on the beach and then they were less frequent and then there were no more flashes from the bay.

Hobo stepped out of the hut and the American breathed a sigh of relief. Mike followed and they walked forward through the dunes to get a better view of the assault. The huge number of craft filling the bay from end to end made it hard to think that this was just a rehearsal, not the real thing. A few years ago, he thought, those might have been German landing craft, and we would have been the ones crouched behind hot, pinking gun-barrels, our backs to the wall. The hairs on his neck prickled again.

A couple of heavy machine-guns were firing from a pill-box set into the dunes a few feet below them and the air was filled with the noise and the stink of hot metal and gun oil. Hobo stared out across the post's field of fire. Mike followed suit. What he saw horrified him. The white tape had been cut to pieces in places by gunfire and shrapnel. Men were running past it, oblivious to its significance and the guns fired on, in short, workmanlike bursts. As he watched he began to see men fall, in ones, in twos, in ragged sticks. Some of them got up again. Some didn't. Hobo saw what was happening too, because he shouted,

'Run to the next emplacement and tell them to stop depressing their guns so far! I'll deal with this one. It's a bloody charade. If they're not careful, they won't have any men left for D-Day.'

As they were setting off from the beach-head an hour later, Charlie gave way for a column of US Army ambulances to come through. Too despondent to speak, Mike watched the trucks lumber past. The Old Man was silent too. Spent, perhaps, after a series of volcanic eruptions down the telephone to Field HQ.

'Where to, sir?'

The ambulances were parking now in a line behind the dunes. Stretcher-bearers jumped down off the tail-boards and started to jog towards the beach. Mike wondered if they still believed the exercise was going according to plan and that the casualties they were going to collect would be lying around, chatting and smoking, happy to be labelled 'wounded'. Hobo had been watching the stretcher-bearers too. Now he looked over at Charlie. 'Back to Plymouth Docks.'

Mike frowned, and Hobo said, 'If they're still going on with it, the next phase of the exercise is a follow-up landing tomorrow morning. The premiss is that resistance will have moved inland, so there'll be no bombardment or firing down on to the beach. We've seen it from the landward side. Might as well see it from seaward. Find out what the hell's happening about wireless communications. The big ships clearly had no contact with the landing craft this morning. It won't do, Dixon. Six weeks to D-Day. How the hell can we hope to establish a bridge-head if we can't even co-ordinate a landing with our own bombardment?'

'Thing is, I'm not sure the Yanks will be very keen to have us right on the spot again, not after this morning.'

'No,' said Hobo, 'I think the Yanks have had enough of our

advice. But the Royal Navy are in charge of the convoy escort. We should be able to get aboard one of our own ships.'

At first it seemed they had missed the boat. The troop transports were already crossing Lyme Bay under Navy escort. Only after some bullying did Hobo discover that the convoy would be swinging round and picking up another three transports at Brixham before heading over towards Slapton. More bullying was required before it was conceded that Hobo and Dixon might join the escort at Brixham that night.

Charlie drove them to the old fishing harbour. The Devon lanes were so beautiful and peaceful, their deep wind-swept hedges in tight green bud and the banks under them scattered with yellow primroses, that it was almost impossible to think of men dying a few miles away. They got held up behind a line of three US Army trucks that were waiting to turn into a field. Looking idly out of the window, Mike saw something odd through the hedge, the arm of a mechanical digger drop down and a minute later rise jerkily up again with its grab full of deep brown soil, which it swung to the side and dropped before pivoting back for another bite at the earth. A soldier came down to open the field gate and one by one the trucks bumped through the gateway. As they drove past, Mike saw a group of soldiers standing with their arms folded, watching the digger work at the hole.

'Sir,' said Charlie. 'Do you think those trucks were … ? I mean, are they going to bury those … ?'

Hobo looked up. 'I'm afraid so, Charlie. There's no way what happened this morning can be allowed to come out before the Second Front. It'd be appalling for morale. I know you understand the Official Secrets Act, but let me be quite clear. You must never speak of this again. Ever. The consequences would be most severe. Do you understand?'

'Sir.'

They drove on in silence, before Charlie said: 'What about those men's families, sir? Will they be told?'

'They'll be told when the time is right. I've no doubt the bodies will be re-buried in due course. The appropriate explanations and condolences will be offered. But not yet, not when telling would be likely to cost a lot more lives. Now, that's the end of the subject. Do I make myself clear?'

'Sir.'

Dinner aboard *HMS Azalea* was cordial, even if Hobo's impassioned monologue on the importance of co-ordinated communications between all branches of the invasion fleet met with nothing more than polite nods. Mike detected relief in the faces of the ship's officers as they rose to go. Perhaps feeling they were falling short on courtesy, the captain invited Hobo up on to the bridge, leaving him alone in the ward-room. 'Thing is,' thought Mike, 'he's right. But he doesn't have the knack of winning people over, not at first. He makes it all sound like too much hard work, when all people want is a quiet life – even in the middle of a war.'

The ship shuddered into life. He hadn't been on a boat since New Year's Eve and the roll under his feet cast him back on to the deck of the MTB that had brought them home across the Channel. He wondered where Bruce was now, and what he would be doing on D-Day. He hadn't seen him since they'd parted in Southampton. The sergeant had tried to say something more to him about Henry Peat as they shook hands. Something about the next time they landed in Normandy being 'third time lucky' and taking Dieppe for good, for Henry's sake. He felt a sudden grip in his stomach muscles at the thought that he would be standing back on D-Day, while a million men took their places in the line to push the Nazis out of Europe. As the ship pitched and a glass slid across the table, he admitted to himself just how much he wanted to be part of it, despite what had happened today on the beach at Slapton. No, because of what had happened today. Because he had an idea now of what had to be done, and how.

He pushed back his chair and went out on deck. The running lights on the ship had been doused and he felt his way along the rail to see if he could make out the convoy stretched out in line astern. But the moonlight was too weak or the distance between the ships too great and the rumble of the destroyer's engines vibrating through her steel plate drowned out any noise astern. Leaning at the rail, he thought about his promise not to ask for a transfer before D-Day and how the Old Man would react to being asked to release him from it. Then he thought about what Charlie would say. There were a million other mothers, wives and sweethearts who had to put up with their men doing their bit. There was nothing special about him. Besides, they weren't engaged. She wouldn't have him, would she?

He straightened up from the rail. No time like the present. If he was going to get bawled out for going back on his word, he might as well get it over with. Halfway back to the bridge the destroyer's super-structure suddenly lit up in blinding clarity. For a moment he had no idea why and then a wave of solid air blew him against the ship's plating and a mighty boom reverberated in his ears. He staggered and turned to look over his shoulder. Another explosion buffeted him and the scene astern lit up in ghastly relief. A great red and yellow blaze surrounded three of the transports that waddled in *Azalea*'s wake, fire leaping into the sky from a fourth ship that was blazing from end to end and beginning to tip and slide into the waves as he watched. His first thought was that it was an explosion in an ammo store. Then he saw tracer fire, red, arcing at one of the ships from the darkness, and further off, more tracer, yellow. As the word 'E-boat' was still forming in his mind, there was another almighty flash and the troop transport directly behind *Azalea* shot out a gout of flame near the bows. The noise of the explosion rolled towards him and before it blotted out all sound he heard a voice say, 'Aye, that's a fuckin' torpedo.' He looked round and realised that he was not four paces from two sailors manning a gun. He could see them clearly now as they clapped on steel helmets and began to traverse the gun towards the explosions.

'E-boat or submarine?' he said, leaning over them.

'Can't see a thing sir, except those fires and tracer. Some of that could be ours, from the LSTs firing at Jerry. Shall we open fire, sir?'

Mike hesitated. He'd seen enough of Allies firing on each other for one day. 'Wait until you can see the bastards clearly. And keep a look-out for torpedoes.' He ran back along the deck and up the steps to the bridge, arriving as another huge explosion rolled forward from astern. The door banged open as he reached it and General Hobart came out. 'Should we open fire, sir? Gunners want to know.'

The General caught his arm. 'Leave them to it in there to give the orders,' he said. 'No point in firing if we can't see the enemy. We might fire on our own. The captain's plotting a zigzag course to avoid torpedoes. Let's hope the rear escort has a clearer view of Jerry than we do.'

They made their way back to the stern. The first troop carrier had gone, sunk in the time it had taken him to run to the bridge and return. The second boat to be hit was blazing at the bows and listing badly. Mike now saw the source of the third explosion. Yet another of the transports had been hit and flames were leaping into the sky with occasional taller showers of sparks belching like magma from the belly of a volcano. All around the burning ships, in the red and yellow reflections, he saw heads in the water. There was no more tracer now and no fresh explosions besides the ones that came from within the stricken boats. He looked at his wristwatch by the fires' glow. He had no idea how long it was since the attack began. Couldn't be more than fifteen minutes. Were they still circling, the sharks? Or had they slipped away as rapidly as they had come?

'You know what's queer, sir?' he said.

'What?'

'I can't see the rear escort. I mean, we were all lit up like Christmas trees for a while there, but I couldn't see another destroyer.'

'Must have been below the horizon.'

'Surely she'd be up closer than that. There were only six transports, at the best of times.'

'I'd have thought we'd have seen her.' Hobo sighed. 'To my mind we should have had MTBs further out in the bay too – an interdiction force that could have engaged Jerry without getting tangled up with our own ships. Imagine what carnage E-boats could cause on D-Day if they came out in force.'

The first officer came down off the bridge with hot cocoa and the news that a signal from Plymouth had ordered *Azalea* not to turn back to pick up survivors till morning in case of further enemy attacks. Dixon and Hobo kept their places at the stern, watching over the remaining transports wallowing in *Azalea*'s wake. Ever further behind them, a reproachful column of flickering flame marked the stricken ships, fighting to stay afloat until help came.

Dawn eased across the horizon at last and *Azalea* stood off as what was left of the convoy headed into land. Hobo and Dixon watched the square backsides of the transports buck and wallow through the waves and heave to and unload, before swinging round and heading back out into the bay.

'Look,' said Mike as a little flotilla of floating Spam tins pushed their way clumsily towards the beach, 'DDs.' He only realised he'd been holding his breath when the last one safely made landfall and collapsed its screens. Normally he would have been elated to see a detachment of Funnies performing as advertised. Not today. As he watched them land, all he could think about was the men they'd left behind in the bay.

Azalea's number one came looking for them. 'We've orders to pick up survivors now, sir. Turns out *Scimitar* was damaged in a collision yesterday and never left Plymouth. We were supposed to get a signal, but we didn't.'

'You mean to say there was no rear escort?' Hobo glared.

The young officer shook his head miserably. He was silent for a minute before he remembered what he'd been sent to say. 'I'm afraid it means we'll be longer getting back to Plymouth. The captain hopes that won't inconvenience you.'

Hobo snorted. 'Not compared with the inconvenience of losing those men, Lieutenant. We shall need every single one we can fish out for the invasion.'

They felt the ship turning and gathering speed. An hour and a half later, it slowed again. Scrambling nets were thrown down the sides of the ship and seamen lined the decks. As a sailor clambered down the nets and reached out with a boat-hook to a body floating face down, an officer shouted, 'Leave him. Our orders are to pick up the living. Someone else will deal with the bodies.'

The ship steamed on. All heads turned, trying to spot a man in the water with life left in him. Corpses bobbed alongside one at a time to start with, then grew more numerous, and still not one man alive.

'Why are they all head down like that?' Mike heard one sailor ask another, and he realised the man was right. Most of the corpses were floating head-down so that almost all that was visible of them was their pack.

'Good God,' said Hobo. 'Their life jackets are round their waists not under their armpits, because they put their packs on first. Damn thing has flipped them over and the weight of the pack has held them under. Their own Mae Wests have drowned them, poor devils.'

They steamed on through a sea of bodies. Mike felt his gorge rise as they passed a rare body floating face up. It was wearing neither pack nor life-preserver. Both had been burnt or blown away along with the face, and the skin of the belly was split apart like an overripe fig to reveal bright pink flesh and grey guts. As the men lining the deck-rail watched the body drift past, a herring gull glided down, perched on the peeled skin and dipped its beak to pull at a loop of intestine. 'Gertcha!' bellowed the petty officer standing next to Mike, waving his arms at the bird. 'Geddout of it!' Somebody dug in a pocket and hurled a volley of coins, pennies and one bright sixpence that flashed in the early morning sun, in the gull's direction. It lifted its head for a moment, querying the commotion, without letting go of the loop of gut. Mike heard a groan and tore his eyes away from the horrid tableau to see a young rating fall away from the rail in a faint. It was a relief to go over and pull the boy up and put his head between his knees, and other men crowded round gratefully too.

Finally there was a cheer from the rail. Dixon left the rating sitting on the deck and rushed back to see a sailor pointing at a life-raft with men still clinging to it. One or two of the men round the raft cheered weakly in answer and the ship turned gratefully towards them. Fifty arms reached down the scrambling nets, pulled the soldiers aboard and smothered them in blankets. The search continued, and from time to time they came upon a lone swimmer or a couple of men clinging to a raft or a piece of floating debris. For every survivor they pulled from the water, they passed five or ten drowned corpses. The few that floated face up were horribly young.

After an hour they made out two small merchant ships approaching from the direction of Plymouth. They were steaming along side by side, making only a couple of knots and Mike assumed they were picking up survivors too. But, as they came closer, he saw that the two ships were linked by a curve of hawser that they were dragging in a loop between them. 'Jesus,' he said under his breath, and he heard other men muttering too as they realised the terrible catch for which the two boats were trawling. 'How many are there?'

Hobo looked haggard: 'Too many, Dixon. Far too many. What a bloody shambles.'

28

MAY 1944, OXFORDSHIRE

By the first weekend of May, the half dozen apple trees in the Hobarts' Oxfordshire orchard were in full bloom, but it was the flowering cherry that was almost enough to stop the heart. Lady Hobart had set out an old swing seat and a couple of deck-chairs beneath its canopy the previous afternoon, but it was Sunday morning now and the family had gone to church. Mike thought perhaps he should have gone too, in deference to the CO's hospitality, although he had had little time for God since the day he first grasped Darwin's theory of evolution – and none at all since Dieppe and Slapton Sands. But when he had stood up, hesitantly, from the breakfast table, Hobo had given him that straight look of his: 'I didn't think you had any truck with this kind of thing, Dixon.'

'Not a great deal, sir.'

'Then sit down, man and enjoy your breakfast. There'll be enough hypocrites in the place without you adding to the scrum.'

'Patrick!' said Dorothea, pulling on her gloves. 'Perhaps Mike wanted to come.'

'He didn't, did you?'

'Not especially, sir. Thanks all the same.'

'He'd much sooner stay here and talk to our Miss Carrington, if she ever makes an appearance. I don't know what's wrong with the girl; she's generally punctual on duty.'

'Yes, well she's not on duty this morning, Patrick. I sent Grace up with a cup of tea and some copies of *Picture Post* and instructions to have a nice lie-in. She looked done in when you got here yesterday. She's only a small slip of a girl, you know, not a great strapping tank-man who can trundle around for days on end without rest.'

'Nonsense, woman. Charlie's tough as old boots, isn't she Dixon?'

'Generally gives that impression, sir, yes.'

Dorothea raised her eyes to the ceiling. 'Blind as bats, the pair of you. Now, we should go, Patrick. It's already a quarter past and I'm not being quick-marched across the square.'

The old house shuddered as Hobo closed the great front door behind them and Mike watched the three heads pass the breakfast-room window. He shook out the paper and poured himself a fresh cup of tea, wondering when Charlie would appear. He was only halfway down the first column of newsprint when he heard her step.

'It's all right,' he said, without lowering the newspaper, 'coast's clear.'

'Don't tell me you bunked off church as well. I feel awful.'

He did lower the paper now. 'So you should. I did at least offer to turn out on parade. You just skulked around till it was too late. Very poor form.'

Charlie's face fell. 'Oh dear, am I in bad odour?'

He put down the paper altogether and picked up the teapot. 'I'm teasing. I think they were glad to be together as a family for once. We'd only have been gooseberries.' He poured the tea and held up her cup and saucer, but pulled it away when she reached out to take it. 'As you're such a sluggard, I'm not going to let you sit here and drink your tea. I'm going to take it out into the garden with the paper. If you want it, you'll have to come and get it.'

'What about my breakfast?'

'You're so late for breakfast it'll only spoil your lunch. And Lady H is determined to lay on the best spread she can, so it'll be doubly rude if you don't have an appetite. Come on.'

'All right, but I need my shoes. I took them off inside the side door when we came back from walking yesterday. They're not there now.'

'Ah,' said Mike, 'I think you'll find them in the scullery, polished to the nines.'

'Really? I must remember to leave the maid a tip.'

Mike smiled. 'Kind of you, but it wasn't the maid. It was him, Hobo. He did mine too. Says it's his Sunday morning ritual at home.'

'No? The CO? Lord, and they're terribly down at heel. What will he have thought?'

'That he works you far too hard for you to have time to visit the cobbler's. He is extraordinary, though, isn't he? Half the time he acts like he's blessed with the divine right of kings, the other half you'd almost think he was a socialist. Anyway, hurry up and put them on. We're missing a glorious morning.'

While Charlie was still exclaiming at the shine a determined Major-General could produce, Mike led the way out into the garden and across to the orchard. He set down the china cups on a little rustic table and lowered himself into one of the deck-chairs. Charlie brushed cherry petals off the faded striped ticking of the swing seat and sat down. Above their heads, the tree stretched its branches, each one laden with pendulous stalks of the most exquisite double flowers in an unnameable colour somewhere between white and pink. The tree's leaves were still furled so that between the branches it was just possible to make out patches of an impossibly blue cloudless sky. But the overwhelming feeling was of enclosure beneath that roof of blossom, of being hidden away in the heart of nature on the march and in its pomp.

Charlie stretched forward to claim her tea, swung her legs under her and leaned back to look up at the show. 'Have you ever seen anything more beautiful than this?'

Mike looked up at it too, and smiled: 'Are you fishing?'

She looked across at him, questioningly, and giggled: 'Good God, no. Of course not. I just meant, this place, this morning, I don't think I can imagine anything prettier. It's so ... well, it's so English, isn't it? Makes you realise why we have to win.'

Mike rested his head on the top bar of the deck-chair and looked up between the lacquered bronze branches at the sky. 'Of course, the Japanese are keen as mustard on cherry blossom. It may be that there's a young suicide pilot and his girl sitting under a cherry tree in Kyoto at this very moment saying the exact same thing about Japan.'

She shook her head in exasperation: 'You're impossible. You always have to counter everything with some irrefutable piece of logic. Were you like this before you met the Old Man, or is it him that has made you so argumentative?'

'I'm not being argumentative. I just don't think you should fall into the pathetic fallacy, that's all.'

'The what?'

'The pathetic fallacy. Burton was telling me about it the other day. It's some art critic's name for the romantic idea that the weather, or inanimate objects, share our feelings or serve our ends. In your case, you could almost call it the 'patriotic fallacy'. This is a beautiful cherry tree, I grant you. But it doesn't sanctify the cause for England, I'm afraid, any more than that cherry tree in Kyoto sanctifies the cause for Japan.'

'Mike Dixon, sometimes I think you're the least romantic man I've ever met.'

'You're wrong, I'm deeply romantic. Wasn't I the one who made you come and sit out here? Why do you think I did that, if not to be able to enjoy two beautiful things at once?'

She looked across at him, and smiled. There was a hint of sadness in the smile, as well as pleasure. At that moment, a little shower of petals fell from the branch above her and dropped into the folds of her skirt. A couple of petals floated on the surface of her tea.

'Oh,' she said. 'It's coming down like confetti.'

'I wish it was,' said Mike.

She put back her head and laughed. 'Now who's got the pathetic thingummy?'

'Don't laugh, Charlie. I want to marry you, that's all. There's nothing pathetic about that, is there?'

She stopped laughing. 'Nothing pathetic. Not about you, anyway. Maybe there is about me. It might jinx you, to be engaged to me. Like it jinxed Bill.'

'There's not much harm I can come to while I'm tied to Hobo's apron strings, is there?'

'Well, not for now. But after the invasion, you know as well as I do, he's going to want to get to France as soon as he can. Then anything might happen. I couldn't stand it, thinking you were carrying my bad luck around with you like a … like a rabbit's foot in reverse.'

Mike pushed himself upright, gripping the sides of the unstable deck-chair, pushed himself forward so far that his weight shifted and he almost tipped on to his knees in front of her. He was there, caught in a limbo between sitting and kneeling, when they both became conscious of footsteps running across the garden towards their outdoor room. It was the Hobarts' maid, out of breath. 'Telephone, miss,' she said, as she dipped her head under the branches and broke in on them. 'It's a trunk call, from a telephone box. Quickly, please miss. Quickly. I don't know how much money he's got left.'

'Who?' said Mike, dropping back into the deck-chair. 'How much money who's got left?'

239

'He said his name was Flight Lieutenant Hartwell. He said he was the young lady's fiancé.'

Charlie and the maid ran back across the lawn to the house and left him sitting under the cherry tree. Small petals, which he noticed for the first time were shaped like tears, drifted down and lay lightly on his trousers and on the sleeves of his sweater. He did not move to brush them off. He did not move at all.

After a time, she came back, and sat down again on the swing seat. She didn't curl her legs beneath her this time. This time, she sat up straight and rested her hands on her knees. He wanted to say: 'Well?' or 'Was it him?' or 'Where was he calling from?' But he found he could say nothing. He could only look at her and, when he did, he knew that Bill Hartwell was back in England, and that she was still engaged to marry him.

'How the hell did he get back to England?' As soon as the words were out, he realised how bad they sounded.

'He escaped. A tunnel, he said. And they drew lots and he got one – and he managed to get on a train and ... I don't know, something about Sweden. I don't know. I wasn't really taking it in. I was standing there in Hobo's hall, holding the telephone receiver, thinking: It's Bill. Really Bill. Talking to me. I'd almost forgotten his voice. And there it was. Talking to me as if he still knows me, as if we still know each other. But I don't know him anymore, and he sure as hell doesn't know me.' She put her hands over her face and rocked backwards and forwards. He wanted to go and sit beside her, put his arm around her and tell her that everything was going to be all right. Something stopped him. A voice whispered to him that perhaps she wasn't ready to pass over a future Member of Parliament for the son of a coal-miner with no qualifications besides half a diploma in engineering.

Perhaps she'd been hedging her bets, and now it would be far easier for her to go on as everyone expected.

'What are you going to do?'

She looked up, sniffed and wiped her eyes with her knuckles. Her voice was very small and un-Charlie-like. 'He's in London for a few days, before he goes back on Ops. He wants me to ask the Old Man for compassionate leave.'

'Are you going to?'

'I think I have to see him, don't you? I owe him that. After all, I've been saying that I could only break it off face to face.'

'And what if he persuades you you're wrong? You said yourself he's very good at getting what he wants. He got you to agree to marry him before. Why not again? He's a damn sight more persuasive than me, at any rate. Damn sight better prospects too, after the war. One of your own type. Not a scholarship boy from the Midlands, wherever the hell they are.'

'Don't, Mike,' she said, tears slipping down her cheeks. 'Don't start that again. It has to be gone through, that's all. I will sort it out, I promise. Please say you believe me.' She reached out a hand to touch his arm but, as she did so, he heard the thud of the front door and used it as an excuse to jump up from the deck-chair.

'They're back from church. I'd better go in. Come in when you've sorted yourself out a bit.' He pushed aside a cherry branch and walked away, leaving her alone, a swirl of petals fluttering down forlornly in his wake.

29

Charlie asked to speak to Hobo as soon as the luncheon things had been cleared away. He led the way to a pretty room at the end of the house with a French window in the Gothick style that looked out over the garden. There was a desk in an alcove, and a swivelling office chair, but it was clear that the room was only Hobo's study part-time and that it mostly served as Lady Hobart's sewing room and sanctum. The evidence for this was a cluster of well-used chintz armchairs, a tea table, a standard lamp and a low Victorian nursing chair upholstered in faded silver velvet, beside which stood a sewing trolley. Several pearl-topped pins and a threaded needle were stuck haphazardly in the side of the nursing chair and pieces of fabric with the shapes of a paper pattern pinned to them lay over the back of one of the armchairs.

He sat at the desk and gestured towards the female seats. 'Take care not to impale yourself,' he said. 'My wife is quite blasé about where she leaves sharp implements. No protocol over the use of live ammo in this house, I'm afraid.'

Charlie took a seat, gingerly, in the one armchair that appeared to display no offensive capability. 'It's good of you to see me, sir.'

'Difficult to avoid you, when you've been cluttering up the house all weekend. What's this about? You and Dixon were giddy as kittens yesterday – but ever since we came back from church it's been as if someone has died. Has someone died?'

'Not exactly. Rather the opposite, in fact.'

'What's on earth's that supposed to mean?'

'I … I had a telephone call, while you and Lady Hobart were at church. And it came as a bit of a shock. It's my … well, my fiancé.

He's managed to escape from a POW camp. He's back in London. In fact, he only has a few days before he goes back on active duty. Wants me to take some leave and go down there.'

'Well, that's splendid news. A home run, eh? All the way from Germany. Good for him. Splendid news. Not like someone dying at all. More of a Lazarus job. You must be ... '

She was trying her hardest not to cry. Her hands gripped at each other in her lap, and he looked aghast at the prospect of her failing to keep the tears from falling. 'You want some leave?' he said. 'Is that it?'

She nodded. 'Please, sir, just forty-eight hours. I need to ... well, I need to go and see how he is. Get things sorted out a bit.'

He stood up. 'You'd better get off down there tonight. Then you can get things fixed up and be back at Rawdon by Wednesday. Ring the station and find out the time of the next London train. Will you have somewhere to stay?'

She looked surprised, as if everything was moving too fast. 'My sister's in Chelsea, sir. I can stay with her. If I could just ring through to let her know.'

'Of course. The telephone – well, I suppose you know where it is by now. How did he know, by the way, where to find you?'

'It took him a while, sir. One of the ATS girls at Rawdon spoke to him first, and eventually they got hold of Piddington and he let on I was here.'

'I see. Well, it's not what we pay him for, but I suppose in the circumstances ... ' He petered out and she realised the interview was at an end. She stood up, and would have saluted, except that she was wearing a cotton summer dress and it didn't seem right. She slipped out of the room and ran upstairs to pack her bag.

Dorothea came upon her husband at the breakfast-room window

observing his ADC, who was slumped in the deck-chair under the cherry tree. 'What's wrong?'

'*Cherchez la femme.*'

'Not *la femme* who's just fled up *l'escalier*, by any chance?'

'The same. How did you guess?'

'Oh Patrick, it sticks out about a yard. They were so happy yesterday. What's gone wrong? A tiff?'

'Not exactly. She's engaged to a bomber pilot who was shot down over Germany. He was missing for quite a while before he turned up as a POW. Now, rather extraordinarily, he's made his way back to England and wants to pick up where they left off.'

'And she doesn't?'

'I think she and Dixon are pretty sweet on each other.'

'So what's she going to do?'

'She's going to London to see the chap and sort things out.'

'Break it off? Or make it up with him?'

'I didn't enquire. It's hardly my affair.'

'And she didn't ask your advice?'

He raised his eyebrows: 'Why ever would she do that?'

'You do have some experience in this sort of thing, Patrick, in case you've forgotten. Romantic entanglements. I expect she's heard the story. So it's just conceivable she would think you might be able to help. If she does ask, you will tell her to follow her heart, won't you? I've certainly never regretted it.'

'My dear, if you think I have any intention of broaching the subject again you are very much mistaken. I nearly got the waterworks just now and you know I'm allergic to weeping females. That's one of the things I admire about you, old girl. You've never been a sniveller.'

She laughed and put her arm through his. 'Patrick, how can you possibly claim you don't have charm?'

He smiled down at her: 'You're teasing me now, aren't you?'

'I am. I'm teasing you and then I'm going to drive that poor girl to the train and give her a little bit of advice, since you're too cowardly to do it.'

As Dorothea's car disappeared through the gateway, Mike asked if he could have a word. Hobo led the way back to his study and lowered himself into his chair again. He waved a hand at the armchairs, but his aide remained standing, hands clasped behind him. 'What is it, Dixon? Something to do with this Charlie business?'

'No, sir. Not that. Something else. I need you to release me from my promise.'

'Oh yes? What promise is that?'

'After the recce to Normandy, you made me promise I wouldn't request a transfer until after the invasion. But I really feel I want to be there, sir, on D-Day. I want to re-join the Royal Engineers. After all, I know as much about the AVRE as anyone. I've been there at enough of the testing and training, I think, to go straight into a tank. I've seen more Flying Dustbins actually fired than anybody except you, I suppose. I think I could command a troop, but if you don't think I'm up to it, I'd be happy with a single tank.'

Hobo leaned back in his chair. 'Out of the question.'

'Why, sir? Don't you think I'm up to it?'

'I've no doubt you are, but you've got a job already. I've told you before, I don't have time to train up another ADC. We shall be chasing our tails right up to D-Day and I need every one of my team pulling his weight. Once we're in France I might be in more desperate need of tank commanders than I am staff officers. Right now, it's the other way around.'

'Then I'd respectfully like to resign my commission, sir.'

The blood started to rise in Hobo's face: 'Not that bloody nonsense again! You can't resign your commission right before the invasion. You might as well talk of mutiny. Of desertion.'

'I'm sorry, sir. But that's how strongly I feel about it. I wasn't fit for much when I first joined the Division. I've learnt a lot since then. And I've seen action, sir, which is more than most of the men. The things you talk about, sir, initiative, adaptability, I think I've shown I have them. We've both seen the casualty predictions. If our goal is to clear four lanes per beach and we take seventy per cent casualties, it may come down to two lanes, or even one. One clearance team could make the difference between getting off the beach and falling back into the sea. I know what's needed, sir, better than anyone.'

Hobo held up his hand. 'Why do I get the feeling I've been hoist on my own petard? Occupational hazard for a one-time sapper, I know, but still. All right, I will consider your request. First I'm going to ask you again, and I want the truth this time. Is this really to do with Miss C? Because if it is, and you're flouncing off to do a far, far better thing than you have ever done, just because a pretty blonde has given you your marching orders then you can forget it. I won't have my officers making bfs of themselves and putting their men in harm's way to make a stupid romantic gesture. So if it's that, you'd better cough it up. Or you and I shall fall out and I *will* transfer you – to a paper-filing job so far in the rear you won't even find out the war's over till years after everyone else has gone home. Do I make myself clear?'

Mike swallowed hard. 'Sir.'

'Well?'

'To be honest, I was planning to broach it with you the night we were on the *Azalea*. Then the E-boats attacked those transports and, well, there hasn't seemed to be another moment till now. So maybe it does have something to do with Charlie. She's got it into her head that she's bad luck for a chap, you see. She has to see that's a load of rubbish now, doesn't she? I mean, with her fiancé making it home. That's not bad luck, is it? Not for him, I mean. So I realised that now there's nothing to stop me doing what I think's for the best.'

Hobo sighed. 'I suppose it's not actually the worst possible moment to lose you. The men are about as ready as they can be. All right, Dixon, seeing as you're hell-bent. You'll need a crash course in radio comms and so forth, but there's no reason you shouldn't go in as a troop commander. In fact, if you don't have a squadron under you in very short order, I shall consider you're slacking off.'

'Thank you, sir. You won't regret it.'

'I'd better not. Because if I hear you've been going in for any Sir Galahad stuff that puts your men's lives at risk just because you're careless of your own, I shall haul you over the coals myself. Understood?'

'Yes, sir.'

'This invasion's going to cost enough lives and enough tanks, more than enough, without anybody throwing theirs away. Anyway, I'm not convinced that Charlie would feel you getting yourself killed improved matters, as far as she's concerned. Don't chuck in your hand too early, that's my advice. If I've learned one thing about life, it's that you never know what card is going to be dealt next. Do you know what I was doing four years ago?'

'No, sir.'

'Four years ago, when we first came to live here, I was a lance-corporal in the Local Defence Volunteers, defending Chipping Campden. I'm surprised you haven't heard the story. I was sent home from Egypt because Archie Wavell didn't like my training methods. Too many officers complained my regime interfered with their polo.

They promised to find me another job. Three months later they dumped me on the retired list. So in May 1940 there I was, standing on a hilltop in the Cotswolds, while disaster unfolded at Calais. A life-time in the army and no way to be of use when I was needed most. I'll tell you, Dixon, if the rifle they'd issued me hadn't been a wooden dummy I might have done something damn stupid. But a few months later Downing Street was on that telephone, asking me to go and see Churchill, and a few weeks after that I was back in the saddle. And they haven't got rid of me yet, try as they might. So, like I said, it doesn't do to chuck in your hand too early.'

'No, sir. Though I can't quite see you in the Home Guard.'

'Well, I assure you I was. Ah, well, I suppose no experience is ever entirely wasted. I like to think we made Chipping Camden pretty nigh impregnable. Anyway, bugger off, would you? I have orders to write – and no blasted ADC to handle it.'

It wasn't far from the house to the railway station at Aynhoe Junction so Dorothea knew she had better make a start right away. 'Well now,' she said, as she steered the baby Austin past the bottom end of the village green and waited for a farm cart to come through the pinch-point in Chapel Square. 'Patrick tells me your fiancé has made a miraculous escape. Sounds rather splendid.'

Charlie fiddled with the catch of her bag, and smiled weakly. 'I suppose it does. I'm being rather a goose and struggling to take it in, I'm afraid. It was so strange, hearing Bill's voice on the telephone, without any sort of warning. He must think I'm a total idiot. I don't suppose I made any sense at all.'

'I'm sure you made complete sense. Anybody would be a bit non-plussed. Rung up like that out of the blue. How long since you've seen him?'

Charlie wound a strand of hair round her finger. 'A year. Or a bit more. He was posted missing in March last year. We didn't hear he was in a POW camp until late June. Now this.'

'Must be awful, being a prisoner of war. The helplessness particularly. My husband was taken prisoner once, you know. In the last war.'

Charlie looked shocked. 'Really? I can't imagine Ho—, I mean ... '

'Oh, it wasn't for long. His plane crashed in the desert and some Turks captured him. It was only a few days, I think, before he managed to get away and get back to his own lines. Anyway, it was long before we were married. I wasn't even married to my first husband in those days.'

The hook went in just as she hoped it would. Charlie's eyes stretched wide. 'Your first husband?'

Dorothea threw the car out of gear as they reached the crown of the hill and let it coast down the long slope to the river, gaining the twin benefits of time and fuel economy. 'Didn't you know? I always assume everyone knows. It was such a scandal at the time I didn't think it would ever die down. The divorce, I mean.'

'Divorce?'

Dorothea laughed. 'Is this how you were on the telephone? Repeating the last word of the poor man's every sentence?

Charlie blushed. 'Sorry.'

'I'm teasing. Not about the divorce. That was real enough. I was already married when I met Patrick, you see. To a perfectly decent man who was, unfortunately, not the right man for me. Patrick came out to India to teach at the Staff College in Quetta, where my husband was also lecturing and, well, after a while it became clear to both of us that he was the right man.'

'Crikey,' said Charlie, her eyes still round with surprise.

'Yes,' said Dorothea, slipping the little car into third as they reached the water-meadow at the bottom of the hill. ' "Crikey" about summed it up. We tried keeping apart, but it didn't work. My husband was very decent when it came to the divorce, actually. But the Army was pretty foul. The Army wives, in particular. It was touch and go for a while whether Patrick would have to resign his commission. Thank God he didn't, because soldiering is what he loves. But there are still people who cut us, who will always consider Patrick a stinker because of it. I've given up trying to do anything about them. All I know is that, however wrong it seemed to the rest of the world, it was the right thing for us and I haven't regretted it for a minute.' They were breasting the old hump-backed bridge over the Oxford Canal now, with only a few yards to go until they would have to turn into the station yard. Dorothea looked across and hoped the girl was bright enough to understand what she was trying to tell her.

'I didn't know,' said Charlie.

'No, well, I'm glad if it's not common currency these days. You needn't go round telling everybody. Though I'm not ashamed. It may count as an advanced sort of view, but I don't believe one should ever be ashamed of falling deeply in love. And in my experience, it's better for two people to be happy than for three people to be miserable.' She drew up in front of the platform and pulled on the hand-brake. Charlie reached for the door-handle: 'Thanks, Lady Hobart, for the lift, I mean. And for a lovely weekend. And for the, well, for telling me about the divorce and everything.'

'Dorothea, dear. Please call me Dorothea. I'm not at all used to "Lady Hobart" yet. It seems rather undeserved, to be a lady all of a sudden, just because one's husband has earned a knighthood. Still, I suppose it's one in the eye for the "stinker" brigade. Good old Winston, to give Patrick his stamp of approval.'

'Yes,' said Charlie, thinking instantly of Freddie Quiller. 'I'm glad about that.' Then she heard the train coming, and jumped out with her bag. As she closed the door, she leaned down and smiled through the open window. 'Cheerio then.'

'Goodbye, Charlie,' said Dorothea. 'Good luck.'

30

He suggested they meet at the restaurant in Maiden Lane he used to go to before the war to rub shoulders with other Oxford Tories.

'If it's still there,' she said.

'Wait, I'll check.' His voice grew muffled and she pictured him in the lobby of his club, his father's club, putting his hand over the receiver and turning to one of the porters. Then he was back. 'Still there. Turbot's not what it was, apparently. One? No, half past twelve. Give us more time.'

Charlie thought, 'Is that what we need?' She said, 'Twelve thirty. I'll be there.'

He was there first. An elderly waiter led the way into the ornately decorated restaurant, and she saw him as soon as they stepped round the glazed screen from the entrance lobby. He was at a little red velvet booth for two, with a tall glass of lager in front of him, reading a folded newspaper. She noticed that his uniform was brand new and it made him look younger than she remembered. The wing of blond hair that used to fall across his forehead was cut short and he was thinner too. But the way he sat there, one hand in his trouser pocket, long legs crossed at the ankle, sucking up the contents of the paper as if he already knew everybody in it and everything about it, was essentially the Bill of old. Then he turned square to face her and the Bill of old was wrenched away. The war had taken him in a moment of violence and left someone else in his place.

'Bill!' she said, and he pushed back his chair and stood up. She reached out to take his hands, sympathy and an overwhelming sense of shame rising up inside her. For a moment he didn't move. Then he let his paper fall on to the tablecloth and held his hands out to hers with a strange little smile. As soon as she grasped them, she realised why. One was a hand like any other young man's hand, larger than hers, warm, smooth, strong. The other was a strangely ridged and shrunken claw, glassy smooth and rough in parts, the fingers stiff and curled in on themselves.

The shock of that never-before-felt touch made her glance down before she looked up again and met his eyes in the face that was Bill's and yet not Bill's. Two thirds of his face was still that of a monstrously handsome blond public schoolboy but at the outer edge of his right eye the old symmetry had blurred and slipped as if the sculptor of a head had dragged a broad spatulate thumb across the damp clay and wiped away the detail of an eyelid, a cheek and an ear.

'You didn't … You said you were a bit banged up, but you were fine. I imagined a broken arm, a rib or two. You never said … '

He slipped his hands out of hers. 'What was the point? By the time the Red Cross tracked me down in hospital, I was over the worst. Jerry doctors aren't bad at this stuff, I'll give them that. They shifted quite a bit of skin back on to my hand before they handed me over to the Luftwaffe.'

'Is that why it took so long to hear you were alive?'

He nodded. 'I think the Jerry surgeon was trying to give me a chance of getting back to something like normal before I was transferred to a camp. Kept me under wraps while they operated on me. Christ knows why, when I'd gone over there determined to knock seven bells out of one of their cities – hospitals, doctors and all. Still, thank God for the Hippocratic oath, eh?'

'Yes,' she said, and could think of nothing more.

'Shall we sit down? We must look like Patience on a bloody plinth and this is Rules, after all, not Trafalgar Square.'

253

'Of course, yes,' she said, and there was the waiter, pulling out her chair and laying a napkin in her lap. Perhaps he'd been there all along. Perhaps he witnessed meetings like this every other day. The way he asked: 'Can I get you a drink, miss?' certainly suggested that it was nothing out of the ordinary.

'A whisky please,' she said.

Bill raised his eyebrows. The glassy smooth side of his face did not stretch, making the gesture curiously lopsided. 'Scotch with lunch, eh? Is that what the girls are drinking in town these days? Or is it the shock? Can't say I blame you. I should have warned you, I know – but, to be honest, I wasn't altogether sure you'd have come if I had.'

'Of course I'd have come.' She blushed, ashamed at how close she'd been anyway to not coming, at how her feet had dragged along the Strand, at the way she'd hesitated outside, at the effort it had taken to push open the door.

The waiter came back with her whisky and menus, and they bent their heads over the list of dishes.

'What do you want?'

'I don't know. Steak? It always used to be good here, didn't it?'

'Steak it is,' he said. 'The biggest they have. Fried potatoes, mushrooms. Do you mind onions? I've a craving for onions. In fact, I've a craving for every kind of food there is. When I first got back, they'd hardly let me eat at all. Doctors were afraid I'd bust a gut. Literally, I think. After a year on soup and black bread.'

'Sounds pretty grim.'

'It was no life for a gourmand, I'll say that. Amazing how important food becomes when you can't get it. Sex and food. Though to be honest, I think most of the men spent more time fantasizing about food than about the other. Sorry if that sounds a bit unromantic.'

She was nowhere near ready for the subject of sex to rear its head. Had forgotten how blunt he was about all that. Relentless when he wanted it. As with anything he wanted.

'When did you get back? You said, "When I first got back" as if it was a while ago.'

'About six weeks. Look, I know I should have let you know before, but they bundled me straight into a long de-brief. Then they decided I was due another spell in hospital – my eyelid needed a bit of work – and I thought, well, I thought it would be better to know what I was doing before I called you. It had been a year already. A few more weeks gave me a chance to stop looking like such a bloody scarecrow, have a new uniform made.' He smiled. 'I know you can't make a silk purse out of a sow's ear, but this lot is a hell of an improvement on what stepped off a Swedish fishing boat a few weeks ago.'

'I wouldn't have minded.'

He laughed. 'Well, I would. It was bad enough seeing your face just now. It's quite a lesson, I can tell you, to find out how much of what you took for granted as being due to your talent, your wit, your charisma was actually just a response to your looks all along. It's funny, because when they first let you look at yourself in a mirror you get a nasty shock and then you think: "Oh well, at least I'm still a clever bastard, at least I can still carry things off by force of person-ality" and you find that actually whatever influence you used to exercise over people wasn't down to your inner qualities at all, it was down to the hair and the teeth and the smile. Makes you feel a prize ass, I can tell you.' He pulled out a pack of cigarettes and offered her one. She shook her head. He put one in his mouth and held the match box in his bad right hand, striking the match against it with his left. He lit the cigarette and tossed the match into the ash-tray. She noticed he smoked it using his left hand. He noticed her noticing. 'I'm quite a handy lefty these days. Don't like drawing attention to the other one. It still works okay really, it's only delicate stuff and heavy work it's not so good for.'

'Like flying?'

'No, actually, flying shouldn't be too bad. That's what I meant about waiting till I knew. I wanted to get back on ops and I wasn't sure they'd let me. I've spent the last three weeks trying to get the buggers to pass me medically fit. Finally talked them into it on Friday. I'd already got my CO to promise I could re-join the squadron if I managed to get passed fit. He isn't very happy about it. I think he thought the quacks could be relied upon to squash me, but he can't go back on his word now.'

'Aren't they awfully heavy to handle, Halifaxes?'

Bill smiled. 'Well, that's the publicity we like to give out for the evening papers. Actually, a girl could fly one.'

The steak arrived and was set down in front of them. He took up the knife in his left hand and gripped the fork in his right. He sawed clumsily at the meat. She put her knife and fork down. 'Do you want me to … ?'

He glared at her fiercely. 'No, Charlie, I fucking don't want you to.'

She looked at her plate and picked up her cutlery again. They ate in silence for a while. He stopped now and then to spoon more onions on to his plate from a metal dish, clanging the spoon against the dish in a way that made her flinch each time. He ate ravenously. She had never had less appetite, though she hadn't seen steak in ages. She cut it mechanically into squares and forced it down, only because it was better than stopping, which would have meant starting to talk again.

Too soon for her, his plate was empty. By accident or provocation, he dropped his fork on the china with a clatter and she jumped again. Several heads turned to look and turned quickly away. He took another cigarette from the pack and lit it, even though she was still eating. She pushed what was left of the meat to one side and put down her knife and fork quietly.

'Sorry,' he said, and went to stub out the cigarette. 'Wasn't thinking.'

'No,' she said, 'it's all right. I didn't want any more.'

'Christ, I know I'm no oil painting. I didn't think it was enough to put people off their food.'

She looked him full in the face and saw what it had cost him to telephone her and ask her to lunch, what it must have been like for him waiting for her to walk in and see him. She saw the bravery in it, and the vulnerability that had never been obvious before. She wished she loved him. If she had loved him, the damage to his face and hand wouldn't have mattered a damn. She was as sure as she could be that if it had been Mike sitting there opposite her, with his looks spoiled, she would have loved him as much as ever. But it wasn't Mike. It was Bill Hartwell, and she knew without a shadow of doubt that she didn't love him.

'Bill,' she said, and found the waiter at her elbow.

'Have you finished, miss?'

'Oh. Yes. Thank you.'

He collected the plates on his arm. 'Shall I bring the dessert trolley?'

Bill looked at Charlie: 'Afters?'

She shook her head: 'But don't hold back on my account. You ... '

'No. Just the bill please, Alfred.'

'Very good, sir.' He gave a little bow and went away. Bill laid his cigarette down in the ashtray and reached out his good hand to take hers. She let it lie, passive, in his grasp.

'Shall we get out of here?'

She nodded, hope rising that he had somewhere he needed to be.

'Where are you staying?'

'With Cec. She's working for Military Intelligence these days.'

'Little Cecilia? Christ, I feel like Rip van Winkle.' He shook his head: 'She got a flat in town?'

'Yes. Just off the King's Road.'

'Could we use it, do you think?'

Charlie didn't follow him for a moment and then she did. Blood rushed to her cheeks and her hand jerked, but he tightened his grip. 'I go back to the squadron tomorrow. It's been a long time, old girl. I know I said I spent most of my time thinking about food, but not all my time – and besides, I'm not hungry any more. You needn't worry – I'm still in full working order from the neck down.'

She kicked herself for not thinking he might want this. She had assumed he'd just want to talk, and that she'd find a way to tell him. But now there was this, and there was him, so altered. 'I don't think we can. There's only one bedroom and her roommate works nights. I'm sleeping on the put-you-up in the sitting room as it is.'

'Have to be a hotel then. There's a strip of them up by Paddington. A chap told me they're clean, and you can get a room for the afternoon quite as the norm. Sign of the times. Would you mind it awfully? It's not what I'd like, but I can hardly take you back to the club, can I?'

The waiter came with the bill and he let go of Charlie's hand for a minute. She hid it in her lap, her mind whirling at the inescapable horror of the situation. The words she wanted to say, had planned to say, circled her mind, and she could no more speak them out loud than spread her arms and fly. Dully, she watched him count money out on to the bill plate and heard him make a bad joke with the waiter. He stood up. 'Shall we?'

She found herself getting to her feet and crossing the restaurant. He was half a step behind and, as they reached the door, she felt the touch of his hand in the small of her back. She shivered, and he said in her ear: 'Steady, old thing. We still need to find a cab.'

She prayed there wouldn't be any cabs about, and that somewhere on the long walk towards Paddington she would rediscover the power of speech. But he flagged a taxi down with ease in Floral Street, and named a street and a hotel to the driver with a familiarity that made her wonder how well he knew it. Even that thought didn't un-dam the words stuck in her head.

When he jumped into the taxi without waiting for her to go first she was surprised at his lack of manners. Then she realised he was anxious that his good side would be turned to her. He took her hand again as soon as she was beside him and, sitting there like that, it was possible to see him still as the almost god-like creature who had lifted his bomber off a Yorkshire runway heading for Nuremberg with half a dozen other young men. She looked down and saw the shiny red claw resting on his right knee. 'Are you really fit to fly?' She was surprised to hear her own voice. He moved the hand out of view.

'Main controls aren't too bad. I'm a bit worried, if I'm honest, about being able to operate the landing gear. It's a pig of a thing on the Hali. Needs a real tight grip. But that's what co-pilots are for, isn't it? Can't sit around with their feet up the whole trip. Fact is, Charlie, if I can get up there and make it to the target, I'm going. Do you know that virtually all of my lot are gone now? I went up to the Squadron last week. They're not at Linton any more, moved to an even more godforsaken bit of Yorkshire. Everything's different. Apart from the CO, who used to be junior to me by the way, almost everyone was a new face. Kids, a lot of them. They looked at me like I was some ancient prophet. Christ, I felt it too. I can hardly sit around while they go off every night. At least I know the score. These days that's worth more than a fully functioning hand.'

The cab drew up outside a terrace of spalled stucco buildings with names like The Lancaster, The Bristol, The Astoria painted on cheap signboards under their Doric porticos. They got out and she hesitated until he put his hand under her elbow and walked her between a pair of grime-streaked columns into The Lancaster. They passed another couple in uniform coming across the hall, and Charlie saw the girl blush and pat her hair, glancing up at the naval officer beside her with the unmistakable glow of illicit satisfaction. She remembered the old inn at Banbury, and Mike writing them into the register as man and wife. Despite the hammering of her heart, anyone could have challenged her at that moment and she would have defied them, so right had it felt. Now, watching the man she was actually engaged to marry talking to the hotel porter, she prayed for someone to step between them and stop what was about to happen.

Nobody stepped between them. Bill came back with a key and then they were in a bedroom. Not a terrible bedroom. As if the bedroom mattered. He sat down on the bed, loosened his tie and tried to unfasten his collar with his left hand. His fingers fumbled it, and she put her handbag and gas-mask holder down on a chair and went over to help him. She thought he might curse at her again, but he just dropped his hand and let her work the stud out of its fastening. As it came free, she looked up and found him staring at her. He reached out and pushed back the hair from her face. 'I'd forgotten,' he said.

'What?'

'How pretty you are. Were you always this pretty?'

She shrugged, embarrassed. 'You're just out of the habit. Of being around women, I mean. Even a glass of water looks delicious when you're thirsty.'

'It's not that. You're no glass of water. It's as if I never really looked at you before. Was I an absolute four-letter type, Charlie? Before. Did I ever deserve you?'

She dropped her head. He raised her chin with his finger. 'I'd try to understand. If you said you don't want to go on with it. If you don't want to be stuck with a crock like me.'

Here was her opening at last, but she found she couldn't take it. So much of who he once was had already been stolen from him that she couldn't bear him to lose anything more. Instead, she eased his stiff new wool jacket down over his shoulders and pulled his arms out of the sleeves, one at a time, like a mother undressing a child. She pushed him back on the bed and climbed on top of him. He sighed and she felt his left hand move up under her skirt as she threw off her own jacket and unbuttoned her blouse.

She felt her muscles flinch away as he touched her through her underclothes. She still bent forward to kiss his mouth. It wasn't the same mouth as she had used to kiss, over a year ago. But it wasn't that that mattered. What mattered, terribly, as soon as her lips touched it, was the realisation that it wasn't Mike's mouth. She drew back a little, but his lips searched for hers and he pulled her head back down to his, stroking her hair clumsily with his bad hand. Realising it was too late to do anything else, she shut her eyes and let him go on with what she had started.

It was over quite quickly. After his spasm, which was accompanied by an almost-despairing cry that she had never heard from him before, he rolled away, again careful to keep his scarred side away from her. They lay on their backs, and he lit a cigarette. Neither of them said a word. It was a grey afternoon and the light in the room was flat. When she could stand the silence no longer, she pulled her skirt down over her thighs and reached for her blouse, crumpled at the end of the bed.

'Do you have to go?'

'I promised I'd meet Cec from work. Haven't seen her in ages. And I have to be back at Rawdon tomorrow.' She didn't invite him to join them, and all he said was: 'I don't know when I shall see you again.'

'No. I'm not sure when I shall get another leave. Things are awfully busy at the moment.'

'I really want to get back on ops, you know.'

'I know.'

'Only trouble is, I don't much fancy getting shot up again. I have the feeling I shouldn't get out of it a second time. I was the only one, you know. When we were hit, I think I must have been blown out of the cockpit. I was alone in the sky, when I came to, just falling. No idea what happened to the crate. There's been no trace of any of the others – I checked. All of them gone. Obliterated. Except me. I don't think I'd have that kind of luck twice, do you?'

'Maybe you won't need it.'

He laughed. 'Oh, you need luck. Over those German cities, you need the devil's own luck. Every night. Thing is, I'm pretty convinced I've used up my ration.'

'Then for God's sake, why go back? They can't honestly want you, with your hand like that. You've done your bit. Let someone else have a go.'

'Some poor kid straight out of pilot training, you mean. Do you have any clue how many aircraft don't even make it back from their first trip? I'm a statistical freak, you know, Charlie – the man who's outlived his generation. I'm like the sole survivor of one of those Pals' Regiments that went off to the Somme. Everyone I joined with is gone now. My crew, obviously. Denys, Bateman, Cooke, even Codrington. All better pilots than me. Better men. That's why I have to go back, don't you see? I belong with my cohort. Dammit, I belong to this war. It's put its mark on me plain enough, hasn't it? There's nothing for me to do except go back.'

'What about all the things you wanted to do before the war? Politics? What about that?'

He toppled a column of ash into a saucer on the bedside table: 'Christ! What a pill I must have been. What the hell made me think I knew how to run the country – at twenty-one? At least the war has done one good thing if it's saved the world from the prospect of William Hartwell MP.' He turned his head on the pillow and looked at her. 'Sorry. Were you counting on being an MP's wife?'

She laughed: 'Always hated the idea, actually.'

'Why the hell didn't you say so?'

'I don't think it would have made much difference in those days, would it?'

He thought for a moment. 'Don't suppose it would. Whatever did you see in me, Charlie?'

She stared up at a crack that ran across the ceiling from the cornice to the ceiling rose. She wasn't sure she knew. The woman she had become, the woman the war had put its mark on just as surely, if not as cruelly, as it had marked Bill, found it almost impossible to recall what the girl she had once been had thought or felt about anything. She tried to remember that fresh spring morning in Putney, the day of the Varsity Race, and what she had felt as he left her clutching that little velvet box. 'That boundless confidence of yours was pretty powerful stuff, I suppose. The way you wanted everything from everybody all the time. The way you made anything seem possible. It was terribly exciting to a young girl.'

'Sounds like maybe I ought to try being an egocentric bastard again, if I want you to carry on loving me like you used to. Trouble is,

I don't remember how it felt any more. To be that sure of everything.'

She didn't know what to say. She swung her legs over the side of the bed, put on her blouse and her underwear and walked round the room collecting her things. He lay and smoked and watched her, but made no move to get up.

'I have to go.'

'I see that.'

She came over to the bed and bent down to kiss him. He watched her steadily as she lowered her lips to his. The contact was gentle and dry, and she was all at once certain it must feel as horribly empty to him as it did to her. Surely now she could tell him the truth.

As she straightened up, he said: 'Don't leave me, Charlie.'

She tried to swallow. Now or never. His eyes were on her, ice blue and as demanding and determined to have his own way as ever they had been. 'I know it's not fair of me to ask, but I think it would make it easier to get in the crate and go over there again if I knew you were here waiting for me. You're the only one left, Charlie. Everyone else has gone now. If I didn't have you to come back to, I think I might just drift off out of it, like a barrage balloon with its hawser cut.'

She stood looking down at him. The damage to his face and neck finished abruptly at the line of his flying-jacket. The skin below the line was pale and young and unmarred. The contrast between the brutalised flesh and the untouched made him seem unbearably vulnerable.

'I'm sorry, you know, to put you through it all again. If I was braver, I wouldn't ask. I came here intending not to ask. But I don't seem to be able to help it. It's your fault for being so beautiful. Can't understand why I didn't remember. You will marry me, won't you, Charlie? It's all I want now.'

She didn't know what to say. She opened her mouth. Nothing came out. The words 'I CAN'T!' beat against her temples from the inside of her skull, like a prisoner beating his fists on a steel cell door. His eyes held hers and she felt herself nodding. She knew she ought to kiss him goodbye, but it was impossible to bend down to meet those stranger's lips again. Everything she was capable of giving him had already been drawn from her. All she wanted now was to be out of this room. 'I have to go, Bill. Write to me. With your new address. We'll ... work out leaves and things.'

He stared straight up at her through the rising smoke from his cigarette with a faint smile, until she could stand it no longer. Then she turned and went away. The room was empty without her in it, as if her going had left only inanimate furniture behind. For a while he lay, as slack as the mattress, as lank as the curtains, until the cigarette burned down to his good fingers and he stubbed it out with a bitter yelp.

He sat up and reached for his trousers, pulling them on one-handed and hauling up the braces over his un-buttoned shirt. He crossed to the window and lit another cigarette. The room gave on to the front of the hotel, three floors above the life passing by on Westbourne Terrace. Behind the dingy net curtain, the single sash window was cross-hatched with blast tape so that looking through it reminded him of the wire fences at the camp. He shuddered and was in the act of turning away when he spotted her. She'd crossed the street from the hotel and was walking fast in the direction of Paddington underground station. For the last three hours he'd been studying her, detail by detail – hair, eyes, lips, hands, waist, legs, skin. Now here she was, presented whole, in long-shot. Not a girl playing at being an adult. Not a wild coltish thing looking to him with bated breath to tell her who and what she should be. Her bright hair shone in the

265

drab crowd, and she seemed to stand straighter and walk faster than the shuffling mob through which she moved. 'My God,' he thought, 'she's so completely alive,' and it struck him that the way she strode through the crowd was the exact way he used to walk. It had always been he who hurried back towards the world and its affairs, and she who was left standing at the window. Now she was the one sloughing off her bedroom skin within a dozen steps of the door while he stood here, haunted by her absence. Haunted by a whole mass of things. As far removed from the hurrying figures in the street as if he was flying above them in a bomber at ten thousand feet, in a cold metal and plexi-glass cell of little ease that he hated and feared and which was the only place he made any sense to himself now.

He watched her until she ran down into the Underground, and he envied her, and he wanted her, and he hated her and he was more determined than ever not to let her go.

31

Charlie had arranged to meet Cecilia in the bar at the Ritz. It was the last thing she wanted, but they had had no time to talk when she arrived the night before and it was months since they had seen each other. The bar was hectic but she instantly spotted Cec, sitting by herself at a small table, with a two thirds-drunk glass of lager beer in front of her. Her Wrens uniform only amplified the impression of a diffident girl who has just been made a Prefect and isn't yet sure what's expected of her.

Cec jumped up and hugged her. 'Thank goodness you've come. The waiters keep looking at me like I oughtn't to be here. I was going to go and walk up and down Piccadilly for a bit till you came.'

'Don't be an ass, Cec. You've as much right to be here as anyone. Do you want another drink?'

Charlie caught the eye of one of the waiters. He shimmered over: 'Yes, miss?'

'Two large whiskies, please. White Horse, if you have it.'

'Of course, miss.'

'Charlie, I don't … '

'I'll drink it if you don't want it. I was just showing him you're an adult. How do you manage to look so absurdly young, Cec? Everyone else looks so tired and old.'

'You don't.'

'God, I do. I feel it anyway. Old as the hills.'

'I bet Bill didn't think so. Come on, I'm dying to hear. It's so romantic. I want to know absolutely everything about it. Is he as handsome as ever?'

'I don't know,' said Charlie. 'Look, before we get into all that, I'd better go and telephone to Rawdon. Let them know I'll be back tomorrow.'

Piddington fielded the call. 'Sorry, miss. They're not here. The GOC had to fly up to Scotland. And Captain Dixon's gone, of course. We're waiting for his replacement to arrive.'

'What do you mean, "Captain Dixon's gone"? Gone where? Scotland?'

'No, miss. I mean he's gone to his new outfit. General Hobart approved the transfer and he left this afternoon.'

'I don't understand, Piddington. You're not making sense.'

'Funny, I could of sworn as I was speaking the King's English. Let me have another crack. Captain Dixon's transferred to the Royal Engineers. He's to have a troop of AVREs.'

'But Hobo made him promise to stay until ... well, to stay. He can't have transferred.'

'I'm sorry about that miss, seeing as he has. Like I said, the general signed the orders himself. And they seemed friendly enough at the end. There was no parting of brass rags. Not as far as I could tell. Will there be anything else, miss?'

'What?'

'Anything else I can do for you?'

'No. Yes. Just let General Hobart know that I'll be back tomorrow, will you, if he comes back and should be asking for me.'

'I don't think he'll be here today, miss. But if he comes, I'll tell him.'

'Thanks. One last thing – Captain Dixon. Do you know where he's been posted?'

'Somewhere in Hampshire, I think.'

'I see. Thanks. Well, see you tomorrow then.' She walked slowly back into the bar and sat down. She felt frozen stiff and in need of something to thaw her out. Cecilia hadn't touched her whisky so she leaned over, her fingers hovering over the tumbler. 'You want that?'

'Not really.'

Charlie picked it up and drained it. Cec looked alarmed. 'Perhaps we should get something to eat. All that whisky on an empty stomach ... '

'I had lunch at Rules.'

'That must have been hours ago.'

'I suppose it was. All right, where shall we go?'

'Trocadero's not far. Be easier if we go before it gets dark.'

The two girls set off along Piccadilly arm in arm. The light was beginning softly to fade, and Charlie realised it had been another beautiful spring day. With the weather in her head set to storm and cataclysm she hadn't noticed it at all, but now, walking with her good little sister's hip nudging her own, she felt her mood lift a little. Of course, everything was a terrible mess. Bill had come back and Mike had gone. And she'd said she would marry Bill, though she didn't love him – and that she wouldn't marry Mike, though she did. It was hardly surprising when the whole world was in a terrible mess. If Churchill and Roosevelt couldn't sort out the mess the world was in, it was hardly surprising if she couldn't sort her little bit of it. She giggled.

'What's funny?' said Cec.

For answer, Charlie hooked her elbow round a passing lamp-post and swung them both round it in a great arc. Cec shrieked and stumbled up the kerb. 'Charlie. Whatever's up? Are you tight?'

Charlie let go of the lamp-post and pondered. 'Maybe I am. A bit. Not enough. Come on.'

The Troc was frantic as ever. Charlie made straight for the Long Bar, but Cec pulled back on her arm, like she used to do when they were little and Charlie was trying to lead her into some adventure that would get them both into trouble in the nursery. 'Not the Long Bar, Charlie. It's always full of soldiers and their tarts. I thought we were going to eat. I want to talk to you without anyone else butting in or trying to buy us drinks.'

Reluctantly, Charlie let them be shown to a table in the Grill Room. As soon as they'd ordered, Cec leaned across and took her sister's hands. 'Now, tell me about Bill. You can't put it off any longer. I'm dying to know how he is.'

Charlie had been meaning to get out of it somehow. Out of telling. But the shining, trusting eyes, the warm, affectionate fingers in hers, the throb of the whisky all worked on her at once and she heard herself saying, 'Awful.'

'Awful? Bill? Why, what did he do? What did he say?'

'He wants to get married.'

'What's so awful about that? You've been engaged for yonks anyway.'

'Not yonks.'

'Yes you have. Yonks and yonks. Since before the war. I was in ankle socks practically.'

'Well, maybe we have. I expect you're right, if it wasn't for the war, we'd have got married ages ago. Or called it off. One or the other.'

'Called it off? Why ever would you call it off? Bill's divine. The handsomest man in England, Mummy always says.'

'I doubt she'll say it anymore.' Charlie hadn't meant that to come out either.

'Why? What's happened?'

There was nothing else for it now. She took a deep breath: 'He was burned, Cec. When he was shot down. That's why it took so long to hear he was alive. He was in a Jerry hospital. Having operations. Skin grafts.'

'Oh. Poor Bill. Is he, I mean, is it ... is it bad? Can you ... did you recognise him?'

'It's not as bad as all that. I mean, it is his face, but only one side. And one of his hands is pretty awful. But it's still Bill all right. He is different though. A lot less sure of himself.'

'Well, maybe that's not so bad. I mean, he was a bit *too* handsome for his own good before, wasn't he? Bit of a honeypot, always surrounded by lots of bees. Maybe it'll be ... '

'Cec, are you're trying to say that now his looks are spoiled he's less likely to stray?'

'No. No, I wasn't saying that. You know I wasn't.' Cec blushed. 'I was just saying, oh, I don't know what I was saying. Just that Bill was always so, I don't know, everything was so easy for him. Maybe now he'll know what it's like to be an ordinary mortal.'

'You're right about that. He's definitely feeling mortal. He's still determined to fly though. Says he belongs with the men he joined up with. Only trouble is – they've almost all gone west while he's been in jug.'

'Poor Bill.'

'Cec, you keep saying that. Would you mind not? It's not helping.'

'Sorry. It's just ... oh Lord.'

'What is it?'

'Don't look round. It's that dreadful ... '

Too late. Charlie had already turned and seen that dreadful Freddie Quiller for herself. What was worse was that he had seen Cecilia and was advancing on their table with a revolting smile. Which failed him somewhat when he realised that the young woman sitting with her back to him was Charlie. By then it was too late to change tack. He faltered, then he squared his shoulders and hitched the horrible smile back into place. 'Cecilia. And Charlotte.' His emphasis on the 'and' suggested it was possible to have a little too much of a good thing. 'What a turn up for the books. Your mother will be so thrilled.'

'Mother's here?'

'Yes,' he glanced behind him. 'Ah, yes, here she comes now. Veronica, you'll never guess who's here.'

'Who is it, darling? Good Lord. Charlotte! Whatever are you doing in London? You never telephoned to say you were coming up. Cecilia, why on earth didn't you tell me your sister was in town? Anyone would think the two of you were going out of your way to avoid me.'

'Don't be silly, Mummy,' said Cecilia. 'Charlie didn't know she was coming till the last minute. It's because of Bill. He's back in England. And of course he wanted to see her, so she got special leave.'

'Bill's in England? How on earth did he manage that?'

'He escaped. Got out of that horrible camp and made it all the way back here. Isn't it wonderful? And with burns to his face too. Charlie says he's ... '

Cec faltered and looked at Charlie. What had she said? What had she been in the middle of saying when Freddie Quiller appeared? Cec wasn't sure she knew.

'Burns? Oh, how killing for him. How bad is it? He's not a candidate for Archie McIndoe, is he?'

Charlie shook her head. 'He's not too bad really. The Germans looked after him, actually. One of his hands is pretty messed up, and one side of his face ... '

'Poor Bill. Such a crying shame that it should happen to him, of all people. He was *such* a beautiful boy. When Archie first brought him home from Shrewsbury, I almost fell for him myself.'

'Veronica. Really!'

'Oh, Freddie. Don't huff. You never saw him, I suppose? No. Well, what is he going to do now? I suppose they'll give him a desk job. He won't like that at all. Not Bill. Still, it's good in one way at least. I mean, there'll be no reason now why the two of you shouldn't get married. You've been engaged long enough.'

'He's going back on ops. This week, actually.'

'But I thought you said his hand was … Oh, well I suppose it can't be that bad if they're letting him fly again.'

'It is quite bad, actually. He's bullied them into passing him fit. You know what he's like.'

'I'm sure the medicos know what they're doing,' said Freddie. 'They wouldn't put him back on ops if he wasn't up to it.'

'Excuse me. As far as I'm aware you've never met Bill Hartwell, so you're hardly in a position to know.'

'Charlie!'

Charlie dropped her chin and stared at the tablecloth. There was a silence, which Quiller broke. 'Still working for old Hobo?'

Charlie nodded, relieved that at least the conversation had moved away from the subject of Bill and marriage.

'I hear he created a hell of a rumpus among the Yanks the other week. Telling them how to run their exercise, when he was only there on sufferance. Couldn't wait to be rid of him, by all accounts. Is there anyone he doesn't fall out with?'

Charlie's head came up again. 'Plenty, actually. Plenty of people think he's the best trainer of a division in the whole Army. Even the Prime Minister says so. It's usually only people who don't do their jobs properly he falls out with.' She tried to make her smile look as sweet and innocent as one of Cec's, whilst watching the colour rise from under Quiller's collar and spread through the broken veins in his jowls. Maybe it was the whisky she'd had. Or maybe it was the day she'd had. Whichever it was, she couldn't resist adding: 'CO says we'd be better off putting the whole of tank procurement under the RAF. He says at least the Air Force understands the importance of machinery in modern warfare. Unlike the Army.'

Quiller spluttered, his whole face purple now. 'The bloody cheek of the man. That's just like him. No loyalty. No discretion. Never mind that the Army's put up with him blowing his trumpet for years with this one cracked note: All-Armoured! All-Armoured! As if nothing and nobody else mattered a damn. Never mind that his ruddy Heath-Robinson devices are making us a laughing stock with the Yanks. Hobo's Funnies. There's nothing bloody funny about them in my book. Well, if he wants any more he can find them elsewhere. I'm damned if I'll lift a finger in his cause from now on.'

Charlie jumped up and pulled her jacket off the back of the chair. She swayed a bit from the sudden movement, but steadied herself. 'Don't you see? You're exactly the type Hobo says would sooner lose the war than get your backside into gear.'

'Charlotte!' said her mother. 'That's an unforgivable thing to say. What the devil has got into you? Apologise to Freddie at once.'

Whatever devil had got into Charlie was not finished yet. Her mouth opened and quite without hesitation she heard herself say. 'What's unforgivable, Mother, is people whose job it is to further the war effort acting more like Fifth Columnists by trying to put a spoke in the wheel of those who are trying to win it. What's unforgivable is that people who should be working every hour God sends actually seem to spend half their time out on the town with other men's wives.'

'Charlie!'

She turned away, wobbled, steadied and marched towards the door. Behind her, she could hear Veronica apologising and Quiller trying to laugh it off in a slightly huffed manner. The clatter of a busy dining room drowned the sound of the two of them consoling each other a little more with every stride she put between herself and their table but she knew for sure now, she could tell by their tone, which was full of complicity even as they struggled with the embarrassment of the bomb she'd tossed into their laps. There was no getting away from the fact that her mother and Freddie Quiller were lovers.

She headed straight for the Long Bar. It might be full of soldiers and tarts, but so, apparently, was the Grill Room. White-jacketed barmen were skittering about in droves behind the deeply florid marble counter. Between her and them the crowd stood four deep and almost everyone was intent on catching the eye of one of the bartenders. It was as if the entire mob had just come out of the desert after a month without water. For all she knew, they had.

She felt sober and chastened. The depth of her bad manners and, worse, her clumsy indiscretion, began to sink in and she felt a horrible chill in her stomach that had nothing to do with the fact that she'd walked out on her dinner. What in God's name would the CO say, when he found out she'd been queering his pitch with Quiller? She felt she might be sick.

A hand touched her arm. It was Cec. The sisters looked at each other for a moment, and then hugged. 'I am a dolt, Cec,' whispered Charlie in her sister's ear. Cecilia rubbed her back. 'You've had a horrible day.'

'You don't know the half of it. Let's get a drink.'

Cec held her at arm's length. 'Wouldn't you sooner come back to Chelsea? I'll make cocoa and we can sit up in bed and tell each other everything that's happened the last few months. I have a life too, you know.'

Charlie felt guilty on another front now. How many fronts was it possible to feel guilt on? Surely, there must be a limit. Surely she

275

must be reaching it. How could she have been so self-centred as not to realise that little Cec probably had her admirers too? Looking as she did, how could she not? She nodded. 'Of course, I'm being an ass. It'll take us ages to get a drink here anyway. Let's go.'

As they walked towards the door something made her hesitate. One of the men standing at the bar with his back to her struck her as familiar. He had his arm draped casually round the neck of the plump little blonde on his left. His right hand was shoved deep in his pocket. As she stood, staring, he dipped his head to catch what the girl was trying to shout in his ear, gave a laugh and tossed his head in the way Bill always used to do when his hair was longer and he needed to flick it out of his eyes. She caught a glimpse of the man's profile as he did it. An unspoiled profile so like the old Bill Hartwell she could almost swear it was him.

Cec, feeling her step falter, must have thought she was going to change her mind and insist on another drink. She tugged on Charlie's arm. 'Please Charlie, let's go. You've had enough for one day.'

Charlie was too exhausted and dizzied even to say how true this was, and in how many senses. Everything she'd done today had been wrong, hopeless, stupid beyond belief. She had absolutely no idea what to do now, and couldn't help thinking that whatever she did it would turn out to be just as wrong as everything else had been. That being so, she allowed herself to be led away to Chelsea and cocoa.

It was an odd sensation to be detached from Hobo. Sitting in the train to Southampton, it occurred to Mike that it wasn't unlike the strange, doubtful silence at the end of a bombardment.

It was hard to believe that he was free. Free for the first time in over a year from the machine-gun delivery of orders and ideas, all to be acted on immediately. Free from worrying about which of Hobo's unexpressed commands he might have failed to anticipate. Free from the grinding urgency of the CO's single-minded mission to bring the Division to a state of battle-readiness in time.

Released from his responsibilities, there was nothing to stop his thoughts running on Charlie. What kept looping in his head was the way she had raised her cheek for him to kiss when they parted at the Hobarts' garden gate. It was the gesture of a cousin, or the wife of a friend, and yet the softness of her cheek against his lips had run through him like electrical current and left him humming like a wire for ten minutes after Lady Hobart's little Austin had taken her away. Whatever she said about going to sort things out, he could not convince himself that Charlie's reunion with her bomber pilot would result in anything other than a resumption of the old status quo. Clearly, the man had far more charm and force of personality than he, to have convinced her to marry him in the first place. Now he was back, the wounded hero of a rare home run from Germany. If she hadn't broken with him when he was a distant ghost, she was hardly likely to do it now. That demure offering of her cheek for him to touch with his lips surely confirmed it. She had had her adventure, and now she would resume the conventional path her life had been meant to take.

That being so, clearly only a fool would keep on hankering after her. If he was going to make a decent tank commander, his mind needed to be clear and focused. The men for whom he was about to become responsible deserved better than to be led by a whimpering, broken-hearted idiot. He made a pact with himself that he would take this one journey to sift through the memories he had of her – all the snapshots in his mind: the touch of her skin against his; her smell, that made him want to bury his nose in the curve of her throat and sob; her throaty little giggle; the flash of her eyes; the way her gloved hands sat on the steering-wheel and her hair rolled at the nape of her neck; the way she threw her head back when … He would indulge himself one last time by bringing them out to examine one by one as England clattered by outside the window. And then he would stop. At Southampton, he would get off the train and leave them all behind, a parcel discarded on the luggage rack. At Southampton, he would give up being a man in love and go back to being a soldier.

Southampton came far too soon. Everyone else in the carriage jumped up from their seats before the train had even rumbled to a stand-still, marshalling their luggage. As they started to file down on to the platform, Mike didn't move.

'All change!' shouted the guard, moving along the corridor. Seeing Mike, he even opened the door to the carriage. 'All change here, please.'

'Yes,' thought Mike. 'That's the ticket.' But into his mind's eye slipped a vision of Charlie, staring up into the sky in a field in Suffolk, shielding her eyes with her hand, watching a Dakota circle overhead. He shut his eyes, as if that would help, and gave himself a stern order. When the image finally dissolved, he hoisted his kit bag off the rack and stepped down on to the busy platform without looking back at what he'd left behind.

An army driver was waiting for him outside the station. As they drove out through the city he saw how badly Southampton had been bombed. Most of the centre was reduced to piles of grey rubble, through which weeds were growing with all the devil-may-care vigour of spring.

'They've caught a packet here, haven't they?' he said to the driver, who grunted, 'Portsmouth too. You'll see. It's the docks they're after. Not that they're too choosy.'

His new regiment was based near Gosport, in a long-evacuated school that overlooked Stokes Bay. He was directed to the headmistress's office, where Tiny Hay-Wood produced a bottle of Scotch and two glasses to celebrate his return to the Royal Engineers.

'Not before time. You'll be leading First Troop. You've got experienced sergeants commanding your other two tanks. They'll keep you on the straight and narrow. Though I'm sure you'll soon get the hang of it – versatile chap like you.'

Mike wasn't sure whether there was a friendly dig in there. If there was he chose to ignore it. 'I'm looking forward to it.'

'Are you? I wonder. You may find it strange being in the dark like the rest of us after so long on the inside track.'

'Actually, Tiny, I'm more than ready for it. Just keep me busy, will you? I don't want to be sitting on my hands.'

'Don't worry, there's plenty to do. We've only just got a full set of AVREs. We're the lucky ones. Regiment's still hellish short. And still no ammo. I hope old Hobo knows what he's doing. If our Flying Dustbins don't get here soon, it'll be like trying to win Agincourt without any arrows. Come on, you might as well meet your troop.'

They downed their Scotch and strolled across hockey pitches where the grass had grown long and lush to a walled kitchen garden, now a secret tank harbour, with camouflage nets strung between ancient fruit trees. The trees were in full bloom and pollen-laden bees criss-crossed the air on flight-paths of their own devising, ignoring the interlopers in their immemorial airfield. Hay-Wood pointed to three Churchills grouped in the farthest corner. 'That's First Troop, parked on the asparagus beds. Used to be the headmistress's pride and joy, according to the old gardener. He drops by most days to suck his teeth in horror at what we've done to the place.'

The side hatch of the nearest tank was open, and from inside came a loud roaring. As they walked up, there was a clang and a large chunk of steel fell out of the hatch and landed at the officers' feet.

'What the devil?' said Mike. Two men standing beside the tank turned and, seeing officers, saluted. A head in a welding mask appeared in the open turret and the mask was lifted to reveal pale eyes in a smoke-grimed face.

'What in God's name do you think you're doing?' Mike poked at what looked like a section of the inside of the turret with the toe of his boot. The newly cut metal was scorching the damp grass and a steamy scent of hot steel and stewing greens rose through the air.

'Just a few mods, sir. It's a bit tight in here, and we thought, like, if we need to get out in a hurry it would help if the turret were a bit wider, like. Especially if we've got Mae Wests on and such, crossing the Channel. They're over-engineered anyway, these old Churchills. Few pounds of steel won't be missed. Honest, you'll never know the difference.'

'I might, if the turret gets hit by a shell.'

'All due respect, sir, if we get an Eighty-eight through the turret it'll tek a lot more than fifty pounds of steel to save you, especially with a full payload of ammo.'

'A lot of crews are making mods like this,' said Hay-Wood. 'I don't see the harm in it if it makes them more confident in the vehicle. That's Lance-Corporal Rendall, by the way. Fifteen years in the Royal Engineers. If he says you don't need it, you probably don't. Chaps, this is Captain Dixon, your new troop commander. Show him the ropes, would you, but don't mollycoddle him, he's quite quick on the uptake. Corporal Williams, your driver, and Hipkiss your gunner. You're to have a co-driver and a wireless operator to make the set. We're waiting on replacements at the moment. Williams will introduce you to the other crews in your troop, won't you Taff? Right, I'll leave you to get acquainted.'

He gave Mike a thump on the back and strolled off towards another grouping of tanks that had made a home amongst the headmistress's soft fruit cages. A third troop had established itself next to what had once been a long greenhouse, the glass pitched against a sunny south-facing wall. For grapes or peaches, thought Mike, his mouth watering at the thought. Most of the glass was gone now, whether from general neglect before the war or shaken out by the Luftwaffe's attacks on Portsmouth he couldn't tell. It was still a sunny and sheltered spot, though, and a tankman lounged in the doorway with a mug of tea. Mike's mouth watered again. Tea at least was something he could get.

There was water coming to the boil in a sawn-off petrol can over a small fire beside the tank. Mike nodded at the gunner, a slight man in his late twenties, whose scrawny neck and prominent Adam's apple stuck out of a battledress top that was far too big for him. 'Why don't you mash the tea, then you can show me round the tank? What's left of it.'

'All right, sir.'

'Hipkiss, isn't it? Haberdasher, am I right?'

The man looked up from lifting the can off the fire with a rag wrapped round his fist. "'S right, but 'ow did you … ?'

'I was in Catterick the day you met Major-General Hobart and told him you minded your own business.'

Hipkiss grinned. 'Thought I was for it that day, sir. Thought I was for the ruddy high-jump and no mistake. Lucky Napoleon said that thing about us all being shopkeepers or he'd have bitten me 'ead clean off.'

'Maybe. So you're a gunner now, are you? Seems about right for a haberdasher. After all, if anyone should be able to tell a yard by eye … '

'That's right. Don't matter if it's measuring calico or chucking high explosive. A yard's a yard, ain't it?' Hipkiss shook a heap of tea and powdered milk into the billy and stirred it. The welder and the driver had come over to the fire and thrown themselves down, waiting for their tea.

Mike squatted on the grass: 'You're all sappers, are you? How do you like being in tanks?'

'We're not all sappers,' said Hipkiss. 'Corporal Williams here, he's Royal Armoured Corps. They don't trust us not to scrape the paintwork, so a lot of our drivers are RAC.'

'Bloody lunatics,' said the Welshman. 'It's not a question of paintwork. They kept knocking the corners off houses. Piles of rubble wherever they went – and that was before they started trying to knock anything down.'

'Well, Corporal, if they're that good at it when they're not even trying, I look forward to seeing what they can do when they mean it.'

'Chance'd be a fine thing, sir.' Hipkiss started to tip the tea into a cluster of enamel pint mugs. 'We still ain't got ammo for the mortar. Be nice to have a chance to get the 'ang of firing it, especially seein' as

282

there ain't no gun-sight. At the moment we're just hopin' it makes as big a mess as they say.'

'If it helps, I was at the trials and from what I've seen it works like a charm. Limited range. Best at about eighty yards. Definitely for assault on static targets, rather than in a running battle. But bloody effective, used properly.'

'So do you think we'll get chance to have a bash with it, before we go into action, like?'

'I hope so, Williams. There's a hell of a pressure on the munitions factories at the moment, but we shan't be much use in the invasion without those mortars. Knowing who's in charge, I have a feeling heaven and earth is being shifted to get them here.'

'You mean that General Hobart, sir?'

'Yes, Hipkiss. I worked on his staff, before this.'

'I can see why you fancied a change, sir. Think I'd sooner face Jerry than him every morning. He's a rum 'un. A stickler, you might say.'

Mike smiled, sentimental already. 'You might say that, Hipkiss. A rum 'un, a stickler and plenty more besides.'

33

Hobo was in a filthy temper. Burton could have crowned Mike Dixon for leaving them in the lurch at such a crucial moment. Just when they were in the home straight, and the Divisional Staff was finally a stable unit. Dixon's replacement was predictably hopeless. All he'd had to do was collate the figures on AVRE conversions to date and how many of the mortar bombs to go with them had been produced. It was only en route to their meeting in Whitehall that Hobo had checked his report and found it was fit for nothing. Dixon would have done it without a murmur. But blasted Dixon wasn't here, and as a result they were without the facts and figures. Burton had tried to placate him but the Old Man had been forcefully blunt: facts and figures were ammunition. Without ammunition, it would be almost impossible to press home the assault he had planned on Freddie Quiller.

As they marched up the steps of the War Office, the doorman snapped a salute and had it returned with a scowl. They were early, Hobo reasoning that to have command of the ground might compensate at least a little for their lamentable lack of fire-power. In the conference room he stationed himself on the far side of the table, opposite the door and with his back to the windows, so that the enemy should be forced to squint into the sun. Burton sat down quietly beside him, hoping against hope that the news would be better than he feared. The other participants in the meeting arrived, singly and in pairs, civilians and army personnel from various departments and sub-departments, men from the industrial firms and Burton watched each one of them falter at the sight of General Hobart and glance around, trying to find for themselves a place where they might avoid his baleful gaze.

Last to arrive was Major-General Quiller. He alone refused to quail before the ferocious stare. 'Ah, Patrick,' he said. 'Good of you to make it. All the way from Suffolk or Yorkshire, or wherever. Only really a routine progress report today. Things seem to be rolling along as smoothly as could be expected, under the circumstances. But I shouldn't second-guess the experts, should I?' He turned to a lieutenant-colonel, who had taken a seat a few places to his left. 'Hawkins, you'd better give us the latest production numbers.'

Hawkins looked a lot less comfortable than his chief. He fussed with his papers and started to read figures from a table in a dull drone, perhaps in hope that the more monotonous his delivery the less likely anyone would be able to make sense of them. For a couple of minutes it seemed to be working. Then he faltered and Hobo pounced: 'Yes, yes. But how many AVREs?'

'Sir?'

'Armoured Vehicles Royal Engineers. How many Churchills have been converted to AVRE to date – and how many are scheduled before the end of May?'

Hawkins er-ed and shuffled his papers about, and umm-ed. He er-ed a bit more.

'For God's sake, man, it's a simple enough question. I have two regiments of sappers waiting for the equipment they need to breach the Western Wall. Most of 'em haven't even used their main armament yet. It's all very well to stand in your turret and shout "Bang!" on exercise, but it'll be bugger all use against an eighty-eight millimetre on D-Day.'

Quiller raised a small, fleshy hand. 'Patrick, please. Surely even you can comprehend that, at a time like this, re-fitting armour is not the *only* priority. The infantry needs equipment quite as badly as you tank boys. Not to mention the RAF. They're getting through bombers like hot cakes every night. Everything has to take its turn, even your Funnies.'

'Take our turn? What do you think this is, Quiller, a ladies' excuse-me? It may have escaped your notice, but we have a rather immovable deadline. We can't all sit around taking turns as if we're at some village hop. There's only a few weeks left to get all the kit we need. If we don't get it, the thing won't fly. It's your job to make it happen, not to sit on your complacent backside like a fairground barker, telling me to wait my turn on the waltzers. So have the decency to stop patronising me and tell me what you mean to do about my conversions.'

Burton could see the muscles working in his face even when he'd finished. Major-General Quiller's, by contrast, had turned a dull burgundy, the flush extending all the way from the slabs of his cheeks to where the wattles of his throat crammed into his collar. Most of the other faces in the room flamed in sympathy or awkwardness. Burton looked down and twiddled with his pen. Hobo was right, of course, but even so …

'Four a week.' Hawkins had finally found his place in the right table. Everyone had forgotten all about him. 'What?' growled Hobo.

'Four a week, sir. To do more, we'd have to re-tool another production line and they're all fully committed.'

'Four a week? How many T4s do the Russians turn out a day, do you think? We'd better pray to God that Uncle Joe Stalin never turns his attentions on us.'

Quiller finally regained the power of speech: 'It can't be done any faster. Hawkins is quite right.'

'Then I shan't be able to deliver the formations I've promised to the Prime Minister and Field Marshal Brooke.'

Quiller threw down his pen and folded his arms. 'Dammit,

Hobart. Everyone knows you like to go running to Churchill and Brooke, telling tales behind the hand. Well, it won't do you any good this time. There simply isn't the capacity. You'll have to make do and mend like everybody else.'

'That's it,' thought Burton. And it was.

'What if your "make do and mend" is the ha'p'orth of tar that costs the ship, Quiller? What will you say then, with a hundred thousand lives on your conscience?'

'They won't … '

'No, of course they won't. Nothing ever will be, will it? Not when you've followed protocol to the letter and everyone's had their tea-breaks. What could you possibly have to reproach yourself for, even if the war is lost? Well, if you won't help me get my kit, I shall have to go to the commercial firms. See what Lord Nuffield has to say.'

Quiller shrugged. 'You're welcome to try, of course, but Nuffield's flat out as it is. His man Scott's here.' He nodded down the table at a thin man in a brown suit. His hair was neatly, sparsely slicked across his scalp and he had the look of an engineer about him, a dog-tired one. 'They're actually doing your conversions at MG already. You can rail at me all you like in that offensive manner of yours. What I'm telling you is the reality.'

Hobo stared at Scott for a minute, until the man dropped his gaze and gave a small shake of the head. The General stood and picked up his briefcase. 'I don't like your damned reality, Quiller. It's going to get a lot of men killed and, what's more, it might cost us the beach-head.'

'If it comes to that, Hobart, I don't like your damned self-right-eousness. Coming in here talking about decency, you of all people. Always convinced your all-armoured idea should take precedence over everything else. If they're any kind of soldiers, your sappers will do their job, with or without a Funny to hide in. I don't see the Yanks clamouring for them. If their demolition boys don't need 'em I don't see why ours do. There's a lot more essential equipment I'll push through before I prioritise one of your pet follies.'

Hobo jammed the briefcase under his arm and walked round the table. Burton stood up and followed. When Hobo reached the door, he turned. 'You're a fool, Quiller. I'm not having my men sacrificed by a fool. I'll get those AVREs if I have to do the welding myself.'

As the echo of the slammed door faded, Quiller unfolded his arms and leaned back in his chair. There was a collective release of held breath around the table. One man coughed. Quiller spoke as if he were talking to the ceiling. 'Sorry about that. As you can see, the man's quite impossible. No wonder they never gave him a corps. That's what this is all about, you know, his last-ditch scramble to build an empire before the war finishes. Well, not by rail-roading me he doesn't. Now, where were we? Hawkins?'

34

Charlie couldn't quite bring herself to believe what Piddington had told her. She had seen what an important member of Hobo's team Mike had become and knew how the Old Man, so quick to sack men he judged no good, hated to let go anyone really useful. But when she walked into the tack-room at Rawdon, Monica was upon her immediately, eyes alight: 'Charlie, you'll never guess what! Captain Dixon's gone and joined the sappers. Nobody knows what's happened between him and Hobo. He was only up here for a day, collecting his gear and now he's gone to be a troop commander with Tiny Hay-Wood's lot.'

'Oh?' said Charlie, trying to mask her disappointment. She dropped her bag next to the table and leafed through the stack of letters that someone had propped against the up-turned stump of a loaf of bread. If he'd really gone, surely he'd have left something for her. Even it was just a line to tell her how much he hated her. Surely he couldn't have left without a word. Ah, there it was. She lifted it out from among the crumbs, her heart thumping, and then she recognised the hand-writing and the postmark: London W1. Gone was the hard pencil and the cheap rag paper. Bill had been reunited with his fountain pen and his royal blue ink, and she saw at once that it gave back to his writing, even left-handed, some of the bold character of the old days. She flipped through the pile again. Nothing else for her.

'Did you hear me, Charlie? I said Mike Dixon's gone. Or do you know all about it already? Come on, Charlie. Spill. Has he had a row with the Old Man?'

Charlie pushed Bill's letter into her pocket and threw herself into one of the armchairs. All of a sudden she was heartily sick of Mike Dixon and all his works. It wasn't as if it was her fault that she'd been engaged before she met him, or that Bill had made it home. She'd told him she needed time to go and sort things out, hadn't she? And … then she remembered what she'd actually done in London and her indignation ran into the buffers.

'Charlie?'

She looked up at Monica finally. The little gossip was almost dying of anticipation.

'I haven't the faintest clue. All right? I wasn't even there when it happened. I was down in London seeing … '

She instantly wished she could bite off her tongue at the root, but it was too late.

'Of course. How could I have forgotten? This Dixon business has got us all in a tizzy and all the time I suppose all you've been thinking about is this brilliant news about Bill. You've actually seen him, have you? God, how incredibly romantic. Tell all, Charlie. I'm all ears.' Eyes shining, Monica curled herself up into the armchair opposite, like a little girl in her nightdress, hair all brushed, waiting for her bedtime story.

For a moment, Charlie considered spilling the beans. Thought about heaving up the whole mess and vomiting it out on to the rag-rug in front of their little fire, like a gun-dog that has gorged itself on rotten meat and come inside to get it up and feel better. She remembered one of her father's labradors, heaving and heaving and heaving, his shoulder muscles knotting under the strain, before the steaming mess slid out of his jaws on to the kitchen floor and, after a minute's inspection, the look of relief on his face as he turned away, wagging his tail faintly, as if to say, 'Ah well, that's that.' It was tempting.

Except that Monica's excited face told her that she wasn't there to give Charlie a sympathetic pat and clean up after her. Any relief to be had from telling the gory details would soon be outweighed by the whole camp getting to hear the story within about two hours. 'He was fine. He's going back on Ops later this week.'

This was far too bald for Monica, who hugged her knees and settled in for a thorough debrief. 'How did he get home? Did he say? He must have had an incredible time of it. I suppose he'll be up for a medal or something. Did any others escape with him?'

Charlie frowned. 'We didn't talk about it. It didn't seem … ' It hadn't seemed important at all. She realised she hadn't even asked. Had it seemed strange to him, that she had showed so little interest in what must have been an epic journey home? What had he made of her running away from the hotel? Had it been him, at the Troc, with that little blonde? Did he go there to make himself feel better because she'd been so cold to him?

She remembered the letter in her pocket. Perhaps he'd realised that it was hopeless after all and was writing to tell her they needn't go on with the engagement. She stood up. 'Look, Mon, don't take this the wrong way, but I've got heaps to do. The GOC might be back at any time and I've no idea if the Killing Bottle has been checked over the last few days. He's bound to be in a filthy mood, with Captain Dixon gone, so I'd better make sure he's nothing else to complain of.' When Monica started to protest, Charlie grabbed her hat and her jacket and fled.

She was relieved to find nobody else in the cart-shed. She climbed into the driver's seat of the Humber, where she ran her hand over the smooth arc of the steering wheel and touched the Bakelite knobs on the dash one by one. She'd spent so many hours in this car now it felt more like home than anywhere else. She glanced in the mirror at the empty rear seats and thought of all the times she had snatched a look at Mike when he was busy talking or listening or staring out of the window with his elbow on the arm-rest and his chin on his hand. It hurt so much that she reached up and twisted the mirror sharply until it threw her own face back at her. 'Stop it,' she told her reflection. She took Bill's letter out of her pocket and tore it open. There were two sheets of watermarked blue paper folded inside. She hesitated for a minute, all at once unsure what she hoped for, before she unfolded it.

My dearest Charlie, he had written at the top. She stopped again. This was affectionate, but not decisive. It could just as easily be leading to a gentle retreat as to a re-doubling of his claim on her. She wanted to know, but could hardly bear to read on. 'Come on, Charlotte,' she told herself, 'don't be wet.'

My dearest Charlie,

I am sorry to have given you such a horrid shock yesterday. Perhaps it would have been fairer to have warned you, but I was awfully afraid you wouldn't come if I did.

Anyway you did come, and what a sight for sore eyes you were. The chaps in my camp were jealous enough of your photograph. It's a good job they have no idea what a poor imitation it is of the real thing. Seeing you was very like seeing real food for the first time after camp rations. I had almost stopped believing in green vegetables and fresh meat, so that when I first had them on my plate it was rather like a miracle set before a man without faith.

It's embarrassing to admit that I'd almost forgotten you were a real girl too. In my head, you had become your picture, forever looking over your shoulder and laughing. Then to have you sitting across the table, drinking, eating, turning your head so there were so many views of you to take in made me dizzy. Perhaps I shouldn't have hauled you straight off to a hotel but can you honestly blame me? A year as a monk is all very well, but even a real monk would be likely to rend his habit at the sight of you.

Anyway, it was just the tonic I needed and I feel a new man. Not quite my old self, but perhaps that's not altogether a bad thing. I told you I thought I might not last long on ops, but since seeing you I feel differently about it. I thought I had used up my luck, whereas now with you as my talisman I feel I might manage to see it through. That's why I want to marry you, Charlie, the first chance we get. Please say you'll do it. I used to think it was only the non-entities who needed marriage and a child to spur them on. Suddenly it seems vital and there has never been another girl I felt would make me so good a wife.

Send me your answer as soon as you can so I can see about the licence. At the same time let me have a current address for Archie, would you? He and I fell out because he got it into his head that I was a supercilious bastard and not worthy of you. He was probably right, but I have few enough friends left these days and I'd like to show him that the war has improved me somewhat.

I shall be on tenterhooks until you write, so don't keep me in agonies.
In feverish anticipation,
Bill

Charlie re-folded the pages and slid them gently back into their envelope. It seemed it was her fate to become Mrs Hartwell after all. Even before she'd finished reading she'd owned up to herself she wasn't strong enough to resist the new Bill, any more than she had ever resisted the old one. Not alone, anyway. Maybe if Mike had been here. Maybe if Mike had still loved her and wanted to marry her, she would have been able to steel herself to tell Bill he would have to survive without her. But Mike had gone away and left her without a single word.

Today was Wednesday. She didn't have to write back today. Or even tomorrow. She would have to write on Friday though, or Saturday morning at the latest.

35

They went on to Suffolk from London by train. 'There must be a way, Howard,' Hobo was saying as they walked out of Ipswich station and climbed into the staff car. 'It's bad enough having so few Crocodiles ready. We have to have the AVREs. We need that reducing power on the beaches from the start. Photo-reconnaissance is saying the concrete's eleven feet thick now in places. We simply have to have those mortars.'

'I know, sir. But we can't expect any more shipments from America before D-Day. MG are doing all they can, working round the clock. Lagonda's tied up producing the fuel-trailers for the flame-throwers and all our own workshops are flat out too. At this rate I don't see how we're going to get there.'

Hobo stopped in his tracks. 'I won't have that, Howard. Not from you. We need a new idea, that's all. We have to get those conversions done by hook or by crook.'

Burton blushed. It was rare these days that he was rebuked by his chief, and never in such a quiet, resolved fashion. He felt he'd let the Old Man down. He straightened his shoulders and breathed out a long breath. 'Of course, sir. We will.'

It was market day and the streets were busy. The General's driver, new to the job and anxious about it, tried a short-cut and soon found himself in a narrow road with a builder's yard down one side. A big wagon, piled up with rubble, was trying to turn into the yard gates and making heavy weather of it. Two men stood either side of the cab, waving directions to the driver. The Humber slowed to a stop as the wagon reversed up for another try.

'What's the hold-up?'

'Sorry, sir. Lorry blocking the road. Sure he'll get it right in a minute.'

He didn't.

'Christ's sake, man. What are we doing in this damned back-alley in the first place?'

'Sorry, sir. I'll back up and go the other way.'

He put the car into reverse, but as he started to move, Burton leaned forward and touched him on the shoulder. 'Wait a second, would you?'

The driver jammed in the clutch and Hobo glared at his Number One. 'What is it, Burton?'

'Over the wall. Sparks. Someone's welding in there.'

'So they are. What of it?'

'It's a builder's yard, isn't it? I expect it's structural steel they're using for construction. It just occurred to me that's something we haven't thought of. We've tried all the big industrial firms. We never thought of builders, did we? I mean, it's not as if converting a Churchill to AVRE is particularly complicated, is it? Surely any skilled welder could do it if they had the plans ... '

Hobo stared at him for a moment. 'Well, let's go and see, shall we?'

'Now, sir?'

Hobo already had the door open: 'Of course now, Howard. If ever the phrase "no time like the present" counted for something, it's now.'

They squeezed past the juddering flank of the lorry, which was still trying to inch its way between the gate pillars. Inside the yard, they looked around for an office. Hobo nudged Burton and pointed to a far corner. Two figures in welding masks were working on connecting a couple of steel H beams. The spitting hiss of oxyacetylene and the smell of hot metal drifted over the yard. At the opposite end of the yard was a small wooden construction, more hut than building with a faded sign over the door: Cockbridge & Sons. As they walked towards it, the door opened and a thin young man with his shirt sleeves rolled up above the elbow clattered down the rough plank steps. He stopped, clearly surprised to find two senior Army officers strolling in his yard: 'Can I help you gentlemen?'

'We're looking for the owner,' said Hobo.

'That's me.' He glanced back at the sign as if to check. 'Cockbridge. Well, Son. One of them, anyway. The others are in the Army.'

'Not you?'

The young man blushed. 'Diabetes. Wouldn't have me.'

'I'm sorry.'

'Me too. Still, someone's got to keep the business going. Anyway, I do what I can. There's plenty of work on keeping the airfields open.' He nodded towards the lorry and its load of rubble. 'We do our bit.'

'I'm sure you do. That's why we're here. Those men over there, your welders. How skilled are they? You see, we have some work needs doing and I had an idea you might help us out.'

'Be glad to, sir. Those men?' He smiled. 'Well, you'd better come and see for yourself.'

As he led the way across the yard, Hobo turned to Burton. 'Fetch the AVRE blueprints from the car, would you?'

Burton returned a minute later with a long roll of drawings. Hobo was standing with Cockbridge by the steel joists. The welding torches were off now and the two welders had raised their masks. Burton realised why Cockbridge had smiled. Beneath the grime of smoke from the torches were two attractive female faces. 'They both worked at De Havilland's before they got married. Kay's got a kiddie now, so she came back to Ipswich and Maggie followed. Their husbands are ground-crew at Woodbridge. Should think they have all the skills you're looking for. Shall we go into the office and you can show me what you need doing?'

Hobo beamed: 'Lay on, Mr Cockbridge. And damned be he and so forth.'

As they followed the young builder back to his HQ, Hobo turned to Burton and grinned like a schoolboy. 'See, Howard. We shall beat Freddie Quiller after all. First Quiller, and then Hitler.'

36

Two weeks after Mike took command of his troop, they moved to a new camp in the New Forest. To their astonished delight they found well-appointed bell tents waiting for them, complete with camp beds and other fancy American mod cons. The Yanks were also running the cookhouse, so the food was better than they were used to – even if Hipkiss peered suspiciously at the hotdogs and bemoaned the lack of good old Irish stew. It wasn't until they woke on the fifth day that the true nature of the camp was revealed. During the night, the barbed wire fences round the perimeter had been completed, the gates reduced to one, and that one was guarded by two American MPs.

'A fucking concentration camp, that's what it is,' grumbled Hipkiss, when it was announced that no one was allowed beyond the wire until further notice.

'You know what it means, don't you?' said Williams.

'It means we're being ordered around in our own backyard by the bloody Yanks, that's what it means.'

'No, pal, it means that this is it. No more exercises. They don't bang everyone up before an exercise. It means this is the real thing. The Second Front.'

'They could of warned us. I mean, no leave nor nothin'. Beautiful, that is. Can't even get out to the pub for a decent send-off. Typical of the army, that is. No bleedin' consideration. I mean, what's my old lady going to think? I promised her I'd be getting embarkation leave. I was told you always get embarkation leave before a deployment. It ain't right.'

'Maybe the army thinks it's more important that the invasion comes as a surprise to Hitler than to Mrs Hipkiss.' Mike had come up behind the two men, who were sitting on camp-stools under a beech tree beside their tent.

Hipkiss swung round to protest. 'That's as may be, sir. I still call it a cheap trick. Especially bein' ordered about by them snowdrops. If we has to be banged up, why can't it be by our own MPs? It ain't right havin' to kow-tow to a load of Yanks. They ain't enjoyed theirselves so much since the bleedin' Boston tea party.'

'Sorry, Hipkiss, it's only for a few days. I came to tell you, they've set up a display of the landing grounds, showing all the landscape features and so on that we need to learn so we shall know where we are. Go along there this morning. I'm expecting you to know it as well as you know the Essex Road by the time we move down to the docks.'

'So where are we going, guv?'

Mike smiled. 'If you believe the labels on the model, we're going to be landing somewhere between Pittsburgh and Detroit.'

'Suits me. I'd like to get me own back on these Yank bastards by invading their sodding country and chatting up their birds for a change. See 'ow they like it.'

'It's France though, sir. Isn't it?' said Corporal Williams. 'I mean, you can tell us that much.'

'I don't think it really matters where we're landing, Taff. All that matters is that it's occupied by Jerry and we need to take it back.'

'It's all the same to me. I've never been abroad, so I shan't know any better, wherever the boat sees fit to land me.'

'Right, well, the more you can learn the lie of the land, the better we'll be placed, especially if we don't come in exactly as planned. Which is highly likely, I imagine.'

He left the men to their grumbling and strolled away through the trees. It was a clear late May morning, and the New Forest was in full leaf, its shade pierced, here and there, by theatrical spots of sunlight. The leaf litter and moss of the forest floor was spongy underfoot and absorbed a portion of the noise made by an encampment of ten thousand men and machines. Mike spotted a comfortable-looking patch of moss between the roots of an old oak and, sitting himself down, pulled a pad of writing paper out of his pocket and unfolded it.

The first letter was to his parents. He hadn't got round to letting them know that he'd left Hobo's staff. He had no way of telling whether the letter would reach them before word of the Second Front came through. He pictured his father standing in the corridor at Rawdon, his cap fidgeting to and fro between his fingers. All that time he'd thought they were blaming him for what had happened to Frank, when actually they were terrified of losing him too. There was a good chance that fear would be borne out but, without Overlord, what chance was there of Frank ever coming home?

In a page and a half he had said all that he could and, as he signed it, without any hesitation this time, 'Your loving son, Michael', he wondered how many other men would sit and write almost identical letters with their backs against these English oaks in the next few days.

The second letter would have fewer facsimiles. Maybe there were others as awkward or that were started and abandoned as many times, but he doubted it. This one had been started a hundred times before he'd taken the notepaper out of his pocket. He'd wanted to send it ever since he left Rawdon, but could never get it to go right. Even the greeting was problematic. 'Dear Charlie' seemed too ordinary. 'My dear Charlie' was too sadly inaccurate. 'Darling Charlie' he scrubbed out once for being importunate, a second time for being presumptuous and a third time because it made his hand tremble to read it. The fourth time he let it stand, because it was the only way he could think of addressing her, and dammit, if he was going to die he might at least call her what the hell he liked one last time.

Once he'd got that down, the rest came relatively easily. The only problem was, when he finished, he realised that he really had almost better be killed on D-Day than ever run into her again. It would be excruciating to meet her, knowing she had read this stuff. He held it in his hand, wondering whether to tear it up and save his dignity. After all, just to have written it was a breach of the pact he had made with himself in the train to Southampton. Yet here he was, still thinking about her constantly, still wanting her, wasting time composing a letter to her that he'd probably never send, when all his attention should be on the men under his command.

He folded the letter into an envelope and wrote her name on the front. There was still time enough to decide whether he was actually going to post it. The very last thing he wanted was to give her time to write back. The very last news he wanted to hear before embarking was that she was going to marry Hartwell or, worse, had already gone ahead and done it. He'd promised the Old Man he wouldn't do anything stupid just because he'd been thrown over, but he didn't entirely trust himself to keep his word if he knew for certain that there was no hope. He remembered the extra few ounces of strength it had taken to swim out against the tide on New Year's Eve, ounces the thought of Charlie had given him. If he needed those ounces again, would they be there if any chance of making her his wife had gone?

'For Christ's sake,' he thought. 'Give it a bloody rest.' He ought to be checking the water-proofing on the AVREs before they took them down to be tested. Making sure the extension pipes for the exhaust and air inlets had been properly fitted too. It'd be embarrassing if the things sprang a leak, but better in a Hampshire pond than in the surf off Normandy.

There was a surprising amount of bustle about the tank harbour. Men were hurrying to and fro with pots of sealant, gun mountings and bits of kit. A three-tonner at the far side of the clearing was unloading drum-shaped objects to a queue of men standing by the tail-gate. He wondered, suddenly anxious, if the order to move had been given whilst he had been writing his letters. Looking around for someone to ask, he caught sight of a familiar figure, hands clasped behind him, talking intently to Corporal Williams and the reason for the manic urgency in the clearing became clear. Williams, normally the most laconic of men, looked extremely unnerved – and equally extremely relieved as he spotted Dixon.

'Here's Captain Dixon now, sir,' he said, gesturing with his chin.

The officer with his back to him swung round and Mike saluted sharply, experiencing as if for the very first time the fierceness of General Hobart's gaze. 'Ah, Dixon. They told me I'd probably find you round here. I was just telling your driver how important it is he learns the details of the landing area like the back of his hand. You've got to din that into them, man. Din it in. I told him to memorise the lie of the land for a good mile in each direction, seeing as the chaps driving the landing craft are likely to be just as much amateur sailors as your men are amateur soldiers.'

Over the General's shoulder, Corporal Williams shook his head at this bit of morale-raising. Mike tried not to smile. 'Yes, sir. I'll make sure they do that. Do you have any idea how much longer we'll be sitting around before the off?'

Hobart gave him a hard stare. 'You're the one who wanted to be back with the men in the line. That means being out of the loop, you know. You can't have your cake and eat it too.'

'No, sir.'

'Truth is, I wish I was going with you. But it can't be helped. I shall follow as soon as I can. We'll need a Divisional HQ over there pretty damn smartish to re-organise things if the casualty estimates are correct. You know we're expecting up to seventy per cent casualties in the first twenty-four hours.'

He saw Williams' eyes widen behind Hobo's back. 'That's pretty high, sir.'

'Most probably pessimistic, but we have to establish that beachhead, Dixon. If we get thrown back into the sea … ' He waved his swagger-stick and whacked his knee with it, as close to a doubtful gesture as Mike had ever seen him make.

'We shan't, sir. We've trained too long and too hard. There isn't a thing Jerry can throw at us that the men haven't trained for.'

'I hope you're right. It's all we can do, anyway, make sure every crew in this Division is capable of working in support of others, or on its own initiative, to combat whatever obstacle it comes up against – on whatever terrain.'

'I honestly think we'll do all right. The men are ready. Of course, we still need our Flying Dustbins … '

'They're here. Two of your chaps are over there collecting your payload.'

He nodded towards the three-tonner. Hipkiss and Taylor were trudging back across the clearing, each one carrying two forty-pound dumb-bells, like slightly resentful circus strongmen. 'Twenty-four per vehicle. That do you?'

'Twenty-four? That should take up most of the room inside the tank.'

Hobo snorted a laugh. 'You were just complaining about not having them.'

'I know. I'd prefer not to be sitting on one in the turret, that's all.'

'Well, the sooner you lob them at Jerry, the sooner you'll have elbow room. Come on, walk me to my car. Carry on, Corporal, and good luck.'

Taff Williams stood to attention and saluted. Hobo returned the salute. They turned and walked (like the old days, Mike caught himself thinking) across the forest's dappled shade. His stomach gave a lurch when he spotted the Snipe. Then he saw the soldier leaning against the driver's door. 'New driver, sir?'

'Eh? Oh, I see. No, she's on leave. Miss Carrington. Most inconvenient when she's the only driver I have that gets a decent move on. This fellow drives like he's on a perpetual Sunday school outing.' The driver, stony-faced, opened the door for the GOC to climb in, but he paused. 'Hope she comes back in a bit better mood, I must say. She's been quite snappish lately. Pretty little thing, though I'm not quite sure the man who takes her on will have an easy time. Still, the ones that are worth having aren't always the easy ones, are they?'

'No, sir,' said Mike. 'I don't suppose they are.' He made a sudden, desperate decision: 'By the way, you don't happen to know how things turned out with that fiancé of hers, do you?'

Hobo looked bemused. 'Why on earth should I? It's hardly my concern – although Dorrie seems to think I should show an interest. Says I'm "in loco parentis" or some such rot. I keep telling her it's nothing to do with me.'

Despite this lack of encouragement, Mike rummaged in his pocket and pulled out the letter: 'Would you give this to Charlie for me? Only, please could you make it as close to the off as possible? I'd prefer it that way.' He proffered the envelope and the older man took it. Then he gave his former aide one last hard stare and pointed at him with the letter. 'I shall give it to her, on condition that you do your job and get off that beach in double-quick time. The Division will have a job to do all the way to Berlin and the fewer replacements I have to find, the better. Remember that, would you?'

'I will, sir. We'll do our best to lay on the Lord Mayor's Show all the way to the Reichstag.'

Hobo nodded. 'Look after your men, Dixon. We shan't have time to train their replacements half so well. You know, Maréchal Foch once said, "It takes 15,000 casualties to train a Major-General." I'm rather counting on you all to show that he was wrong. Apart from anything else, I'd hate to see a Frenchman proved right on a point of military theory.' With that, he drove away, leaving Mike on the edge of the clearing, wondering if he would ever see the terrifying old features again.

37

Charlie's leave coincided with a rare heatwave in Yorkshire. The train windows were open and the leather edges to the carriage seats burned the backs of her legs when she first took her seat. The sunshine was so bright and the sky so blue that it reminded her of a summer train ride from Marseilles to Nice before the War. Except that the landscape outside the window was unmistakably England, with trees freshly in leaf and the May blossom still bridal on the hawthorn hedges. She changed at Leeds. The train for Selby was already in and she climbed into an empty carriage and sat down in a window seat, waiting for it to pull out. She glanced out at the other passengers getting on to the train, and realised that quite a few of them were couples. And not only couples, but couples accompanied by family groups in suits and dresses, their best clothes.

As she was still deciding what to make of it, the carriage door opened and a woman and a man climbed in. The woman, very young and wearing too much make-up, a tailored skirt and jacket and a hat the exact colour of a sherbet lemon, stared at Charlie resentfully but seemed to resign herself to having to share the compartment and plumped down in the seat nearest the corridor. The man, maybe a year or two older than his bride but still with a rash of acne painfully shaved round his neck, put their small cardboard suitcases up on to the rack, side by side, before taking the seat opposite her. He leaned back and crossed his right ankle over his left knee. 'Well, thank God that's over.'

'Ron. Shhh! The window's open. They'll hear you.'

'I don't care if they do. Yer mam's pie-eyed, any road. All that yarting she did at t'church. Anybody'd think it were a wake, not a wedding.'

'Ron, don't be awful. She were overcome, that's all.' A whistle blew somewhere down the platform and the couplings jerked. 'Ooh, we're off. Quick, let's give 'em a wave.' The young woman jumped up and barged past Charlie's knees to get to the window. The bridegroom stopped in his seat and Charlie noticed him staring hungrily at the tightly clad rump as his bride thrust her top half clean out of the window and waved goodbye to her hitherto nearest and dearest on the platform. A chorus of responses returned and, as the train pulled away, Charlie caught sight of a plump woman waving a handkerchief, which she snatched up to her nose and blew into loudly enough for the sound to carry to them over the noise of the accelerating locomotive.

The long platform slipped behind, and with it several other wedding parties. Whit Saturday, thought Charlie. Supposed to be a lucky day to get married, wasn't it? Her fingers brushed against Bill's latest letter in her pocket. She started to draw it out, then changed her mind and left it where it was.

The bride squeezed herself back through the window frame and banged past Charlie a second time. 'Sorry,' she muttered sulkily and plumped down again opposite her husband.

'You could of waved, Ron.'

The groom rolled his eyes. 'I've only got a forty-eight hour pass. I've wasted enough of it staring at your mam and dad with a daft grin on me face. Give us a bit of peace and quiet, won't you?'

'Well, really, that's nice. Our wedding day and all you want is peace and quiet.'

'I do, yes. While you're at it, why don't you take that ruddy hat off? You look a right sight in it.'

Charlie saw the bride's mouth pucker into a little 'O' of shock. She looked away, out of the window. When she risked another glance, the girl was dragging at a hat-pin and lifting her going-away hat off. She dropped it on the seat beside her. Tears spilled down her round cheeks as she did so and the boy opposite, with his legs still crossed and his arms folded now too, stared out into the corridor, avoiding her miserable gaze.

It took about an hour to get to Selby, the country flattening out as they left the Vale of York and headed towards the Wash. The happy couple mended fences a few stops out of Leeds. By the time Charlie stood up to unlatch the door, they were sitting on the same side of the carriage, the girl giggling and squawking as Ron whispered in her ear, his thin arm all the way around her, stroking her breast and giving it a little squeeze whenever he thought Charlie wasn't watching, which brought about an extra little squawk each time he did it. The affronted hat lay forgotten on the seat opposite.

She stepped from the train without a backward glance at connubial bliss. At first, there didn't seem to be anyone on the platform. Then she saw a movement near the ticket office and there he was, a tall slim figure stepping out of the shadow into the sunshine. Dropping her suitcase, she ran down the platform and threw her arms round his neck: 'Archie! What on earth are you doing here?'

Her brother smiled: 'It wasn't easy. Most leave's been cancelled. Luckily, I happened to be up at Brigade HQ and the adjutant owed me a favour. Even lent me his car on condition I was back by noon tomorrow. Bill made me swear not to tell you he'd asked me to be best man. He wanted it to be a surprise. It was a bit of a surprise to me. I thought you were dead-set against getting married while the War's still on.'

Charlie disengaged herself and took a step back. She looked at the ground. 'It's Bill's idea. He's got it into his head that it will bring him luck, protect him when there's a flap on.'

Archie frowned. 'Do you think he ought to be flying at all? His hand's a hell of a mess, and one of his eyes isn't much better. I can't think how the MO passed him fit.'

She looked up now, into his face: 'Can't you? He's still Bill, after all. When he wants something … '

He walked off to pick up her suitcase. When he came back with it and they were going out through the station, he said, 'Well, he certainly wants you. When he wrote to me a couple of weeks ago, he seemed very anxious that I shouldn't kibosh the idea. Not sure why he thought I would.' He stopped by an MG and loaded her suitcase into the back.

Charlie walked round to the passenger seat. As she turned the door-handle she said, 'He seemed to have the impression you'd fallen out with him – because of some bad behaviour on his part.'

Archie paused, one hand on the corner of the windscreen, and frowned as if he was trying to remember Latin verb endings. 'I suppose I did. It seems an awfully long time ago. Our idea of morality seems to hinge on more serious things these days than a bit of under-graduate loutishness. And if anyone's had cause to grow out of his caddish tendencies, I'd say it's Bill.'

To Charlie's relief, the noise of the open car prevented any further attempt at serious conversation. Crossing the Pennines, she had had the feeling that something might still happen (a train derailment, a bombing raid?) to stop her having to go through with the wedding. But Archie being here made the thing certain at last. It wasn't what she wanted, but he was right: these days morality wasn't about who you slept with, or wanted to. It was about life and death and being brave. Bill's belief in her as a talisman might be a lot of nonsense, but if it gave him the strength to go up into the hostile sky every night then surely giving up her own selfish desires was a sacrifice she shouldn't be too cowardly to make. Besides, she hadn't heard a word from Mike Dixon, who had clearly thrown her over. So it wasn't as if her selfish desires were likely to be fulfilled even if she didn't keep her promise to marry Bill.

The wedding took place in a tiny Norman church a mile from the airfield. Beforehand, at the village inn where Bill had booked two rooms, Archie presented Charlie with a bundle that contained an ivory silk and lace wedding dress that Cecilia had helped him excavate from the storerooms at Eaton Place. It had been the height of Paris fashion in 1919 and Charlie had seen photographs of her mother carrying it off with an élan she seemed to have been born with, her father standing stunned beside her. She held it out in front of her and gazed at it for a minute, then laid it down on the bed. 'Thanks Archie, but it's not that kind of wedding. Anyway, I'm not sure it's a lucky omen, mother's dress. I was planning to wear uniform. I know it's hardly glamorous, but Bill will be in his. It seems right, somehow.'

So the hideous khaki skirt and jacket, shirt and tie it was, surrounded by Air Force blue. The Squadron Leader's wife contributed an incongruously pretty bunch of old-fashioned scented roses and myrtle sprigs from her garden. Apart from Archie, the congregation was all on the groom's side: his Squadron Leader and wife, the members of his crew and a few of the other pilots. Bill's new co-pilot, a former school-teacher in his thirties called Spalding, acted as the second witness. They signed the register in the little vestry, which was damp and smelled of musty hymn-books and mouse-droppings. Charlie put down the home-made bouquet to sign her name and when she saw the space for her father's signature she all of a sudden wished he had been there to give her away. She hadn't invited him, because that would have meant inviting her mother, and her mother would have made the whole thing public and official and altogether unbearable. She might even have insisted on bringing Freddie Quiller.

Bill's family weren't there either. Or maybe they were. She had the feeling he considered the men of his crew brothers, even though he had known most of them only a few weeks. They came on to the pub after the ceremony, with the vicar in tow, and downed pints of beer cheerfully for a couple of hours before pushing off, a couple at a time, back to the mess. Apart from Spalding, they all seemed like schoolboys, and called Bill 'Uncle'. He appeared not to resent it, and the way he moved and sat, the self-contained quietness of his manner, did seem to fit a man at least in middle age. It was almost impossible to think he was still only in his mid-twenties. The Bill of Boat Race Day belonged to another life.

When Archie offered to leave them to have supper alone, Charlie clutched his hand and told him not to be an ass. So they sat beside the old inglenook, its hearth swept clean for the summer, at a round tilt-top table for three and ate a game pie followed by a rare piece of Wensleydale cheese with pear chutney. Charlie had little to do as Archie and Bill talked about old times at Shrewsbury and Oxford, a procession of stories and laughter punctuated here and there with the names of friends and acquaintances, most of whom seemed to have bought it at Calais, in Singapore, over Berlin or breaking out of Tobruk. None of them mentioned what lay just around the corner.

Finally, there was nothing else for it but bed. Charlie kissed Archie and looked back once as Bill led her by the hand up the winding stair behind the bar. She tried not to make the look a desperate one, but realised she might have failed when he met her eye and put his glass down on the bar, too hard. She tried a little smile, and he smiled back, but they knew each other too well to be fooled.

The inn was ancient, and its bridal suite was a big, under-furnished room with wide elm floorboards that sloped down from the doorway towards the bed so steeply it would have been possible to lie down and roll there. The bed was a carved oak four-poster with heavy tapestry curtains. It was the room Charlie had changed in earlier and her mother's wedding dress still lay across the eiderdown.

Bill picked it up. 'What's this?'

'Oh,' said Charlie. 'Archie brought it in case I wanted to wear it. It was mother's.'

Bill laughed and held it up against him. 'She must have been quite the flapper in her day, Veronica. How is she? Magnificent creature. I had something of a pash on her when I was seventeen or so.'

'That's funny,' said Charlie, lingering in the doorway. 'She told me recently she had a bit of a thing for you too.'

He laughed again, and spun around holding the dress as though he was dancing with the wearer, until the uneven floor caught him and he stumbled. He righted himself, clutching the bed-post and looked over at Charlie quickly. Her face was blank and she hadn't moved. He bunched the dress in his good hand and dropped it on the floor.

'I never did anything about it, you know. I haven't always been a saint, Charlie, but that's over now. I don't suppose I was all that different from a lot of other men that went to my sort of public school and my sort of college. I thought it was my right to grab anything I wanted. I suppose I only wanted to fight because it would allow me to show off on the battle-field too. I didn't bother about what I was fighting for. I despised anyone who bought that stuff about patriotism. And I still wouldn't go in for King and Country exactly, but I have something to fight for these days. I have to do it now for my friends who've gone, and for all the men who are still fighting to smash Hitler and stop him smashing us.' His face worked with emotion, the unscarred two thirds of it flushed and mobile, the remainder taut and shiny and dead. It was seeing him like that, more than what he said, that made Charlie step away from the door and go to put her arms around him. She was his wife, after all.

38

On 3 June, the Royal Engineers received orders to break camp. After a week of glorious sunshine, it was a bleak, gusty morning, with a smattering of rain in the wind that grew heavier as the day progressed.

'Just my luck,' grumbled Hipkiss, as he packed the space inside the side-hatch with water-proofed bricks of explosive. 'First trip to the Continent and the weather turns to shite.'

The second AVRE in the troop carried a fascine, and Mike stood by as the fat roll of chestnut palings was winched up on to the tank and secured with hawsers. Sergeant Ridpath swung himself up on to the AVRE. Mike watched him scale the eight foot bundle of palings, unspooling the wire connecting his headphones to the tank's W/T system. There was just enough give in the line to let him perch on top, silhouetted against the sky. It was no place to be under a hail of shrapnel – or around snipers. The alternative was to rely on the driver's vision through the triplex glass block in the front of the tank – like peering through a fish tank that hadn't been cleaned in about a hundred years.

The third tank in the troop mounted a small box-girder bridge. The bridge, thirty feet of it, was canted up about fifty degrees from the horizontal for travelling, and when all three tanks were ready to move, he stood back and looked at the strange convoy. Even though he'd been closely involved, it was hard now to imagine how these preposterous-looking machines had come about, each in response to a specific problem. What if they had it all wrong and the obstacles they expected failed to materialise? What if there were other defences they hadn't foreseen and against which these contraptions were no use at all?

'Too late,' he told himself. 'Too late to think like that.' They were on the move, all of them, the Crabs, the Crocodiles, the Bulls-horns, the Bobbins, the AVREs, the swimming tanks – Fred Karno's Armour. Soon enough they would know if a year's frantic, tireless work had been well spent or a monumental miscalculation.

They travelled to the docks on low-loaders in an endless river of ordnance. The men fell silent as the scale of what they were part of finally came home to them. As he looked out across the teeming docks, it seemed almost impossible that man could have organised such a spreading mass of stuff. It felt more like a great storm gathering over the water. It felt like force on a scale that only Nature could invoke.

Finally their turn came to reverse up the ramp. With the fascine and the bridge-carrier, there was only room on their landing craft for four AVREs and two Crab flail tanks. The special purpose AVREs embarked first and had their tracks pinned and chocked to the deck. Next came the Shermans, their long rotors hung with clanking chains like strange military threshing machines. Finally, he reversed his AVRE on to the left side and Tiny Hay-Wood drove his command tank on to the right. The ramp went up and the two men looked at each other, turret to turret, knowing that when it was lowered again it would be on a scene no man on the invasion force had ever seen before. And that some, maybe most, of them would not live to look on it for long.

As daylight faded, the landing craft cast off and slogged out into the Solent, where it moored up to a buoy. They jostled away the night in a cold and lumpy swell. It was almost impossible to move about between the tanks. The men slung tarpaulins across the vehicles and huddled between them as best they could, trying to brew tea and keep from getting soaked through.

'How long do you think it'll be before we're off?' asked the gunner as dawn broke, the rising sun no more than a hint of a suggestion behind a dense wall of cloud.

Mike shrugged. 'Your guess is as good as mine, Hipkiss. I imagine they'll aim to land around first light. Probably move into formation later today, sail through the night and arrive about this time tomorrow.'

Hipkiss groaned. 'You mean we've got another twenty-four hours on this stinkin' hulk? My innards won't take it. And what are we supposed to do for kip? It's bloody impossible to get any shut-eye.'

'Ours not to wonder why, eh, Hipkiss?'

'Right you are, sir. You're almost as bad as old Hobo, with his seventy per cent casualties and calling us "amateurs". Very nice from the CO after all the hoops we've jumped through for him.'

'Thing is, we're all civilians and amateurs compared with him. If he tells us to expect high casualties, it's because he doesn't want us to fall apart when we start to lose tanks.'

'There you go again, looking on the bright side. Right little ray of sunshine, you are. Fancy a smoke, sir? It's the only thing that keeps me mind off me poor guts.'

Mike pulled a cigarette from the gunner's freshly issued ration and smiled to himself as he fished in his pocket for a box of matches. Hipkiss was notoriously stingy. It really must be the end of days if he was offering round his fags. He struck a light first time, despite the wind, and offered it to the gunner between cupped hands. He felt the hot lick of the flame as the wind swirled it around his palms like brandy in a snifter and lowered his head quickly to the match as soon as Hipkiss stood back. Cigarettes alight, the two men puffed out smoke that the wind wrapped round their heads before snatching it out from under the tarp and away over the water.

'Wonder if they can smell us coming. The Jerries, I mean.'

'I doubt it. Wind's from the West. They're more likely to smell us in the Low Countries than France. With any luck, Jerry'll think nobody would be barmy enough to launch an invasion in this lot.'

'If they think that, they don't know our top brass very well, do they, sir?'

'No, Hipkiss. They don't.'

All through Sunday they waited. Mike figured they must move by mid-afternoon, then by early evening. When they were still on the mooring at ten he had to face the fact that the operation had been delayed. The probable reason was becoming more and more apparent as the wind rose notch by notch and the rain sheeted down harder and harder until, looking out across the water in the last of the light, he could see nothing of the vast fleet he knew lay there.

The weather grew steadily, horribly worse through the night. A full gale drove rain horizontally into every crack and cranny of the comfortless open boat, while the men cowered miserably between their tanks. All except Taff Williams, who had contrived for himself a kind of rat's nest inside the Churchill, wedging himself in with all sorts of odd packing, stopping up draughts with the precious softback books the wireless operator Davis had stowed on a new steel shelf that was part of the crew's modifications. When Mike peered in on him through the side-hatch the driver appeared to be as fast asleep as a hibernating dormouse. Part of him wanted to shake the one boot he could see, out of sheer jealousy, but he decided it was good to have at least one man in a fit state to fight and shut the hatch again.

Hipkiss was being horribly and repeatedly seasick, despite the pills they had all been given, and the stink of vomit and urine billowed across the decks, mixed with the smell of oxtail from cans of self-heating soup that those who could stomach food fired up from time to time. The men had grumbled a bit at the bulk and weight of those soup tins when they were first issued. Now they seemed like a good deed in a naughty world.

39

Hobo and Burton drove up to Southwick Park at 04.00 on 5 June. The colonnaded white mansion loomed out of the pelting rain and darkness, looking so like a Georgian plantation house that Burton didn't wonder Eisenhower had chosen it as his HQ. The British General Staff, by contrast, were huddled underground in the base of one of Palmerston's old Napoleonic forts on the top of Portsdown Hill. No more than a few miles away as the crow flies, but a world away in its feeling of embattlement. Perhaps that's the difference the Blitz has made between us, thought Burton. The Americans still haven't been made to believe in their vulnerability whereas we're all too clear on the point.

Torrents of rain were being pushed sideways by the gale and the two men were soaked in the few seconds it took them to hurry from the car to the shelter of the portico. As Burton brushed the wet from his shoulders inside the front door he saw that the same officers were standing around in the same attitudes as they had been when they'd last gathered here six hours before. Now the weather was undeniably worse. Burton frowned. It already felt as if they had been gathering in this room every few hours since the beginning of time. He nodded to one or two men he knew as he headed over to the fireplace, where Hobo had taken up post with his foot on the fender. Monty's Chief of Staff, General De Guingand, was crossing the room.

'Any news, Freddie?' asked Hobo.

De Guingand stopped and shook his head. 'Stagg's not here yet. Probably hanging on by the scrambler till the last possible minute for the latest weather charts.'

'Surely it can't go on like this without a break. It's June, for God's sake.'

De Guingand smiled ruefully. 'Tell that to the weather gods. It's not the sea state that's the problem so much, though the men will be pretty sick and your swimming tanks might not get their day I'm afraid, Patrick. It's the cloud cover that's the killer. It's still right down on the deck and the Air Force are saying there's no way they can put in an effective bombardment unless there's at least a thousand feet clear under the cloud base. More, if we want to drop paratroopers anywhere near their objectives inland.'

It was Hobo's turn to shake his head. 'We can't keep putting it off. It was bad enough this morning, having to postpone by a day. If we can't go on Tuesday, it'll be the most god-awful snarl-up.'

'If we can't go on Tuesday we'll have to abort and bring the men back ashore to rest and re-provision. Refuel the fleet. It'll take us a fortnight to be ready again, with tides and so forth. Apparently, Stagg's gone back fifty years in the records and can't find a single set of charts for June as horrendous as these.'

A gust of cold air rattled the glass in the French windows as the front door slammed again. A tall figure in RAF uniform, a study in anxiety, hurried towards the library with a roll of charts under his elbow. 'There he goes,' said de Guingand: 'Six foot two of Stagg and six foot one of gloom. I wouldn't be in his shoes for all the tea in China.'

'No,' thought Howard Burton, 'who'd want to be in charge of weather forecasting when the lives of a hundred and sixty thousand men and the whole course of the war depend on the shape of a North Atlantic depression? It could be the Armada all over again, with the luck running against England this time.'

The company watched the double doors to the library where Eisenhower and the other top brass were waiting close on Stagg. The silence held firm. After a year of frantic planning and preparation, at this moment of enforced pause nobody seemed to have anything to say. Minutes passed. Burton felt as he had when Mary was in labour with the girls, nervous and helpless, wishing it would all be over. He smiled at the thought of them in their old quarters at school, before he remembered that Mary had had to move to a rented house in the village to make room for his replacement as house-master. Before he had chance to dwell on the quick jab of regret this gave him, the double doors opened and Eisenhower came out. Monty was behind him, and Bradley. A glance was enough to see that they were resolved. Eisenhower stopped in the middle of the room. 'OK, gentlemen, we're going. D-Day is June sixth. Let's get on with it.'

There was a collective murmur – everyone started to move at once, like characters in a fairytale released from a spell. Hands were shaken. Backs were patted. Montgomery cast about with starling-like intensity until his gaze alighted on the trio by the fireplace. He came striding over. 'Well, there we are. Stagg's now saying there should be a break in the weather around dawn tomorrow, and that's the best we're going to get. We don't know quite how long it'll lift for, but we should have fairly clear skies from early morning till midday. Just got to make the first blows count. With any luck, we shall catch them on the hop. Are you ready, Patrick?'

'My men are, Bernard, but I'm having the devil's own job persuading transport to allocate shipping space for my Divisional HQ. They claim all they can give me is room for one vehicle until D+Seven at the earliest. That's no damn good. By D+Seven my Division will have been pulled about all over the place, probably be totally bent out of shape. I need to be there to take charge by D+One at the very latest. Can you make some room for me?'

Monty pursed his lips. 'Sorry, old man. We have to give priority to fighting men for the first few days at least. The build-up's crucial. We're having to leave all sorts of equipment behind. Your chaps'll have to make shift for themselves for a bit. I'm sure you've trained 'em well enough to do it. They're certain not to be shrinking violets if they've come up in your school.'

Hobo wasn't to be diverted by flattery. 'No, but even so. I'm damned if my HQ should be classified as supplies. It's not dental chairs and spare left boots we're talking about – the whole effectiveness of the Division's at stake. You know our machines are designed for specialist tasks. I'm warning you, Bernard, if they get dragged into acting as standard battle tanks or infantry support we shall lose them too fast to be able to replace them and then we shan't have them when they're really needed. If I'm not there to defend them from all sorts of fool requests ... '

Montgomery held up his hand. 'Sorry, Patrick. You'll have to bend somebody else's ear. I have far too many things to do. Come along, Freddie, I need you.'

De Guingand grinned apologetically at Hobart and hurried after Monty. Hobo raked their backs with a fierce look. Jerking his head at Burton to follow him, he headed out into the storm too. Wind and rain threatened to tear their caps from their heads, so that by the time they reached the car Burton felt as if he'd been to sea in an open boat. He felt a pang of sympathy for the men who were there in fact, waiting in the Solent without shelter or news. They didn't know it yet, but the waiting was almost at an end. It was hard to take in the simple fact that the moment had come, that everything they had been working towards tirelessly for the last fifteen months was finally to be tested in the crucible. And before that, by the blind power of Nature on the rampage. He hoped to God it wasn't going to be a total disaster. Maybe Hobo was thinking the same, because they sat in the dark in silence for a minute before Charlie said. 'Everything all right, sir?'

Hobo cleared his throat. 'It's on. Weather's supposed to lift in the next twenty-four hours and give us some respite until about noon on Tuesday.'

'Pretty filthy at the moment. I hope they're right.'

Neither man replied for a moment, then Hobo said. 'So do I. Now, back to Fort Southwick. Shall we?'

'Sir.' She pressed the starter and the engine caught. Then, as she reached for the gear lever, she turned her head: 'May I ask a question, sir?'

'What's that?'

'The Sherwood Rangers. Do you know if they're likely to be landing on D-Day? My brother's with them.'

Burton leaned forward and spoke gently. 'I believe they're slated to be in the first wave, Charlie, yes.'

She nodded. 'Archie'll be glad about that. He hates waiting about almost as much as I do.' She paused and plunged on. 'I suppose Captain Dixon will be there too, won't he?'

'Dixon?' Hobo sounded irritable, as if he'd still not forgiven Dixon for his defection. 'Yes, yes. He should be well to the fore. I shouldn't worry about him too much. He's got his head screwed on. Oh, now, there you are, I'd quite forgotten. He gave me something for you when I saw him a couple of weeks ago.' He unstrapped his attaché case and felt around in it in the dark. He pulled out an envelope and dropped it on the passenger seat beside her.

She took her hand off the gear lever to touch the paper: 'What is it?'

'How should I know? I mean, I doubt it's a council rates demand. But I've no idea what's in it.'

He sat back. The car still didn't move off and Burton realised a pair of blue eyes was looking at the CO through the rear-view mirror. Even in the minimal glow from the headlamps he could see that the expression in them was colder than usual. Hobo must have seen it too because he defended himself in the only way he knew, by attacking. 'Don't look at me like that, woman. He specifically asked me not to give it to you until just before the off. I've no idea why, and I didn't ask. I got the impression he wanted to get some things off his chest. He was pretty convinced, you know, that he stood no chance once your fiancé turned up again.'

The eyes flicked down and then met his again. 'You mean my husband, sir.'

'What?' Hobo and Burton spoke in unison. Charlie turned her head and faced them both down.

'We got married, sir. That's why I needed a forty-eight hour pass the other week. For the wedding.'

'Oh. Oh, I see,' said the General, sounding not a little put out. 'Well, why on earth didn't you say so? I expect you'll be going off and leaving me in the lurch now too, will you?'

'Not while you still need me, sir. Bill's back on ops, so I'd only be sitting about, waiting and worrying every night. Far better to be getting on with my job.'

'Well, that's something, I suppose.' Hobo sounded placated. 'I say, do you want to give me back that letter of Dixon's? Maybe, in the circumstances, he might rather I hadn't handed it over. I can always tell him I forgot it. Damn nearly did, as a matter of fact.'

Charlie put her hand down protectively over the letter. 'No. Honestly. If he meant me to have it then I think I ought to know what he has to say. I shan't embarrass him over it, you can be sure of that.' She trod down hard on the clutch, stirred the big gear-box and set off down the driveway towards the horizon, which was already showing the faint edge of a grey dawn. On any other day, Howard Burton might have spent the drive back up the long slope of Portsdown Hill thinking about how Mike Dixon would cope with the knowledge that the girl he was pretty obviously mad about had married another. But this was the day before D-Day and Mike Dixon was only one man among many thousands who might not live long enough to receive any more news from home, good, bad or heart-breaking. 'Sufficient unto the day,' thought Burton, thinking of his father, who used to say it rather often, 'is the evil thereof.' His father had been an army chaplain in the last lot. Maybe that was when the quotation had entered his canon.

40

As the light began to gather on their third day in purgatory, the rain eased off. Mike went to stretch his cold cramped legs, high-stepping carefully over ropes and cables, making a circuit of the shoe-box deck. For the umpteenth time he looked hopefully at the naval crew in the rudimentary shed of a wheelhouse. For the umpteenth time they shook their heads. He worked his way up the opposite side of the deck and, when he reached the bows, he ran into Tiny Hay-Wood, his collar turned up and his hands thrust deep in his pockets, apparently with the same idea. They stood and stared out at the dawn in silence. Across the water were scattered hundreds of other grey blurs, ships and boats waiting, just like them. The sky, though, was still empty of aeroplanes. Tiny slowly turned his head a fraction to glance at him, over a hunched shoulder, reminding Mike of a cold, wet owl. 'Do you think they can have decided to go for a night attack, after all? Because otherwise, we've definitely missed the boat for today.'

'I wish we bloody had missed the boat. I don't fancy tossing around like a cork in this for much longer, do you?'

Mike shook his head, dislodging raindrops that ran down his neck and he shivered. Hay-Wood dug in a pocket and produced a hip-flask. 'Drink? Seems to be the only thing that helps.'

'What is it?'

'Rum. Navy issue.'

'No thanks. Can't abide the stuff. Never was cut out for the Navy.'

'I suppose not. If you don't like rum, that only leaves sodomy and the lash. Not a very enticing prospect. Unless you were at Eton.'

Hay-Wood grinned and took a long swig from his flask. He knew full well Mike Dixon hadn't been to Eton or anywhere like it. Somewhere over the last few months it had ceased to matter to either of them. He took a step closer and said, in a low voice, 'What do you think it'll be like, when we do get over there? Seriously. I mean, at least you were at Dieppe. Me, all these years of training, first with the ghastly gas, now under old Hobo. Seems a bit of a farce that I've never fired a shot in anger yet. Can't help wondering if I shall know what to do when that ramp goes down.'

Mike smeared a rain-drip off the end of his nose with the back of his hand. 'You'll know. Just rev up and go. Hope the Crabs and DDs have landed as advertised. Even if they haven't, we get on with the job. There's no point hanging around. Just keep moving.'

'That's right, old man. Keep moving. Wish we could *get* moving, that's all. When we do, I shall say a few words to the men. Egg them on a bit. Bet it'll be the same thing all over these boats. Bits of cod Shakespeare mumbled out by chaps who never paid a blind bit of notice in Eng. Lit. Still, has to be done, eh?'

'I don't imagine it matters much what you say. We'll all be glad enough to know we're going to be off this bloody boat soon, even if Jerry is waiting at the other end.'

'Do you think they have a clue what's coming? Jerry, I mean.'

'Let's hope not. Let's hope they haven't got an inkling.'

'Wonder what they'll make of the Funnies. Do you think the swimming tanks have any chance of making it to shore in this muck?'

Mike shrugged. 'I hope the Navy have the good sense to take them in close before they launch. We could do with their fire-power. Don't fancy trying to do the whole job with Flying Dustbins.'

'Can't wait to see the look on Jerry's faces when these big dinghies come sailing up and – ta dah! – turn out to be Shermans in drag.'

Mike smiled and prayed that the Germans were going to be as surprised as Tiny imagined. As far as he knew, MI5's search for the man he and Charlie had seen signalling on the beach at Linney Head had come to nothing. He supposed they had concluded it was a wild goose chase and called it off, but those flashing lights still worried him. In the next few hours he would finally find out whether he'd been right to lie awake. If the Germans were expecting the DDs, they'd be pouring fire on to them, doing their best to sink them before they came ashore. He thought of the crews stuffed tight inside the hulls of the submerged Shermans in their Mae Wests and breathing apparatus. Brave men. He hoped whoever had been watching the trials on that Welsh beach that day had reported a complete shambles, and not a fearsome secret weapon worthy of counter-measures.

41

It was getting light by the time Charlie set Hobart and Burton down at the entrance to Fort Southwick. They had camp beds in the bowels of the old stone fort. Charlie's billet was with nine other ATS girls and Wrens in a draughty tent in the east ditch. It hadn't seemed too bad when they arrived in sunshine three days before, but twenty-four hours of heavy rain had turned the ditch into a lethal bog. She tucked his letter deep inside her jacket and slid down the soaking grass into the ditch. Picking her way through a cat's cradle of guy ropes in the flat dawn light, she hoped the other girls would be asleep so that she could read it in peace. The wind was still blowing hard, and the ditch was filled with the noise of ropes creaking and canvas flapping under strain. It was impossible to tell which tent was hers until she spotted a red scarf that one of the Wrens had tied near the top of the canvas as a marker. The scarf was soaked and bedraggled now, but it spanked furiously in the gale and Charlie trudged towards it with relief.

She pushed aside the canvas flap and stepped inside, quietly as she could in boots clodded with mud. Apart from the throbbing of wind against canvas, all was still. The cramped double row of camp beds was occupied by figures in the various attitudes of sleep, curled, stretched, twisted and all as yet oblivious to the coming morning. Tired, thought Charlie. Everyone is so damned tired. And likely to get more so yet.

Luckily, her bed was on the end of a row and she lowered herself on to it, trying not to make a noise that would stand out from the creaking and buffeting of the wind. No one stirred as she bent to unlace her revolting boots. The laces were wet, swollen with mud, and her fingers were filthy by the time she'd worked the knots free. She rubbed her hands down her trousers and lay back, only undoing the top two buttons of her jacket so that she could pull out her letter.

There was enough light now to read but, for a while, she did no more than stare at her name on the envelope. She realised she had never seen his handwriting before and yet she knew it was his. Of course she knew it was his, because Hobo had given it to her. Even besides that, she felt as though she recognised it. The strokes of the pen were just like him somehow: straight, unembellished, but compellingly attractive. She remembered him leaning back in Hobo's deck-chair under the cherry tree, teasing her about the pathetic thingummy. If he was here now, no doubt he'd be ragging her for falling into it again. She smiled and caught her breath at the sharp, painful realisation that that had been their last happy exchange, the last thing they'd shared before the Hobarts' girl came running across the lawn and everything was ruined.

The Hon Miss Charlotte Carrington. How had he known she was an 'Honourable'? She was pretty sure she'd never mentioned her father was a baronet. It would only have made him stupider about the difference in their backgrounds. Someone had told him though – probably that little tittle-tattle, Monica. One more reason he had to hate her. As if there weren't enough. She'd begged him to trust her to sort things out when she went to London. Then Bill had succeeded in making her feel the only 'honourable' thing to do was to marry him after all. Why was it everything right felt wrong, and everything wrong felt right? It seemed a bad joke to be saddled with being called 'Honourable' when she couldn't feel less like it if she tried.

She flipped the envelope over and opened it. There were two, no, three sheets of onion-skin thin paper inside. From the way the writing sloped across the pages and the nib of the pen had torn through in places, she guessed that he had written it with the pad propped against his knee. She imagined him struggling to find a quiet corner in a cramped assembly camp to sit down and write to her. To say what? He had been so angry at Hobo's house, after Bill telephoned. Then he'd made certain of not having to see her again. Clearing out as soon as he could. If only he'd waited until she got back from London. If only he'd written to her the way Bill had written. But he'd gone off and left her without a word. What had she been supposed to do? She hardly dared to start reading, and yet she couldn't bear to carry on not knowing what he thought of her. She unfolded the pages and read: *Darling Charlie.*

She stopped and closed her eyes. Tears stung instantly and she rubbed a hand, hard, over her face to discourage them. Then she opened her eyes and started again:

Darling Charlie,

Well, here we are. I am back where I feel I belong, waiting to do what we've all been training for so long. I hope I shan't be too rusty, after a year of meetings and memos, to be any good to the men, because they are a grand lot – and they seem to be gaining a bit of confidence in me, so I hope I shall do something to deserve it.

Sorry, this already seems a very banal letter. I am not in the habit of writing to you, and probably never will be now. Worse luck. But I couldn't bear to leave things as we left them the other week. It was a rotten parting, wasn't it? I was just so miserable and confused.

I went back and asked old Hobo straightaway for this transfer – and that was a good thing, which I don't regret. But I was also jealous and angry – and that I do regret. I have tried my damnedest not to think about you, Charlie. I have tried to shut your face and your name and your voice out of my head every day since you got on that train to London – to go to him – but it's no good.

It's no good, and it may never be any good. I love you. I fell in love with you the very first time you gave me a lift from Rawdon station and I have loved you ever since. I want to marry you, and if I can't marry you, I can't see that I shall ever want anyone else. There, I've said it. You've probably made it up with Bill and will find this excruciating, but I don't care. Of course I do care horribly, but laying my cards on the table is more important than my dignity at this moment, so there we are. I may feel differently about it later, or I may soon feel nothing ever again, so it seems best to be a clean old man about it while I still can.

If you are already Mrs Hartwell, or planning to be, then I know you will have the decency to destroy the evidence of my humiliation and, if we should happen to meet up one day, to pretend you never received this letter. But just in case there is any chance that you still feel as you once felt, or thought you felt, I'm going to make no bones about it. If you love me and not him, then for God's sake break your engagement and marry me. This war will be over one day. Soon, if the job we have on goes as well as we hope. When it is we shall have earned the right to live our lives in the way that makes us happy. Shan't we? If not, what the hell has it been for?

Well, darling, that's all. Please don't worry that the way we parted will make me do anything stupid. On the contrary, I shall be trying my utmost to come back safe, just to get your answer. So, if it's bad news, please don't send it yet. That way I shall 'keep buggering on' as Churchill says, hoping for the best.

Did I mention that I love you terribly, terribly much?

Yours, always and forever,

Mike

PS You are not a jinx, Charlie. You are the best luck a man could ever have.

The irony of this was too much and Charlie began to cry – not just as if her heart would break, but in the clear and irrefutable knowledge that it actually had done so.

She woke to find herself curled up on her blanket, still fully dressed, apart from her boots. She had the sensation that she had lost something precious, though she couldn't immediately think what. Glancing wildly around, she spotted sheets of paper scattered across the muddy ground-sheet, and remembered. She leaned over and picked up Mike's letter. The ink had run slightly in the top corner, but the ending with his name and postscript were unmarked. Her hand trembled. She couldn't bear to read the whole thing again. She folded the paper over her fingers so that all she could see was the last few lines, starting with the war being over and living in the way that makes us happy. She read those two or three times before she tucked the letter back inside her jacket.

The tent was empty now. The rest of the girls must have gone on duty. She could get into bed properly if she wanted and catch up on the sleep that had been on short ration since she arrived from Yorkshire. But the empty tent was cold and cheerless, noisy too, with the wind still booming. She grabbed her sponge bag and towel and made her way through the wind and rain to the latrines, where she scrubbed her teeth and washed in stinging cold water. Her hair was a fright. She combed and pinned it up as best she could without a mirror, thankful for once for the ugly ATS cap with its leather strap over the crown badge. It was eleven by the time she'd finished, and still two hours till she would be wanted again. She'd missed breakfast and it was too early for lunch. She was at what was commonly known as 'a loose end'. It wasn't her kind of thing.

She threw her washbag and towel back inside the tent and paced along the ditch until she found a muddy gulley that led to the fort's brick outer rampart. The bank was steep and slippery and she was out of breath by the time she reached the gravel road running alongside the moat. The gale that was whistling across Portsdown Hill almost blew her back into the ditch. Taking the wind in her face, she turned her back on the fort and gazed down over the spreading expanse of Portsmouth harbour below. It was a view so vast, so panoramic that she doubted God had a better. Yesterday, every dock and mooring had been packed with ships and boats and every road with lorries, tanks, jeeps and guns. It had been like looking down at a great ant's nest the moment after a child had stirred at it with a stick. She had wondered if Mike was down there, Archie too. Now she knew they must have been. This morning the harbour was emptying. Most of the smaller craft had already gone, and even the great ships of the line were steaming out of Port Solent, Gosport, the Hamble and Southsea, trailed by their straight white wakes. Soon, the ants' nest would be deserted, as every member of the colony set about its instinctive task.

She looked at her watch. 11.30. 'This time tomorrow,' she thought. 'This time tomorrow they'll be in battle. This time tomorrow either of them might already be dead – and I'll still be here, watching and waiting. Not knowing.' She kicked morosely at a loose stone on the road. Overhead, a formation of heavy bombers wheeled and lost height as they came into land at one of the Hampshire airfields. Charlie watched them sink below the horizon, one after the other, like a flock of stiff-winged geese. 'Halifaxes,' she thought. She stared in the direction they'd gone and wondered if Bill would be in action tomorrow too, part of the aerial bombardment, yet another layer of the invasion. It was the first time she'd thought about what he might be doing on D-Day. Ashamed, she tried to share out the terror she felt over Mike and Archie equally with Bill. But it was no good. It just wouldn't stretch.

She turned away and did her best to think of something else. What could she do that was useful in the little time left before General Hobart took himself off to France too? There'd be plenty of time after that to worry and hate herself for the stupid mess she had made.

Finally, she decided to take the Humber round to the motor pool and check the oil and tyres. She hadn't had a chance since they drove down from Yorkshire two days ago. Very lax. The instructors at Camberley would have had her guts for garters. She was thoroughly wet by the time she reached the car, and the windscreen steamed up as the moisture evaporated from her sodden wool tunic. Scrubbing at it with her sleeve, she braked hard as something rumbled across the yard right in front of her. It was a tall tracked vehicle with sloping panelled sides and the US Army star on the side. She watched it go by and drove in and parked up by a row of Yank jeeps. A group of men stood in an open shed round a small brazier stoked with petrol-soaked logs. She ran for shelter. 'Gosh, it is foul, isn't it?'

'Sure is, lady,' said one of the men in overalls, a good-looking boy with his dark hair crew-cut, the texture of velveteen. 'If this is an English summer, I hope I'm long gone before winter.'

She smiled at him. 'It's not normally this bad. In fact, winter isn't normally this bad. Where are you from?'

'Boca Raton, Florida. Where oranges grow like apples do here.'

'Ah, oranges.' Charlie sighed and stretched her hands out towards the smoky yellow fire. 'I used to love oranges. I even dream about them sometimes. I see why you need a fire anyway. It's not exactly tropical here, is it?'

The American laughed: 'No, ma'am. That would be British understatement, I guess.'

'Yes, well, we're good at that. It helps us to cope with the weather, rationing, the Luftwaffe. Pretty much anything rotten, actually. You probably don't need understatement in Florida. It's a bit of a godsend round here. I'm just going to check the oil in my car. If I need a top-up, can you help me out?'

The mechanic wiped his hands on a rag and stood up from the crate he'd been leaning against. 'Sure thing. Do you want me to take a look at it for you?'

Charlie looked affronted. 'I'm not completely feeble. It'd just be easier to top it up here than have to go off and requisition an oil can from stores, if you can spare a drop.'

He gestured towards a pile of oil drums. 'It'd be the US Army's privilege to assist a lady, ma'am.'

She decided to return the Southern charm. 'Thanks. That's jolly good of you. What are you doing here anyway? On your way to France?'

He leaned back against the crate and looked crestfallen. 'We were. Now they say it could be weeks till they have room for mechanics and spare vehicles, so we're kicking our heels.'

'Can't you go across in those?' She nodded at the massive amphibious truck that had nearly run into her. It was parked now, one of a row.

'The Ducks? They're OK for short trips. Not designed to be ocean-going. I think they have them lined up for crossing the Rhine. That's why we've been bounced to the back of the line. Not enough big rivers in Normandy to make it worth taking them over yet.'

'Huge things, aren't they?' She wandered over and hopped up on to the step by the driver's door to have a peek inside.

'Biggest we've got. They can take a jeep. Other stuff besides.'

'Really? Could you show me round one when I've checked the old girl's vitals? I've driven most things, but I've never had a go at an amphibian.' She gave the American one of her most winning looks.

42

When the landing craft containing Dixon's troop finally cast off, the men were almost indifferent to their fate. Hipkiss would certainly have volunteered to face a firing squad, given a choice between that and another hour moored to that bouncing buoy. Their orders were to form up on the south side of the Isle of Wight before setting off in a great motley fleet, mismatched for speed, power and armament but united in purpose, for France. Beyond the shelter of the island, the lumpen seas grew even more threatening, waves higher than the gunwales rolling towards the flat-bottomed vessel, looming up out of the rain, sliding down under one side of the boat and rocking it violently as they towered up again on the other. The steel hawsers bracing the tanks to the deck thrummed and creaked, and Mike clambered round each of his AVREs. He had once seen a tank break loose on a landing craft and slide around the deck, crushing three men before it came to rest. He found Corporal Williams about the same task, helping the driver of one of the AVREs to tighten the cables around the roll of chestnut palings hoisted up behind the turret. 'Has it slipped?'

Williams looked up from winching in the cable: 'Been rocking a bit, sir. On the really big waves, like. We don't want it skew-whiff, in case it jams in the exit ramp. Be a shame for the boys to have this lovely long cruise and have to go home again without seeing the seaside, wouldn't it?

Mike smiled. 'I suppose it would, Taff. Where's your life preserver?'

'In the tank. I was using it as a pillow. I'll put it on when we're nearly there.'

'Put it on now, and tell the others. There's more boats out here today than Sunday afternoon on a boating lake. A ship of the line could run us down in this murk and never notice. Be sure to wear it right up under your armpits too. Not round your waist, for God's sake.'

A mirror-flat sea studded with corpses slipped into his mind's eye as he tramped away. He sent up a silent prayer that the foul weather would at least have confined the E-Boats to base. As soon as the prayer, or thought, or wish formed in his head (and he noted that it formulated itself as 'Please God' though he was further from believing in anything of that sort than he had ever been) it occurred to him that the coming days were likely to yield sights just as horrible and as hard to forget.

Just after midnight, the boat's commander called Dixon and Hay-Wood to the wheelhouse and showed them his orders. He was to land them on the Eastern sector of the beach known as Sword at H-hour: 07.35.

'Will we be there on schedule?'

'So long as the Luftwaffe doesn't turn up, we should get there on time. Not sure we'll all arrive in the right order though. Your chaps in those DD tanks might have a bit of a rough time of it. It's still blowing Force Six at the moment. I thought those jalopies weren't designed to cope with anything above a Force Three.'

'They're not,' said Mike. 'They'll have to launch pretty close in to the beach if the sea state stays like this. They're not bad boats in the right conditions – but when they go down, they go down like stones.'

'Yes, well, I wouldn't count on them arriving when and where you expect them. We'll do our best to deliver you lot on time at any rate. I should try and get some shut-eye if you can.'

'That's fine, Lieutenant,' said Hay-Wood. 'If you could send the steward along to make up my cabin, I'll think I'll have a last hand of canasta and a cigar on deck before I turn in.'

The Navy reservist raised a mug of cocoa in mock salute. 'Keep that up, sir. Sense of humour's bound to come in handy tomorrow morning.'

The night passed in an hallucinatory fog of engine noise and rolling seas and the growing fear of every man aboard that their hellish voyage might never be over. Dawn brought visibility and visibility supplied the realisation that the great armada had been toiling along on every side and was finally approaching its destination. The sea was filled with ships. In the circumstances it was impossible, even for men afflicted like Private Hipkiss, not to feel nausea give way just a little to awe.

When land was still maybe five miles off, the naval bombardment started. The first thing they knew about it was the huge naval shells lumbering over their heads, big as freight wagons, followed by a series of massive booms from their point of origin, an eruption of smoke clouds on shore and mighty crashes as the sound of the explosions travelled back across the water. At first it was possible to tell the sounds apart, but within a couple of minutes the barrage grew into solid deafening noise on all sides. The procession of shells flew thick as machine-gun bullets and, craning his neck at the sky, Mike knew if he hadn't seen it he could never have imagined it. Every fibre of his body humming with the vibration from the ship's engines and the pressure waves in the air, he climbed on to the back of his tank to get a look over the gunwale. What he saw was a wall of smoke and seaspray. Glancing over, he saw Tiny Hay-Wood was already in the turret of his tank, binoculars trained on where the shoreline ought to be. 'What can you see?' he shouted across. Hay-Wood didn't move. Mike vaulted across on to the other Churchill. He tapped on his friend's shoulder and shouted the question again. Tiny shook his head. Mike leaned over the turret and cupped his hands to Tiny's ear. Finally, he nodded and leaned over to scream back, 'Not a thing! I was just getting my bearings when the Navy went and covered up the target. How the hell are we supposed to hit our marks if we can't see them?'

Mike put his mouth right up to his ear again and yelled: 'It'll clear. If there's less stuff to break through when it does, so much the better.' He sounded more confident than he felt. He thought of the tank he'd seen destroyed at Slapton Sands by a naval shell. He hoped this time the Navy had its range and timing right. What was the alternative? No naval barrage? He'd seen at Dieppe how that turned out.

He vaulted back on to his own Churchill and peered down into the body of the tank. They were all there. Corporal Williams in the driving seat, Davis at the wireless, Hipkiss, Taylor, the co-driver, fiddling with the lap gun, and Corporal Rendall, the sapper NCO, sitting hunched on the tool-box in the cramped space behind Williams' driver's seat. Rendall was the only regular soldier and a good deal older than the rest of the crew. Mike noticed that he went about his business quietly and calmly which, when your business is handling high explosives, struck him as a sound way to do it.

He fitted his headphones over his beret and checked the set was switched to intercom. Their orders were for radio silence, so there was nothing coming in from the world outside except the hiss and crackle of static. He spoke into the mouthpiece. 'Have we got one up the spout, Hipkiss?'

'Yes, sir.'

'Good. I'm in the mood to do some damage this morning.'

More hiss and crackle, and beyond it the terrible percussion of the barrage. 'You there, Williams?'

'Sir.'

'Davis?'

'Yes, sir.'

'Taylor?'

'Sir.'

'Rendall?'

'Sir.'

'Good. Look, we'll be second off when the ramp goes down, so we follow Major Hay-Wood until we clear the surf, and we let the Crabs through and support them whilst they set off beating a lane. The DDs should have landed before us, so with any luck they'll already have quelled a bit of the fire.'

'What if the DDs aren't there, sir?'

'Then we shall do our best to knock out a bit of the opposition and make sure the lanes go through. Forcing an exit off the beach is our first and only priority. If we lead the way, others can follow. Clear?'

A chorus confirmed that they were, so there was nothing to do but wait for the shore to re-appear through the smoke and for the ramp to go down.

He looked at his watch: 07.15. Twenty minutes to H-hour. A spout of spray shot up over the side of the boat and the whole thing shuddered. A shell fired from the shore. The typhoon of noise from the battleships behind them lessened. The barrage was ending. Machine-gun bullets rattled off the hull and now he could see them spearing the water all around. Smoke from the barrage was already drifting up and revealing the shore, a long line of shingle and sand pierced with tall wooden staves, metal gates and hedgehogs. And behind the mess of beach obstacles, on top of the sea wall and between the houses, came the bright winking flash of the enemy guns.

Tiny had his field glasses to his eyes again. He should be able to see the landmarks now. The lighthouse a mile or so to the west at Luc-sur-Mer, set back on the hill. The village houses of Colleville-sur-Mer lining the beach directly in front of them. The old casino on the headland. Tiny dropped his glasses and looked round at Mike. He raised a thumb and grinned. The ship's engine began to rev higher and they surged through the waves. The sub-lieutenant had said his orders were to take the last mile at full speed. This must be it then, the last mile. And hope to God there were no mines. He held his breath, not letting it out until the boat grounded out on the beach. The engines gave a final roar as the helmsman pushed forward to be sure they weren't caught on a bank or an obstacle. Apparently satisfied, he throttled back. Naval ratings hurried forward to operate the ramp and Mike dipped his chin to the intercom to tell Williams to start the engine. He felt rather than heard the big tank throb into life and saw a puff of blue smoke drift from the exhaust of Tiny's tank.

Another LCT ran ashore right alongside and he tried to work out who was getting off next to them. As the other boat's ramp went down there was a huge crash amidships and a spout of red flame and smoke shot up into the air. The detached turret of a tank spun lazily in the air. Hatch covers and the twisting strip of a track fell back into the burning boat. There was other falling debris too, identifiable as helmets, weapons and pieces of what had been men a moment ago. More explosions followed and a thick plume of black smoke spiralled from the inferno. Heat from the fire rolled over him and he scoured the beach for the source of the shell, but there was too much smoke. Anyway, their own ramp was dropping now, slowly at first, before slamming down with a splash that reared up on either side. As soon as the ramp was down, Hay-Wood's AVRE began to move forward. Another shell landed off their starboard bow and sent a huge cascade of water down on their heads. Mike spluttered and wiped stinging salt from his eyes. He took a last look around before he closed the turret, reducing his field of vision to what he could see through the front periscope. Tiny's tank lurched into view. As it crawled doggedly to the end of the ramp, he caught himself praying they were close enough in. The tank hesitated and started to move forward again. He swallowed his relief and spoke into his mouth-piece. 'Let's get on with it, Taff.'

Bullets pinged and whined off the hull as they surged down the ramp and then they were in the water, moving forward up a slight gradient. The waterproofing seemed sound, but water still sloshed through the crannies in the upper works as waves rolled in behind them and Mike heard Corporal Williams yelp and curse as he got a shock from the electric battery mounted right by his seat. 'Keep going, Corp. Soon be on dry land.'

'Nearly there, sir.'

'Good. Any of the DDs landed yet?'

'Can't see nothing besides Major Hay-Wood's arse, sir.'

'Well, stay behind him while I have a look around.' He pushed open the two halves of the turret-lid again and took a breath before he stuck his head out. The noise was astonishing, a percussion of pressure waves beating down on his head. He could see flashes issuing from gunposts, but the overall din made it impossible to distinguish one gun firing from another. It was like watching a silent film. As far as he could tell, they had landed pretty much as expected. Big craters and twisted wreckage showed the naval barrage had done its job, but there was still plenty of stuff blocking the way inland. He couldn't spot any DDs. Other Funnies were landing up and down the beach though. The two flail tanks that had been behind them on the landing craft were inching forward through the surf, rotors raised. 'Good show,' he thought. A second later the left-hand Crab was hit by a shell and crumpled to one side, its rotor pointing up at the sky, chains swinging crazily against the drum.

Angry at himself for jinxing it, he glanced back and saw an almost continuous wall of landing craft heading for the beach. Above them, flying in chevron formations tight as a sergeant's stripes, a mass of aircraft headed inland. Bombers to beat up the roads and rail-lines. Good. Keep the Germans from bringing up reinforcements. The mighty drone from a formation like that would normally have drawn all eyes. Today, with the cacophony on the beach he wouldn't even have known they were there if he hadn't chanced to look up. He dropped back down into the turret and shut the lid. He felt the reverb as the two halves of the clam-shell closed, but his ears refused to distinguish even that sound from the rest. He spoke into the intercom and was almost surprised to hear his own voice: 'Davis, get me the command tank.' And when he was on the right channel, 'Red One, Silver One here, one of our flail tanks has been knocked out. Shall we start clearing a lane? Over.'

Tiny's voice came crackling through the din: 'Silver One, yes, we'd better get on with it. Can I borrow your demolition chap to help mine out in front? Over.'

'On his way. Out.' Switching back on to intercom, he said: 'Rendall, hop out and start clearing by hand in front of Major Hay-Wood's tank with his sapper. Take a Bangalore torpedo.'

'Sir.'

Rendall struggled out of his Mae West, grabbed his steel helmet and collected a sackful of charges. He opened the side-hatch, pushed out one of the six-foot tubes of explosive and followed it. Mike felt but could not hear the hatch clang shut after him. Through the

344

forward periscope he watched his crewman run, head down, towards the other Churchill and a couple of minutes later the tank started to crawl forward. The sappers must be doing their job.

Some infantry were already ashore, landed early, and a group of soldiers rushed to take cover behind Tiny's tank. Peering out at the poor bastards cowering there, Mike wondered if there were more hunkered down behind him. He made a note not to go into reverse unless he absolutely had to.

Without warning, the beach rose up and blasted itself through every crevice and gap in the tank's plating. He was blind and suffocated, choking on sand, and thought himself deaf too until the roar of an explosion told him he wasn't and made him so, all at once. He had still not even begun to recover from any of these assaults on his senses when the whole tank reverberated like a struck church bell as something heavy smashed into the turret and the turret smashed into his head.

There was a moment, maybe more than a moment, when he knew nothing about anything. Then he found himself rubbing at his eyes. Tears washed out a bit of the sand and, though his eyeballs were scratched and sore, he could see again, blurrily. Hearing was another matter. There was a wild jagged buzzing in his head that drowned out everything. He tried shaking his head, but stopped when he felt everything sliding towards darkness. He leaned his forehead against the periscope and peered out, expecting to see Tiny's tank in front. It wasn't there.

There was a sound in his left ear, above the buzzing, the crackle of a voice on the intercom. He couldn't make out the words. He could hardly hear his own voice when he spoke. 'What's that?'

The voice came again. It was Williams, clearer this time. 'It's gone. Major Hay-Wood's tank. Blown to buggery.'

He put his eye to the forward periscope and squinted through the grimy prism. His heart gave a great thump. There was a crater in the sand and dark wet marks and lumps of debris at the edge of the hole. Of the leading AVRE there was no sign. He felt, rather than heard, the ping of bullets against the tank's plating and cleared his throat. 'Don't just sit there, Corp. Keep moving.' His voice, tinny through his headphones, sounded like another man's entirely, repeating the advice he had given to Tiny thirty-six hours ago. Much good it had done him. Yet it was still the best he had to give himself or anyone else. He was in no state to come up with anything better. His head was pulsing from the blow the turret had dealt him and his ears still rang. He felt wetness trickling down his neck and when he touched his right ear his fingers came away red. He wondered vaguely about his ear-drum. When he'd become conscious of still being alive, his first thought was that they must have been hit by a dud shell. Now, twisting round to peer through the rear periscope, he saw a big irregular hunk of metal lying on the beach behind the tank and he realised that their turret had taken a direct hit from the gear-box or cylinder block of Tiny Hay-Wood's disintegrating tank. There were other, less identifiable, lumps lying nearby. He did his best not to think about what those had once been.

There was no sign of Rendall, or the sapper from Tiny's tank, or of the soldiers who had been sheltering behind him. Bullets pinged and whined off the tank's plating and he realised he hadn't yet got rid of the tank's water-proof sealant so that they could revolve the turret. For that he needed the cover of the Crab's man-made sand-storm. He peered through the rear periscope and was relieved to see the remaining flail tank was still moving towards them. He prayed neither of them would be hit before they could make inroads up the beach. While he waited for the flail tank to come up, he went back to the forward periscope and watched as a stick of men fell raggedly to a machine-gun hidden in the dunes. Frustration at not being able to get on with it made him forget the throb and buzz in his skull. Where was that bloody Crab? At long last, it crawled past, its flailing chains raising a cloud that rolled back over them. He flicked on the intercom: 'Taylor, Hipkiss – I'm going to blow the water-proofing. As soon as I do, hop out and clear it off the turret.'

He pressed the button and there was a thud as the explosive charge blew off the caulking. The two men wriggled out of the sliding hatch, and flung themselves back in again half a minute later, choking and spluttering from breathing in flying sand. He got back on the intercom: 'Hipkiss, can you get a bead on any of their guns?'

There was silence for a minute, before the haberdasher, still spitting sand, said, 'I reckon I can 'ave a go at that fifty millimetre. It's a bit more than eighty yards, but I might be able to slot 'im.'

'All right, let's see how well you can measure him up. Fire when ready.'

The short barrel elevated and turned slowly on to Hipkiss's target. The tank shook and bounced on its axles as the mortar fired its load. He felt his teeth rattle and grabbed for a hand-hold inside the turret as the recoil threw him back and forward. Next thing he heard was a cheer through his headphones as the concrete emplacement dissolved in a cloud of smoke and cement. Williams' voice came through the intercom. 'You got him, Nev boy. Posted it right down 'is fuckin' throat.'

'That one's for Rendall, sir.'

'Yes, Nev. That one's for Rendall,' and he sent up a prayer, not caring if it was absurd to be addressing it to a god he didn't believe in, that they should not be hit at least until they'd fired a few more petards for Tiny Hay-Wood and his crew. 'Now, pull back in behind the Crab, Corporal Hipkiss, put another one up the spout, would you?'

Hipkiss opened the front hatch and wriggled out to depress the mortar spigot and load another Flying Dustbin into the barrel. He did it faster than he'd ever done in training and slammed the hatch shut again. 'Why in fuck didn't they make these things load from inside the tank?'

'Sorry, Nev. Still, gets you out in the fresh air.'

'Which I wouldn't mind, sir, 'cept it's raining out – and hard stuff at that.'

Before they followed the Crab on its long slow odyssey across the beach, he turned to the rear periscope to see what was happening behind them. Away to the right, in the very corner of his view, a beach-master in white hat and braid and carrying a swagger stick, had set up a post with four loudspeakers on the top and was directing traffic, waving it all up the beach. Not all of it was going, though. Groups of infantry were huddled around the beach obstacles and behind disabled tanks and other vehicles. Medical parties were attending to wounded men and stretcher-bearers were running across the beach, heads sunk in between their shoulders, trying desperately to keep their ends up and their heads down. He glanced out to sea again and spotted what looked like a little fleet of tins of Spam, making slowly for the shore. Better late than never, he muttered to himself, and turned back to the battle.

43

The news arriving at Fort Southwick was sporadic and fractured, and the first news of all was the worst possible. The American DD tanks due to land on the beach code-named Omaha had been launched seven thousand yards out and had virtually all been lost before reaching shore. Hobo looked up at his Number One with tortured eyes when he read the signal. 'Good God, Howard,' he said, 'Do you think it's going to be a complete disaster?' Burton shook his head firmly, trying not to think of the men trapped in those ship-wrecked tanks, and insisted, 'No, sir,' with far more conviction than he felt.

Bad news from Omaha continued to drown out the gradually encouraging reports from the British beaches. By mid-morning, the Americans had made so little progress in disabling the beach defences and had suffered so many casualties that the rumour racing round the fort was that General Bradley might fall back and abandon the attempt. Everyone knew well enough that all the beaches had to be taken if the Allies were not to be driven back into the sea. For an hour the entire invasion hung in the balance and the old stone tunnels stank as powerfully of claustrophobia and impotence as if a besieging enemy had been encamped around the moat. When their nerves could barely stand it any longer, a signal finally arrived to say that the Americans had cleared a lane off Omaha. Relief flooded the fort, and Hobo and Burton could turn their attention to what was happening elsewhere. They were deep in a pile of paper trying to piece together the state of play when the door of their room flew open and a flushed Charlie burst in, breathing hard from running all the way down the hundred odd steps from the surface. So excited that she forgot to salute and blurted out, 'I've got it, sir.'

The General looked up over his reading glasses. 'Got what?'

'A duck, sir.'

He pulled the glasses off now and swung them in her direction by the arm-piece. 'What are you talking about, woman?'

'Well, sir, I overheard you telling Colonel Burton the other night that the shipping people would only let you have space for one vehicle … '

'That's so. The idiocy of it, one vehicle a Divisional HQ does not make.'

'It might if it's a duck. Mightn't it?'

He glared at her for a moment more, sat back in his chair and tapped the arm of his spectacles against his teeth. 'By "duck", I take it you mean a DUKW, not a thing that quacks and waggles its tail?'

He glanced at Burton, who shook his head in tolerant amusement.

'Of course a DUKW, sir. And it's amphibious, if that's any use. You could get all sorts in there, radios, motor-cycles, maybe even a jeep if everyone budges up a bit. I was talking to the Yanks in the motor-pool yesterday and they were saying they had all these DUKWs and no way to get them over the Channel for weeks, it looked like. I didn't immediately think much of it. Then I remembered you saying you could only take one vehicle, and I thought … '

'You thought we might borrow one and the Yanks have so many they'd never notice?'

'Something like that, sir. It's not as if they're doing any good sitting in Portsmouth.'

Howard Burton cleared his throat. 'It's not a bad idea actually.'

Hobo shrugged. 'Although I hate to say so, it might be the best of a bad lot.'

Charlie grinned, a big triumphant grin. 'I'm glad about that, because I've already asked them, sir, and they said if I could get a letter from the CO of an Armoured Division, with an undertaking to hand over the vehicle to the US Army once you're in France then they'd sign one over to us. I don't think they thought I could do it, sir.'

Hobo smiled. 'I don't imagine they did. I don't imagine they had a clue who they were dealing with.' He turned to Burton. 'Get a letter sorted, Howard. I'll sign it and Miss Carrington here can run round and deliver it. I'm sure she'll enjoy the look on their faces. Oh, and Charlie, you'd better ask them to detach one of their drivers to come with it.'

'Sir,' said Charlie. Then something occurred to her, and she turned away quickly so that the CO shouldn't see what she was thinking.

44

The first time Dixon looked at his watch it was nearly 15.00 and they were on the road to Caen. He couldn't have said exactly how the hours since they completed their lane off the beach had passed. Firing and being fired at, directing his troop, and the rest of the squadron, talking to HQ on the net and trying to hear what was being said, while all the time his ears were still thrumming and singing from his bang on the head. His left ear, though he didn't say anything about it to the others, was pretty much out of commission. His right was not too bad. There was just an awful lot of noise in it.

They parted company with the Crab at the head of the beach, leaving it to flail round in a circle and right back down to the water's edge, doubling the width of the lane. Flagged down in Colleville-sur-Mer by a captain in the East Yorks who had lost three men to a sniper, Hipkiss obliged by demolishing the church tower where he was suspected of hiding. As the crew cheered the heavy downpour of masonry with philistine enthusiasm, Mike couldn't help thinking of Burton and the Great Sage on Brancaster beach discussing the merits of Norman church architecture. They'd have a bit less to talk about after today.

Half a mile beyond Colleville, the troop was rolling along nicely when a shell hit the front plating of the Churchill. The impact rang through the tank but was followed by no flames, screams or shredded, flying metal. It must have bounced off. Dixon ducked to the periscopes to try and see where it had come from, just in time to see Sergeant Johnstone's tank behind him veer off on to the grass verge. There was a dull thud and the thirty foot bridge canted up over the front of the tank dropped heavily on to what Dixon at that moment recognised as an anti-tank gun emplacement. Johnstone's tank swung back towards the road. There was no sign of any more activity under the bridge. He switched over the intercom, 'Thanks, Johnstone. Not exactly what they had in mind when they gave you that bridge.'

'Sorry, sir,' came the reply. 'I've been looking for somewhere to drop it all day. Anyway, more than one way to skin a cat.'

The troop's third tank did find a nice big shell hole for its roll of chestnut palings but, when the sapper corporal jumped to check how it had fallen, the lower half of his body disappeared in a cloud of blood. His torso slammed back against the tank and slid down to lie against its track. Mike had been talking to him from his turret as he jumped down and the man seemed to hold his eye for a long moment. He tore his eyes from the ravaged body and looked across at Ridpath in the tank's turret. He had seen the explosion and the cloud of blood spatter across his hull, but couldn't see the aftermath. Mike shook his head. Each caught the other's horror and looked away. Williams pulled their tank over to the verge and Taylor and Hipkiss slipped out of the side hatch. Treading gingerly, they picked up what was left of the body under the arms and carried it over. Hipkiss shouted up: 'Shall we bury him?'

Mike shook his head and yelled back: 'I'll radio the position back to HQ. Padre'll come up and bury him as soon as it's safe. Get back on quick.'

The two men stood indecisive for a moment, until a mortar crashed down a few yards away and they laid down their burden and dived back in through the hatch.

A few minutes later they received orders to move up to Ouistreham, where there was a fight going on for the lock-gates across the Caen Canal.

'Do we have any infantry in support?' Mike asked the officer from Brigade who radioed the orders in. 'We're pretty vulnerable against mobile artillery or Jerry tanks.'

'We'll get infantry there as soon as we can.' The strain in the voice that came over the ether was clear above the static. 'But the East Yorks have been hit pretty hard. Do what you can. Four Commando are adamant you're the chaps they need. Take ten AVREs and hold there until further notice.'

'Sir.'

At the canal they found the commandos hunkered down under a wall by the lock. Their CO was lying propped against the masonry with a field-dressing over a shoulder wound. Germans were moving about on the far bank. One man stood up and stared at the tanks over the top of the sand-bagged embrasure. Someone took a shot at him from the British side and he ducked out of sight.

Mike jumped down from the tank. His legs nearly buckled under him as he landed, stiff from hours cramped up in the turret. He danced about a bit to get rid of the pins and needles, aware he must look a right charlie. He squatted down by the officer. 'What do you want us to do, sir?'

The major, who had brick dust in his hair and was chalk-white from loss of blood, looked at him and said with an effort: 'Just make them see sense, would you? Pour some hot stuff on to them and persuade them to give it up as a bad job. They've blown the eastern span of the bridge and I think they've got the lock-gates wired, but we have to take control of the lock whether they blow it or not.'

'Are they likely to bring up reinforcements?'

The major shrugged and clearly wished he hadn't. He coughed, and didn't enjoy that much either. 'They're holding out as if they might be expecting some. Then again it may be sheer bloody-mindedness.'

'Let's find out, shall we?'

He climbed back on to the AVRE. As he put his leg into the turret, a wasp buzzed past his nose and whined off the hull of the tank behind. He swung his other leg in rapidly and dropped straight down inside, missing his seat and thudding his knees into the back of the gunner, who complained. 'Ow, sir.'

'Sorry. Sniper.'

He clambered back towards his seat and stood on the man's hand this time.

'Ow again, sir.'

'If you will always be getting in the way, Hipkiss. Try taking your mind off it by giving Jerry a burst of BESA fire, would you? And we'd better have a go at the lock-keeper's cottage. I think it has rats in it.'

'Can't have vermin about the place, sir.' The mortar-man revolved the turret towards the tall narrow house on the far side of the lock and fired. Brickwork and roof tiles erupted in a cloud. Through the periscope, Mike watched a roof timber fly end over end and land thirty feet away. There was scurrying movement under the rain of debris and Taylor fired away, the belt of ammunition rattling through the machine-gun and piling up on the floor of the turret.

The other AVREs joined in and machine-gun bullets started to come back over the canal and crack against the hull. A bigger shell, probably a mortar, landed behind them, rocking the tank with a hot wave of blast and noise that made Mike's ear ring in agony. The firing went on for what seemed like ages, then he looked out to see men standing up behind the sandbags with their hands raised. 'Hold your fire!' he said.

'What's up, sir?' said Hipkiss.

'They're surrendering, I think.'

'You sure, sir?'

'Of course not. I've never seen a German surrender before. But it looks like it does in the pictures.'

'I don't trust 'em. It could be a trick.'

'What am I supposed to do, Hipkiss? Let them stand there all day with their hands up?'

'We could shoot them. Then we'd know it wasn't a trap, wouldn't we? What are we supposed to do with prisoners anyway? There ain't no room for 'em in here.'

'We're not shooting them, Hipkiss. Not if they have surrendered. Four Commando can look after them – it's their show.'

Even as he spoke, three commandos were up and jogging towards the lock-gates. Another came running over to the AVRE. Mike opened the turret and stuck his head out. The commando shouted up: 'Looks like they're giving up. Have you got a sapper who can make the gates safe?'

Mike shook his head. 'Sorry, we lost ours. The only one left in my troop is two tanks back. Look after him, they're becoming a rare breed.'

The commando jogged on, and came running back a few seconds later with McDonald, the demolition corporal from Johnstone's tank, following close behind. A bag of explosives bounced at his shoulder.

By 17.00, the commandos had clambered over the de-fused lock-gates to occupy the east bank, the AVREs were deployed on the west and a troop of German POWs was heading to the beaches under armed escort.

'What now, sir?' asked Hipkiss.

'I should say we have some tea and hope we get relieved by the infantry with Bren carriers before Jerry thinks about coming back with mobile artillery of its own and a Tiger or two.'

'Right. I'll make a brew, shall I?'

356

'You do that, Hipkiss. And shove another Dustbin up the spout on your way out, would you? Just in case.'

At long last, the day that had seemed to have no beginning, only an infinite preamble of heaving seas and glowering sky, was drawing to a close. Or at any rate a halt. With the light going and no sign of a counter-attack on the lock-gates, Dixon's troop was detached to join up with the rest of the squadron. Darkness was falling fast when they turned off the road to Benouville. The remains of their squadron, a squadron of Shermans and four or five Crabs of the 22nd Dragoons were already there. He noticed the absentees. Babington-Browne, finally looking more like a soldier than a schoolboy, jumped down from his Crab and came over to ask about Major Hay-Wood. Mike shook his head.

'There's no chance he got out?'

'No chance at all, I'm afraid.'

'Bad show.'

Mike nodded. Babington-Browne scuffed at the grass with his boot. 'We lost Major Elphinstone – sniper on the beach. And did you hear about your CO? Shell hit his tank while he was still on the LCT. Never even made it ashore.'

Mike remembered the boat next to them exploding on the way in to the beach. 'Colonel Cocks is dead?'

Babington-Browne nodded. 'And if Major Hay-Wood has bought it too, I suppose that puts you in charge of the squadron.'

'I suppose it does.' There didn't seem anything else to say. They backed the tank into a corner between two apple trees. The scene was powerfully like their old billet at Stokes Bay. Except the blossom had finished here and the stalks that had borne it were already swelling into tiny inchoate fruit. That wasn't the only difference. That other garden had been in England, home, and now seemed safe as houses. This one was on the front line, as close as anyone could draw it. In occupied territory. And who was to say that by morning the line might not have moved?

As soon as Williams killed the engine the crew tumbled out of their various hatches and lay on the grass to smoke. Mike looked up at the sky and saw there were only a very few minutes of light left. He let them devour their first cigarettes before he squatted down beside them. 'I know you're all in, but we still have work to do. Hipkiss, cook up some compo stew. Davis, go round and check the tracks, oil, water. Taff, make sure the battery isn't showing any ill-effects from that sea-water. We shall need sentries. And before anyone goes to sleep, I want you to wash your eyes carefully with fresh water. I don't want anyone waking up in the morning with gummed-up eyelids. We shall need to look where we're going tomorrow, just as much as today. Questions?'

'Any chance of a lie-in, sir?'

He smiled. 'When we reach Berlin, Hipkiss. Until then, it's bright and early all the way. Oh, and bed down close to the vehicle, would you? We might have to move in a hurry if there's a counter-attack. Wouldn't want to leave anyone behind.'

As they moved off about their maintenance tasks, stiff from twelve hours in a cramped and comfortless steel box, Mike climbed on the back of the tank and untied the rope securing their bedrolls to the hull. He held the bundle with one hand while he wrestled with the knot and his palm came away red and sticky. There was a dark wet patch on the top bed-roll and brown and grey drips next to it on the hull. He wiped his hand on the seat of his trousers and turned the bed-rolls over so that the stain was on the bottom. As he jumped down and threw them out in a semi-circle, Private Taylor came walking across the orchard, carrying his mess-tin with greater than usual care.

'What have you got there, Taylor?'

'Milk, sir. Fresh as you like. One of the boys in Red Two found a cow in the field over there and he's milking it. There's a bit of a queue. But it's a pretty big cow, sir.' He smiled, his teeth glowing white in his grime-covered face, and Mike felt a sudden rush of relief and something like gratitude that, apart from poor Rendall, his crew had at least made it to the end of the first day of the invasion alive and scrounging.

He went to check on the other tanks, not only his little troop but also the other troops that made up what had been Tiny's squadron and was his, for the moment at least. Smoke-blackened and caked in sand and mud, the tanks hulked in a long, brutal row. There was nothing poetic or beautiful about them and yet he felt an odd tenderness for each one.

When he had done the rounds, he crouched beside the stove and let Hipkiss pour him a mug of tea. He propped his bed-roll against a tree and lay back against it, cradling the mug. As he took a first testing sup at the scalding liquid, Babington-Browne crossed in front of the tank and called over, 'Officer's mess set up in the farmhouse. Food's on the go.'

Mike leaned his head back against the bark of the apple tree, and let out a long breath that might easily have been mistaken for a sigh. He hadn't been more than about ten feet from his crew ever since they left the New Forest and it seemed unthinkable that he should abandon them now to their compo stew and bed-rolls and go off to the comforts of a French farmhouse. They had come through D-Day together and they were his men. He was happy where he was. He'd decided to ignore the invitation when Private Hipkiss looked up from poking the fire and grinned at him. 'Best get off, sir. You belong with the brass. The brass, not the arse.'

As he walked over to the back-door of the farmhouse, it felt weirdly familiar. The cobbled yard, with its mingled smell of straw, mud and cow dung, and redundant bits of machinery strewn about in corners, reminded him of Freddie Mee's yard so fiercely that he had to suppress the urge to pull off his cap and knock at the door. Over-compensating, he turned the handle and pushed harder than he needed, so that the door bounced off the wall with a crash. Four officers standing in the kitchen jumped as one man. A couple grabbed for their revolvers.

'Steady on,' said Babington-Browne. 'Nearly scared the living daylights out of us.'

'Sorry.' He glanced around the kitchen. It too bore a resemblance to Mrs Mee's kitchen. The scrubbed wood table surrounded by rush-seated chairs. A black-leaded range with a big stew-pot on top. A broad pot sink with dishes on shelves underneath. Tiled floor and blackened beams across the ceiling. So many of the same elements and yet all subtly different and foreign. The table with a narrower top and a different grain to the wood. The chairs with strangely curved backs and legs. The range knobbed and rounded and the stew-pot made of coloured enamel. Most different of all was the smell. Mrs Mee's kitchen had always been a savoury-sulphurous mixture of yeasty bread and carbolic soap, whereas this French kitchen was impregnated with onions and coffee. He sniffed a deep sniff. The smell was all-enveloping, the onion in particular having a stronger, higher, sweeter note than he'd ever come across. Even the onion clamp on the farm didn't smell as strong.

A major in the Sherwood Rangers Yeomanry turned and stuck out his hand. Mike shook it. 'Royal Engineers? You the sappers in the AVREs?'

Mike nodded.

'Good to have you along. How many of you made it?'

'I'm not entirely sure yet, sir. My troop's in one piece, though we've lost a couple of our demolition NCOs. My squadron leader bought it on the beach and we saw the CO's landing craft blow up as it landed. I've heard various people on the radio but I need to get on to Brigade HQ for the full picture. How about you?'

The tall Major shrugged. 'Not too bad. We came in on Gold. Most of our DDs made it, though a couple of them had their engines swamped by the tide. With a bit of luck we should be able to recover them when the support teams arrive.'

Mike smiled. 'I'm glad they made it. When I saw the sea state I was afraid they might all go under. The ones on our beach were a bit late arriving, but I saw a fair number coming in behind us. Rather glad not to have been driving one myself in this weather.'

The Major nodded. 'Quite. I was happy to be in the standard Sherman. Always seemed a pretty crackpot idea to me, but I suppose it's worked. Odd sight we must have been, what with the mine-destroyers beating the beach like a big Indian rug and you boys chucking your mortars about. I watched one of the flame-throwers clear out a couple of pill-boxes. First set of Jerries bailed out on fire.' He laughed. 'Second lot didn't hang around to get grilled.'

Mike smiled. 'The Old Man'll be happy. Have you heard how the Yanks got on? They weren't keen on taking any of our Funnies except for DDs.'

The major shrugged again. 'I heard they had a hell of a job getting ashore on Omaha. Made it in the end though.'

Mike thought of the American sappers in their light boats. There was a noise behind him and he turned to see a small door open and a young woman appear at the top of some steps that must lead down into a cellar. Her arms were filled with brown bottles, each stopped with a cork tied in with string. She advanced, smiling, and unloaded them on to the table. Then she fetched six short pressed glass tumblers from the dresser. She cut the string away from the first bottle and levered out the cork with her thumbs. It flew out with a pop and a whiff of gas and she hurried to pour the over-flowing liquid into the glasses. Shyly, she handed the first one to the Major and the second to Mike. The others gathered round and helped themselves.

'Your very good health,' said the tall Major, raising his glass to the French girl.

She snatched up the last glass from the table. '*Libération!*' she said. '*Victoire! Mort aux Boches!*'

The Major laughed. 'That's the spirit, mademoiselle. *Vive la France!*'

'*Vive la France!*' echoed Mike and the others. He took a deep pull at his glass. Cider. Good cider. This at least didn't seem foreign. He tipped his head back and emptied the glass. The others were doing the same. The girl, bright-eyed, smiled and began to saw at the string on the second bottle.

They dined on chicken stew and soft creamy mashed potatoes so good that when Mike felt a pang for his men and their compo stew he quelled it with another huge forkful and a swallow of the red wine that had come out of the cellar hard on the heels of the cider. When dinner was over they cleared the table and opened out their maps. The beaches lay five miles behind them. Ahead was Caen. He was pleased to see that they had overrun their D-Day objectives by quite a way. Whether they continued to move inland at the same rate would depend on the speed and strength of the German counter-attack. And that depended on whether the German High Command believed this attack was the main invasion, or still expected General Patton's army massed in Kent to attempt a second landing in the Pas de Calais. The fact that there was no army in Kent was one of the biggest intelligence gambles of the war. If it was working, it might pin at least two elite SS Panzer divisions up near Calais. If the Germans had seen through the ruse, every tank they had in France or Belgium would be on its way to Normandy by now.

After dinner, a despatch-rider arrived from Brigade HQ with news and orders for the morning. He poked his head in at the kitchen door and grinned at the array of bottles on the table. 'Is there a Major Carrington here?'

The tall Major stood up.

'Carrington?' said Mike, before he could stop himself. 'No relation to Charlotte Carrington?'

The Major smiled. 'My little sister. Of course. I should have twigged when you said you were Hobo's ADC. She would have been driving you as well as the Old Man. You must know her pretty well, I suppose.'

Babington-Browne leaned back in his chair and clasped his hands on top of his head: 'You're Charlie's brother, are you? Well, it's a small world. What a great girl. We were all in love with her at Rawdon, even Mike here, I dare say, though he plays his cards pretty close to his chest.'

'Well, I'm sorry to disappoint you all,' said Archie, turning away to the despatch rider, 'but she's off the market for good. I went to the wedding a few weeks ago.'

45

Mike woke abruptly. One minute he was in a black, bottomless sleep, the next he was sitting up with his eyes open. He knew he had to remember something and for a moment he couldn't think what. Then the events of yesterday flooded through him in a torrent. He was in France. The invasion was underway. Tiny was dead. Charlie had married someone else. He shut his eyes and lay back down, but there was no way back to the unconsciousness that already seemed like a lost Eden. His men were outside and light was already filtering in through the dusty, cracked glass in the parlour window. The war would be back on at any moment.

He had slept on a narrow straight-backed settle. This entirely comfortless piece of furniture was upholstered in cold shiny sateen. The horsehair it was stuffed with pricked through the cover and it smelled of its considerable age. As he sat up, his stiff back told him he'd have been more comfortable stretched out on his bed-roll next to the tank, but Hipkiss had got it right. Everyone would have found it odd if he'd shunned the officers' mess – and oddness was not a reassuring quality for a commander to display in battle. Of course, if he'd stayed with the men he might have avoided meeting Archie Carrington, but he knew Nigel Babington-Browne's love of gossip well enough by now to be sure his not getting the news from the horse's mouth would only have delayed his hearing it for a few hours.

He went quietly through the empty farmhouse kitchen, relieved there was no sign of Babington-Browne or any of the Sherwood Rangers. As he walked towards the orchard it struck him that there was no thud of guns yet and the birds were celebrating the start of a new day. He wondered if they had sung through the bombardment yesterday or flown away in terror and returned just now to their old perches, thinking the barbaric noise and perturbation of their air was over. Poor, optimistic creatures. There was something odd about their singing, though. He turned his head from side to side and realised he was only hearing it through his left ear. He shook his head, pinched his nose and blew hard – which had no effect besides causing a sharp stab of pain in his head. He put his fingers to his right ear and felt a crust of dried blood and wetness. Inspecting them, he found fresh blood. It definitely didn't look good about his ear-drum.

When he reached his Churchill, three of the crew lay close by on their bed-rolls in attitudes of such total stillness that he felt a sudden thrust of fear. They had passed so many dead men yesterday, some of whom looked as if they might only be sleeping, that the sight of his crew like this made him wonder if it wasn't just as possible that they were just as dead. He stretched out his boot and trod lightly on Taff Williams' out-thrown arm. The driver grunted and relief flooded through him.

He crossed to the ragged hedge that separated the orchard from the field behind and unbuttoned his fly. As the warm stream spattered on to the base of the hedge, his eyes rested idly on the pattern of leaves and twigs. He straightened his back and took stock of himself: ear not too good; non-fatal headache; eyes scratched and sore from flying sand and cement dust; stiff back; odd bruises from banging around inside the turret. Not much to show, really, for a day that had left so many men dead or maimed. Nothing, really, except for a dull, throbbing ache in his chest that had nothing to do with the war, or at least nothing to do with the Germans. His other minor injuries would heal in a few days and be forgotten anyway as soon as he got in the tank and started up. It was only that great hollow drum-beat that troubled him. It seemed foolish, his heart beating away when there was no longer any reason to do it. His dream of marrying Charlie was over. He would never spend another day with her. Never see her … something broke in on his line of thought. His eyes were trying to relay a message to his brain – something about the hedge – a solid shape amid the shimmering green. The shape resolved into a field-grey uniform, crouching in the cattle-cropped grass no more than thirty feet away. He stood still. For a moment he thought it might be a German corpse, until he saw the gun in its hands. If he moved, the soldier was sure to fire. If he didn't move, the man was probably still going to fire. He had taken his revolver out of the turret last night and laid it by his bed-roll before he went off to the officers' mess. It was still there, ten feet away. Stupid, he thought, what a bloody stupid way to die. But at least it'll be over. At least it won't hurt any more. He watched the German swing his machine-pistol up to his hip and round to bear on him. He shut his eyes and whispered her name one last time. The gun stuttered loudly and he shuddered at the punch of bullets ripping into his chest. Except they didn't. He opened his eyes. The German soldier lay in a grey heap. He spun around. There was no one else in sight. No sign of what had happened, except for a small dribble of smoke rising from the holes drilled along the barrel of the lap-gun on his tank.

As he stared at the smoke, the front hatch fell open and Private Hipkiss's head poked out. It was wreathed in a broken-toothed grin. Mike had never seen anything more beautiful.

'Was you going to let the bastard shoot you, sir? I hope you've got better tactics than to just stand there when we come across our first Tiger.'

Mike laughed. It felt good. He was alive and he could laugh. 'Sorry, Hipkiss. Thanks for stepping in.'

Hipkiss grunted: 'Well, it's not the best time to be breaking in a new officer, is it? Not when we've just about got you house-trained. What if they sent us some real snooty type as a replacement? Or a school-kid. Or both. No, we'll stick with you for now, sir, if it's all the same.'

Mike walked over to pick up the holster with his revolver in it. 'It's all right with me, Nev. And I promise I'll try to be a bit quicker on the up-take in future. Keep a look-out for a bit longer, will you? I'll round us up some tea.'

He headed back towards the farmhouse. There had been a nearly-full bottle of Calvados on the kitchen table, left over from their toasts the night before. He hoped it was still there. Hipkiss and the other lads would probably appreciate a nip in their morning tea.

46

Early on D+2, Hobo demanded an inspection of his new HQ. Charlie drove to the motor pool with a mixture of pride and trepidation. 'It's not too bad, I suppose' said the General, when he'd crawled all over the big truck and was standing in its belly. 'Given that beggars can't be choosers. What do you say, Burton? Do you think we shall be able to run the show from here?'

'It'll be cosy. Skeleton team, say six officers, wireless operators, small signals section with a motorcycle. Drive a jeep in last and load that up too. I should say we'll manage until we can afford something bigger.'

'Make us sound like a couple of newlyweds viewing a studio in Pont Street, man. Still, I think it will do. It'll have to do, dammit. Well done, Miss Carrington. Good show. Now, where's the driver?'

'Ah,' said Charlie, feeling her knees go a little slack. She stiffened everything and stood up straight. The turret swivelled and she found herself looking down the barrel. 'That's the only drawback, sir. Yanks have had to call a man over from some way away. He won't be here till later this morning.' Charlie tried not to let her eyes slide away from the CO's and willed herself not to blush.

'He'd better be, because if there's any chance of an earlier crossing than the one we've been allocated, I shall jolly well want to be on it. Do you really mean to tell me the Yanks don't have any spare drivers knocking around here in Portsmouth?'

'Apparently not, sir.'

'Extraordinary. What about one of our chaps?'

'They're not keen to let anyone who's not been properly trained on the amphibious equipment take her over, sir. Sorry.'

Hobo looked at his watch. 'Ah well, Burton. Get the loading sorted. I'm going to check the latest signals. Charlie, get my jeep ready, would you?'

Charlie drove the jeep up behind the DUKW and stopped. The vehicle was surrounded by heaps of radio equipment, stores and members of the Divisional Staff. The jeep was piled with spares and as many jerry cans of petrol as she had been able to scrounge. Also, tucked down in the back, under some spare track links was a small kitbag and a blanket. A steel helmet was jammed in the door pocket. Rather than her usual skirt, she was wearing the jodhpurs of an ATS truck driver. Not wanting to attract attention, she sat in the jeep, hoping they would finish loading so that she could drive aboard unnoticed. Activity continued all around her. She glanced at her watch. It was just after eleven and they were due to sail at two. She hoped it would still be light when they landed in Normandy.

'Charlie?'

She jumped and looked up to find General Hobart standing by the jeep. 'Where in blazes is this Yank driver?'

'I don't know, sir. He should be here by now.'

'Go and find him, would you? I want to be down at the docks in good time. Don't want to get stuck in traffic.'

'No, sir.' Charlie threw the jeep into reverse and drove off to the opposite side of the yard. She got out near the maintenance shed and killed a few minutes chatting to the mechanics. At twenty past eleven, she reckoned it was time to take her life in her hands. She climbed into the jeep and drove back to the DUKW. Most of the stores had disappeared inside the belly of the whale and two soldiers were pushing a despatch motorcycle up the ramp. She lined the jeep up with the tracks of the ramp and turned off the engine until they were ready for her.

'Well?'

She jumped again. 'Awfully sorry, sir. There's no sign of him anywhere. Nobody seems to know what's happened. They swear they sent a message for him, but he's not here.'

'Then they'd better bloody well detach another driver from the pool here.'

'Thing is, there aren't any drivers here with the Ducks at the moment. Only mechanics. The drivers have been deployed over to Kent on exercises until there's room on the transports for them.' She wasn't sure where this particular bit of embroidery had come from. All it would take was for a couple of Yank drivers to come strolling over and climb into the other Ducks and she'd be found out and on a charge.

'So what in God's name are we supposed to do?'

She took a deep breath. 'Actually, sir, I've been down here quite a bit the last couple of days and the mechanics have been showing me the ropes on the Duck. I've driven it up and down the yard a few times and they've taught me how it all works. So … '

'Charlie, are you quite mad?'

'No, sir. I don't think so.'

'Then do you think I'm mad?'

'Of course not, sir.'

'Well, you must believe one of us is certifiable if you think I'm going to allow you to drive this thing on to the front line. There's not a single woman landed in France yet, and won't be until the situation's a good deal more secure.'

'With respect, sir, that's not exactly true. There are women in France already, aren't there? Millions of them.'

'That's different. There are no ATSs on the front line. It's out of the question. Burton.'

Howard Burton, who was talking to some other men near the front of the DUKW, cocked an ear and glanced towards his CO. Charlie knew she was about to be defeated if she didn't press on. 'Sir, please. You're going to need a good driver in Normandy. It's what you're always telling people: fit the right man to the right job. It's why you put Royal Armoured Corps drivers into the sappers' tanks, and picked Cockney market traders as wireless operators. Well, driving you is my job, and I'm thoroughly trained for it. More than anybody. I know how you want to be driven and I think I've proved I can react in a tight spot.'

Hobo pointed his finger at her. 'Don't try and be clever with me, Charlie. You may be a good driver, but you can't be the right man for this job for the very simple reason that you're not a man. There are no facilities for women in Normandy yet and I simply don't have authority to take you. If anything were to happen to you, there'd be hell to pay and I don't have time for it, frankly. It's completely out of the question. Burton.' He turned and started to walk away.

'Sir?'

He glanced back sharply, his face shading from irritation towards anger. The look alone would have been enough to quell most people. 'That letter you gave me the other night. Captain Dixon asked me to marry him. He didn't know I was marrying Bill. Lady Hobart tried to warn me not to do the wrong thing but I didn't listen. I promise I won't get distracted, but if we should link up with Captain Dixon, at least I can tell him that I want to put things right. God knows how, but … '

Hobo checked his watch for the umpteenth time. He looked around the yard again and, still seeing no one who looked like an amphibious truck driver, sighed. 'Oh, for Christ's sake. Load that jeep in the back and secure it, and get ready to drive this thing to the docks. If we can't pick up a driver on the way I suppose we'll have to take a chance. Just keep a low profile or we shall both be in the doghouse.'

Charlie bounced in her seat with excitement. 'You won't regret it, sir, honestly.'

Hobo scowled and said, 'I will if you get your head shot off. Idiotic girl.'

Down on the transport deck, Charlie was sick. She rested her head against the side of the DUKW's cab and tried to keep down whatever was left in her stomach. When everyone else had gone up on deck, the CO had ordered her curtly to stay with the vehicle. He was clearly of the view that, having made her bed, she had better lie on it. She'd glared after the retreating backs but, a few minutes later, she was relieved they weren't there to see her retching into a drainage gully.

When she finally heard footsteps clanging along the ship's metal gratings, she peered through the dim lighting at her face in the rear-view mirror. She looked ghastly so she quickly pinched her cheeks to draw colour back into them. The last thing she wanted was to look like a weak and feeble woman before they'd even started.

'Still here, Charlie?' said Lt-Colonel Burton, opening the door of the cab.

'Still here, sir. Are we nearly there?'

'Not far off. Here.' He held out a paper bag. Grease had seeped through the corners and the smell of bacon fat filled the cab. Charlie felt her gorge rise.

'Only fair, after all the sandwiches you've brought me.'

'Thanks, sir. Just what I fancy.' She got the words out quickly and clamped her teeth shut. She took the sandwich and threw it on top of the dash-board as soon as he turned away. But the smell, the normally tantalising, now torturous smell, snaked its way through the air. A wave of nausea rose up and she fought it down, trying to breathe through her mouth. She tasted bile and shut her mouth hard. That meant she had to breathe in through her nose and the smell was stronger than ever. There was only one way to get rid of it. She ripped off the grease-proof paper and shoved the sandwich into her mouth, attacking it with small, rapid bites. 'Kill or cure,' she told herself as she swallowed, praying that no one would be watching if she had to run back over to the grating. But, funnily, as soon as she was halfway through, she began to feel better, and when it was gone, she even licked the grease off her fingers. The door opened again. 'Better?'

'Much better. Thanks.'

'Thought it might be what the doctor ordered. Pretty lumpy down here, I bet.'

'A bit, sir.'

'Mind if I hop in? Need somewhere quiet to dash off a letter before we land.'

'Be my guest.'

When he'd climbed up into the cab, he started pulling things out of various pockets: folded sheets of blue paper and envelopes out of one; a fountain pen out of another; a pipe from a third.

'You know you can't light that down here, sir.'

He grinned at her. 'I know, Charlie, but I always have it on the go when I write to my wife. I figure just chewing on it will help. This sort of letter isn't the easiest to write, you know.'

'What sort of … ? Oh,' said Charlie, suddenly understanding.

He looked at her, then held out the blue paper. 'You should write one too. We encourage all the men to do it before they go into action.'

She pulled a couple of sheets of paper out of the wad and fished in her jacket pocket for something to write with. Propping the paper against a map case from the door pocket she chewed the end of the pencil she'd come up with. Colonel Burton had already begun to write, his elegant copper-plate hand moving steadily across the paper. He didn't seem to find this sort of thing difficult, after all. Charlie didn't have a clue what to say. There was no point in explaining herself to Bill.

If she was killed it would be simple cruelty to leave word telling him why she'd gone to France. And it was too impossible to explain herself to Mike in the few minutes before they landed. It would have taken her days, probably, to find the right words. And what would they matter anyway, if she was dead before he read them? In the end she wrote a note to the one man who had always understood her adventurous spirit best – her father. She made no reference to the mess she was in, simply to her desire to do her bit, and her hope that he would be proud of her. The letter was so short that she caught Colonel Burton up and they sealed both envelopes together. He folded his and put it in the top pocket of his battledress. Then he rubbed his hands and smiled at her. 'Be off in a minute. Got your stuff?'

'Some here, some in the jeep.'

'Good, put your Mae West on, will you? In case we hit a mine on the way in. There are still a good many floating around, I believe. So keep your fingers crossed.'

She held up her hands to show him they were.

'Good. When the ramp goes down, we'll be getting off quick as we can and following a marked lane up the beach. I imagine there'll be a fair bit of debris lying about, so let's keep our minds on the job, eh?'

She realised that by debris he meant knocked-out tanks, maybe even dead bodies and that he was trying to prepare her. 'Don't worry, sir. I know my job.'

'I don't doubt it.'

She climbed down and walked round to the back of the DUKW. Hobo was there, giving orders to his staff, who stood in a silent circle. Nobody took any notice of Charlie as she climbed up the ramp and opened the door of the jeep. She dug out her life-preserver and strapped it on. She pulled her steel helmet out of the door pocket too.

374

Back in the cab, she put on her driving gloves and swapped her cap for the helmet. As she tightened the chin-strap, the passenger door opened and Hobo climbed in. He looked at her, but said nothing. She had no idea how long it would be before her insubordination was forgiven. Then the engine note of the big ship changed, the motion altered and there was a terrible rasping and scraping beneath them as they jerked and ground to a halt. The high whine of hawser motors started up and Charlie saw a line of light crack open in front of them. The line widened into a slot, then into a box as the bow doors swung open. The hawsers screamed, the ramp dropped down and the beach lay in front of them. She tried not to gawp, tried to concentrate on revving the engine and finding first gear in the unfamiliar box. Two naval ratings waved her forward and the DUKW rolled slowly out into the light. Water surged and ebbed around the bottom of the ramp. She could see wet sand a few yards ahead. It looked like a comfortable wade, so long as there were no mines washing around in the shallows. Holding her breath, she inched the big truck forwards. At the end of the ramp, she felt the front wheels sink into the sand, grip and begin to turn, forced forward by the rest of the driving wheels still on the ramp. She kept a gentle pressure on the throttle and felt the wheels bump one by one off the ramp until the DUKW was in the water and wading towards the shore. Keep going, she begged silently. Keep going. And it did. Until they were on solid wet sand and she could hear the water draining out of the chassis in a gush.

'Well done.' The CO spoke quietly. 'Now there are the poles marking a swept lane. Take us up there, can you?'

Behind them, in the body of the DUKW, she could hear officers talking, pointing things out. She willed herself not to look around. Willed herself to keep her eyes on the lane ahead. It was enough that the air was heavy with the smell of oil, cordite from exploded shells and another sweet, metallic smell she suspected she knew and chose not to name. It was enough that even within the lane she was following there were shell holes where the sand was stained black, and lumps of metal and wire, twisted girders, abandoned packs and broken-down vehicles. It was enough that this place bore no relation to any beach she had ever seen in her life, in her dreams or in her nightmares.

'Stop.'

Charlie braked hard. The big truck skidded slightly on the uncertain surface and swayed to a halt. There was a thud from the back and a quick burst of laughter. She guessed that someone hadn't been quick enough to brace themselves. Hobo already had the door open and was jumping down. She relaxed her hands on the wheel and allowed herself to look around for the first time. A hundred yards ahead, the beach ended in a run of dunes. Behind the dunes lay a row of houses. The remains of houses. What must, until two days ago, have been smart seaside villas were now a tumble-down wreck of sliding roof-tile and skeletal rafters, the remains of their rendered walls spattered with a dreadful acne of shell- and bullet-holes.

In front of the dunes, to the side of the track, stood a tank that had carried a Bobbin carpet-laying attachment. One of its tracks had been blown off on a mine and lay unspooled behind it while the bobbin itself had been hit by shell-fire and sprawled shattered in a mess of torn canvas and spokes over the tank's hull. If it had looked an improbable weapon before, she couldn't help thinking the battle had quickly proved it utterly ridiculous. Her heart pounded in her throat and she was suddenly terrified that all the Funnies had suffered the same fate. Through the open passenger door she saw Hobo striding over to another tank. From the size of it, she instantly recognised it as a Churchill, but it was a Churchill that had been through hell. The turret was a mess of twisted metal and black smoke streaks ran down over the hull and stained the sand. The short snout of the petard identified it as an AVRE. She turned off the engine and jumped down from the cab. The ground was hard and corrugated by the passage of a thousand tracked vehicles, the sand fused together into a stained grey substrate. As she walked round the front of the DUKW her eyes were on the tarpaulin that lay on the ground a yard or so from where the General was talking to a short, balding man with his shirtsleeves rolled up above the elbows. On the tarp lay three or four objects. They were laid neatly, a six inch space separating each from the next, which was the only kind of order or dignity that could be lent them, for the objects themselves were grotesque, irregular, twisted and unnatural. They were unrecognisable. Certainly unrecognisable as the young men they had been two days before. Almost unrecognisable as anything that could ever have been a man, or a part of a man.

The stranger looked up and flinched at the sight of her. He reached down quickly and flicked the edge of the tarpaulin so that it doubled over and covered the carbonised fragments of the AVRE's crew. She looked at the canvas for a minute longer, before she looked up at the man. 'Who were they?'

Hobo turned quickly. 'Charlie, get back in the vehicle.'

'Who were they?'

The balding man had brought a pipe out of his trouser pocket and was trying to light it. She noticed that his hands were filthy, black and greasy. Normally, Hobo would have had him on the carpet for such a flagrant lack of respect. Today, he just said, 'Fifth Assault Regiment. Seventy-seventh Assault Squadron. Second Troop, the padre thinks. A Sergeant Tucker and his crew.'

A Sergeant Tucker. Not Captain Michael Dixon.

'Look here, padre. Do you want me to detail men to come back and help you? When I link up with my Brigade HQ I can detach a graves party if you want.'

The padre sucked at his reluctant pipe and shook his head slowly. It was clear he was weary to the bone. 'No thanks, sir. It's best the men who have to fight in tanks don't get too close to this kind of thing. I'd sooner do it myself. I've promised myself I'll account for everyone. The least we can do, really. Identification's not always easy … ' His eyes drifted to the tarp and he took another suck on the pipe. 'I'll bury them up on the verge and mark the graves. Let the families know. They'll be re-buried later somewhere more suitable.'

'It's a rotten job, padre. Glad someone's doing it.'

'I hope to be put out of it soon enough. Soon as you like.'

'We'll do our best. Now, do you have any idea where First Armoured Brigade HQ might be by now?'

The padre raised his eyes and squinted towards the dunes. 'They were in Benouville yesterday. Took a while to see off Jerry there, but they'd reduced it by nightfall. Should be on the outskirts of Caen by now. I can't say for sure. I left them to it and came down here after breakfast. You should find them somewhere along that road.'

'Right. We'll get after them. I need to get recovery vehicles working down here.'

They both turned and looked down the beach, where a line of abandoned tanks showed the state of the tide when the assault had begun. The wreckage was making it hard for the mass of new transports to land their next wave of troops. 'Yes, sir. I've been all along those vehicles. Most aren't badly damaged. Just swamped by the tide, I think. Some chaps must have been concentrating on firing inland and got taken by surprise. Rough day.'

'The sooner we pull them out of there, the sooner we can get 'em repaired. Sea-water won't be doing them an ounce of good. Right, padre. Plenty to do. Time I got on with it.'

'Be careful on the road, sir. Snipers are still pretty active. Enemy's building up again north of Caen. They were talking about two new Panzer regiments moving into the area this morning. Situation's not entirely resolved yet, I should say.'

Hobo saluted and the padre saluted back. His lips brightened into a faint smile, but his eyes were preoccupied and he turned back toward the burnt-out AVRE before they had made a move to go.

Charlie started up the DUKW again. Neither of them said a word as she put it into gear and set off toward the dunes. They drove in silence through the wreckage of a village, which was or had been Lion-sur-Mer, according to the pocked signboard. Turning towards Ouistreham and Caen, they found themselves in a slow-moving stream of traffic as the road funnelled newly landed troops towards the front. Hobo soon wore out his small store of patience, swearing every time there was a hold-up to skirt a shell-crater or a broken-down lorry. He leaned back and stuck his head into the rear of the DUKW and she heard him say, 'Have you got Brigade HQ on the radio? No? Why the hell not? See if you can raise Nigel Duncan. He should know where in blazes they've got to.'

There was a gap of a few minutes before Colonel Burton stuck his head into the cab. 'We've found Brigadier Duncan, sir. Says Brigadier Watkinson is between Benouville and Caen. Been tied up with a Jerry counter-attack most of the day. They'll be going into laager shortly. We're working on getting a map reference for Brigade HQ now.'

As night was falling, they came to the outskirts of yet another village and turned off into a courtyard next to a long, low Norman farmhouse. Jeeps and lorries were drawn up outside the house and tank-tracks led through a gateway that had had one pillar reduced to rubble by a shell or careless driving. Beyond the gateway, Charlie could dimly see the shapes of tanks lined up against the walls.

'Take her through into the farmyard, Charlie,' said Colonel Burton peering through from the back. 'We'll disembark the other vehicles and kit and see who's here.'

She nosed the DUKW through the gateway, mounting the left-hand wheels up on the rubble and landing with a thump on the other side. The wheel jerked in her hands as the DUKW swayed and she realised for the first time how tired she was. When she turned off the engine, Hobo jumped down from the cab and she heard the others' boots thudding along the metal floor and the truck sway as each man jumped down. She didn't move. She was all at once weighed down by a huge feeling of inertia, that unseen force Hobo hated most in the world. While she'd been driving, she had just about been able to keep from thinking about the brewed-up AVRE on the beach. Now it flooded her senses and threatened to sweep her away on a tide of dread. With Bill, she'd never had any sense of whether he was dead or alive, but she'd told herself that was because she didn't love him. With Mike, she had always felt that she would know. Now she was overcome by terror that this growing foreboding was the feeling she had searched for inside herself when Bill was missing and never found. She laid her head against her forearms and wished she hadn't come.

When the driver's door was flung open she looked up in alarm, expecting the CO or Colonel Burton. Instead it was a soldier in dirty battledress, with a beret pushed back from a dust and dirt-spattered face so that there was a little rim of clean skin between the grime and his hair line. Before she could move, he reached into the cab and lifted her out, pulling her into a hug before her feet had touched the ground. 'Charlie, what in hell's name are you doing here? Has your GOC completely lost his mind?'

For a moment she couldn't speak. Then, 'Archie,' she said. 'Bloody hell, Archie.' She grinned up at him and stamped out a treacherous flicker of disappointment that the filthy tanker was not Mike. Only her brother. Only the person she was second happiest to see, safe and alive, in all the world.

'Don't blame the Old Man. I talked him into it. Tricked him into it, really.'

'Well, you're a dolt. It's not safe for you here. Not in the slightest. We lost one of our tank commanders to a shell blast this morning before we even left laager. He'd nipped along to the next village. Got caught by mortars coming back. Not a mark on him, but a stopped clock all the same. After going right across North Africa. Very decent poet too, by all accounts. If it could happen to him it can happen to anyone. More likely now, actually. There could easily be a couple of Panzer divisions on their way from the Pas de Calais. We're expecting a counter-attack any time.'

He glared at her, sore red eyes in a black face. Charlie pouted and, catching herself at it, started to laugh.

'What are you laughing at, dolt?'

'You, Archie. Us. Don't you see we're acting exactly like when we were children, and you were off climbing round the chimney stacks at home? God, how you hated it when you turned round and found I'd got up on the roof behind you. "It's too dangerous for girls", you used to say. But I never slipped off the roof and cracked my skull, like you said I would. Did I?'

'Charlie, for Christ's sake, this is not a kids' game. It's a battle. It's bad enough my men dying, without having to worry about my little sister getting blown to pieces as well.'

She stuck out her chin. 'Don't worry about me then. I shall be all right. And if I'm not, well, why should I be any different from all the men who're being killed, anyway? I am in the Army, you know, just like you. I don't know what should make me so worthy of special protection. I'm doing a job that needs doing and I'm good at it. Good as a man. So, please don't make a fuss, Arch. Be a dear.'

She tilted her head and gave him the round-eyed look that had usually worked when they were children. He sighed. 'All right, but I'm warning you, Charlotte, if you go and get yourself killed, you will never hear the end of it.'

'Deal,' she said, and realised that seeing Archie had given inertia the bum's rush. She was suddenly starving. 'What are the odds of scrounging something to eat round here?'

'Funnily enough,' he said, as they picked their way across the farmyard, 'I met a couple of chaps who knew you. They were here the night of D-Day. Chap in the Dragoons, and a captain in the sappers. Northern, scholarship type. Said he used to be Hobo's ADC. Could have knocked them both over with a feather when I told them I'd just been best man at your wedding.'

She stopped. Archie walked on. 'Taciturn kind of fellow. Dixon, was it? Hardly said a word all night. And, extraordinary thing if he didn't pinch a bottle of our Calvados in the morning to give to his crew. They went off with grins as big as Cheshire cats. Bit off, we all thought.'

He turned round to look for her. 'What's up?'

'Oh, Archie,' she said. Tears welled up and she pressed her forearm over her eyes to stop them from falling. She could not cry. She would not cry. She had persuaded the GOC to let her come to France to do her job, not to be weak and womanish, no matter what happened. She rubbed her sleeve across her face and let her arm drop to her side.

'What is it?'

She looked up at him, dry-eyed. 'I've made the most terrible mess of things, Archie. That's all. And I don't know if I shall ever be able to put them right.'

47

The next morning would have heralded a beautiful June day, if the month of June hadn't been swept away by a revolutionary calendar so that, rather than the ninth of June, it was D+3 that dawned fine and clear. After a night of broken sleep on a bed-roll in the back of the DUKW and a sketchy breakfast, Charlie was making her way back to the farmyard to check over the vehicles. She felt light-headed with tiredness, her thoughts circling endlessly round the look she imagined on Mike Dixon's face when Archie dropped his bomb. It was a relief when Lt-Colonel Burton came up alongside and started chatting to her as she side-stepped the rubble in the gateway.

'Morning Charlie,' he said. 'Terrible mess these Sherwood Rangers make. No respect for vernacular architecture. I have a feeling that gateway was seventeenth century. Maybe a bit earlier.'

As Charlie turned to reply, there was a high-pitched zip and Burton dropped flat on the ground. Charlie stared at him for a moment, wondering what on earth he was playing at, before it dawned on her that they were being sniped. She threw herself down beside him. Heard another zip and a high whine as dust puffed out of the broken stonework beside them. Put her hands to her head, wishing she was wearing her steel helmet, which was in the door pocket of the Duck. 'Sir?' she whispered, eyes screwed shut in the childish hope that if she couldn't see the bogeyman then the bogeyman wouldn't be able to see her. Burton said nothing. She slid her hand over to claim his attention, but on the way her fingers found a warm and sticky puddle.

She opened her eyes, even though doing so would render her visible to the sniper, and looked at her fingers. Bright red. Turned her head and saw a pool of blood spreading out from beneath Colonel Burton's body. How easily the mind moved from thinking of Colonel Burton to thinking of Colonel Burton's body. She refused to accept her mind's callous conclusion. Thumped him on the shoulder. 'Sir. Come on, sir. We have to get out of here. Colonel Burton, please!'

But Burton said nothing. She shut her eyes again and waited for the sniper to fire again. Before he did, the ground shook under her, then there was a terrible bang and the sound of a landslide. Charlie opened her eyes and peered around. The house on the opposite side of the road was enveloped in a grey cloud. Before she could work out what had happened, she felt her arms grabbed and she was half-dragged, half-carried into the courtyard and propped up against the wall. As a soldier knelt down to check if she was hurt, she saw two others run past with a loaded stretcher. The body on it looked terribly still.

Hobo had called a conference of his commanders for 09.30. A trestle table was set up beside the DUKW with a map pinned across it by the weight of four French cobbles. Jeeps began to arrive in the farmyard and dirty, tired-looking men clambered out. Charlie watched them come, watched them shake each other's hands, clap shoulders, ask each other questions, bow heads or smile depending on the answers. She was sitting in the jeep with the door open, waiting to be wanted, even though she knew she wouldn't be wanted for a couple of hours. She needed something to do, but there was nothing, and nowhere to go.

The gathering group of officers was almost out of earshot, but not quite. A major from the 22nd Dragoons strolled up, and Charlie heard him ask where the Old Man and Howard Burton were. The others all looked away. Someone muttered a reply and jerked his head towards a mucky patch of grass behind the cattle trough, where a heap lay covered by a blanket and a pair of boots stuck out, the toes scuffed and spattered with stone dust.

'My God,' she heard the Major say. 'How the hell … '

'Sniper,' said one of the others, dully. 'Bastards are all over. They sneak back in the night. Seem to have orders to target our officers.'

'What happened to the one who got Burton?' The Dragoon Major hunched his shoulders unconsciously as he asked the question.

A captain in the sappers gestured with his chin. 'See that ruin across the road? Used to be the local priest's house. Sniper was in the attic. Firefly took it out as the bastard was trying to pot the Old Man's driver into the bargain. Sledgehammers and nuts, I grant you, but there's nothing like a seventy-five millimetre shell to settle a sniper's hash.'

The joke was a thin one and died as General Hobart came striding towards them. Charlie watched him cross the spot where she and Colonel Burton had lain side by side, where the patch of blood splashed on the broken stones must still be wet. If he glanced down she didn't catch him do it, but his face was pale and stern when he reached the group of men. They saluted him and he gave it back, putting them at their ease. 'Gentlemen, it's good to see you all. More of you than I feared, fewer than I hoped. Good show so far. The value of our equipment has shown itself in battle. I didn't doubt it would. We're getting good notices for it. PM's delighted. So is the CIGS. Now, who are we waiting for? Where's Tiny Hay-Wood?'

'Didn't make it off the beach, I'm afraid,' said the Dragoon Major. 'Whole crew bought it. Your old ADC led his squadron for the rest of the day.'

'Dixon?' said Hobart. Charlie strained to hear. Even though he dropped his voice, Charlie heard his next question, 'Where is he now?'

The Dragoon shrugged. 'He was laagered here on D-Day. Haven't heard anything of him or his lot since. We've been kept busy flailing every grass verge between here and the beaches last couple of days.'

'What the devil have you been doing that for? You're meant to be clearing minefields, not mowing the grass.'

'You might try telling that to the infantry commanders, sir. They've taken this idea of us as council street-sweepers a bit too far in my book. They're petrified about mines, so they send us up the road first for reassurance. We're going through flails like there's no tomorrow.'

Hobo snorted. 'Idiotic! I knew this would happen. That's why I was desperate to get here quickly and restore some kind of order. What about the rest of you? Who else is being sent on jobs you're not designed for?'

It seemed to Charlie they all spoke at once. The Old Man glared around. She knew who he was looking for. Knew who would normally have absorbed the first wave of his exasperation. Who would have let it break over his head and, when it had passed, would have offered a quiet, sensible suggestion for dealing with the unbelievable idiocy of the world. But calm, humane, intelligent Lieutenant-Colonel Burton was no longer at his CO's side. He was lying under a blanket with his dirtied boots pointing at the sky. The other officers seemed to know who the Old Man was looking for too. They stood silent, one or two of them glancing towards the body, before looking away.

'Right. I shall be having words with the infantry commanders. Make them see that if they want this Division to be available for the jobs only we can do they'd better stop squandering our machines on stupid tasks. We shan't be able to replace men or tanks nearly fast enough if they get thrown away.'

'Problem is, sir,' said the sapper, 'when the infantry's struggling to make headway in a place, they get a big fillip from seeing us come along and blow the buildings Jerry's holed up in to buggery. Commanders are starting to call us up every time they go in, for the effect it has on morale. If there are Tigers about, they expect us to take them on too. We've lost quite a few machines that way already.'

Hobo snorted again. 'I don't care a fig for their damned morale. Not if it's got at the cost of my men and machinery. It's got to stop. And it will. Before you head back, give Piddington the names of the commanders who are misusing you and I'll go and straighten them out. I need your casualty lists too. Piddington!' The little clerk stuck his head out of the DUKW. 'Sir?'

'Nobody's here from Fifth Assault Regiment RE. Find out where they are and get their commander on the net.'

'Who is it, sir?'

'If I knew that, Piddington, I wouldn't be asking you. CO and some of the other senior officers didn't make it off the beach. No one seems to know who's left. Get hold of Captain Dixon, would you?'

'Sir.' Piddington ducked back inside the truck. Hobo turned to the map on the trestle table. 'Now, gentlemen, if you'd be kind enough to show me exactly where your units are at the moment I can fill you in on what we're expecting from the enemy, now they've finally realised the invasion's under way.'

The men gathered round the table and, as the guns crashed into life not far off, Charlie could no longer hear what they were saying. She sat staring at the old stone wall for a minute. Then she unbuttoned the top pocket of her jacket and pulled out an envelope that was folded and already turning soft and ragged at the creases. She unfolded it and extracted some thin pieces of paper that the morning sun shone through. She spread the pages open gently and read, '*Darling Charlie*

… ' Her throat tightened and the words blurred on the page. Quickly, she re-folded the letter. As she tucked it back into her pocket she touched another envelope, the one containing her note to her father. Then her eyes drifted to Colonel Burton's body.

Slowly, she got out of the jeep and walked over to where he lay. She knelt down and lifted the edge of the blanket gently, though it made no difference to the man under it whether she was gentle or not. The sniper had got him in the back and there was a great dark patch in the middle of his tunic, where the bullet had run right through. It had spread to the seam of his top pocket, and would spread further. The padre who came to bury him would collect his belongings, including his letter to Mary, but by then it would be unmistakably stained with his blood. Charlie stumbled over unfastening the pocket flap and when she drew the envelope out it trembled in the sunshine. The thinnest streak of red ran along the bottom edge where it had sat against the pocket seam. Charlie rubbed at it with her thumb and it blurred to a faint smudge. Carefully avoiding looking at his too-familiar handwriting she slipped his letter into her pocket for safe-keeping with the others.

When Hobo's conference ended, Charlie saw him pause and glance at where Colonel Burton lay. His face emptied of its usual purpose and he looked, for a moment, lost and old. She realised that he couldn't believe Burton was dead, any more than she could. His eyes drifted away from the body and met hers, and as he saw her watching him he braced his back and walked on. She was, all of a sudden, glad she had come. With Dixon and Burton gone, she was the last of the old Rawdon gang who knew Hobo best. 'All right, sir?'

He climbed in beside her and stared out of the windscreen. 'He was a good man, Charlie. A very effective officer. And a pretty good history master too, I expect.'

'He was very clever, sir. And very kind to me.' She felt her voice waver and she shut up.

'It's a damned shame,' said Hobo. 'But it can't be helped. We've a job to do. Let's head towards Caen and see what's going on.'

As they were bumping over the cobbles towards the gateway, a Dingo scout-car came hurtling into the farmyard. Charlie jammed on her brakes and, seeing her at the same moment, so did the other driver. Only the pile of rubble in the gateway checked the scout-car's speed enough to bring it to a halt nose to nose with the jeep.

'What the — ' exclaimed Hobo. 'What kind of bloody maniac comes round corners at that speed? If he's one of ours, I'll have him out of the Division before the day's out.'

He jumped out of the jeep as a captain in dirty battledress and a tanker's beret, with a piece of whitish sticking plaster on one side of his face, climbed out of the scout-car and saluted.

'Dixon!' said Hobo. 'What in blazes are you playing at? When I call a conference, I don't expect my commanders to come careering in forty minutes late as if the hounds of hell are after them.'

'Sorry, sir. I got bracketed by Eighty-eights on the road. Had to do a bit of haring across country to get here.'

If he expected this to cut much ice, he'd forgotten his old chief. 'Well, you missed the conference. Long and the short of it is that our equipment is being pulled about pretty badly and I'm just off to have a word with a few people about employing us in the right way, not willy-nilly, as they've been doing up to now. You might as well come along for the ride. I'll fill you in on the way – and you can return the favour.'

Hobo leaned in through the window of the jeep and said to Charlie, 'I'm going back to see Piddington for five minutes. Then I expect to be able to get on with fighting the war. Understood?'

Charlie nodded.

'Good.' Hobo turned back to Dixon. 'You might as well navigate. Take us round those Eighty-eights, if you'd be so kind.'

'Sir,' said Mike and swung himself into the jeep. Hobo marched off. It was only then that Mike glanced at the driver. His face showed a moment of pure shock before it hardened. 'Mrs Hartwell?' he mumbled, staring down at his filthy hands.

Charlie, who had been looking at him, watching his every word and gesture from the moment he climbed out of the scout-car, watching him though she could hardly bear to do it, when it made her heart beat as if it would burst out of her chest, reached out slowly with her left hand and slipped it over one of his. He didn't try to take his hand away but his fingers lay motionless under hers. Then he moved them. Pulling his hand away. She caught her breath, tried not to cry out. But no, he was only turning it palm upwards to grasp hers. She looked at his fingers, black with oil and mud or blood, felt grittiness in his palm and, above all, his pulse thudding weightily against hers. She found herself wishing they could sit like this for the rest of their lives. Whether that amounted to a day or fifty years seemed not to matter much.

Hobo gave them the barest five minutes. Not enough time even to start to talk. When the fierce old face loomed at the window, Mike gave him a quick, confused smile, and jumped out to let him into the jeep. When he had settled himself in the back, satisfied he had done everything that Dorothea could possibly have expected of him, he looked at the backs of the two familiar heads in front of him and said, 'Now, if we could possibly get a move on. I was three days late getting here and it's high time we got a grip of this Division.'

'Sir,' said Charlie, and put the jeep in gear. As they drove out of the farmyard she was careful to avoid Colonel Burton's blood, which was already turning dark and sticky in the sunshine. Even so, dust from her tyres floated down and settled on its rusty surface. Other vehicles passing through the gateway that morning took fewer pains. Some drove straight over the stain, carrying the blood away on their tracks. Others pulverised the fallen stones by the wall to a fine drifting dust that settled over everything in their wake. By the time those who survived the day returned, no trace of the stain would remain. Men who had known Burton would spare him a thought as they came back to harbour, perhaps, if his death had not already been overlaid with all the other deaths they had seen that day. But tomorrow the war would move on and they would follow where it led, leaving him behind, buried by the remains of a Norman gateway dating from the seventeenth century. Or maybe a bit earlier.

HISTORICAL NOTE

I first saw the name Major-General Sir Percy Cleghorn Stanley Hobart on a deed of easement relating to rights of light from a bathroom window. My bathroom window. I was researching the history of a 700-year-old house, newly mine, and the name seemed one to conjure with. The very first article I found online hinted at a fascinating character, and Kenneth Macksey's excellent biography, *Armoured Crusader*, haunted me for several years before I had the idea of seeking to make Hobo's story better known by including him as a character in a novel. As part of my research, I read his thirty-year correspondence with Basil Liddell-Hart, which only increased my admiration for him as a man who never stopped fighting for what he believed was right, against his own side as well as against the Germans.

Hobart is not as famous as he deserves to be. When Churchill plucked him off the scrap-heap in 1940 it was one of his most brilliant pieces of talent-scouting. Hobo's Funnies were used in every major operation throughout the campaign in North-west Europe, supporting every front line divison of the British and Canadian armies and many units in the US Army. The professionalism and adaptability of even junior ranks due to Hobo's rigorous training was attested to by the commanders of many units whose actions they supported. By February 1945, the 79th Armoured Division comprised 17 regiments, mustering over 1500 tracked armoured fighting vehicles and 21,430 men. It was the largest single formation in any allied army in North-west Europe and the only all-armoured formation in the British Army.

One of the final tasks undertaken by Crocodiles of the 79th was to burn down the huts and gallows of the extermination camp at

Belsen. In May 1945, Major-General Hobart was present at Luneberg Heath when Field Marshal Montgomery accepted the German surrender. The 79th Armoured Division was disbanded at the end of the war and Hobo finally retired from active duty at the age of sixty. He first worked for the Nuffield Organisation before leaving his Oxfordshire village to become Lieutenant-Governor of the Royal Hospital, Chelsea as well as one of the three Commandant Colonels of the Royal Tank Regiment. He retired in 1953 and died in 1957.

Allied casualties on D-Day were lower than anticipated, with around 10,000 men killed or wounded across all the landing beaches. General Eisenhower paid tribute to the 79th Armoured Division's role, saying that without its contribution he doubted whether a beachhead would have been established. The heaviest losses were on Omaha beach, which was both better defended and the only beach where none of Hobo's Funnies was successfully deployed. The American beach demolition engineers, carrying their explosives in dinghies, suffered nearly fifty per cent casualties within thirty minutes of landing. By the end of D-Day the forces landed at Omaha had progressed only nine hundred metres inland, whereas forces landing on the other beaches had penetrated up to six miles.

The tragedy at Slapton Sands in April 1944 during Exercise Tiger was not reported prior to the invasion, and there is still no true consensus as to how many American soldiers and sailors died. Some were buried ashore in unmarked graves and their families informed that they had died in the D-Day landings. Independent researchers estimate that over 1000 men died, more fatalities than on any of the invasion beaches on D-Day other than Omaha.

Numerous German spies were sent to Britain but most were captured and either executed or turned to become double agents, passing back to Germany vital misinformation about the location of the planned invasion. So far as we know, the Germans had no foreknowledge of Hobo's Funnies. On D-Day, however, no one could be sure if the element of surprise was intact.

Apart from Hobo himself, other characters in this novel based on real people include: Professor J D Bernal (the Great Sage), Sir Malcolm Campbell, General de Guingand, Group-Captain Stagg and Sergeant Bruce Ogden-Smith, who did actually take part in a New Year's Eve reconnaissance of the invasion beaches, although his companion was not Lieutenant Michael Dixon but Major Logan Scott-Bowden of the Royal Engineers. The lost trowel and the consequent dropping of a plane-load of trowels is also true.